H.L. Davis
Collected Essays and Short Stories

H · L · DAVIS

Collected Essays

and

Short Stories

UNIVERSITY OF IDAHO PRESS

For Bettie

H.L. Davis
Collected Essays and Short Stories

Contents

Introduction

THIS volume brings together for the first time essays, stories, sketches, and criticism of H. L. Davis (1894-1960), whom Thomas Hornsby Ferril called "probably the most important writer of the modern West." Summing up Davis' achievement, Paul T. Bryant, in the only book-length study of the author, wrote that he was "one of the few twentieth-century writers who have opened the West for literary settlement and given us back our essential cultural unity. In this effort, H. L. Davis was an original . . . ." These are well-earned words of praise. But the plain truth is that Davis has not received the critical recognition he deserves. Among the luminaries writing between the two World Wars, Davis presently stands in the fifth or sixth rank. He has earned a better fate.

To correct this oversight and to encourage the rediscovery of Davis' work, the University of Idaho Press here publishes long out-of-print pieces as *H. L. Davis: Collected Essays and Short Stories*. The sources of this collection are three. This volume reprints the whole of *Kettle of Fire* (1959), a book that included eight travel essays, one story entitled "The Kettle of Fire," and a critical essay—"Preface: A Look Around," published originally in the *New York Times Book Review* in February of 1954 as "The Elusive Trail to the Old West." Six additional selections in this volume—three stories and three sketches—come from *Team*

Bells Woke Me and Other Stories, first published in 1953. Davis wrote most of these tales and sketches between 1929 and 1939. The last title in this collection is *Status Rerum: A Manifesto upon the Present Condition of Northwestern Literature Containing Several Near Libelous Utterances upon Persons in the Public Eye,* first published in 1926 in an edition of two hundred copies at The Dalles, Oregon. With James Stevens as co-author, Davis declared in this Manifesto his literary independence from the stereotyped Western tales that had dominated the marketplace and held the imaginations of readers since the days of the dime novel. Now a rare book, *Status Rerum* appears here for the first time since 1926, along with commentary by Don Love and Warren Clare.

Before Bryant's *H. L. Davis* appeared in 1978, Davis' biography had been a jumble of half-truths and lies, created by Davis himself. For years, he hoodwinked people with tall tales about his life, claiming, among other things, military service against Pancho Villa on the Mexican border during World War I, residence as as student at Stanford University, and the birthdate of a younger brother Percy, who died in 1910. Bryant's sorting of fact from fiction establishes the following outline of Davis' career.

Harold Lenoir Davis was born October 18, 1894, at Rone's Mill, near Nonpareil, Oregon, the son of Ruth Bridges and James Alexander Davis, both of whom traced their roots to Tennessee. Harold's father, who at age six lost a leg in a sawmill accident, was a country school teacher, and the family moved frequently as his employment changed. Between 1894 and 1906, the Davises lived in Looking Glass, Drain, Ten Mile, Roseburg, Yoncalla, and Oakland, Oregon. Following a two-year residence in Antelope (1907-1908), the family settled in the Columbia River town of The Dalles, Harold's home until 1928. After graduating from high school in 1912, Davis worked as deputy county tax assessor and a surveyor before trying to enroll at Stanford University in 1917 to study engineering. Without sufficient tuition money, he returned home immediately to work until he was drafted into the army on September 23, 1918. Davis served fewer than three months at Fort McDowell, California, before being honorably discharged and returning to The Dalles to work at various jobs, including bank clerk and time keeper on a railroad gang.

Between 1919 and 1939, Davis established for himself a modest literary reputation, first as a poet, then as short-fiction writer, and finally as a novelist. Harriet Monroe's prestigious *Poetry* — then printing the verse of such notables as Frost, Eliot, and cummings — published in April 1919 eleven of Davis' poems. For this work, he won the 1919 Helen Haire Levinson Prize for poetry. Davis published some thirty-nine poems between 1919 and 1933, mostly in the pages of *Poetry*, and received accolades from Carl Sandburg and Robinson Jeffers. Jeffers recognized in the poems an authentic Western voice, whose rhythms, manner, and vision were "like no one else's." And though *Status Rerum* — a satiric assault on the vapid and self-congratulatory literary establishment of the Northwest — was good sport, it earned Davis few friends.

But poetry did not pay, and in the late 1920s, at the urging of H. L. Mencken, to whom Davis had sent some poems, he turned to writing short stories and sketches. Though Davis had written with James Stevens or under Stevens' name two tales published in *Adventure* in 1928, the first story to appear under his own name was "Old Man Isbell's Wife" in Mencken's *American Mercury* of February 1929. Delighted, Mencken asked for more, and Davis had trouble keeping his editor supplied. Three sketches — all reprinted in this volume — followed shortly in the *Mercury's* pages: "Back to the Land — Oregon, 1907," "A Town in Eastern Oregon," and "Team Bells Woke Me." Of the ten sketches Davis wrote between 1929 and 1933, these three are among his best.

Of the short stories Davis wrote, mostly in the 1930s, "Old Man Isbell's Wife," "Open Winter," and "The Homestead

Orchard"—all reprinted here—number among his best. Like most writers in this period, Davis turned out pot-boilers to make money,[1] but he wrote during this time more than a half dozen stories that merit continued study, among them "Flying Switch" (1930), "Shiloh's Waters" (1930), "Extra Gang" (1936), "Beach Squatter" (1936), and "A Flock of Trouble" (1941), retitled "The Stubborn Spearmen" in *Team Bells Woke Me*. "The Kettle of Fire," also included in this volume, was Davis' last story. Though he cannot match in productivity such contemporaries as F. Scott Fitzgerald, who wrote some 200 stories, Davis created a few tales that match the best work of such short story writers as Fitzgerald, John Steinbeck, and Willa Cather.

In 1928, Davis left Oregon with his new wife, Marion Lay, whom he married on May 25 of that year. They moved to Bainbridge Island, Washington, where he and James Stevens had a radio show featuring folk tales and music on Station KEX in Seattle. Pressed for money, the Davises moved to Arizona in 1930, back to Washington in 1931, and to Mexico in 1932. Davis had received a Guggenheim Fellowship in 1932, and he and Marion lived first in Mexico City and then in Oaxaca, where he worked on a novel. *Honey in the Horn,* published by Harper & Brothers, won the Harper Novel Prize in 1935 and the Pulitzer prize for fiction in 1936. With these awards under his belt, Davis' career looked promising. He had served a long apprenticeship, had written some solid verse, had created several fine stories, and had received national recognition for his first novel.

But trouble dogged him in the next few years. Following their residence in Mexico, Davis and Marion, on their way to New York City, spent the winter of 1935 and the spring of 1936 near Nashville, Tennessee, where Marion suffered a prolonged illness. After she regained her health, they visited Baltimore and New York City before settling in mid-May of 1937 at "Deer Lick," a ranch they had purchased near Napa, California. The Davises' marriage, evidently never on solid ground, collapsed, and in

1942, Marion sued for divorce, which was granted in 1943. A quarrel with Harper & Brothers over royalties for *Honey in the Horn* also preoccupied Davis, who prepared legal action in 1947 before the matter was settled out of court. Harper & Brothers did publish *Proud Riders* (1942), a collection of Davis' poetry, but he did not publish another book until 1947. His new publisher, William Morrow and Company, would issue the rest of his books.

Though Davis published a few stories in the early 1940s, the twelve-year hiatus between *Honey in the Horn* and *Harp of a Thousand Strings* (1947) obviously damaged his reputation as a promising novelist. But settled in Napa, California, with his domestic and publishing problems resolved, Davis resumed his writing. After *Harp of a Thousand Strings,* Davis completed *Beulah Land* (1949), *Winds of Morning* (1952), *Team Bells Woke Me* (1953), *The Distant Music* (1956), and *Kettle of Fire* (1959). Reviewers consistently praised his achievements in the novels. He married Elizabeth Tonkin Martin del Campo on June 2, 1953, the same year that his essays comprising *Kettle of Fire* began appearing in *Holiday* magazine. In 1956, he suffered acute arteriosclerosis, which required amputation of his left leg in a Mexican hospital in October. Though the amputation bothered him greatly, he continued writing. He was working on a novel tentatively titled "Exit, Pursued by a Bear" when he died of a heart attack on October 31, 1960, in San Antonio, Texas.

At his death, Davis had published "forty-two poems, twenty-four short stories, ten sketches, eleven travel essays, a scattering of critical essays, and five novels."[2] Compared with the body of work created by John Steinbeck or Willa Cather, Davis' corpus is small. But in the experimental rhythms of his poetry, in a half-dozen or so stories, and in his sketches and travel essays, Davis created pieces full of wit, humor, and craft. His best work still has bite and appeal, still stands as art of a high quality, indeed. But it was in the novel that he achieved his finest work. *Honey in the Horn* and *Winds of Morning* are novels that repay revisiting because they rely on the Western landscape and characters for telling archetypal stories rich in folklore, symbol, humor, and language. *Harp of a Thousand Strings,* a much underrated novel, stands in texture and complexity as an international tale that mixes the best of Mark Twain and of Henry James, an unlikely couple. These three novels need reprinting so that a new generation of readers can discover Davis' work.

Slowly, scholars are making Davis' work easily available for reassessment. *The Selected Poems by H. L. Davis,* with an introduction by Thomas Hornsby Ferril (Boise, Idaho: Ahsahta Press, 1978) was a first step. Now *H. L. Davis: Collected Essays and Short Stories* (which is really the Selected gathering of his work) offers readers two critical essays, four stories, three sketches, and eight travel essays. This book should contribute to resuscitating the reputation of a writer who still speaks to readers — and speaks well.

What will readers find in these pages? They will find a cantankerous, tough-minded literary critic with definite ideas about what Western writing should and should not be, a teller of tall tales that always go somewhere, a humorist who is still funny, an essayist who looks around Oregon and discovers he is on the track of his own past and that of human history, an iconoclastic social critic suspicious of "Community Betterment" and "Civic Improvement" and yet still amused by the downright damnfoolishness of the human race, and a short story writer fascinated with grotesques and outsiders who struggle to earn their dignity and who discover that they, too, belong within the human community.

As Davis noted in both *Status Rerum* and the "Preface" of *Kettle of Fire,* he believed that Western writing must always be lodged in place, but that writers who could not make their work rise above local color to the universal were no writers at all. Davis strove in his own work to embue the specific with the universal and archetypal, rather than simply the immediate and the ephemeral. In the "Preface" to *Kettle of Fire*, Davis encouraged Western writers to avoid romantic and stylized views of their past. He warned that Western writers particularly needed to be wary of both the "colorful" and the "sordid."

The "unity" Davis refers to in that preface is the unity between past and present, between genuine art and life, between conflicts of the human heart beginning with Adam and Eve and those conflicts continuing on to Oregon and the American West. Without discovering that unity, Western writing was doomed to insignificance and triviality. Later in *Kettle of Fire*, Davis says, "Landscape counts in the place, but people count more." Linking Western history with human history made Davis the kind of regional writer that William Faulkner was for the South and Nathaniel Hawthorne was for New England.

The eight travel essays of *Kettle of Fire* nearly always begin in the physical world and end up "somewhere else." The essay "A Walk in the Woods" illustrates Davis' method. After describing his adventures on Northwestern trails, Davis says near the middle of his essay:

> *A parable of some kind could be worked up from looking into mountain water on a still day. At a distance, it reflects what is around it—grass, trees, sky; when you lean close, the reflection is of yourself. Lean close enough to drink from it, and you will see down past all the reflections to the reality of underwater life—bugs, worms, tadpoles, fingerling trout, drowned weeds, sprays of reddish lichens. But the water itself, through which both reflections and reality exist, is so still and colorless that it is never really visible at all.*

This passage, reminiscent of Henry David Thoreau's writing about Walden Pond or Robert Frost's going out to clean the pasture spring, illustrates how Davis' visiting the sites and sights of Oregon often leads to insights. As an observer and writer, Davis finds all the perspectives of the "mountain water on a still day" revealing yet mysterious. The observer of nature can discover the reflections of the world, as well as reflections of himself. But the careful observer can also penetrate the "reality of underwater life," which for Davis is symbolic of something resembling our unconscious life. The attentive observer of that life becomes a see-er. Though Davis is not a transcendentalist, he sees nature as possessing symbols that allow man transcendent perceptions about himself and his world. The eight travel essays abound in such moments as the one from "A Walk in the Woods."

"Oregon," the first essay in *Kettle of Fire,* opens with Davis recording a "saying in Oregon that people who lived there could change their whole order of life — climate, scenery, diet, complexions, emotions, even reproductive faculties — by merely moving a couple of hundred miles in any direction inside the state." However, after returning to Oregon "from three different directions," Davis concludes that perhaps the state is a sufficient place because it is not a collection of separate localities," but "one single and indivisible experience. Everything belongs in it, and it all comes together." The way Oregon "comes together" is through the perceptions of the writer, here Davis himself.

In bringing together the newness and oldness of Oregon, Davis tells about meeting a young doctor who has recently moved West and considers the state "new country." The doctor, a gatherer of local lore, tells Davis about a building that had once been a dance hall with a wild Western past. Davis says the building was "merely a hotel" with "no wild times, no dance-hall girls, no big-money gambling." The only shooting to occur there, according to Davis, involved his grandfather, a hard-shell Baptist preacher, who fired a double-barrel shotgun from the hotel's third floor after officiating a wedding. Thinking he saw shadows near the corral after the wedding, Davis' grandfather hurriedly loaded his shotgun, jamming his nightshirt tail down one barrel so that "the shot yanked him out of the window headfirst." Davis continues:

> *He fell three floors into the middle of the wedding*
> *celebration with his shirttail in flames around his*
> *neck and scared almost everybody to death.*
> *Several guests collapsed, and some ran eight or*
> *ten miles without stopping. My grandfather*
> *sustained a broken arm and second-degree*
> *burns, and miscarriages were claimed by two*
> *ladies and denied heatedly by three others,*
> *including the bride.*

Davis reading of the wild and woolly West, filled with misspent shots (his grandfather's) and miscarriages, locates comically the real story of the hotel's past, but does not deny the possibility of tragedy. Davis' version of the story is simply corrective.

Davis amplifies his reading of this anecdote clearly in "Oregon." He writes:

> *The difference between that uncolored incident*
> *and the rip-roaring type of conventionalized fan-*
> *tasy is the difference between* tradition *and* illu-
> sion *(my emphasis). Tradition is what a country*
> *produces out of itself; illusion is what people*
> *bring into it from somewhere else. On the*
> *record, the illusions have considerably the better*
> *of it. People keep bringing them in. Those who*
> *kept the traditions going kept drifting away and*
> *scattering, to New York and Washington and*
> *California, and places in the Middle West. Still,*
> *it will go on producing new ones probably. It*
> *always has.*

The truth of the matter, as Davis says, is that all people have both illusions and traditions. The Westerner gains his traditions the hard way (as do all people), by stripping away the illusions. But with the mobility of the Western populace (and the American, for that matter), the process of stripping away illusions and creating enduring traditions is a cyclic process that has repeated itself since the beginning of time. Though Davis does not say so, Oregon is as good a place for discovering tradition as is Troy or Rome.

The eight essays in *Kettle of Fire* are travel pieces, but when Davis gets on the road, he is searching for larger truths. Exploring the country of his youth gives Davis an apt opportunity for looking around. He casts his affection for and his chagrin with his native land into essays that are meditations on nature, on his past, on his region's past, and on the sameness and difference of human experience. In tone, these essays are a curious mixture of the voices of Thoreau and Mark Twain, but the voice that emerges from these small gems is Davis' own.

Though Davis' travel essays contain social criticism, the three sketches — especially "Back to the Land — Oregon, 1907" and "A Town in Eastern Oregon" — have as their main purpose commentary on Oregon society. In "Back to the Land — Oregon, 1907" Davis writes ironically of the 1907 homestead rush. The homesteaders arrive, not in romantic procession, but in the spring mud that plugs roads so that no "horse could set foot without sinking to his belly." And though the homesteaders have kinships with the earlier pioneers, they are not heroic folks. These homesteaders are looking for land, for a place to begin again, but as Davis repeats, almost in refrain, "There was nothing to see except the homestead rush — a rickety wagon, or two, or a half-dozen, wallowing through the street; women and bawling children and sallow, middle-aged men beating the tired horses forward with the brutality of a desperate hope."

Davis quotes a ranch foreman to make his point about the

quiet desperation and foolishness of these searchers for new land, and the foreman turns out to be right. In the last section of the sketch, all the homesteaders have left the land. What remains is their cats and pack-rats. Davis says, "If there is ever a monument to busted homesteaders, the pack-rat deserves to be on it. He is nature's one victim of the homesteaders' never-failing curse—a fury for beginning things and leaving them one-fourth done. It may have been from them that he learned his habits. I used to think so." But the tone of Davis' irony at the end of his sketch is merciful. He feels "abashment and shame" when he comes upon an abandoned homestead because he senses that he is prying into people's secrets. But he has seen such cycles of homesteading before and speculates that they will occur again.

The irony of "A Town in Eastern Oregon" is much harsher, much like Mark Twain's irony in "To a Person Sitting in Darkness." As a revisionist social historian, Davis documents how the town of Gros Ventre, much like The Dalles, sought "civilization." He documents with wit and satire the battles that mark Gros Ventre's history—first against the Indians, then against the soldiers protecting the town, then against the freighters, then against the steamboaters, then against the saloons and bawdy-houses. These reforms occur in the name of civilization, "Social Betterment," and the "Spirit of Helpfulness." But Progress has cost Gros Ventre its livelihood, and Davis adds,

> *They didn't, it is true, foresee that the consequence would be death, but it is altogether likely that they would have gone ahead with it, even if they had. It was the same instinct that operates in a soldier on the firing-line who, having turned down a hundred chances to rush a machine-gun and be a hero, will straighten up squarely in the line of fire to scratch a place on his leg.*

Davis' portrayal of the Gros Ventre citizens as not only self-destructive, but stupid, won him few friends in The Dalles.

"Team Bells Woke Me" is a more nostalgic sketch, for here Davis recounts the folklore and the characters of the teamsters who drove wagons before the coming of the railroads. As a boy, Davis is the initiate of Tamarack Jack, who takes the youngster in tow and introduces him to the business of freighting. Tamarack Jack, "one of the best frieghters on the line," gives Davis a chance to meet such characters as Greene Tucker, an ex-Indian fighter, and Frank Chambeau, who "hugged and kissed his horses." Most of all Davis remembers the music of the team bells. The "railroad splurge" of 1910 ended this era. And much like Mark Twain, who recalled his Old Times on the Mississippi, Davis recalls with affection those just-gone days. The sketch ends, "Merely to have taken away the team bells at morning ought to be enough to get them all [financiers and farmers] immortality. I hope it will." Once again, Progress has taken a toll.

Of Davis' stories, "Old Man Isbell's Wife" is a remarkable achievement. For an early story, it is more than remarkable. Davis spins the yarn of two grotesques, Old Man Isbell, who is "eighty-five years old, slack-witted, vacant-minded, doddering, dirty, and a bore." The other grotesque is his unnamed wife, who is twenty-eight, "close to three hundred pounds," and has "to shave her face regularly to keep down a coarse black beard." The two marry in order to keep the townspeople from putting him away and in order for her to have his pension and care for him. The "fat woman" believes that marriage should give her respectability with other wives, but they exclude her. The only wife to pay attention to the "fat woman" is the narrator's mother.

Only when Old Man Isbell dies do the townspeople call on the "fat woman," and when they do, they discover her seated on her husband's bed re-enacting with him his fevered remembrances of Indian fighting, of corralling a runaway stage, and of standing off wild horses. When the townspeople return, they find the "fat woman" "had gone to sleep by herself, beside her dead husband; a fat woman, twenty-eight years old, beside the corpse of a man eighty-five." Old Man Isbell's wife tells the narrator's mother, "I was proud of my husband. The things he'd done, and the risks he'd been through, when the men in this town was rollin' drunks and wrappin' up condensed milk."

Davis manages to endow his two grotesques with dignity largely through the way he tells the story. The story is a story within a story within a story, a fact that gives Davis distance on his characters and keeps him from falling into sentimentality about this strange pair. The outside narrator (presumably the son) tells a story that his mother (another narrator) has told him. The mother tells him the story she has heard from Old Man Isbell's wife. The outside narrator, the son, functions somewhat in the same fashion as Faulkner's narrator in "A Rose for Emily," for like Faulkner's narrator, the son reflects the views of the townspeople, but also comes to know the inside narrative. So the direction the story moves is from the outside narrative to the inside narrative of Old Man Isbell's wife herself. That structure makes Davis' story work well.

But "Old Man Isbell's Wife" is also a story about story telling, as well as the tale of the two grotesques and their humanization by the outside narrator. Old Man Isbell is himself a story teller, but the narrator speaks at least twice of the Old Man's being a bore. The narrator reports:

> *The dullness of his speech was a gift of God. He had lived in his eighty-five years through the most splendidly colored history that one man could ever have lived through—the Civil War, the Indian campaigns in the West, the mining days, the cattle-kings, the long-line freighters, the road-agents, the stockmen's wars—the changing, with a swiftness and deci-*

sion unknown to history before, of a country and its people; yes, and of a nation. Not as a spectator, either. He lived in the middle of every bit of it, and had a hand in every phase. But, for all the interest it gave to his conversation, he could just as well have spent his life at home working buttonholes.

"I remember Lincoln," he would say. "I drove him on an electioneerin' trip, back in Illinoy. Him and Stephen A. Douglas. I drove their carriage."

One would sit up and think, "Well! The old gabe does know something good, after all!" Expecting, of course, that he was about to tell some incident of the Lincoln-Douglas debates— something, maybe, that everybody else had missed. But that was all. So far as he knew, there hadn't been any incidents. They electioneered. He drove their carriage. They rode in it. That was all that had impressed him.

Later, the narrator says, "Old Man Isbell remembered the exact thing, and, that being done, he stopped. He ought to have been writing military dispatches. Or had he?"

So to the town Old Man Isbell is a literalist and a bore. But as he re-enacts his adventures during his last hours, the Old Man re-creates for his wife his adventures; she is a participant. The narrator, describing the Old Man's fever, says that at the end Old Man Isbell "had burned his brain down to the last nub." For his wife, the Old Man's re-creation is not a bore; it is resuscitation. And in the act of resuscitating his adventures, Old Man Isbell escapes the role of bore and literalist and becomes, like the narrator of the story, a story teller who brings life to his tale. Because Old Man Isbell in his fever frees himself from his literalism, he can create, just as Davis himself creates, a story with power and art. It is, finally, the recreating of tales that endows Old Man Isbell and his wife with a dignity that allows them to escape their grotesqueness. The fire of creation in the Old Man's brain kindles the imaginations of the narrator and his mother, but especially the narrator. Thus, on one level "Old Man Isbell's Wife" is about the power of story telling.

"Open Winter" and "The Homestead Orchard" are more conventional stories in theme and technique. Both are initiation stories that take place in Oregon and that employ Christian symbolism to convey their themes. In "Open Winter," Beech Cartwright, a young skeptic, rides with Pop Apling, his guide figure, through a landscape where Beech learns the nature of evil and of his own worth. He learns that hope is possible and that human dignity often comes at a high cost. The journey tests Beech physically, morally, and intellectually; at the end of the story he is a proud rider herding into town the horses he and Pop Apling have been responsible for. Similarly, in "The Homestead Orchard" Old Ollivant and his son Lucas recover mutal trust and love for each other after traveling through a dangerous landscape. In these tales, Davis works his craft well.

Paul Bryant has called "The Kettle of Fire," Davis' last story, "an artistic anomaly and an interesting if unsuccessful attempt to pull together and sum up most of the major themes" in his short fiction. Drawing on the story of Prometheus, Davis sends his protagonist, Sorefoot Capron, to find fire and bring it back to a wagon train in distress. Capron succeeds after an adventuring that Bryant compares with Gulliver's travels. But this story, as Bryant argues, remains pretty much at the level of fable, which may not be a bad thing for a story to do. All of Davis' stories bear further examination.

These are some of the delights readers will discover as they work their way through this collection of H. L. Davis' work. Though Davis was not a prolific writer, he wrote well in several forms — in poetry, the essay, short fiction, the novel, and the sketch. I hope this volume encourages old admirers of Davis to take up the work of elevating him in the ranks of American writers, not just writers of the West. For those discovering Davis for the first time, we old admirers issue an invitation to help us with that task.

Notes

[1]Paul Bryant, in *H. L. Davis,* lists the pot-boilers as follows: "Wild Horse Siding" (1931), "Wild Headlight" (1933), "Spanish Lady" (1934), "Shotgun Junction" (1934), "The Vanishing Wolf" (1935), "A Horse for Felipa" (1935), "Railroad Beef" (1935), "Mrs. Elmina Steed" (1936), "Cowboy Boots " (1936), "World of Little Doves" (1941), and "A Sorrel Horse Don't Have White Hoofs" (1941) (p. 48). Bryant's list should stand as a good one.

[2]Paul T. Bryant, "H. L. Davis," *Fifty Western Writers: A Bio-Biliographical Sourcebook,* eds. Fred Erisman and Richard W. Etulain (Westport, Conn.: Greenwood Press, 1982), p. 73.

Robert Bain
University of North Carolina
at Chapel Hill.

Preface: A Look Around

THERE has been a freshet of books on the West lately—
history, biography, fiction, travel, even things like ethnology
and dendrology and economics, not to count the ones I must
have missed. Some are undoubtedly good—some would have
to be, out of so many—but curiosity about which ones they
are and what is good about them tends to be overshadowed
by speculation as to why, all at once, there has been such an
outpouring of them.

The explanation, I think, can be found only through a
certain amount of casting back into the past. The West, because of circumstances beyond anybody's control, got off to a
better start than it was able to live up to. Pioneer settlement
of the Northwest began in the eighteen-forties, and the Oregon question, which was the most feverishly debated issue
in the Presidential election of 1844, was followed by the ac-
quisition of the Southwest from Mexico, by the California
gold rush and smaller mining booms in Oregon, Idaho, Montana, Colorado and by furious wrangling over possible routes
for a transcontinental railroad. Everything that happened
in the West was national news, and everybody who could
struck out for the West to be in on it.

The Civil War stopped that splurge dead. Public interest
shifted, naturally, to the great battles in the East; everybody

who could hurried back to be where things were really happening. The West became a sort of backwash, populated by hand-to-mouth mining promoters, seedy politicians, Chinese coolies and Border State draft-dodgers. There was nothing in the West to write about that anybody was interested in, and writing, except for the war poems of Bret Harte, leveled down to light travel sketches and newspaper whimsies.

The West was left to work its way to civilization by itself —and the end of the war brought no revival of interest in it. What people wanted to read about in the post-war years was not the West but the South, where their war had been fought and where reconstruction, with its attendant feuds and scandals and recriminations, was in full swing.

The writers whose work had been associated with the West mostly gave up: Bret Harte and J. Ross Browne went to Europe, Mark Twain moved East and settled down to write *Life on the Mississippi* and *Tom Sawyer*—both about the South, but not, it should be noted, as the war had changed it. The period he wrote about was the eighteen-forties and fifties. And it should also be noted, because it is an important point in this casting back for causes, that all the other Southern writers of the time were doing the same thing— Maurice Thompson, Joel Chandler Harris, George W. Cable, Richard Malcolm Johnston among them. The Eastern magazines were full of their stories and sketches about life in the South; always and without exception it was life in the South before it had been knocked apart and buried under the wreckage of war and post-war turbulence and change. Their writing was not description but exhumation based on nostalgia.

About the new South that was coming into being around them they wrote nothing; they left that to visiting writers from the North, New Englanders like J. W. de Forest and

J. T. Trowbridge and Rebecca Harding Davis. It was a fair division. Any outsider with a talent for reporting could see and put down what the destruction of the war had been like; only the insiders could know what had been destroyed.

I have touched on this briefly because it brings out something at the very heart of most American writing—perhaps of most writing everywhere. A certain layer of time and history is necessary before material becomes manageable. A man writing about what is around him has to take things too much as they come, whether they fit together into any unified impression or not. Using material from some vanished past, the author can select more discriminately. And what he digs up and what he makes of it will be something more than a mere account of facts. It will be something drawn from and colored by his own memory and feeling.

In the West, the past receded too slowly to need digging up. In the South, the Civil War made a break between past and present. In the West, there was no hint of ghostliness about the past, no veil through which a writer could reach to select figures and incidents. The things that had happened in the eighteen-fifties went right on happening through the eighteen-seventies: Indian outbreaks, land booms, mining stampedes, railroad building, buffalo herds, cattle drives—more and bigger ones, mostly, but the same incidents, the same people, the same directness and incongruity and disorder that had made even reportorial writing about it a guess-and-fumble business from the outset.

The few specimens of Western fiction that appeared during this period have to be seen to be believed. With tremendous stories happening all around—Texas cattle drives North, the tick-fever wars on the Missouri border, the railroad construction race through Kansas to the Indian Territory, the sweep of settlement west across the Great Plains— the plots twitter along on the level of sewing-circle gossip, and some of the attempts at Western idiom are embarrassing to read even now. In the late eighteen-eighties, with the publication of Theodore Roosevelt's Dakota ranching sketches and articles on the Southwest by Frederic Remington and one or two others, the past finally began to move back where it belonged. Indians, these writers all noted, were no longer dangerous except as possible carriers of trachoma and vermin; the buffalo herds were gone; cowboys no longer carried firearms as a part of their clothing; the country, except for mosquitoes and real-estate promoters, was as safe and as sedate as a church.

Having a past that newcomers to the country could no longer look at for themselves was something. However, it was not until the century's turn—and the advent of such modern phenomena as economic recession, union labor riots, fighting through the mining areas of Nevada and Idaho and Montana, threatened railroad and shipping tie-ups in Oregon and outbreaks of violence over squatter evictions in California—that writers finally got around to realizing what the region's historical possibilities were. It would be hard to say which of them got to it first. Besides Theodore Roosevelt's series of books on *The Winning of the West*—the first whose work caught on with the public were Owen Wister and Alfred Henry Lewis, neither of them Westerners. Lewis was a St. Louis attorney; Wister was a young Philadelphian not long out of Harvard.

Others followed close behind them—first a few, then dozens and scores, some specialists, some competent craftsmen, a few of both and many not much of either. But Wister's *The Virginian,* Lewis' *Old Cattleman* series and Roosevelt's *The Winning of the West* were the works that showed them all where to dig and what to look for. Western writing has been dipping out of their rain barrel for at least the last fifty years. All the books on the West have been a result, in one way or another, of what they did; not only the thousands of mediocre ones but, if there is anything in the theory that every good book is written as a revulsion against some vast accumulation of tasteless and sentimental trash, the good ones as well.

They might have gone on being the model for Western writing for another fifty years, probably, except that a new past has appeared. The changes in the West over the past twenty years—and most notably since World War II—have been profound and sweeping. New towns have risen up, old ones have spread out over three and four and sometimes ten times their old areas, old landmarks have been leveled and new ones set up; new people have come in, new types and faces and customs, thousands and hundreds of thousands of them, with new ideas about which things in the country are worth keeping and which need to be altered or discarded.

The glaring and incongruous realities from which the early writers reached back into a more colorful and manageable past have become a part of the past themselves. Much of what seemed sordid and incongruous about those realities was a result of the colorfulness that had gone before; it is becoming clear now that they were all of one piece, and perhaps neither as colorful on one side nor as sordid on the other as they had seemed. It is becoming clear, too, that the early writers in their reaching back into the past must have missed something about it, since they failed to establish any unity between it and the world out of which they wrote. All the new changes in the country, its overgrown towns, its leveled forests and stopped-up creeks, its swarms of new faces and jangle of strange accents, are a consequence of something that has happened somewhere.

The past needs to be searched through again to find out what the link is, to find out the things about the new past that the early writers ignored and the things about the older one that they overlooked or threw away. The link may be difficult to find and difficult to be sure of when it is found, but more and more people are coming to understand that it is worth trying for. All these Western books are one way of reaching back after it.

Oregon

It used to be a saying in Oregon that people who lived there could change their whole order of life—climate, scenery, diet, complexions, emotions, even reproductive faculties— by merely moving a couple of hundred miles in any direction inside the state. Maybe they still can, but there is not that feeling about coming back to it after a long time away. I have tried returning from three different directions now, and touching it at any point unfailingly brings all of it back on me, not a collection of separate localities but always as one single and indivisible experience. Everything belongs in it, and it all comes together: the gray high-country sagebrush ridges of the Great Basin where I once herded cattle, the rolling wheatlands fronting on the Columbia River to the north where I lived as a youngster, the greentimbered valley country between the high Cascade Mountains and the Coast Range where I was born and grew up—where people sometimes lived all their lives without having any idea what the naked earth looked like. Except for the cultivated tracts, there were not a dozen acres in the country without a stand of Douglas fir trees.

Beyond the Coast Range is the open coast, and it belongs in the experience too. I used to hunt deer there every fall. My grandfather homesteaded down one of the little coastal rivers in the eighteen-seventies, and my mother lived there as a girl. The country was not logged off then, and there were no roads. The family marketing had to be done by taking a homemade canoe down the river, and the children explored the neighborhood by walking on fallen logs where hundreds of gaily colored garter snakes collected to sun themselves during the afternoon. It must have been an intrusive kind of place to grow up in, with white-topped combers jarring the granite cliffs like dynamite blasts and the long wall of black spruce and cedar tossing and roaring in the spring gales, and swarms of huge gulls screaming and fighting over the salmon that got washed out on the sand bars in the spring spawning runs. It would be the same now, probably. Cliffs and combers and gulls are still there, and so is the timber, black spruce or fir or cedar, not bent or twisted by the sea wind but standing straight and rigid against it as the gray cliffs in which they are rooted. They do let down a little along the creeks and old clearings; there are intervals where they leave room for masses of grayish-green alder and dogwood and maple. There is not much variety of color in the country. Except when the flowers are out, it is mostly variations of green, and even autumn alters it very little: a few blots of yellow in the maples, sometimes verging on white, a few streaks of pink in the dogwoods, though hardly enough of either to break the monotony. The extremes of temperature are too small to color leaves very brilliantly. In some places the alder leaves merely die and fall off without coloring at all.

The wildflowers do make a difference. They are all through the woods and grasslands when spring opens: dogwood, wild cherry, sweetbrier, flowering currant, mock orange; ground flowers like lamb's-tongues, cat ears, blue camas lilies, red bird bills, patches of buttercups and St. John's-wort, wild violets that are not purplish like garden violets, but the intense sky blue of jaybird feathers, and yellow violets, trilliums, blue lilies of the valley and pink swamp mallow, besides skunk cabbage and water lilies, which are mostly ugly. Wild asters, foxgloves, azaleas and rhododendrons come later in the summer when the berries are beginning to ripen—wild blackberries, black raspberries, black haws, wild strawberries, red and black huckleberries.

Wild berries were a staple article of diet for farm families in Western Oregon a generation ago. Some species, like the native wild blackberry, were scarce in many sections then, because hurried and careless picking destroyed the vines. They should be taking a fresh hold now. Picking them always took hard work and time, and it is easier nowadays to buy such things at the market, so the berries are left for the blue grouse and bears, which don't object to hard work and have more time than they know what to do with anyway. People in some areas used to depend on the mountain Indians to come through the country with their pack trains every fall, peddling huckleberries and wild blackberries, as they always wandered through peddling muddy water cress out of dripping gunny sacks every spring, but those signs of the changing seasons ended a good many years ago. Indians nowadays do their wandering mostly in automobiles, the same as everybody else, and seldom with anything to sell.

The berries go on growing, nevertheless. There are places in the scrub oak and bracken of the red-earth foothills where, in late April or early May, the wild strawberries are crowded so close together under the broom grass and bracken that you will crush a handful at every step; there are huckleberry swales in the higher mountains where the bushes are bent flat to the ground with the weight of their berries, and trails show where the bears have had to fill up on bitter ashberries as a corrective against overindulgence in them; there are wild blackberry patches in the old timber burns of the back country where, in the late spring, the drumming of ruffed grouse sounds like a battery of rivet guns running full blast.

Some of the country's most common and useless-looking types of vegetation have stories back of them. The evergreen blackberry vine, which tangles itself over all the old fences and abandoned homestead clearings, was brought across the plains by the women of the first emigrant train in 1843, and watered and tended carefully during the entire journey as something to plant in their new gardens. Once it was started, they discovered that the native wild blackberry was far superior to it in size, flavor and accessibility, so it was left to run wild, and in many parts of the country it has become a serious pest. The Spanish moss, which grows in long skeins and festoons on the oak trees of the lower valleys, belongs on the opposite side of the ledger. None of the early settlers had imagined there could be any possible use for it until one winter in the early 1850's, when a deep snow buried all their pastures and they discovered that their cattle were keeping alive by eating Spanish moss from the low-hanging tree branches. Since most of the moss grew higher, the settlers took to cutting the trees down to keep a supply of it within reach. After the first few days, the cattle would come charging through the snow whenever they heard the crack of a tree about to fall, and the children of the settlement had to be stationed around it with clubs to keep the cattle from stampeding in and being crushed under the tree when it came down.

The moss has never been used for anything since, but the memory of help given in need takes a long time to wear off. A great-uncle of mine, who came to Western Oregon as a youngster in 1852 and lived there till he was past ninety, told me once about standing guard in the snow with the other children during that winter, and added that he had never since been able to look at Spanish moss without a vague stir of gratitude, or at cattle without a deep feeling of dislike. He had five or six children, all born and brought up in the valley country where he spent nearly all of a long and useful life. None of them stayed there after they were grown. They all moved away, and scattered according to the usual pattern for such families: one to New York, one to Washington, D.C., a couple to Los Angeles, one to some city in the Middle West. They used to come back on visits sometimes. They are all elderly now; some may be dead.

The constant drifting away of second generations from this country, and the influx of new people from other states, may have something to do with its persistent sense of newness, of everything being done for the first time. The growth of the towns probably helps too. Many Western Oregon towns have trebled in size since the war; most have doubled. There are old buildings still left in them, but they are usually overshadowed by an environing swarm of new stucco supermarkets, car and tractor showrooms, chain-saw and logging-truck repair shops, real-estate offices, Assembly of God tabernacles, drive-in movie theaters (generally referred to as "passion pits"), country-club residence subdivisions, antique and curio shops, and places offering such out-of-the-way amenities as fortune-telling, agate testing, and stream-lined bull service.

Even if it were possible to account for all these new and varied enterprises in detail (what, for instance, is there about bull service that anybody could streamline?), trying to trace out the original lines of these towns runs into all kinds of confusions and bewilderments. The local residents are usually not much help. Traveling through the lower valley country last spring, I stopped at one of the newer towns to have a surgical dressing put on an infected finger. The doctor's office was upstairs over the drugstore. From the window, there was a view of two motels, a service station, the highway bridge over a small creek, and a gaunt old three-story frame hotel, tall and shabby and narrow-windowed, shedding loose boards and patches of ugly yellow paint behind a clump of huge half-dead pear trees. The doctor saw me looking at it as he worked, and remarked that it was a real relic. It had been a kind of roadhouse for gold miners back in the early days, he had heard: saloon, dance hall, gambling house, that kind of business.

"Some rip-roaring old times there when it was new, I guess," he said. "Shootings, big-money gambling, one thing and another. Dance-hall girls, and all that. It could tell some wild old stories, I guess, if it could talk. It is a kind of an eyesore, the shape it's in; a firetrap too. It ought to be fixed up or got rid of, or something. We could have a real town here if these State people weren't so fussy with their restrictions."

He was young, sociable, and interested in a lot of things. He was originally from Wisconsin, had come out during the war as medical officer in an armored division that carried on field training in the desert around Fort Rock, and had decided to stay on afterward and grow up with the country. I asked which State people seemed the most bothersome, and whether there weren't other places where they were less stringent. He said it was the highway department, mostly, though none of them were easy to get along with if you wanted to do anything.

"All their regulations about what you can build and where, and what you can do and what you can't do, till you'd think we were some bunch of mental cases that had to be told to come in out of the rain," he said. "There are other places, I suppose. Still, I don't know. I like this one. All this new country, and seeing things to do with it. You don't get that in the older places. It's worth something. There's a kind of a feeling about it."

New country, I thought. Down the little creek that was

visible from his office window was part of the old trail over which Ewing Young and ten herders drove 600 head of cattle in from California in 1837. It was something of an achievement, by all accounts. His herders quarreled among themselves so fiercely that he had to sit up nights with a loaded gun to keep them from killing each other, and he dared not attempt to reconcile them for fear they might get together and decide to kill him. He got cattle and herders in safely, despite difficulties, and other herds followed. By 1842, the trail was a main route of travel. And not over an hour away was a town on the Umpqua River where the Hudson's Bay Company had a fort and trading post in 1834, and French Prairie near Salem was all wheatfields and orchards by then. . . . What was Wisconsin in 1834? Indian country, like most of Maine, and Minnesota, and Louisiana, and Northern New York, and all of the Tennessee Valley. Oregon is not new; it is older than most of them. Its population turnover gives it an illusion of newness, that is all. However, the doctor was right about one thing: there is the illusion, the same as in the beginning, and an illusion is enough, if it can be made to last.

His ideas about the old hotel having had a rip-roaring past were all wrong, though: colored by too many moving pictures, probably, or by some older resident trying to make the country sound interesting. Merely a hotel was all it had ever been: an overnight stop on the old stage line across the mountains from the coast, with the usual accommodations for man and beast. There had never been anything rip-roaring about it: no wild times, no dance-hall girls, no big-money gambling, probably no great amount of money to gamble with, if gold mining had been its main source. There was gold mining back in the hills in the early days, and some even up to a few years ago, when high operating expenses forced most of it to close down, but none of it ever produced much. A sheep herder prodding around in a dry creek bed on the Upper Rogue River in the early 1930's took out more actual gold in a single afternoon than most of the early-day miners ever saw, or the old hotel either. My grandfather, who was a Hard-Shell Baptist clergyman, used to hold religious services in its main lobby every month or so when he was circuit rider for the district. He was not in the least rip-roaring, though he was responsible for the only shooting the place ever had recorded against it; not exactly a conventional one, though it was disastrous enough in its results.

It happened, according to family tradition, one night after a wedding in the hotel at which he had been invited to officiate. After the ceremony, he withdrew to an upstairs room and went to bed, leaving the guests to their dancing and celebrating, which usually lasted till daylight. Along past midnight, he was roused by some disturbance in the horse corral that sounded as if prowlers might be sneaking up to spring the gate and stampede the horses. Raising an alarm seemed a waste of time, in such an emergency, so he rummaged an old muzzle-loading shotgun out of a closet, rammed down a double load of powder and shot, leaned out of the window and let go both barrels at the shadows outside the corral gate. Nobody ever found out whether he hit anything or not because, loading the gun hurriedly in the dark, he had rammed the tail of his nightshirt down one barrel along with the powder, so the shot yanked him out of the window headfirst. He fell three floors into the middle of the wedding celebration with his shirttail in flames around his neck and scared everybody almost to death. Several guests collapsed, and some ran eight or ten miles without stopping. My grandfather sustained a broken arm and second-degree burns, and miscarriages were claimed by two ladies and denied heatedly by three others, including the bride.

The difference between that uncolored incident and the

rip-roaring type of conventionalized fantasy is the difference between tradition and illusion. Tradition is what a country produces out of itself; illusion is what people bring into it from somewhere else. On the record, the illusions have considerably the better of it. People keep bringing them in. Those who kept the traditions going keep drifting away and scattering, to New York and Washington and California and places in the Middle West. Still, it will go on producing new ones, probably. It always has.

There used to be an old sawmill and logging settlement back in the deep timber on the eastern fringe of the valley country, where my father taught school when I was not much over two years old. It was a small-scale sort of operation, with no prospects of expansion, because its local market was limited to a scattering of homesteaders and cattlemen around the neighborhood, and distance and bad roads made hauling its lumber out to the railroad impossible. Still, between the homesteaders and some half-breed fragments of an old Indian tribe back in the hills, there was enough to run a school on while it lasted. Afterward, the mill closed down, the homesteaders moved away, the Indians were rounded up and shipped north to the collective reservation at Siletz, and the school and settlement were abandoned for a good many years. Recently, after back-country logging had been put back on its feet by such new wrinkles as tractors, hard-surfaced roads, power chain-saws, truck transportation and a rising market for building material, a big lumber company bought up the old camp and the timber back of it, built a fence between it and the main road, and hired a watchman with experience in handling firearms to keep campers and hobos and log pirates out.

There was nothing about the old logging camp that I wanted particularly to see. I had lived in it when too young to remember it; the stories people used to tell about it afterward were associated with them, not with the place. It was the lumber company's watchman I went up there to call on. I had known him from years back, when I was on a Government survey in one of the national forests up in Northern Oregon, and he was guide and camp wrangler for a symphony-orchestra conductor from New York who liked trout fishing, or thought he did: a strutty, playful old gentleman who sang resonantly while fishing, and naturally never caught anything.

The watchman didn't have to work as a guide, being very well off from speculating in orchard lands around the Cascade foothills, but he liked the woods and would rather be working at something than sitting around doing nothing. He used to come over to our camp of an evening and tell stories about being sent out to track down people who had got themselves lost back in the deep timber. He held that anybody could get lost in the woods, there was nothing disgraceful about it, he had been lost in that very country half a dozen times himself, though he was accounted an authority on its geography and landmarks. Whether it turned out seriously or not depended on the kind of intelligence a man used after he got lost. A fool would never admit that he was lost; no matter how completely bushed he was, he always knew his location and directions exactly, and got himself worse lost trying to make them work out. The watchman said he had brought out lost hunting parties in almost a dying condition who were so positive he was taking them in the wrong direction that some of them had to be dragged to get them started. His stories were not only diverting but helpful. I have been lost in the woods a couple of times since then myself, and without them I would undoubtedly have done pretty much what he said the fools always did.

The hard-surfaced road back to the old logging camp had strung the twenty-mile stretch of adjoining country so full of small cottages and shacks and chicken-farm lean-tos that there was hardly any country left until I got within sight of the old logging-camp buildings and the lumber company's fence and padlocked gate. Beyond that, everything changed. There was a dirt road, sprinkled with dead fir needles, with a dusty spot showing where quail had wallowed. The big Douglas firs stood straight and tall and motionless up the sidehill, not crowded together as they are in the rainier mountains near the coast, but scattered out between clumps of hazel and vine maple and open patches of white-top grass and pink fireweed. There were no rusty car bodies or can dumps or barnyard manure piles in the creek. It rattled past clear and bright and untroubled, reaching back through thickets of red willow and gray alder and sweet bush to some old stump land overgrown with evergreen blackberry vines. There was a grouse clucking somewhere up the hill, in a sort of anxiously persistent tone that for some reason was restful to listen to. It was impossible to tell where it was coming from: sounds in timber country have a curious way of seeming to come from the air itself rather than from any tangible thing in it.

The old logging-camp buildings were all nailed up and deserted, except the one nearest the road. It had its windows unboarded, with a school election notice tacked to the door above a wooden-seated chair, and a tin tobacco box alongside containing a few rusty nails, a fire warden's badge, a carpenter's pencil, some loose cigarette papers, and a half-box of .22 cartridges. The watchman was nowhere around. I left my car at the gate and climbed over it and walked up the road a few hundred yards to look around.

There were deer tracks in the road, a doe and two fawns, and big-foot rabbit tracks, and a blue grouse hooting in the firs somewhere, but it was not altogether as the Lord had left it. People had lived here once, up the dirt road for miles back into the hills. My mother used to tell about some of them: an old cattleman, enormously wealthy, who kept eight squaws, one at each of his line camps, and had children by all of them regularly, though he was then past seventy, and a town named after him which is still flourishing. And one of the young half-breeds who drew a knife on my father in school, and then tried to make up for it by bringing him presents—potted plants, ornamented mustache cups, dressed turkeys—all of which turned out to be stolen; and another half-breed, a youngster of about fifteen, who used to write poems, each stanza in a different-colored ink, and peddle them around the settlement at two bits a copy. People used to buy them and never read them. And another cattleman, middle-aged and quarrelsome, was supposed to have set himself up in business by murdering and robbing an old Chinese peddler, and had a mania for giving expensive wedding presents to every young married couple in the community, even those whose fathers he was sworn to shoot on sight. . . . There were more of them. It had been a big community once. There had probably been as many people in it as there were in the chicken-farm cottages down the creek, and they had stayed there at least as long. But they had marked it less, or maybe the marks they made were the kind that healed over more easily. A few were still visible: some old stumps grown over with vines, some half-burned fence posts showing through the fir needles, part of an old corduroy wood road running uphill into the salal, with rabbit fur scattered in it where a hawk had struck. The creek had taken out some of the old marks, seemingly. A tangle of whitened driftwood piled high above a cutbank showed that it had sometimes flooded. There were scuff marks across a strip of sand below the cutbank where some beavers had dragged sticks to use in building a dam.

They had their dam finished, and the cutbank was partly

undermined where they had started a tunnel to their nest. It was nothing to be proud of, as far as workmanship went. I had always heard that beavers had a sort of obsession for work, and spent all their time at it because they enjoyed doing it, but the dam didn't show it. They hadn't cut down any trees for it at all, though there were dozens of alder and willow saplings within easy reach. They had merely made it a tangle of dry sticks from the driftwood, most of them no bigger than a lead pencil. The whole thing was so childish and flimsy that they had to weight it down with rocks to keep the creek from washing it away. It was some sort of commentary on modern times, probably, but a man gets tired of having the same thing proved over and over again. It was time for me to go back, anyway.

The company watchman was sitting in his chair by the door when I got back to the gate. There is always a certain trepidation about meeting somebody you haven't seen for twenty years, but he hadn't changed much. He had always been grayish and scrawny, and he was merely a little grayer and scrawnier. He apologized for being out when I came, and said he had been down arguing with some of the chicken-farm people who kept trying to sneak through the company fence and dump garbage upstream in the creek. He didn't know why it meant so much to them to dump it upstream, and they hadn't been able to explain it very convincingly themselves. Their main argument seemed to be that it was a free country and the creek belonged to everybody, and the lumber company had no right to go around telling people what they could do and what they couldn't. It looked sometimes as if they couldn't stand to see anything in the country left as it had been before they got there. It preyed on their minds, or something.

"There's not much left for them to worry about," I said. "Not around here, anyway."

"It's no better up north," he said. "There's highways criss-crossed all through the mountains up there. A highway into the mountains lets people see what wild country looks like, if they can find room to drive between the log trucks. Nobody ever figures that the wild country might not want to see what people look like. It's like that old saloonkeeper up on the Columbia River that had himself buried in an Indian graveyard when he died, because he'd decided that Indians were better to associate with than white people."

I remembered the story. Everybody had been deeply impressed by his wish to associate with Indians after he died. Nobody had thought to find out how the Indians felt about associating with him. It turned out that they were not impressed by the prospect at all. After he had been buried in their tribal graveyard, they moved all their graves somewhere else and let him have it all to himself. Building a main highway into a wild country is like driving a red-hot poker into a tree and expecting the sap to start circulating in it. The living tissue of the tree draws back from it, and the sap goes on circulating around it; or else the tree dies.

"There's wild country left," the watchman said. "More than you'd think, from the way they've fixed things down the creek below here. It's not much different than it used to be, if you figure it right. You've got to figure it in time instead of mileage, that's all. It used to take a day for a man to drive up here from the railroad with a team and wagon. You probably drove it in less than an hour, and you're surprised that it's all built up. If you'll take a team and wagon and take out on some of these old corduroy wood roads into the hills for a day, the way you'd have done twenty years ago, you'll run into all the wild country you want. You may have to chop some logs out of the road and fight yellow jackets off the horses, but it'll be wild. The animals and everything else."

"Not all the animals," I said, and told him about the beaver and their scamped job of dam-building up the creek.

"They're Oklahoma beavers, I expect," he said. "Moved out from the Dust Bowl back in the hard times, more than likely. You've got to remember that they've been through a lot, and that it don't do any good to stand around and criticize. What they need is help. You ought to have chewed down a few trees for 'em, to get 'em started off on the right foot."

It was not the first tribute to the Oklahoma temperament I had heard, though most were less indirect. "Are they as bad as that?" I said.

"We're none of us perfect," he said mildly. "They're not exactly the kind of company I'd pick to be shipwrecked on a desert island with, but there's points about 'em. I had a crew of sixty of 'em fighting a little brush fire in some second-growth timber on Thief Creek last fall, and they were as conscientious as anybody could ask in a lot of ways. Paydays and mealtimes they never missed. They even fought fire off and on, till it got within about three-quarters of a mile of 'em. Then they dropped everything and legged it out of there at a gallop. Well, they have to learn. It takes time."

"It sounds as if it might take a lot of it," I said. "More than either of us will ever see, probably."

"I've seen 'em come in like this before," he said. "Some as bad, and some worse. They spread back into places like this and dumped garbage and slashed trees and strung fences and tore up grasslands and fixed everything around to suit themselves. Then they got old, and their kids grew up and moved away somewhere else and sent for 'em and a lot of 'em died out, and now they're all gone. They never last. They think they will, but they never do. They swarm in here with their car wrecks and bellyaches and litters of children, and they pile in to fix the whole country over, and it civilizes 'em in spite of themselves. Then they pick up and go somewhere else to show it off. I may live long enough to see it here yet. Hell, lots of people live to be over ninety nowadays. It'll happen, anyway."

It was looking past externals to an underlying purpose in the country, whether it was the right one or not. And it may have been the right one. Years before, when I was time-keeper for a Greek extra gang on the old Deschutes Rail-road, the foreman of the outfit used almost the same terms in trying to explain about some squabble that had got stirred up among the men. The details were a little involved, and he finally brushed them aside and attacked the root of the problem.

"The trouble with these fellows is that they ain't been over here in this country long enough to know anything," he said.

He was Greek himself, from some small coastal village in the province of Corinth. He had left home when he was young, because of some parental difficulty: he had sneaked his father's muzzle-loading pistol out to see how it shot, and the load of slugs and scrap iron tore all the bark off two of the old man's best olive trees, so he ran away to keep from being skinned alive. "All these fellows know is how things are back in the old country. They think that's all they need to know, and it ain't anything. They ain't civilized back in the old country."

The idea that an expanse of Eastern Oregon sagebrush where horse-Indians still wandered around living in tepees and digging camass could represent a higher stage of civi-lization than the land that had cradled Sophocles and Plato was so startling that I laughed.

"Well, it's the truth," he said, "them people in the old country ain't civilized. They don't know what it is to be civilized till they've been over here awhile. It takes a long time for some of 'em."

"You ought to be civilized by now, anyway," I said. "You've been over here a long time."

"If I was, I wouldn't be out in a place like this," he said. "I didn't say this country got people civilized. I said they found out what it was like to be civilized, that's all. That's as far as I've got."

It did work out to some kind of system. The older generation found out what civilization was; the younger absorbed it, and moved away somewhere else to show it off: Joaquin Miller from his parents' farm in the Willamette Valley to Canyon City, and to England, and to his final exhibitionistic years in California; Edwin Markham from Oregon City to California and to his end in New York; John Reed from Portland to New York and Mexico and to his tomb in Red Square in Moscow. . . . Civilization? At any rate, it was something.

I got a camera from the car to take some pictures of the old logging-camp buildings. It was not difficult to pick out the one we had lived in from the stories my mother had told about it. It was the one with the high front porch; she had told about two drunk half-breed Indians rolling and fighting under it one night on their way home from town, and how she lay in bed listening while one of them beat the other to death with a rock. She was alone in the house; my father was away at a teachers' conference in Roseburg, the county seat.

The watchman looked the camera over, and said he had been intending to get one himself. He wanted to take some pictures of the country to send his son, who lived in Hollywood.

"San Fernando, I guess it is, but it's the same thing," he

said. "He works in Hollywood. He's got one of these television shows, 'Know Your Neighbors,' or something like that; interviews with people, and things like that. He's doing well at it, but it don't leave him much time for anything else. He can't get away much. It'll be a big thing some of these days, but you have to stay with it. If you don't you lose out."

The country north through the Willamette Valley is lovely in the spring, with long expanses of green meadowland and flocks of sheep and dairy herds and clumps of wild apple and plum and cherry flowering against the dark fir thickets along the streams. The towns have a certain New Englandish look about them, emphasizing a difference between their culture and that of the country around them that has existed from the earliest days. The townspeople came originally from New England, and were traders and small merchants and artisans. The settlers in the rural areas were mostly open-country cattle raisers from the Mississippi Valley—Missouri, Arkansas, Tennessee, Kentucky. The two cultures have never mixed, and there has been little sympathy or understanding developed between them. Each is admittedly indispensable to the other: country people need towns, and towns have to live on the country, but there is not much enthusiasm in accepting the necessity.

A highway turns east from Salem across the Cascade Mountains by the Santiam Pass, following an old toll road built by cattlemen in the 1850's as a driveway by which to move their herds from the Willamette Valley to the open-country sagebrush and bunch-grass ranges of Eastern Oregon. It couldn't have looked like much of a move, as far as appearances went. The Willamette Valley grasslands are green, luxuriant, well-watered, and usually open for grazing throughout the entire year. East of the mountains the country is arid, colorless, baked dry in summer and whipped by blizzards in winter, its sparse clumps of whitish-green bunch grass not sodded, but spaced out two or three feet apart from each other with naked red earth showing between each clump, or sometimes hidden so close among the sagebrush roots that an outsider will wonder how cattle turned out on it are managing to keep alive, when they may have been put there to fatten for market. There is not much nutriment in grass that has had too easy a time of it; it will keep cattle alive, but not put weight on them. The bunch grass, which has had to fight for every inch of its growth, is far superior in nutritive value to any of the deep sod grasses west of the mountains. There might be some suspicion of a moral back of this, except that cattlemen are not interested in the moralistic aspects of the subject. Nor are their cattle.

Last April I drove east by the highway over the mountains through Santiam Pass. Deep snow all through the pass and in scattered drifts far down into the timber. Blue Lake down in a deep basin to the south, still and deserted; the snow roofs of the summer cabins looked peaceful and attractive. Not a living soul in any of them. Mount Washington towering back of the lake, its huge snowy peak striking into the blue sky like a spear. Snow in patches even below the level where the fir timber changes to yellow pine; salal bushes in bloom among the pines, hanging full of little pink bells like heather, the shallow drifts of old snow under them splotched with pale yellow where their pollen had shed. No wild life in the fir timber, not even birds. A few magpies among the pines, and a tiny lilac-throated hummingbird working on the salal blossoms. Near where the pine thins out into scattering juniper, a little town called Sisters, where sheepmen used to load their pack trains for the camps in the mountains; remote, quiet and dusty, a movie theater showing some tired B-Western picture. A youngster of about sixteen at the gas station gave me some directions about roads, and then said, "What does television look like?" . . .

North through the Warm Springs Indian Reservation. Open juniper and grassland, the timbered Cascade Mountains off to the west, a few cattle and some scattering wheatfields. The agency was about the same as it was twenty years ago: the store and gas station probably new. Some young Indians in a car, apparently from Klamath or somewhere south, on their way to a spring salmon festival at Celilo on the Columbia River. I noticed that a couple of them had their hair marcelled, apparently to get rid of the Indian straightness. It didn't seem much of an improvement. Until recent years there were only dirt roads through the reservation, and it was even lonelier than it is now.

. . . North to the Columbia River at Celilo. It was late afternoon, and twenty years had not changed it much: the gigantic blue shadows reaching down from the gray-black cliffs over the white sand and dark water were still enough to make a man catch his breath and forget to let go of it. No picture can do what the place itself does; the pen-and-ink drawing that Theodore Winthrop made of it for his *The Canoe and the Saddle* in 1860 comes no farther from it than any of the modern photographs. They all miss the intensity of tones, and the scale—the cliffs a thousand feet high, the shadows half a mile deep and twenty miles long, the rapids thundering spray into the air higher than a man can see. The houses scattered in the rifts of cold sunlight have a helpless look, as if the whole thing stunned them. . . .

The salmon festival appeared to be all over with. Several dozen out-of-state cars were pulled up alongside the old Indian village (a huddle of unpainted board shacks along the river, dirt-floored and completely unsanitary, which seem now to have become merely a show piece; the Indians live in some large white corrugated-iron barracks on higher ground, which look very clean and thoroughly dull) and tourists were poking around asking questions of a few middle-aged Indians, with some squaws watching from an old Cadillac sedan. They had on their best clothes, and seemed prim and a little self-conscious. It couldn't have been much of a salmon festival. In the old days, the centerpiece of a salmon festival was always a wagonload of canned heat, and the ceremonies usually wound up in a big free-for-all fight. It was a little dangerous sometimes, but the guests did have something to talk about for the rest of the year.

The river seemed muddy, possibly because of blasting downstream for the foundations of a new hydroelectric dam at The Dalles. When finished, it will back the river up so there will no longer be any rapids, or any salmon fishing either. Probably it is as well. It can't be good for human beings to live as anachronisms, and a salmon festival that has to restrict itself to merely serving salmon is too meaningless to keep on with.

. . . South through the Sherman County wheatfields to Antelope. The wheat towns remain unchanged, at least: no new buildings, the old ones all still standing, though some seemed vacant. The great divisions of color in the wheatfields were beautiful: bright green winter wheat, black summer fallow, white stubble, running long curves and undulations across the ridges to the sky line and into the gray sagebrush to the south. A flock of sheep grazing along a little creek bed at the edge of the sagebrush, with the herder's camp wagon drawn up behind a clump of junipers; not much of a camp wagon, merely a small high-wheeled trailer with a stovepipe stuck through the roof. The herder came out and stopped to talk for a minute: an elderly man, gray and stocky and taciturn. He complained of the long winter, which had been hard on the sheep, and offered to trade his high-powered rifle for my .22 pistol, because there was no longer anything around that a man could use a high-powered rifle on. He had herded sheep most of his life, he said, and didn't mind it. A man could get used to anything. It was easier nowadays, with cars and radios, than it had been. He had a radio in his camp wagon, and liked to listen to it, except the commercials, which made him want to buy things when he was miles from the nearest town and couldn't. His son was in college, he said, studying law, in Los Angeles.

Antelope had not changed in appearance since I lived there as a youngster. It was still a quiet, grayish little town with tall poplars lining the streets and a creek valley spread out below it. The only thing different was the people. They had been mostly Indians and Highland Scots: big lumbering men, some with the reddest hair I have ever seen, who talked English in a curious half-falsetto tone, when they could talk it at all. The only languages one commonly heard on the street were Gaelic and Chinook jargon. It had been a homesick experience, trying to get used to them at first. Now it was a homesick feeling not to find any of them left.

The newspapers had a follow-up story about the salmon festival at Celilo. There were a few touches of the old tradition in it, after all; according to the reports, some of the guests got drunk and got to fighting, and the venerable Celilo chief got poked in the jaw and was confined to his bed, feeling terrible. The stories gave his age as somewhere around eighty-two. It must have been all of twenty-five years ago that he appeared as a witness in a Federal-court hearing involving some old fishing-rights treaty, and gave his age as eighty-eight. Still, anybody is entitled to feel younger at a party than at a Federal-court hearing.

. . . South to Bend. The road follows the high country along the rim of the Deschutes River canyon, with a view of all the big snow peaks to the west: Mount Adams, Mount Jefferson, Mount Hood, Mount Washington, the Three Sisters,

Broken Top. Sometimes, when the air is clear and the wind from the north, you can see Mount Shasta to the south. A man working in this country during the summer falls into the habit of counting these peaks from the north to south regularly every day, and watching to see how their snow lines are holding out against the heat.

In the irrigated lands north of Bend, there were ring-necked pheasants all along the road. They stay close to it, knowing that it is against the law to shoot from a public highway, but not knowing enough to keep out of the way of traffic. I counted eight that had been killed by cars, in ten miles.

The general notion about company towns is that they are ugly, spirit-destroying, and deliberately sordid and monotonous. Bend and Klamath Falls are both sawmill towns, dominated by big lumber companies. They are the two loveliest towns in Eastern Oregon, and perhaps in the entire West. Certainly there is nothing in California that can come anywhere near either of them.

. . . Southeast to Lakeview. The road from the Deschutes River into the Great Basin is through two great national forests, the Deschutes and the Fremont, with pine timber for miles on both sides of it. There are ice caves off to the north a few miles, probably originally blown into some body of molten lava by imprisoned steam, and not much to see. A cave is a hole in the ground, and ice is ice. The short dark-colored underbrush among the pines is used as summer grazing by the cattle herds east in the Great Basin, its foliage being highly esteemed for its meat-building properties. The stockmen call it "chamiso"; erroneously, since it bears no resemblance to the chamiso of Arizona and California, which is worthless as forage, is pale gray instead of dark, and grows only on ground open to the sun, never in woods.

This country has never been notably accurate in picking names for things. The little blue-flowered ground plant known here as "filaree" is not in the least like the afilerilla of the Southwest, and is not even the same botanical species. Nobody could possibly confuse the two, one being a flowering plant and the other a flowerless grass, so the misnaming must have been accomplished in the dark, or maybe it was mere cussedness. There are dozens of similar cases. The Douglas fir is not a fir, but a spruce; the Port Orford cedar is not cedar, but a sub-species of redwood; the sagebrush is not sage, but wormwood. Some local breeds of trout are really grilse, what the restaurants serve as filet of sole is either sea perch or flounder, and their lobster (which has no claws, merely antennae) is probably some kind of overgrown prawn.

. . . There are a few little towns scattered along this corner of the Great Basin: Silver Lake, Paisley, Valley Falls. They are old and a long way apart, with a subdued sort of charm about them—gray poplars lining the streets, old houses set back against the willows along the creek, lilacs and bleeding heart and white iris coming into bloom behind the gray picket fences. The little creeks hurry past bright and swift and eager, though there is nothing much for them to hurry to. Since the waters of the Great Basin have no outlet to the ocean, the only end its creeks can look forward to is stagnation in some of the alkali lakes down in the desert.

One of the towns had a small roadside lunchstand run by an elderly couple who had owned a cattle ranch in one of the valleys back in the old wagon-freighting days. The old gentleman came out and visited while I had lunch. He was bright, alert, and quiet-spoken. Nobody would have guessed him to be much over fifty, though he must have been considerably past that to have been running a cattle ranch so far back. He spoke of some of the old wagon-freighters, and said he had lost his ranch in the depression, and had been in the country so long he couldn't bring himself to strike out for a new one. There was no chance of starting over again where he was; all the small ranches had been wiped out in the bad times, and the country had fallen into the hands of four or five big cattle syndicates, which ran it to suit themselves. They had everything bought up—homesteads, small ranches, Government land leases—and they hung onto it. A small outfit would not stand a dog's chance trying to buck them. They were the main reason that the town was dead. With the syndicates sitting on everything, there was nothing for new people to come in for.

"They must bring in some business themselves," I said. "You can't run cattle outfits that size without a payroll."

"It don't amount to much," he said. "Not the way they run things, with cross fences and branding chutes and trucks and tractors and everything done by machinery. When they hire a cowboy, they don't ask him if he can stay on a horse or handle a rope. What they want to know is whether he can repair a truck and dig postholes. In the old days, any of those outfits would have kept seventy or eighty men on regular. Now they get by with a dozen apiece; fifteen, maybe. They pay 'em well, I hear. More than they're worth, to my notion. Most of 'em couldn't work for me for nothing. Assembly-line mechanics, that's all there is to 'em."

We talked about men we had both known. One had started a bootlegging business in a small sheep town up north, and when things began to slow up and the businessmen began to close down and move out, he decided to take over all their businesses and run them himself, to keep the place going. Now, in addition to his bar, he ran the drugstore, the grocery, a hay and feed business and the barbershop, besides handling a small line of dry goods, notions, plumbing supplies and fuel. He also repaired shoes, sold hunting and fishing licenses, ran a branch of the county library, and was agent for a laundry and dry cleaner in one of the bigger towns.

"I hope he stands it, handling all that," I said. "He must be old by now."

"A man will stand a lot to hang on in a place he's got used to," the restaurant man said. "Anyway, he's not old. He can't be much over sixty."

. . . All the Great Basin is high country. The altitude of the flatlands around Picture Rock Pass is over 4000 feet, and the mountains are twice that. In the short timber northeast of Picture Rock Pass are mule deer; to the southeast, around Hart Mountain, there are antelope. In between, lying under the huge hundred-mile length of mountain scarp known as the Abert Rim, is a chain of big alkali lakes—Silver Lake, Summer Lake, Abert Lake, Goose Lake. Some are over thirty miles long. During cycles of scant rainfall, they are dry beds of white alkali, as they were during the 1930's, and in 1858 when Lieutenant Philip H. Sheridan camped in the area on some obscure Indian campaign. When the cycle turns, they run full of water again, as they are beginning to do now. The water is too alkaline for any use except as scenery, and Abert Lake has a pronounced odor, but it is pleasanter to live with than the dust clouds, and the uselessness seems a small thing when the great flocks of wild ducks and geese and black-headed trumpeter swans begin to come down on it in their northward migration every spring.

There is something wild and freakish and exaggerated about this entire lake region in the spring. The colors are unimaginably vivid: deep blues, ferocious greens, blinding whites. Mallard ducks bob serenely on mud puddles a few feet from the road, indifferent to everybody. Sheep and wild geese are scattered out in a grass meadow together, cropping the grass side by side in a spirit of complete tolerance. Horses and cattle stand knee-deep in a roadside marsh, their heads submerged to the eyes, pasturing the growth of grass underneath the water. A tractor plowing a field moves through a cloud of white Mormon sea gulls, little sharp-winged creatures, no bigger than pigeons and as tame, following the fresh-turned furrow in search of worms. A flock of white snow geese turning in the high sunlight after the earth has gone into shadow looks like an explosion of silver.

The black-headed swans trumpeting sound like a thousand French taxi horns all going at once. If you happen to be close when they come down, the gigantic wings sinking past into the shadows will scare the life out of you. It is no wonder that the Indians of this country spent so much of their time starting new religions.

. . . Frenchglen, Steens Mountains. Nobody hears much about the Steens Mountains. They are near the southeastern corner of the state, a 10,000-foot wall separating the Great Basin on the west from the tributaries of the Snake River on the east. There is a wild-game refuge in a creek valley along the western rim, with antelope and pheasants and flocks of wild ducks and geese scattered all through it.

. . . The little lake high up in the mountains looked about as it did when we used to ride up over an old wagon road in the late summer to fish for speckled trout. It was small, not over a quarter of a mile long, and not shown on most maps at all. The thickets of dwarf cottonwood around it had not grown or dwindled, the water was rough and dark and piercingly cold, and the remains of old snowdrifts in the gullies back of it still had the curiously regular shapes that looked, at a little distance, like spires and towers and gables in a white town. There was no town anywhere near; the closest was over a hundred miles away. It looked as quiet as it always had at sundown—the dark water, the ghostly cottonwoods, the scrub willows along the bank, a few scrawny flowers spotting the coarse grass. About dark, a wind came up, and it began to rain and kept it up all night. By morning it had eased up a little, but the wind was stronger and it was spitting sleet. Being snowed in, in such a place, was not a tempting prospect. I loaded the soggy camp rig into the car, turned it around gingerly in the mud, and headed out.

There was a sheep camp in the cottonwoods at the head of the lake where the road turned down the mountain. The camp tender was striking camp to pull out, the tent hanging limp on the ridgepole and flapping cumbrously when the wind struck it, the pack mules standing humped against the grains of sleet and gouts of foam from the lake that kept pelting them. The sheep were already on the way out; they were jammed so close together down the road that it was impossible to get the car into it. I stopped, and the herder called his dog and went ahead to clear a lane through them.

It was slow work trying to crowd them off into the cottonwood thicket and there was open ground beyond, so I waved to him to drive them on through to where they would have room to spread out. He nodded, and came back to stir up the tail-enders. It was not a big herd; three hundred, maybe, mostly old ewes, hardly enough for two full-grown men to be spending their time on. He got the tail-enders started, and stood back and dropped the cottonwood branch he had been urging them along with. I expected him to say something, but he looked away, watching the dog round up a few stragglers. He was about forty, heavy-boned and slow-looking and bashful, as if he was trying to avoid being spoken to. It struck me what the reason might be, and I took a chance on it.

"De Vascondaga, verdad?" I said.

That was it. He had been trying to dodge around admitting that he didn't know English. A good many Basque sheepherders in that country didn't.

"Si, Vizcaya," he said. *"Aldeano de Zarauz."*

Vizcaya was one of the Basque provinces. Vascondaga was the collective name for all of them. He was from the country adjoining some town named Zarauz.

"Hace mucho?" I said.

"Dos anos," he said. *"Mas o menos."*

He was not being exactly co-operative. I would have given a good deal to be able to sling a sentence or two of Euskera at him, just to see him jump, but wishing did no good. Spanish was the best I could manage. I tried a change of subject.

"It is slow moving a camp with pack mules," I said.

"We work with what we have," he said.

There didn't seem much left to say on that. I tried the weather.

"Que tiempo malo," I said.

"Hay cosas peores," he said. "There are worse things." He was loosening up a little.

He had something specific in mind, I thought. If he had been over here only two years—"You saw the Civil War in Spain?"

He nodded, and took a deep breath. "Nobody sees all of a war. I saw people shot. I saw our house burned. My father was shot. I didn't see that, but I saw enough."

"You are *desterrado?*" I said. It was a polite expression the Spaniards used for a political refugee. It meant something like exile.

"A little," he said. Then he took it back. "No. I am not *desterrado.* This is my country, here. It is the only one I need."

His handful of lumbering old ewes plodded down the open slope in the wind. The mules flinched and humped uneasily as a blast rattled sleet against them. Some torn leaves from the cottonwoods skimmed past.

51

"Some people would call it bleak," I said. "Weather as cold as this."

"Nobody can know what is good until he has seen what is bad," he said. "Some people don't know. I do."

He went to help the camp tender with the packs. I drove out of the cottonwoods and through the sheep and on down the mountain. It was Oregon, all right: the place where stories begin that end somewhere else. It has no history of its own, only endings of histories from other places; it has no complete lives, only beginnings. There are worse things.

Fishing Fever

ONE thing about fishing that most fishermen are not conscious of and most non-fishermen uninformed about is that it gives its devotees a slightly peculiar set of values—not distorted, exactly, but a little transfigured and elevated and outside what ordinary people might expect. The case of a friend of mine who works in the Government atomic-energy plant at Hanford in the State of Washington may illustrate how it sometimes works. He came back this spring from a fishing trip along a small creek that empties into the Yakima River a few miles from where he is employed, and reported various details about the state of the water and what flies the trout were rising to and how they had to be handled. He also mentioned that while he was fishing some of the downstream holes late one forenoon, he had happened on a couple or three buffalo grazing a strip of dead bunch grass between the county road and the creek. It struck him as unusual to find buffalo wandering loose along a main county road within picnicking distance of so modern a development as an atomic-energy plant—actually they must have been almost in sight of it—and he had thought for a moment of going back to his car and bringing a camera to photograph them, to prove that such things could happen.

It was too bad he changed his mind. The buffalo were not

strays from some circus or carnival company, as might have been supposed. They were real native wild buffalo, from a small and scattered herd that had inhabited the broken country called the Rattlesnake Hills in the Big Bend of the Columbia River since long before any white men had ever seen it. Washington Irving's *Adventures of Captain Bonneville* mentions their being there in 1833, though even then they were so wild and cautious that the Indians never hunted them, and seldom even saw them. Two or three loose specimens from the only completely untamed buffalo herd in the United States might have been worth a photograph or two, at least. My friend admitted that he should have got his camera and tried it. The trouble was that they were between him and his car, and he couldn't get to it without herding them down toward the creek. If they waded into it, they would muddy the water and spoil the fishing the rest of the way downstream, and he couldn't bring himself to risk that. Fishing, after all, was what he had come out there for. Photographing buffalo was all very well, but he was not prepared for it, physically, emotionally or temperamentally. He even regretted having a camera along to feel tempted by. Next time, he had decided, he would leave it at home so he could feel free to concentrate on essentials.

Fishing fever can do that to a man's sense of proportion. It can also color his judgment in matters that have nothing to do with nature or wild life at all. In the Pacific Northwest, where I was born and brought up, it once reached far enough to have a permanent effect on the country's history. Back in the 1840's when the Oregon boundary question was in controversy between the United States and Great Britain, a British admiral was sent out by his government to report on whether the disputed territory was worth holding onto. His report went into considerable detail about its worthlessness and savagery and remoteness, and added, as a final clincher, that the salmon in the streams and coastal waters were the most worthless part of it, because the blasted things wouldn't rise to a fly. In the light of all the evidence, he recommended handing the territory over to the United States, hide, hair, horns and fins, and good riddance, which was done. There is no record that his government ever gave evidence of displeasure over his recommendation. He had reported according to his lights as an officer, a patriot and an angler. No government could have asked more.

He was a little sweeping in stating that West Coast salmon wouldn't rise to a fly, though the oversight was not very important. There are times during the spring spawning run when they will rise to a fly, or to anything else within reach that is moving, but that phase only lasts a few days out of the year, and since nobody can ever tell when it will occur, it is hardly worth counting. The Indian system of seining or dip-netting at the foot of a rapid is still the most reliable way of catching them, and it bears much the same relation to sporting fishing as the Chinese method of catching fish with a trained cormorant, or the practice among the Nevada Paiutes of circling a river-shallow and clubbing them to death. The admiral was right in disdaining such low business, and in feeling that any region where it had to be resorted to was unworthy of membership in the Empire. His moral rigidity not only changed international boundaries and shunted a good many people into United States citizenship who might otherwise have been subjects of the Crown, but it may also have laid down a tradition of picayunishness in Northwestern angling. People who acquire their first experience of fishing in the Pacific Northwest are always a little sniffish about fishing techniques elsewhere, and about any kind of fishing that does not involve either trout, steelhead or salmon. Fishing for anything outside those three species is not really fishing at all, but merely something for school kids to piddle at with a bent pin and a switch and a length of string.

It is true that there are not many other species of edible fish in Northwestern streams—a few sturgeon in the Columbia River sometimes and an annual run of eels, which used to be dipnetted and dried by Indians for their winter food supply and shunned vigorously by everybody else—but even when some other edible species turns up it is likely to be viewed with suspicion, merely because it is outside any of the accepted categories. Once I dropped in on a sheep camp on the Upper Columbia River and found the two herders arguing acrimoniously over a tin bucket half-full of some largish high-keeled fish with heavy scales, which they had snagged out of a nearby slough and were having trouble identifying. One held that they were chubs, the other insisted that they were squawfish. It was not a point that could be easily compromised, so they had got down to personalities, which was not settling anything.

One thing they had managed to agree on. The fish, whatever they were, were mud eaters and unfit for human consumption, and they would have to be got rid of when the argument was over. I took a close look at the bucket, not being quite sure what either chubs or squawfish looked like, but being willing to learn. The fish were neither one nor the other. They were small-mouth bass. There were a dozen or fifteen of them, and some must have weighed close to a pound and a half. I explained to the herders what they were and that they were considered highly edible in many parts of the country where nothing better was available, but they were not much impressed. They seemed to suspect that I was trying to stay neutral by siding against both of them, and they went on with their argument as if I hadn't said anything. I left them building up a fire to burn the fish so their herd dogs couldn't get at them, and still arguing, sometimes changing sides on each other for the sake of variety. The argument mattered more than the fish, seemingly. Sheep herding is a draggy life, and anything that will make red-hot conversation is always welcome.

Even among the three categories to which fishermen in the Northwest are restricted by tradition and prejudice, there's room for individual preferences. A really confirmed salmon fisherman will hardly ever consider any other form of fishing worth talking about. My grandfather, a Hard-Shell Baptist clergyman, was of that stripe, and once flogged one of his sons for reminding him that it was Sunday when he was stringing up his tackle to head for the creek where the chinooks were cavorting like squirrels in a brush fire. When salmon fishing is good, it is lively enough to suit anybody. Nothing gets around faster or fights harder than a chinook, once he is hooked, and a man's glands would have to be down pretty low to resist the waves of varying emotions called into action in getting him worn down and landed. Still, the skill required is only in landing him, not in hooking him to begin with. No amount of art or guile can induce a salmon to take a lure unless he feels like it, and if he does feel like it, nothing can stop him. It is the same with steelhead. A steelhead will strike anything that moves at the depth where he happens to be feeding. If you can figure out what the depth is and sink your bait exactly to it, the rest is merely a matter of hanging on and praying that the tackle will hold.

By trout-fishing standards, this is missing out on two-thirds of the fun. The best part of fishing, to a trout addict, is in figuring out a lure that the trout will fall for when they are not especially interested, or in some technique of casting or handling that will get a bait past the swarm of eager fingerlings near the surface to reach the big ones on the bottom, or some similar refinement that will make use of some idiosyncrasy of nature to circumvent the trout's sluggishness or cussedness. To such people, there is a more genuine sense of accomplishment in casting a Number Twelve fly thirty feet against a cross wind through a two-foot gap in the underbrush and hooking a reluctant trout than there is in landing a thirty-pound salmon after a fight lasting an hour and a half.

Even in trout fishing there are distinctions. Rainbow trout, because of their unusual hardiness and ability to stand transplanting, are almost the only species to be found in the Coast streams now, besides being common in the Andean lakes of South America, in New Zealand and even in some parts of Africa. They are a beautiful fish, resilient and high-spirited and adaptable almost anywhere, with a peculiar habit of changing coloration to suit their environment. In a sunlit stream with a varicolored bottom they will develop streaks and splashes of vivid scarlet against a ground of blackish-green, while in shaded mountain lakes with a heavy snow cast they breed to a pale leaf-gray with no markings at all. They are used almost exclusively in restocking Western streams, replacing the earlier speckled mountain trout, which have long since been crowded out by competition from livestock, irrigation projects, sawmills, chlorinating plants and people.

The speckled mountain trout was the species I knew earliest. There used to be nothing else in the small lakes and snow creeks of the high mountains. They were also in the upland streams of the Great Basin, where, since there was no such thing as trout transplanting then, they must have been ever since the post-glacial period. In spite of their touchiness about being crowded—or maybe because of it—

I still think they were the finest trout to fish for that ever existed. They were not large: the biggest ones were from twelve to fifteen inches, and the average was less, but they had fire and dash and spirit, and when they came after a fly they put the whole works into it. A rainbow or a golden trout will sometimes fritter around for an hour making feints and passes at a floating object, out of mere curiosity or idle-mindedness. A speckled trout never moves till his mind is made up, and when he does move he means it. He grabs a fly before it is even in the water and is halfway to the next county before the astonished angler recovers enough presence of mind to take up slack. There is nothing shilly-shally about a speckled trout. Whatever he does, he does for all he is worth. Rainbow trout are more adaptable and easier to handle, and they afford healthful recreation for thousands of weekend sportsmen who catch them out of every creek within range of a main highway as fast as the trucks from the State hatcheries can pour them in, but there is not the same feeling about them, or about that kind of fishing, for that matter. It lacks something; you can tell it by the grim, set-featured expressions of the anglers.

This tank-truck system of delivering trout to anglers is a highly practical and efficient one, though the people who run the tourist accommodations don't always seem as appreciative about it as one might expect. In a roadside lunchroom on the Chelan River in Central Washington this past summer, I remarked something to the waitress about some fishermen who had been flycasting across a long riffle near some tourist cabins for half an hour without any noticeable result except to get their lines tangled together a few times. She said she supposed they were practicing: the truck from the hatchery was not due till the end of the week, and there wouldn't be any fish in the river till it showed up.

"It only puts in enough to last through the weekend,"

she said. "Sometimes they don't last even that long. These hatchery trout are half-tame anyway, and you could catch them with your hands if it wasn't for all those tourists splashing around squabbling over them."

It didn't sound very absorbing. "You'd think they'd try out some of the creeks back in the mountains, instead of just waiting around like that," I said. "It would be less crowded, and they'd get away from traffic and see some new country."

"They don't want new country," she said. "They've got what they want, right here, traffic and all. They like it."

And still, this shift from the old outdoor spirit of self-reliance and exploration to a dependence on weekly fish deliveries by truck has a bright side to it. There are a lot of small back-country creeks where the hatchery trucks never come, because of their remoteness or inaccessibility or something. In the old days, when fishing meant going where the fish were, even the smallest of them got fished out thoroughly before the season had been open a week—sometimes sooner. Under the new system of trucking fish where the fishermen are, the wilder and smaller streams are left alone, and some of them that were once hardly worth fishing at all have come back surprisingly.

There was one where I stopped for a day last spring, out in the sagebrush country in Central Oregon; a little string of rain pools at the bottom of a rimrock canyon, called Buck Creek, which joins the Deschutes River a mile or so below the old Indian salmon-fishing ground at Sherar Rapids. It is very small and shallow; a man could step across it almost anywhere, and in the old days it was not considered worth bothering with except as a source of minnows and crawfish to use for bait in the big whirlpool below the rapids. I had walked upstream along it for a few hundred yards to look at an old Indian burying ground where a few beautifully made arrowheads sometimes got washed into sight by the spring rains. There were no arrowheads, but when I tossed a cigarette butt into the creek, the shallow pool churned and came alive with trout rushing to strike at it. I had no flies, only a few small bait hooks that I had got down the Coast and nothing to bait them with, and it was too early for grasshoppers; so as an experiment I tried baiting with a catkin from some willows along the bank. They grabbed at it as if it were money from home. They would probably have grabbed another cigarette butt as readily if I had wanted to insult them with one. I caught a couple of dozen from the one small pool in twenty minutes, and could have run it up to a hundred from the pools farther up the canyon if there had been anything to do with them.

One such place could have been an accident, but there were others. There was a creek back in the desert country a few weeks later where I sat for an hour watching a pair of hawks at work picking ten-inch trout out of a hole at the edge of an old hay meadow and carrying them away to a rim-rock cliff a mile or so distant where they evidently had a nest. I don't know how much of a brood they had to provide for, but in the hour I spent watching them they lugged away enough trout to have foundered three or four full-grown men, and they were still at it when I left. Shooting at them would have scared them off, maybe, but it wouldn't have helped the trout much. The creek went dry in its lower reaches every summer, and saving them to dry up with it didn't seem any more humane than leaving them for the hawks, and considerably less picturesque.

There was still another small mountain creek out in the sagebrush near the Nevada line where an elderly Polish couple used to run an overnight station for travelers, with broiled trout as the staple item on their bill of fare. The old Polish woman had never managed to learn English in the forty years she had been living there, but she could go out back of the barn at any hour and in any season, with a cane pole and a dilapidated black-gnat fly with no leader, and come back in fifteen minutes with half a dozen trout running three-quarters of a pound apiece. Nobody else could catch anything out of the creek except water dogs in those days, but when I tried it this past summer there were trout in every hole, and they rose to almost anything that was thrown at them. Some of the sheep herders around the neighborhood thought the old woman had cast a spell on the creek while she lived there, and that it wore off after she moved away. But they were also prepared to argue that killing a spider would bring on rain and that food cooked by electricity introduced harmful electrons into the digestive system, so the theory didn't count for much except to give life in that part of the country a slight added interest, which it could stand. There were fish in the creek and they were biting, and it was more than they had ever done when the old Polish woman lived there, anyway.

Shifts of population have wiped out fishing in many places, but that also can work two ways. There used to be a wild stretch of burned-over hill country up the Oregon coast adjoining the Siuslaw National Forest where I went deer hunting sometimes in the fall. The only road into it then was a crooked wagon track down the open beach, with a few loose planks strung out across the worst places to keep cars from losing traction and miring down. There were small creeks every few miles that had to be forded with a rush and a prayer because of quicksand, and anybody rash enough to risk being overtaken by an incoming tide could catch a horse-load of fish out of them in a morning—trout, salmon trout, steelhead, salmon, candle smelt—depending on the season. A new main highway has gone in since then, the whole coast country has filled up with people and towns, and the creeks have been converted into logging ponds and spillways for municipal sewer systems. There is an embarrassed feeling about going back to country like that, trying to figure out old landmarks that have been built over by glass-fronted residences and realty offices, buying color film and the latest magazines in a supermarket and remembering having killed an eight-point buck deer between its front entrance and the garden-supply emporium across the street. It really was not so long ago as it sounds—twenty years, maybe. If any of the townspeople were told about it now, they would undoubtedly conclude that it must have been done with a flintlock rifle, back around the time of Lewis and Clark. Anything that happened in the country before they moved in is all lumped together as pioneering, whether it happened in the administration of Jefferson or Hoover.

Back of one of the new towns there was an old pack trail that wound up into the hills, following an almost-dry watercourse for a couple of miles and ending at a little clearing and a clump of empty cabins where a man I knew had taken up a homestead back in the early 1920's. He was middle-aged then, with a good many years of assembly-line work behind him, and he had picked the place as a peaceful and uncompetitive location where he could live out the rest of his days, untroubled by urban pressures and work schedules and hurry and people. He had put in several years of hard work clearing the place and making it livable: felling trees, grubbing stumps, clearing brush, splitting rails and shingles, building fences and cabins and sheds and lugging furniture up the trail from the road, mostly on his back. I don't know whether he ever got it completely arranged to suit him or not; the population boom along the highway drew him away from it, as it drew all the people from those little back-country homesteads, and he was running a logging-camp commissary and lunch counter somewhere down the coast and doing very well at it.

The work he had done on the place was being taken back by the wilderness. Mountain laurel had overgrown his fence and garden, the sheds and cabins were sagging and half unroofed, and his beehives had all been tipped over and ripped apart by bears. Most of the things he had carried up the two miles of trail on his back were still there, though dilapidated—the cast-iron kitchen stove, the heavy old oak dresser, some walnut rocking chairs, a big nickel-plated kerosene lamp, a set of old-fashioned steelyards for weighing deer, a wheelbarrow: all things that represented hard work and hopefulness and illusion, all thrown away, rusting and falling apart in the bracken and dwarf alder and wild huckleberry that were beginning to push up even between the floor boards of the cabin.

The one thing that kept the feeling of futility and disappointment from being unbearable was the pond he had built for his water supply. It was merely a dammed-up spring that spread back into a pool about twenty feet across, mud-bottomed and overgrown with alders, and so shallow in most places that leaves fallen into it stuck half out of the water. But there were big speckled trout in it. I counted half a dozen that must have been fifteen inches long, lying close to the surface and paying not the slightest attention to me, though I could have knocked two or three of them out with a stick if there had been one handy. They couldn't have been planted there, because none of the hatcheries cultivated speckled trout, and they couldn't have come in from anywhere else, because the pond was completely landlocked, with no intake or outlet that they could have come by. It lightened the oppressive feeling about the place to have them there, wherever they had come from, and to know that Nature, instead of merely wiping out and burying man's errors of judgment, was turning some of them to use for her own purposes. Nature is more ingenious than we sometimes imagine, and she is accustomed to working over our mistakes from having worked over plenty of her own.

The problem of how fish get into waters that are completely landlocked is always fascinating to speculate on— the native trout that were in the upland streams of the Great Basin when the first whites came to the country, the annual run of huge indigenous suckers up the Truckee River in Nevada, unlike any other suckers in the world and with no point of origin except where they are now; the tiny little semisardines in the half-alkaline Lake Texcoco in the Valley of Mexico, the golden trout in the glacial lakes of the California High Sierras, the whitefish of the lovely little Lake Zirahuen in Michoacán: none of those waters have any outlet anywhere. There is no way that fish could have got into them from anywhere else. Could they have hatched out of the rocks all by themselves, or might it have been the mud? Neither seems altogether satisfying as an explanation, and still, they had to start somewhere. Did the pre-Columbian Indians know about fish planting?

I have never been able to work out any reasonable answer for it, and I never stop trying. Once, out pigeon hunting at the edge of a small village in the desert country of Northern Mexico, I got so absorbed in studying a swarm of odd-looking little yellow-and-black-spotted fish in an irrigation ditch that I forgot all about the pigeons in the nut palms overhead. Since pigeons were a regional delicacy and the fish weren't, I ruined the reputation of Americans as a practical-minded race for the entire village. The ditch was nothing but a small desert seep; it came out of the ground in one place, wandered through some gardens for half a mile, and went back into the ground again. None of the people in the village had any idea where the fish had come from or how long they had been there: always, they were inclined to think, though the subject didn't interest them much. The village was not especially interesting either, I thought. It is only because of the fish in the irrigation ditch that I remember it now. An interest in fish or fishing can communicate itself to things around it sometimes, and sometimes they need it.

Sometimes such an interest can get itself mixed into a man's individuality until it is hard to tell where he stops and it starts. I was staying for a few days at a run-down old hotel in one of the little Northern California hill towns last fall, and was sitting on the whittling bench outside the front entrance talking with the proprietor about some of the Indian reservations in the neighborhood when a man came riding down the street toward us on horseback. He was somewhere past middle age, gray-haired, trim and stately-looking, dressed in store clothes and a white shirt, with a crutch laid across his saddle pommel like the long rifle in a Frederic Remington painting of a typical frontiersman. When he got close, I saw that he had a fishing rod strapped to the crutch. The hotel man nodded to him as he rode past, and said he lived in some old mining cabin a mile or two out of town, and had been a schoolteacher until he got too old and crotchety for it. Now he didn't do much of anything: drew a small pension, trapped a little in the winter, drafted legal documents that were not important enough to hire a lawyer for, wrote letters to the county newspaper for people who liked to pop off in public and wanted some big words thrown in for style—odds and ends like that. He managed to make out. The country didn't offer much of a field for him, what with his lameness and his education.

"There's places that might," I said. "He don't have to stay here, does he?"

"He thinks he does, I guess," the hotel man said. "He's

at work lining out some old mining road that hits a little creek back in the hills. He aims to have it put back in shape and start some kind of a sportsmen's resort along the creek somewhere—charge a dollar a day for fishing and camping, or something like that. He thinks there'll be money in it. It might work. He claims there's trout up there so thick you can write your name in 'em with a stick, and I guess there are. He brings out plenty of 'em."

"Patching up one of those old mountain roads can run into money," I said. I had tried it once myself. A helicopter would have been cheaper; so would a monorail railroad, or a ski run, or almost anything. "It's a long trip in here from any of the main highways too. He might not get customers enough to pay himself out on it."

"Hell, he'll never do it anyway," the hotel man said. "He gets too much fun out of keeping his damned creek to himself. There ain't a week goes by that he don't come swaggering in with a big string of trout to slap people in the face with. He gets a lot out of it. A man's got to have something to be proud of, I guess."

"It's a wonder somebody don't try to find out where this road into his creek is," I said. "You could trail him."

"I don't care where it is," the hotel man said. "Let him keep it to himself, if it's any satisfaction to him. I've got a creek of my own back in the breaks that'll beat hell out of anything he's got."

There really is a sort of sustaining feeling about having a creek somewhere that other people don't know about, or in knowing something about it that they have missed. Mine is not a creek, exactly, but the backwater of an old hydroelectric dam across a small river that runs into the Columbia from the snowfields of the high Cascade Mountains in Southern Washington. The backwater forms a lake eight or ten miles long, though there are only two or three places in it where the fishing amounts to much. The country on both sides is logged-off stump land grown back to small second-growth timber and underbrush, the old sawmill sheds and bunkhouses are buried in rhododendron and wild black-berry vines, and there are the remains of a few old orchards that were bought out by the hydroelectric company and vacated when the dam went in. The water in the lake is deep and inhumanly cold, with an odd ash-green cast that makes it look opaque, though it is clear and colorless in the shallow places or when dipped out in a bucket. It seems odd to associate age with anything as contemporary as a hydroelectric installation, but it has been there a good many years: long enough for the vegetation and wild life to have become completely adapted to it—from the marten and wood ducks nesting along the shallows and deer and ruffed grouse in the old orchards to the trout that were originally rainbow-colored and have changed to the pale gray-green of the lake water in the deep places.

The trout stay deep and out of sight during the morning low water in the lake, and it is impossible to sink a spinner far enough down to reach them without fouling it in the tangled boughs of some old orchard that got flooded under when the dam went in. Around midafternoon, the floodgates are closed to build up the water level for the peak load that comes in the towns down the river after sundown—the quitting-time rush, the show windows and electric signs lighting up, the electric ranges and water heaters being turned on for dinner. The water rising somehow changes the afternoon light to a luminous white glare and strikes the air over it into a silence that feels as if something had stunned it. In the middle of the hush, in an expanse of smooth water where the reflection of light is so intense it hurts your eyes, the trout begin rising, breaking the glare and the silence with little rainbows of water drops as they come out of the water and slap back into it. It is like being suspended between two separate worlds, one among the drowned cabins and dead orchards at the bottom of the lake, the other of the towns down the river with their quitting-time rushes and electric ranges being turned on and show windows lighting up, feeling and knowing them both without being touched by either.

Silence and passion. . . . The trout work best on a Number Eight stonefly trailed about an inch below the surface on a long line. Some of them run two or three pounds apiece.

A Walk in the Woods

NOTHING leaves a man's thoughts so much room to circulate and develop free from distorting influences as walking through the woods, plodding aimlessly along some half-overgrown trail through the timber to see what is around the next turn, or maybe the next one after that. It shouldn't matter much whether anything is there or whether the trail goes anywhere. To a detached and contemplative mind, a trail that goes nowhere has as much food for reflection about it as one with practicality and usefulness. Sometimes it can have more.

Once I followed the weathered tracks of a farm wagon through some broken pine-timber country in Southeastern Oregon, mostly for the sake of following something, and finally came on a wagon standing rusty and weather-bleached in the middle of an abandoned camp. With it were a half-rotten old tent, a pile of tattered bedding, a few dishes, some rocks piled for a fireplace, some battered cooking utensils and pieces of harness scattered around with grass grown almost over them and a woman's ivory-backed hand mirror hanging from a tree limb by a piece of baling wire. There was nothing to show what kind of people the outfit had belonged to or why they had come there. The land was worthless, the grass sparse, the trees scrawny and twisted and there was no water. They may have taken to the woods to settle a quarrel, or to hide from the authorities, or to hunt for a lost gold mine, or maybe they were a young couple eloping. One explanation was as good as another. The less one knows about such things, the more room there is to guess at them.

To a person used to walking in the woods, an obvious purpose in anything can knock all the interest out of it. Small things like fir seeds drifting loose in the sunlight or grouse feathers scattered in a clearing where a hawk struck can turn out to be unforgettable, while incidents that a practical world might regard as triumphs seem mere passing distractions—the more dramatic, the more annoying.

When I was young a great-uncle of mine in Southwestern Oregon took to wandering around the open timber that lay along the creek bottom below his hay meadows in his old age, and spent almost all his time at it, always carrying a double-bitted ax to keep his neighbors from inventing fool theories about why he was doing it. He was interrupted in his excursion one morning by the hired man, who had snagged a large Chinook salmon in the creek while the horses were watering and was having trouble keeping his line from tangling with the horses' feet. My uncle got the horses out of the creek and helped bring the salmon to land as absorbedly as if he had hooked it himself. Then, after a moment's reflection, he picked it up and hove it back into the creek, threw the hired man in after it and went silently back to the house for the rest of the day.

It was a long time before I came to understand what he had been so resentful about. Salmon was a useful article of diet, and anybody already occupied with a couple of horses was likely to need help in landing one. His strenuousness began to seem rational one fall when I was out with a deer-hunting expedition in a logged-off area of the Coast Range Mountains in Western Oregon. I had injured my right hand in an automobile accident and couldn't handle a rifle, so I spent the time lazing around camp while the rest of the party tramped the hills looking for deer which, as usually happens, kept themselves painstakingly out of sight until the hunting season was over.

Lying around camp got monotonous after a few days, so I started out to explore the line of an old logging railroad that followed a little creek back into the mountains. It wasn't a hunting trip, there were no firearms left in camp to hunt with, and I couldn't have handled a gun anyway.

I did take a folded-up paper sack, on the chance there might be blackberries along the creek, but I didn't use it. There were too many things worth watching—coveys of mountain quail dodging through the salal brush, always with one quail perched on a low limb as a watchman; bumblebees in the patches of fireweed; places where the old logging train had derailed and scored the weather-cracked gray ties for fifty feet with its wheel flanges, and where a trestle across the creek had burned out, leaving the rusty rails hanging helpless in mid-air like half-melted sticks of candy; deer and rabbit trails leading down through the underbrush to the creek, and some bleached crawfish shells scattered along the wet sand where a marten had dined; a flock of band-tailed pigeons that settled on a big madroña tree to eat the scarlet berries, not perching on limbs as birds ordinarily do, but clinging to the outside foliage as if they had been pasted on it for ornament, and then flapping away in panic because one of them lost his hold and let out an alarmed squawk; a huddle of board shanties that had been a logging camp, with galvanized oil drums and some cast-off overalls peering shyly from among the wild blue asters and a greasy old donkey engine bolted to a stump with red-hipped wild roses growing over it, covering its dirt with cleanness.

Finally a wild blackberry patch did come into sight near

the end of the logged-off area. It looked tempting, and there was no sign that even bears had molested it, but it was in a swale at the bottom of a long slope overgrown with mountain laurel. There was no sign of a trail through it, and it was so high that even the fallen trunks of a few huge firs uprooted in some windstorm were almost hidden by it. I sat down on a piece of crumbly rock in the middle of the right of way to decide whether the blackberries would be worth my climbing all that way down.

There were reasons for doing it and reasons against it. The blackberries would be something to show the deer hunters when they got back to camp; but it was past midafternoon, picking them would take time and there would be the job of climbing back through the underbrush after they were picked, which was tiresome to think about. The whole subject was tiresome; I wished the blackberry patch hadn't been there, or that I hadn't seen it.

The sky over the fir timber had a curious effect of depth and tenseness about it; the spaces behind the sun were as vast and lucid and quivering as the space in front of it. I got up, deciding that the blackberries were too much trouble, and the rock I had been sitting on crumbled into pieces. I picked up a piece and tossed it down the slope as a sort of parting flourish, and a three-point buck deer started up from his concealed bed in the underbrush, took a long jump to clear a fallen tree, landed in a deep hole that had been too overgrown for him to see and broke his neck. He was dead when I climbed down to him, his head wrenched so far back that one prong of his antlers was driven an inch into his shoulder.

He was too heavy to carry uphill through all that brush. It was all I could do even to move him, with only one hand usable, but it would have been sinful to leave a whole deer for the buzzards when the hunters in camp had been walking their legs off for a week trying to get sight of one. So I did a one-handed dressing job on him with a pocket knife and lugged the haggled sections back to the old logging-camp shanties to wait for a pack horse. It was backbreaking drudgery, lacking the slightest feeling of communication with wild nature, but even if it had been easy I would have resented it. To get a deer by tossing a rock into a brush pile was not a triumphant climax to the day's impressions. The only gain was that I knew for the first time how my great-uncle felt about having to help land the salmon when he had intended to go out walking. He was a little ahead of me in having a hired man handy on whom to take out his injured feelings. It must have helped.

Walking through a completely wild and untracked stretch of woods never has much in it that is worth remembering. A forest in a primitive state, especially in the West, is invariably cut up with gullies and choked and tangled with underbrush and dead branches and fallen trees. Getting through it on foot and keeping directions straight make such demands on the mind and muscles that there is no room left for any fleeting wayside impressions.

Following a trail is always better, any kind of trail is better than none. Even a deer trail or an overgrown trap line will lighten the strain of remembering landmarks and deciding which way to head next. Once, on a Government survey in the mountains of Central Washington, I spent most of a day plodding through a beautiful high-altitude stand of mixed white pine and cedar along a faintly marked old trail, and had a thorough good time. There were chipmunks and pine squirrels and ruffed grouse, and I got so absorbed watching an old she-bear with two half-grown cubs on a rock slide across a canyon that I strayed off the trail a couple of times and had to go back and hunt for it.

Toward midafternoon, the trail ended in a scattering of bleached bones between two fallen trees, a bent piece of rusty iron and some links of chain sticking up from among the deep pine needles. It was the skeleton of a big timber wolf, with a heavy steel trap locked around one of its forelegs. Following the trail had landed me in the middle of nowhere, and I had to backtrack till almost dark to find out where I had been. Still, it had been serene and leisurely and reflective, and I didn't regret it. Once, while the old she-bear was working her way up the rock slide, one of the cubs sat down and refused to keep up, and she came back and turned him across her knee and spanked the stuffing out of him. Setting a compass course would have been more efficient, but it wouldn't have led to anything like that, or I would have been too busy crawling through underbrush and climbing dead logs to notice it.

Nothing knocks the color out of walking in the woods like forcing some purpose into it. Carrying along a camera gives a man the sneaking feeling he ought to be taking pictures. It is even worse with a gun. Even the most unobtrusive shooting iron will stir in a man an involuntary alertness for some excuse to shoot something. He is not walking, he is hunting. If he doesn't see anything to shoot, the hunt is a failure; if he does, the walk is a failure.

The kind of walking that holds its color longest usually starts with something small and trivial—an odd noise in the blackberry thicket back of a roadside shanty, which turns out to be a loose board flapping or a broken-down windmill creaking. Or maybe it's something moving in the weeds at the turn of the old wood road beyond the shanty's back fence that might be a cock pheasant or sunlight reflecting from a blackberry leaf, or a haw bush with a handful of ripe haw berries on it in a patch of yellowing bracken a dozen yards on, or a trout jumping in a deep hole below a rickety pole bridge, or a stretch of corduroy road beyond it, with skunk cabbage and coarse yellow waterlilies and black-ringed snakeweed crowded where the water seeps out into the black leaf mold below it.

A parable of some kind could be worked up from looking into mountain water on a still day. At a distance, it reflects what is around it—grass, trees, sky; when you lean close, the reflection is of yourself. Lean close enough to drink from it, and you will see down past all the reflections to the reality of underwater life—bugs, worms, tadpoles, fingerling trout, drowned weeds, sprays of reddish lichens. But the water itself, through which both reflections and reality exist, is so still and colorless that it is never really visible at all.

Sometimes the clearings along the old wood roads turn out to be merely wild grass meadows reaching into the timber, or the remains of an old homestead hayfield, its old fence rails matted so deep under dead grass and wild blackberry vines that it is hard to tell what they were intended to enclose. But these clearings do sometimes come up with something unexpected.

It is hard to imagine human beings living in one of those back-country areas, reached only by old wood roads that look scarcely passable for a pack horse, but some people do. It was only a few years back, following a rocky old wagon track along a ridge through the oak timber in Northern California, that I ran into a regular assortment of them. First I found some woodcutters stripping tanbark from a patch of oaks, then I saw a young cowboy of not over eighteen, big and tow-headed and bashful, living in a homemade camp wagon between two rows of half-dead olive trees and herding a couple of dozen scrub cows to pasture on some worn-out vineyards, filling in his spare time by laying a fieldstone terrace in front of his camp wagon after a pattern in a magazine. Then I met an alert-looking little man in a summer shirt who came down the wood road carrying a camp hatchet with a couple of dogs following him. He explained that he had a permit from the mortgage company to trap its lands down the ridge, and was out marking trees for one of his trap lines. He had a couple of lines already in among the abandoned farms down in the timber, and though he hadn't made much of a start at catching strictly fur-bearing animals, he had caught over ninety full-grown outlaw house cats, not counting under-sized ones.

A mile or so farther on, where the gray-green oaks gave way to thickets of small Douglas fir, I saw what looked like an abandoned farm in the middle of some grassland halfway down the slope of the ridge. It was a huddle of gray board shanties with a faint trail of scrawny, climbing rosebush wandering through the tarweed. Four or five full-grown deer were eating green plums and wormy apples from the overgrown orchard while a half-dozen fawns pranced and circled and chased one another around what was left of a high picket fence that had been put up to keep them out. When the door of one of the shanties opened and an old man came out, they merely edged away from him and went on stripping the twisted old trees of their underripe fruit. The man went over to the well curb and hung a cloth on it to dry, picked up a dead limb, and went back indoors with it, taking no more notice of the deer than they did of him.

It seemed a comedown for the country, as I thought it over. Here was a man of supposedly mature judgment who insisted on living on a worn-out farm and lacked get-up enough to keep it from falling to pieces around him, who picked up dead tree limbs for fuel instead of cutting a few solid oak trees into cordwood, who couldn't even rustle up a firearm to keep the wild animals from overrunning him.

In the old days, homesteading in these remote areas was a sign of courage and independence and resourcefulness. A man did it because he felt capable of standing up to Nature at her meanest, and preferred that kind of tussle to being beholden to his fellow men. Now, seemingly, it was a sign of worthlessness; people clung to these run-down weed patches to shirk the responsibility of standing up to anything.

That was probably true as a general observation, but as it turned out the old man shuffling out among the deer was not a good illustration. A heavy-set younger man working in another old orchard farther up the ridge explained that the old man's place was run down so badly because he was blind. The deer weren't afraid of him because they knew it. The old man had stayed with his homestead because he was used to it and knew where to find things without having to see them. People hauled in supplies for him when they thought of it, and he drew a small pension from somewhere.

The heavy-set man who explained all this was something of a specimen himself—big, red-complexioned and awkward-looking, with a week's beard caked whitish with orchard dust. He had only one eye, which shifted incessantly as he talked, like the antennae of an insect, and he seemed to be straining between agonizing self-consciousness and desperate wistfulness. His name was Hulse, or something that sounded like it, and his orchard had been in his family a long time. He was one of four brothers born and raised on it. The others had run into trouble, and he was the only one left.

"They was a little bit headstrong sometimes, and these newcomers around here always go out of their way to make trouble for people," he said. "So they had to leave the country for a while, so I've got the place on my hands till things blow over. One thing is, it makes it easy for people to find me. When they want to know which one of the Hulse boys I am, I can tell 'em I'm the one that's never shot anybody."

Walking through these back-country areas you learn that letting a place run down can bring gain as easily as loss. In the high Cascade Mountains of Central Oregon there used to be a washed-out freight road that followed a creek past a scattering of abandoned farms located along an old lumber flume. It was a good place to walk and reflect in, because the country changed color and character every mile or so and made a man feel that he was covering ground without having to exert himself. At first it was open and dusty, with grayish clumps of scrub oak, deer brush and dwarf pine drooping in the heat and quail whistling in the dead grass or yellowing the sunlight with dust from a wallow among the pine needles in the road. Then the road edged down close to the creek through a stretch of logged-off Douglas fir grown up in little thickets of willow and hazel and blue elderberry. The farms were small and close together and crowded against the old flume line as rigidly as beads on a string. The buildings were small and paintless—too small to be lived in, some of them looked—with the remains of a flower garden in front and a few dozen scrubby and twisted fruit trees alongside where white-tailed deer came to feed on the rusty pears and little red-streaked apples.

Down the slope toward the creek where the ground had been fertilized by the ashes of a brush fire there were great swales of ripe, wild blackberries, torn into ragged lanes by the bears who had fed on them. New coveys of big blue grouse clucked and pecked at them like flocks of chickens. Nearer the creek where the shade was deeper, there were clumps of black raspberries and hazel bushes loaded with nuts as big as plums. Among the huckleberries under the deep fir and alder along the creek there were little sharp-

79

tailed grouse known locally as native pheasants, and whole packs of ruffed grouse all clucking at once, and sounding like somebody picking a comb over an empty rain barrel.

The glare of light that struck through the deep timber came from the clearing around the remains of the old sawmill. All that was left were a few fire-blackened timbers and scraps of rusty iron scattered around a rectangle of naked ground, a weather-blackened sawdust pile cut with blots of dark yellow where the deer had made a trail across it and a half-wrecked log dam that had backed up the creek for a mill pond. There were broken boards and timbers scattered in the dead grass where the flume had been wrecked, and several neat green-lettered signs were tacked on stumps, marking the boundary of the national forest. The signs showed what the sawmill had been doing and why it was no longer in business. One of the standard lumberman's tricks in the uninhibited old days was to buy up a small patch of forest land adjoining some big tract of Government timber, and then to forget about property lines and log off everything in sight until somebody in authority showed up with a crew of surveyors and a court injunction. The lumberman would then pull out, expressing deep contrition for the error, and go do the same thing somewhere else.

Halting such operations protected public property against private pillage, but it usually bore hard on the back-country settlements, which had come to depend on the mill as a market for their produce. Closing this one mill had wiped out a community of from two or three hundred human beings. All the work they had done to bring the country from a wilderness to the production of something useful had to be written off as wasted.

Not that it was all wasted, if one took a long view of it. Nature had come in again after they moved out, and was producing probably four or five times as much usable food from the abandoned clearings and stump lands as they had managed to wrest from the country with all the work they had put into it.

It would be impossible to place any concrete value on walking in the woods, but one can sometimes make a tentative estimate from what people have been willing to pay for it. Eight or ten years ago I was spending a winter on a hill ranch in Northern California. Walking out through the oak timber after a big three-day rainstorm, I ran into the elderly Italian vineyardist who owned the adjoining farm. He was strolling thoughtfully along an old horse trail through the wet leaves, his hands tucked under the bib of his overalls, a big man, heavy-set, red-faced, slow in his movements—a nice old fellow. He was somewhere around seventy, and his vineyard, on which he did most of the work himself, was accounted the best-kept in that part of the country. He explained that he was walking around to see if the rain had brought out any mushrooms.

We sat down on a dry boulder to visit a little, and he got to telling about himself, how he had worked on a farm in Northern Italy as a boy, had run away to Switzerland, gone to work in a machine shop in Zurich, married a Swiss girl and started saving so they could come to America. He worked in Zurich for eight years, at the end of which the Swiss girl eloped with a traveling salesman, taking his accumulated wages with her. He moved across into Germany, working in machine shops and iron foundries all the way down the Rhine as far as the Ruhr, and then across to England, where he worked for a few years in Sheffield and Birmingham.

He finally saved enough to come to the United States where he worked for awhile in New Jersey and Pennsylvania, and then came west to California. He worked for a San Francisco iron works for eight or ten years, and then in one of the big railroad shops, until he had enough money saved to buy his vineyard and the equipment to work it. It had taken time. He had started working toward it in his early youth, and he had got it only when he was on the verge of old age. That was too long, probably. Still, people always had to wait too long for what they wanted, and he had at least done better than some. He had finally got it and had been on it ten years, and here he was, out hunting mushrooms in the oak timber and having a good time at it.

"I don't think you'll find many mushrooms," I said. "It's too soon after the rain for them."

He sat on the rock and looked at the sweep of wet yellow grass down the hillside, the leafless gray-tan oaks and black oaks, the dark-green live oaks and holly oaks, the bright green of the pepperwoods and manzanita shrubs.

"I don't care much," he said. "I like to walk around and look. It don't matter much if there's any out or not. I worked forty-six years to get so I could walk through the trees like this and not care whether I got anything out of it or not. Now I'm seventy-two years old, and I've got to do as much of it as I can."

Puget Sound Country

THE Puget Sound country, which lies about as far to the northwest as you can go in the United States, used to stir up one peculiar reflex in the writers who wrote about it seventy or eighty years ago. All of them, no matter what else their accounts included, always managed to mention that it was like the Mediterranean area of Southern Europe. It is probably a little late to hunt for an explanation of this unanimity now—some early touch of Western hyperbole, maybe, or it could have been merely that they wanted to convey something of the new country's size and spaciousness, and picked the Mediterranean because it sounded impressive enough to do it.

Whatever their reasons, it was not much of a comparison. Puget Sound does spread out over a considerable area—from its southern extremity at Olympia, it is 150 miles to the Canadian boundary at Blaine and 200 miles to the village of Neah Bay, on the Juan de Fuca Strait—but it would be more accurate to compare it to some smaller tributary sea in the Mediterranean rather than to the whole thing: the Dalmatian coast of the Adriatic, maybe, though that would apply only to size. In everything else, it is like nothing except itself. Its cities, big and populous and pushing, reach to the very edge of the wild country from which they were carved, mostly within the memory of people still alive. Bears still raid poultry farms within sight of some of these cities, and there are sixteen Indian reservations within a day's drive of Seattle. The climate sometimes blazes into midsummer in late May and sometimes strings out a cloudy and overcast late February so far into the summer that some of the trees only begin coming into leaf in July. The rainfall, for which the region has always been famous, varies according to location. In Seattle it averages around 58 inches annually. On the western slope of the Olympic Peninsula, less than a hundred miles away, it reaches 180 inches annually. Sometimes, however, it can vary even in its variability. There are years—1953 was one—when Seattle and Tacoma stay chilly and rainy through two-thirds of the summer, while the side roads west along the coast are dry and dusty, the little creeks low and half-choked with leaves falling early.

But Nature holds on hard in this country, and its powers of readjustment and renewal are probably higher than anywhere outside of the tropical forests of Central America. When I lived on Bainbridge Island, roughly opposite Seattle on the western side of the Sound, some twenty-five years ago, there was a retired sea captain a few houses away who took it into his head to keep the trees cleared off the hundred-foot strip of land in front of his house so they wouldn't interfere with his view of the shipping moving back and forth from Elliott Bay across the Sound. Since cutting them would merely have brought up a wilderness of sprouts from the stumps, he used a portable capstan to pull them out by the roots and be done with them for good. He spent most of his time pulling and sawing them up, with a Japanese houseboy helping him. When I left at the end of three years, the trees were more than keeping even with him. Looking from any distance at the handsome stand of young firs and madroñas crowding against his front windows, it was difficult to see where any had been pulled out at all, though his whole back yard was piled high with cordwood. All the towns around the Sound have grown bigger in the years since I lived there, but, though the sawmills have also got bigger and log trucks are everywhere, the timber has kept up by growing bigger too.

It is hardly likely that the wild life of the country has fallen behind the timber in holding its own. A few years ago at a party in Hollywood, I got to trading reminiscences about the area with a woman who had lived for a couple of years in a beach cabin somewhere along the southern end of the Sound, west of Tacoma—Carr Inlet, or some such locality. She remembered so many of the same things I did—grouse, pheasant, bear, deer, wild blackberries and raspberries and red huckleberries, windfall apples from the abandoned homestead orchards, clams, oysters, salmon, fishing for sea perch from the dismantled old lumber docks, dipping out candle smelt from creek inlets with a bucket (some people preferred a wire bird cage) when a run was on, hunting for wild strawberries under the upland bracken in the late spring—that it was hard to believe our dates of residence had been as far apart as they turned out to be. She had lived there in 1951-52. I had left in 1932. Twenty years seems a long time for any part of the West Coast to have remained as much the same as we both remembered it. There are places that have struggled up from savagery to a passable degree of civilization in twenty years; or down, depending on how one looks at it.

It is not that the Puget Sound country resists change more stubbornly than the rest of the country. Things change here perhaps faster than in most places, only the changes tend to work both ways, so that a loss in one direction is apt to be made up by a gain in another. Twenty-five years ago, Tacoma was primarily a sawmill town, with the red glow of giant sawdust burners lighting the main north-and-south highway through it like a bank of outsize exhaust pipes valving off fire from hell. Now the town has spread out into such things as wood-pulp and fiber-board mills and the smelting of copper concentrates from mines in Mexico and Central America and the Philippines. Twenty-five years ago, anybody in Seattle who had ventured to hint at the possibility of a slump in Alaska salmon fisheries and export trade with the Orient would probably have had to leave town. Now, though Alaska canneries are running only one week out of the year and trade with the Orient has dwindled to a shadow of itself, nobody seems to mind, and the town goes barreling along bigger and livelier than ever. Merely the expansion in aircraft manufacture has more than made up for the loss. The Boeing statisticians estimate that their company furnishes employment for one out of every six persons in the entire town. Twenty-five years ago the proportion would have been less than one in sixty.

The countryside keeps the same balance. As late as fifteen years ago, a man with a small skiff and some fishing tackle could move into some deserted lumber-camp shanty on one of the back reaches of the Sound and live fairly comfortably merely from fishing and clam-digging and berry-picking, possibly filling in with a moderate infusion of out-of-season hunting and log-stealing if he liked such non-essential trimmings as a radio and an outboard motor and store-bought cigarettes. A man could still do that, probably, given a certain amount of doggedness, a thorough knowledge of the country, and the ability to spot neighborhood game wardens at long range, but it would be harder. It would mean living monotonously and going without a lot of conveniences most people find it hard to dispense with for any long period of time. Living close to Nature for a few weeks every year or so is an excellent spiritual restorative, but having to depend on

Nature for a livelihood year in and year out takes the fun out of it. The wild country has changed, of course, the same as everything else, but the real change may be in the way people look at it.

Nevertheless, monotony in diet doesn't mean as much in this country as it might in other places. Variety in food becomes important when the food itself is insipid or low in nutritive value, but the food of this coastal region is the best in the nation. It was not because of ignorance or lack of enterprise that the local Indian tribes, living in one of the finest big-game countries on the continent, never bothered with hunting. Their community houses and high-prowed seagoing canoes show an understanding of functional design that an ignorant people would be incapable of, and several of the coast tribes—the Makah and Quillayute, for instance —killed whales from their canoes in the open sea, which is hardly a sign of a lackadaisical temperament. They abstained from hunting, evidently, because they had weighed the inevitable work against the probable returns, and had decided that the percentage was not good enough. The food from the rivers and the sea and the beaches was all anybody could possibly need—halibut, candle smelt, crabs, salmon trout, oysters, clams (one species of clam grows as big as a pie plate), ducks, geese, blackberries, salmonberries. With all that at hand, why should anybody spend his time trudging through dripping underbrush in search of deer or bear or elk, which not only took work and patience to track down, but had to be dressed and carried home afterward?

The reasoning holds good for the country today. The food is still the best to be found anywhere. Some of the more highly skilled logging-camp cooks in the old days, according to legend, used to balk at working in Puget Sound camps because there was nothing in the available provender that they could show off their artistry on. All the victuals needed, they complained, was to be walloped onto a hot stove and then shoveled into a plate.

The most important thing in the Puget Sound country is the Sound itself. The water is more a part of everybody's life and consciousness than anything else in it. Its mountains and woods and inland river valleys are all well enough for a weekend of fishing or skiing or hunting or flower-picking, but what happens on the Sound is the thing that really counts—the deep-sea shipping, the halibut fleet, the ships on regular run to and from Alaska, the ferries to the islands and across the Strait to Canada, the trade with the Orient, lumber ships from Europe, ore ships from Latin America, cannery tenders and trading schooners from the north, houseboats where people live, tugboats inching laboriously through the rough water of the Strait bringing log rafts from Neah and Clallam Bay to the mills at Port Angeles, stylish yachts and cabin cruisers flitting through the island channels past swarms of dingy Indian trolling skiffs, little single-masted canoes, gleaming plywood speedboats, freight scows, outboard dinghies salvaging drift logs from the beaches. There is every kind of craft on the Sound, big and little, old and new, slow and fast, handsome and ugly. Name it and they've got it.

The log rafts are scarcer and smaller nowadays, but they are still to be seen sometimes along the Strait and the waters to the north. A full-sized seagoing log raft beating out through the Strait on a clear day, with the dark blue water rolling half over it, used to be something to remember—the great spread of round-backed logs lying almost motionless in the rough water, the smudgy little tug straining and fretting so far ahead that it seemed headed out to sea all by itself except for the tow cable whipping a track across the waves. Sometimes, when a tide was running up the Strait and a raft was being towed out against it, a man could watch the tug laboring and the cable whipping and sawing water and the logs washing under and lifting for two or three hours without being able to see that it was moving at all; but, like the hour hand of a watch, it did make progress even when it didn't look it.

Unionization of the Northwest logging camps has had several long-range consequences that could hardly have been foreseen when it first started. One has affected the Seattle and Tacoma newspapers. At least half their classified advertising used to be announcements of logging-camp jobs—rigging slingers, doggers, choker setters, buckers, fallers, donkeymen, peavymen, cat skinners, swampers, bull cooks, a long string of lively and colorful-sounding occupations. Now there are no such advertisements at all, and the classified ads run mostly to real estate and used cars, the same as everywhere else. Another has changed Seattle's old employment-agency square, once known as the Slave Market, where loggers out of work used to congregate to watch the daily blackboards being hung out with men-wanted lists—a picturesque place, like nothing anywhere else, surrounded by odd little hole-in-the-wall shops dealing in tattoo work and restoratives for waning virility and dream books and paper-backed copies of Cornelius Agrippa's treatise on black magic. It is all quiet and respectable now. The shops are gone, the loggers do their congregating somewhere else, if at all, and the neighborhood has become as sedate and decorous as a church cake sale. Civilization is probably to blame. It always smooths out regional peculiarities such as these, given time. One can't help feeling sometimes that it might find more important things to smooth out, if it looked around a little, but that is daydreaming. It never does.

Tacoma and Seattle are the two big cities on the Sound,

though some of the others, like Olympia and Everett and Puyallup (some note should be taken hereabouts of the awful place names in this country: not only Puyallup, but Humptulips, Skykomish, Duckabush, Enumclaw, Chuckanut, Mukilteo—and there are even worse ones), are coming along fast, and it may very well be that in time they will grow together into one solid urban area, as has happened with the towns around San Francisco Bay and Los Angeles, and with most of the small outlying villages around Seattle.

Tacoma lies farther south than Seattle, on an arm of the Sound not far from its extreme southern tip. It has one of the most important harbors on the West Coast, though its clear, warm days and the open grasslands around it, usually sear by midsummer, make it seem like an inland town rather than a seaport. It has always been a working town, and still is; and it has always taken its coloring from the work it has had in hand, and still does—sawmills, ore smelters, railroad yards, deep-sea shipping, plywood and fiberboard mills, and the big Fort Lewis Army and air-training bases all add to the feeling of restlessness and movement about it. Work impregnates the very atmosphere; the smelters and the big sawdust burners around the sawmills used to do most of the impregnating, but they have been backed into the wings in recent years by the fiberboard factories, which contribute not only color but smell. It is not an especially disagreeable smell; people brought up around the Chicago stockyards would consider it beneath their notice, and the local residents are probably right in maintaining that one can become so accustomed to it as to find ordinary back-country ozone a little flat and wishy-washy. They are also undoubtedly on sound ground in defending it as a heartening sign of prosperity. Still, it is a smell, and one can't help feeling that if prosperity had to have a sign, it might have done better at picking one.

Nobody seems able to pin down what there is about Seattle that gives it so much more the feeling of a seaport than any other seaport town in the Northwest. The location and topography have something to do with it, probably. It is built on a series of hills which rise on the west from the long half-arc of deep-sea docks and ferry slips and lumber wharves facing the Sound, and slope down eastward again to the twenty-six-mile sweep of Lake Washington, where the yacht basin and Naval Air Station and the University of Washington are located. Across the lake are a few villages, still small and scattered, and beyond them the high timbered backbone of the Cascade Mountains that make the divide between the coastal rivers and the Big Bend of the Columbia River.

It is impossible to go more than a block or two anywhere in Seattle without catching sight of open water and deep timber in some direction. It adds something to a city to be able to look out of it into natural countryside—not an imitation of it, as parks always are, but real forests and canyons and mountains and expanses of water reaching somewhere out of sight.

Landscape counts in the character of a place, but people count more. It may be because of its early Alaskan background that Seattle has always run heavily to colorful characters. Let me mention a couple of them to show at least what contrasts the town has been capable of. One was an old Chinese who first came to Puget Sound as part of a shipment of coolies to work in a salmon cannery. He worked himself into the business of contracting laborers to the canneries on commission, installed a corps of expert gamblers to take the laborers' wages away from them on payday, and wound up a multimillionaire. He made regular inspection tours of all the canneries where his laborers were employed, and it used to be one of the sights of the country to watch the old boy disembark from the cannery boat accompanied by a retinue of a dozen or so armed bodyguards, valets, masseurs and umbrella holders, all marching two by two behind him down the gangplank. The other was an old Danish captain of a coastwise lumber steamer who spent most of an afternoon once holding forth about the decline in standards of seamanship brought about by modern progressiveness. He wound up a long string of illustrative anecdotes by relating that, back in the old days, the shipping company he had worked for showed its appreciation of his services after an especially hazardous voyage by keeping a taxicab waiting for him in front of the best red-light house in town for three days, with the motor running. Such things didn't happen any more, he said, and he was undoubtedly right about that.

Seattle's cultural antecedents are predominantly Scandinavian, though there is not much to show it outside of the names on store signs and a noticeable tendency to fair complexions among the people on the streets. There are a few smörgasbord restaurants and a few shops displaying Swedish furniture and Danish housewares and such things, but not as many of either as there are in San Francisco or Los Angeles. The general tendency is to shy away from Scandinavian traditions rather than to cling to them. An architect in Seattle told me once about being hired to build a country house on one of the islands in the Sound for a client, a member of an old New England family, who wanted something patterned after the traditional farmhouse in Sweden. The carpenters, being mostly from Sweden, were delighted to be put to building a kind of house they could remember from their childhood, and pitched in with wholehearted enthusiasm, contributing suggestions and adding extra touches and dropping around after hours and on Sundays to admire and argue about it as if they had a proprietary interest in it. But their own houses, which they had built and mostly designed themselves, were all perfectly ordinary Midwestern frame-and-weatherboard-and-gimcrack structures, uncomfortable and unsightly and badly lighted and worse ventilated, the kind one sees on back streets all over the United States. They were enraptured over the idea of an American wanting a Swedish farmhouse to live in, but when it came to living in such a thing themselves, they went blank. They would as soon have thought of arraying their wives in blue woolen stockings and five or six knitted petticoats apiece. They wanted the things around them to be American, even if the result was uncomfortable and a trifle ugly.

When I lived in Seattle, I used to fritter away the afternoon sometimes at the Pike Street Market. I revisited it recently and discovered that it is nothing like what it was in my time, but at least I had fair warning about it ahead of time from the taxi driver who took me there.

"I remember about 1908 or '09, when the farmers used to drive their wagons in from the country full of truck they'd raised," he said. "They'd back 'em up along the street and sell out of 'em to people on the way to the docks. Climb up in the wagon and pick out what you wanted and bring your own paper sack for it, that was the way it was then. Towards evening, when it was time for 'em to be heading out in the country to milk the cows and get the stock fed and they didn't want to haul all their truck back with 'em, you could buy things pretty reasonable. It's nothing like that now. The stuff they sell and the prices they want for it ain't any different from an ordinary chain grocery store. Things change. A lot of 'em have changed around here."

The rain was coming down so hard his windshield was blurred in spite of the wipers going full blast. He slid down a hill and through a crowded intersection on his brakes, leaning out of the window to see where the openings were.

"You can get used to anything," he said, wiping the rain

out of his eyes. "Some people complain about it sometimes. The people that run the ski resorts up around Mount Baker claim they lose business on account of all this rain. No use driving all the way up there to look at scenery if it's raining so you can't see it when you get there. Still, when it don't rain there's brush fires, and smoke so thick you can't see a hundred feet anyway. It's nice when there's a clear day. They've been scarce around here lately."

I said it seemed a little early in the year to expect any run of clear weather. He agreed absently, and observed that things weren't as easy as they used to be. The fault, he thought, was airplanes.

"I'd think airplanes would be more help than harm around here," I said. "The Boeing plant keeps a lot of people at work, doesn't it?"

He conceded the point readily enough. It was not exactly what he had in mind. "The people that work for Boeing are mostly outsiders," he said. "Came in here from the Middle West, Texas and Kankakee and Dakota and places like that. It's all right for them, I guess. Any place is better than where they came from, probably. The people that belong here, they can't do as well as they used to. When things got a little skimpy in the old days, a man could always move up some river and peck around fishing and prospecting and one thing and another, and if he needed money he could cut cordwood and sell it to the steamboat for enough to tide him over. You can't do that any more. They run airplanes into all the back country now. You can't run an airplane on cordwood."

Since there are no rivers in the Puget Sound country navigable for steamboats, and no airplanes into the immediate back country that I knew of, it was not too hard to figure out that he was following the old residents' habit of lumping developments in Alaska with those of Seattle as if they were one and the same. To the old residents, of course, they always have been the same: a sort of back-yard-and-front-parlor relationship that has kept the two regions mutually complementary and permanently inseparable. For at least the past fifty years, anything that happened in Alaska has registered a more immediate impact on Seattle than any event in its own back country possibly could; something like the St. Louis merchants and bankers of the 1850's, who knew more about events in Santa Fe and the California gold fields than about settlements in Missouri forty or fifty miles from their own city limits. With them, it didn't last long. In Seattle, obviously, it had.

The taxi driver was right about one thing, at least. The Pike Street Market had lost originality and color in the twenty years since I had last known it. Some of the stalls had a few out-of-the-ordinary things on display—salmon trout, barrels of rainbow trout, inkfish, codfish tongues, salmon-egg caviar—but the general level, as he had remarked, was not much different from any chain grocery. There were the same things on the shelves, similar prices, the same vague semiboredom about the people looking them over and the clerks watching. One thing that may explain the general list-lessness and flatness is the disappearance of the Japanese who used to run most of the cut-flower and vegetable stalls. They always showed a sense of decoration in arranging their merchandise, and I had not realized before how much it helped. I was sorry they were gone, and that I had never bought anything from any of them when they were there.

Some people do keep up with the Puget Sound back country, but it usually has to be forced on them. One was a man who had a house across the county road from me when I was living in a small community on the north end of Bainbridge Island, facing across Agate Pass toward Hood Canal and the Olympic Peninsula. He was an Icelander, and he used to make running translations of modern Icelandic poetry from memory during the long winter evenings when there was nothing else to do. In the summer he used to work as second mate of a salmon-canning steamer working the Alaskan inlets, besides picking up additional income from gillnetting and trading knickknacks to the Eskimos when the steamer was tied up putting away salmon. That was all done and over with now, knocked in the head by the falling off in the Alaska salmon runs. Now he spent his summers working with the Forest Service in the Olympic Mountains, helping to cut fallen trees out of the trails after a windstorm, mending telephone lines, packing supplies to lookout stations, helping to spot fires when there was a long dry spell, hunting for summer tourists who got themselves lost, things like that. None of it amounted to much, but it filled in.

He told of going out once on a Forest Service patrol plane to look for fires after a lightning storm, and of flying low over one of the rivers where four or five bears were out on a long mudbank waiting for salmon that got washed ashore after spawning. One old she-bear saw the plane coming, and reared up and hauled back to slap at it, apparently taking it for some species of predatory bird. She miscalculated its speed and, trying to correct her bead on it, overbalanced and fell off the bank backward into three feet of thin mud.

The other bears all sat watching curiously as she hauled herself out, mud-plastered and mad, and she drew back and slapped one of them over the bank into the same mudhole, probably suspecting him of wanting to snicker at her. He crawled out, also mad, and slapped one of the smaller bears into the mudhole, whereupon the whole pack of them piled into a free-for-all, clawing, cuffing, biting, gouging, and filling the air so full of sand and mud and hair that it looked as if the whole river had exploded. The Icelander didn't know how it had come out. The plane moved away while the fight was still going on, and when it turned and flew back all the bears were gone. None of them had been hurt much, apparently, or they couldn't have got themselves out of there so fast.

"It must have been worth watching," I said. "You wouldn't see anything much livelier than that in Alaska."

"You'd see bears, if you wanted to," he said. "They're big up there too. These bears around here, there's lots of 'em, but they're little. They don't amount to anything."

"There's salmon around here, and they're not little," I said. "They're not running short, either. I've seen people catching them."

"Tourists," he said. "They play at it. In Alaska, catching salmon is work. I like it better when it's work."

A new highway connects Bainbridge Island with the Olympic Peninsula on the west by a huge and imposing high-level bridge across Agate Channel. It comes out on the main-land in approximately the middle of the Port Madison In-dian reservation, and then leads south through Bremerton to pick up the extreme inland tip of Hood Canal at a little roadside station called Belfair.

None of the Indian reservations in this country have any-thing about them that looks particularly Indian. The dif-ference between them and ordinary back-country landscape, usually, is that there are no isolated houses or clearings on the reservations: the people live in villages. It is only white settlers hereabouts who live out in the wild country by them-selves. The Indians have always preferred living clustered together, and still do. The Port Madison reservation does have a few scattered shanties and hayfields bordering the highway near its southern boundary, but they may not be Indian: I noticed that the hay, which had been cut, was draped across the fences to dry like a Monday's wash, as is sometimes done in Finnish communities in the Middle West.

From the reservation as far south as Bremerton the country is mostly small hay and dairy farms. From Bremerton on south to the point of Hood Canal, it is wilder: clumps of small second-growth fir, bordered with vine maple and wild lilac and hazel between openings of redtop grass and bracken. The wild flowers in this part of the country run so much to white—marguerite daisies, dogwood, elderberry, vine maple, chokecherry, wild lilac, thimbleberry, wild blackberry, bear grass—that the outcrops of pink rhododendron and wild roses and yellow buttercups seem to have wandered in by mistake and to be trying to work their way out again. This type of cut-over brushland is always a better place to find wild game than the deep and untouched timber. I jumped three deer in a willow swale a couple of miles out of Bremerton, and a covey of a dozen or fifteen ruffed grouse flew up from the roadside into some alders and sat peering down inquiringly as I drove past. From the point of Hood Canal on north, where the timber was heavier and there were no stumplands, I saw nothing except a few chipmunks.

Hood Canal is something of an oddity of Nature. It is really not a canal at all, but a natural salt-water arm of the Sound, some eighty miles long and half a mile wide, so straight and uniform in width that it is difficult to believe it was not laid out with engineering instruments. It is a beautiful body of water, clear and bright and tranquil, with beautiful country bordering it: dark firs lifting above a wall of pale-green underbrush, brightened underneath with thimbleberry and tall spikes of pink and white foxglove.

There was not much traffic along the road except a few logging trucks, but a woman at one of the roadside lunchrooms said it was about average. There was never what could be called a rush season; still, there was never really any slack season, either. She had kept her lunchroom open through November and December, and people dropped in at about the same rate as during the summer months. She wouldn't want them to come in any greater numbers than they did, because it was impossible to get help. The loneliness seemed to be the main objection. Hired help nowadays didn't like to work too far from a town.

"I'd think you'd find it lonely sometimes yourself," I said. It seemed a little isolated. She said no, there was too much to keep busy at: berrypicking, keeping things up, one thing and another.

"It looks a lot more isolated than it really is, anyway," she said. "There's people living all along this road. They leave the trees standing so you can't see their houses, but they're almost as close together as in a town."

I asked if there was someplace around where they worked. She said no, most of them were retired people who had come there to live because they liked it. That was all they did, she thought.

"A lot of them are from California," she said. "I'm from California myself. I ran a tourist camp in San Rafael for several years before I moved up here."

If she had been looking for something different from San Rafael, she had certainly found it. There could hardly have been a more complete contrast. "What made you decide to leave it?" I said.

"Several things, I guess," she said. "Too much to do all the time. Too crowded. I got sick of looking at all those swarms of people."

All mountain lakes are beautiful—that is their business, as Heine remarked about something else—but Lake Crescent, up near the northern edge of the Olympic Peninsula, outdid itself for me under the gray morning light, with mist tatters drawing loose from the dark timber after a night drizzle. Its surface was like glass, black-green in the deep shadows, almost blinding white where the clouds moving across the sky reflected in it, though the sky itself was only a watery pale gray. Some mallard ducks waddled down past the hotel flower beds toward the water, picking things out of the wet grass as they went. The young man at the hotel desk said they didn't belong to the establishment. They were wild, and had merely picked it as a place to spend their summers. They didn't go in the water much, though they spent most of their time hanging around it. We talked about the fishing. He said there were plenty of fish in the lake— Beardslee and Crescenti trout, which were found nowhere else, and rainbows and cutthroats—but that the fishing never amounted to much when it was cloudy. In clear weather they would usually come after a fly: a flying ant seemed to work the best on them. There was steelhead fishing in the creek that led out of the lake, though he hadn't tried it for a long time; the creek was brushy, and there were log jams along it.

I asked about a cutoff road that could get me to the shore of the Juan de Fuca Strait. It showed on my map as unimproved, but the young man said it had been graded and hard-surfaced in the last year or so, and would probably be all right in spite of the rain.

"And the log trucks," he said. "They're pounding it pretty hard, I hear, getting out logs for the pulp mills and the shingle mills around here. Still, they haven't had time to beat it to pieces yet. It takes two or three years for them to ruin a hard-surfaced road completely, and they've only been at it since last summer."

I took the cutoff road and ultimately came to Neah Bay, the principal village of the Makah Indian Reservation: a small place on the northwest tip of the Olympic Peninsula facing across the entrance of the Juan de Fuca Strait a few miles in from Cape Flattery and the open sea. It has a Coast Guard station, one or two gasoline stations, a few shops that sell or rent fishing tackle to tourists, and a dozen or fifteen blocks of small wooden houses, some unoccupied and most unpainted, where the Makah Indians live. There is a long sand beach where two or three huge flocks of sea gulls roost and a few people wander around hunting agates and digging for clams, and a long shallow harbor filled with motor launches, mostly for rent to people who come to troll for salmon in the Strait. The history of Neah Bay goes a long way back, for a place so small and so little known. The Spanish viceroy of Mexico established a military post there in 1789, giving it the official name of Puerto Nuñez Gaona. Until 1795, when it was abandoned under pressure from Great Britain, it seems to have been a fairly busy port, with trading vessels putting in from such far-off places as Macao, Canton, Bengal, Boston, Bristol, and Portsmouth. Afterward it dwindled away to nothing, and now it has grown back into an Indian fishing village, so small and so far from anything that most people have never heard of it and few have ever been there.

Nobody could call it a pretty town. Still, the sun was out all along the road into it, and the light on the weathered old houses and the white gulls and the rough water in the Strait gave it a brightness and sparkle that was almost as good. There were clumps of pink wild roses on both sides of the highway that looked as if they had been planted as a hedge, and big bushes of yellow lupine and Scotch broom in the open fields.

I turned down one of the side streets to take some photographs, and opened the luggage compartment of the car to hunt for a wide-angle lens. A couple of little Indian boys came out of one of the houses and stopped to watch.

"You are moving here?" one of them said finally.

They were nine or ten years old, probably. Their English had no definable accent, but there was a painstaking stiffness about it, as if they were having to think of the right words as they went along. The luggage compartment did look a little like moving day. There was everything in it, as the saying used to have it, except the kitchen sink and the lens I was looking for. I said no, and thought they looked a little disappointed. A new resident in town would have been something to talk about, at least. They tried again.

"You are selling something?" the other one said.

It seemed too bad to disappoint them a second time. I explained about taking pictures, to temper it down a little. Then, to change things around, I asked what kind of fish people were catching out in the Strait.

The two boys looked at each other doubtfully, probably feeling that any question so useless must be loaded somehow. The first one finally decided to risk it, and said that they were fishing for silvers, meaning silver salmon.

"Does your father rent boats to people, or take them out to fish?" I said.

They looked at each other again. "Our father don't rent," the first one said. "He catches."

"Not around here, though," the second one put in. "He catches out. Away out, a hundred miles out. He don't fish like these people."

They had stopped looking at me. They were looking out past the gray houses and the pink masses of wild roses and the gulls and the swarm of little fishing boats rocking in the bay, toward the bluish outline of Vancouver Island in the distance and a long black-hulled freighter hammering in against the rough stone-colored water of the Strait. It was as if the ship were using some thoroughfare that was theirs. The people who belong here have always been like that, I thought, the Makahs and Quillayutes driving their high-

bowed canoes west to their whaling and north to their seal-
ing grounds in the spring, the old residents dreaming of
Alaska and its rivers and of prospecting and salmon fisheries
and steamboats. The country keeps its own life so well because they have never taken time to bother with anything so
close to home. For them, it has always been a place to look
out from at something far out—Macao, Bengal, Canton, the
Alaskan rivers, anywhere.

The Brook

ONE fall, a good many years ago, I was working on a General Land Office survey of some high-altitude timber in the Cascade Mountains of Central Washington. The timber was mixed white pine and cedar running along the flank of a high ridge, with an undergrowth of red fir so dense and close-spread overhead that we had worked through it for two days without seeing any sunlight except, sometimes, as a faint and elusive patch of ghostly radiance about as big as a man's hand, and with no water except where some accidental snow-seep had been dug underground for storage by one of the little mountain marmots. On the afternoon of the third day, the ridge tapered down and spread out into a clearing: a grassy tract of level ground where two little mountain streams came together, closing it in on two sides in the shape of a triangle. It was at the bottom of a small canyon, but it was the only part of the woods where the sun reached at all —the dark-gold autumn sunlight of the mountains that sometimes seems tangible enough to dip one's hand in—and somebody had built a log cabin on it, with the door and windows taking the afternoon sun exactly where it reflected back from the junction of the two streams.

There were many cabins in remote parts of the woods then, put up by wandering sharpshooters to pin down homestead rights on valuable timber. Most of them were merely the four walls, roof and two windows required by land-office regulations, with no great care shown in finishing even them. This one had real workmanship in it: the logs all of a size, with the corners squared and the tops and bottoms grooved and slotted to fit together without chinking, the hand-split planking of the floor and partition dressed smooth and joined tight, and the slab doors set in casings and fitted with iron latches and hinges instead of the cast-off harness straps commonly used in homestead shanties in that country. There was glass in the windows, and a fireplace. Everything about it showed that whoever had built it had intended to live in it. It never had been lived in, and, considering the location, never could have been, because of the communications. It was thirty-five miles from the nearest wagon-road, with twelve miles of the roughest and wildest kind of mountain country between it and even a practicable horse-trail. We had back-packed in to finish with our survey, but we had to do it only once. For a man to settle himself in a place where everything had to be back-packed in over twelve miles of mountains would have made any ordinary brand of foolishness look spindling; and still, I couldn't help sympathizing with him. The sight of running water always gets hold of something inside me, and the little sunlit rise of ground between the two streams would have made me feel like doing exactly what he had done. I wouldn't have gone as far with it as he had, but I knew how he must have felt, squaring his logs and siting his windows to look out on the water sweeping past the russet alder and pink dogwood and yellow rock-maple, and I envied him the lonely exultation he must have felt in working it all out without anybody around to remind him how impractical it was.

It would have been different, probably, if he had figured out some way to live in the cabin after he got it finished. Admiration for a place by running water is something I can understand and share, but asserting possession over it always sets the wrong way with me, as I suppose it does with most country-raised people. There was an elderly retired wheat-farmer in one of the mountain valleys of Central Oregon once who took it into his head to build himself a house astraddle of one of the creeks that ran through it, with a trap-door in the kitchen floor through which he could haul up trout within only a couple of steps of the frying pan on the stove. None of the neighbors seemed exactly carried away by the idea, and none of them acted quite broken up when the spring floods knocked his house off its foundations and he had to be carried out to high ground by a party of rescuers swimming their horses in to reach him. He had no business trying to yard off the creek for himself to begin with; and catching trout within reach of the frying pan was impractical, because it left out of account that they had to be cleaned before being cooked.

A brook reached its highest importance when it ran through a town. Few in the Northwest do nowadays, having been tunneled under in the interests of street-lines and real-estate subdivisions, or else ditched off to make a log-pond for some sawmill, but the town I lived in had one in years past, and it helped immeasurably in keeping one's consciousness widened out beyond the limits of the town itself, which were narrow in more ways than one. Merely watching its changes from season to season was keeping track of what was happening in places upstream as remote from anything the town knew as if they had been in a different hemisphere: the water surging under the street-bridges clouded yellowish from an early rain in the high farmlands, or milky pink from some fall of wet snow carrying down red earth from the timber, or shrunk to a dark thread when some hard mountain frost had slowed down the springs that fed it. To know the brook was to live in a big section of country instead of a small one, and in a variety of different climates and types of scenery and economics and social values instead of merely one.

It was not much of a stream, even for a brook. There was no place in it deep enough to swim in—it was too cold for swimming anyway—and except in the spring freshets a man could jump across it in most places and wade it without getting in over hip-deep anywhere. But it did touch a big and varied assortment of country in its thirty-mile course from the town, ninety feet above sea level, to its source in some mountain snow-springs seven thousand feet up, and there was always something about it worth seeing at any time of the year. Even in the dead of winter, the clouds of pale-red willow and smoke-blue alder holding patches of old snow against the black water were beautiful, and looking at them could bring to mind what it must be like up at the headwaters—the green-white quaking aspens buried in snow halfway up into their branches, the little forest-ranger cabin with only the line of its gray roof sticking out above the drifts, the tops of a dark fir clump twitching and shedding snow from some yarded deer moving in it to keep warm, snow sliding down from a dead tree-snag in a cloud of gleaming diamond-dust, the shadow of a hawk across the snow, the shadow of a big white snowshoe rabbit squatted against a dead log—to know a brook is to know all of it at once, so that looking at one part of it will bring up what it is like at any given moment along its full length.

Some brooks have sections that, for one reason or another, are not worth turning out for at any season. Every part of this one was good during some part of the year. The salmon trout made their run around late March and early April, and they could be caught along the truck farms and small orchards at the very edge of town, and sometimes even in the town itself. Beyond the truck farms, the brook ran in a long shallow riffle over colored pebbles, closed on both sides by a grove of tall black oaks where the ruffed grouse came around the middle of April to carry on their courting ceremonies. The noise the water made rattling over its bed of pebbles was so loud in places that a man had to raise his voice to be heard over it, but the noise the cock-grouse made drumming among the oaks was so thunderous and startling that it would drown out any ordinary speaking-voice completely. I have read somewhere that the cock-grouse produces his drumming sound by beating his wing-tips on a hollow log or a stump, and I wouldn't argue the point against published authority, but there were mornings in the spring when I could hear at least two dozen grouse drumming in as many directions simultaneously, and the entire oak grove didn't have more than half a dozen stumps in it, and no hollow logs at all.

Their courting always seemed to get results, whether it was done according to the books or not. By early summer, the oak grove and the hills back of it and the patches of undergrowth along the brook would be alive with full-fledged families of them, the two old ones and anywhere from ten to a dozen three-quarter-grown young. They usually stayed clear of the orchards above the grove because the ground under the fruit trees was kept plowed so it had no cover, but there was one good-sized orchard belonging to two elderly unmarried brothers who had killed each other in some family argument, and since they had no heirs it had been left to grow up in a tangle of deer-brush and wild sweetbrier and wild hay that drew grouse coveys during the early summer by the dozen.

The grouse-hunting season didn't open until October, but the grouse in the old orchard were so plentiful and brazen that sometimes the temptation to take time by the forelock a little was more than flesh and blood could resist. Once, having let go and knocked down a couple of them that kept whirring up in my face and then settling twenty feet ahead to do it again, I had to spend the whole afternoon hiding in the tall grass from a neighboring orchardist who had been appointed deputy game warden for the district, and, panting for something to use his badge on, combed the orchard up, down and sideways until dark trying to find me. It was too big an area for him to cover thoroughly, and the grass where I was hiding was full of dead-ripe windfall apricots, so I didn't make out too badly, except that I had dropped my gun and the two grouse somewhere back in the deer-brush when I heard him coming, and I had to stay till daylight the next morning to find them. It was uncomfortable, especially in the cold hours before dawn, but the discomfort didn't outlast the night, and the first sun on the tall grass-heads, the sleek dark water of the brook lit with yellow flashes where the light caught it, and the flights of little white-and-gray birds almost striking their wings in it as the light changed it from dark to pale-green, have lasted unchanged and undimmed over all these years. It was a pity about the two grouse: they were bright harmless creatures, worth a lot more to look at than to eat, but it was the truth that four out of five of them always got hauled off by predatory animals before fall, so shooting them may merely have been getting in ahead of some coyote, bobcat, lynx-cat, weasel, hawk, eagle, or something else that might have made more ragged work of it. They were too speculative and incautious to have stayed alive long.

Beyond the abandoned orchard the brook ran in a series of deep pools and small waterfalls past a colony of Swiss-French who had settled there far back in the eighteen-seventies and had kept themselves steadfastly apart from the people around them ever since, still speaking only broken English, or, in a considerable number of cases, no English at all. They were vineyardists, and since neither the soil nor the climate around them was adapted to grape culture, some of their neighbors held the theory that they kept to themselves to avoid being twitted about their foolhardiness in staying with it, but there was something deeper than that back of it. Once, when I was working as a county sheriff's deputy, one of their men got killed from ambush under circumstances that could hardly have meant anything but a carefully prearranged murder. We hurried up to investigate, thinking that a little extra zeal and expeditiousness in the case might help to convince the people in the colony that they were members of society the same as everybody else, and that the State felt itself as responsible for protecting their lives as it did for collecting their taxes. We discovered, after questioning eight or ten of them, that they were not only not interested in having the case cleared up, but were doing their utmost to keep us from finding out anything about it. It was some issue among themselves, apparently, and whether they were pleased with the way it had been settled or not, they were determined to keep outsiders from mixing into it. They were successful, too. We were never able to get the slightest hint from any of them as to who had done it, or why, or anything about it. Living with a murderer in their midst should have made some of them nervous enough to drop a few chance remarks after the excitement had died down, but it didn't seem to. They weren't of a nervous temperament.

The string of deep pools that the brook made in passing their farms was the only part of it that abounded in crawfish, possibly because the table-scraps they habitually dumped into it were a diet that crawfish throve on. Elsewhere along the brook they were scarce, usually no bigger than a man's thumb, and almost black in color. In the pools fronting the vineyard colony they were big, dark red, and swarming into every pool that held forth the shadowiest promise of anything to eat. Once I left a string of half a dozen medium-sized trout in the shallow water at the edge of a pool to go talk to somebody up on the road, and, coming back after three-quarters of an hour, discovered that crawfish were piling four or five deep over the whole string and had eaten the trout almost up to the gills. One would have expected them to spread farther on upstream to widen their food supply instead of having to fight over it constantly, but they never got beyond the limits of the vineyard colony. Something about its atmosphere or temperament may have been congenial to them.

It was curious what changes of color the brook water went through in the short mile between the end of the colony vineyards and its entrance into the deep canyon leading up to the falls. Along the alder-shaded pools fronting the vineyards, it had a darkish cast, a little like the fluted edge of an obsidian arrowhead held up to the light. Farther up, in the open sunlight among the wild gooseberry thickets where a big flock of prairie chickens bedded during the afternoon, it was the dark steel-blue of a new gun except at the riffles which were greenish-white, and in the wild tumble of foam-streaks and rapids where it came out of the shaded canyon it was dark gray-green, as it sometimes was in its course through the town when winter was breaking up. Above the rapids it was blocked by an old beaver-dam that had backed it up and spread it out over the canyon floor in a sort of slough, with a foot or so of water covering a mixture of swamp-grass, dead weeds and bushes, and mud. There was no way to get through it except by wading, which involved some risk because of the deep under-water holes that the beavers had dug as rear entrances to their houses out in the main backwater. It was impossible to see where they were, and stepping into one of them meant dropping ten feet straight down a narrow shaft full of thin mud and ice-water, with no time to yell and no room to elbow out again. Beavers are useful and industrious animals, but it used to strike me sometimes that there was something a little self-centered in their habit of changing the course of a stream and the character of the land adjoining it, merely to work out a few private entrances to their houses.

The upper end of the canyon was deep and narrow, with the brooks sliding dark and unbroken down a channel worn out of black stone. There was one place in it so deep that one could look up from it at the sky and see the stars shining, even in the middle of the day. Beyond were the falls, which filled the canyon for nearly half a mile down with spray like a heavy rain. A trail up a steep rimrock-slide led around them to the upper country.

The upper country was the best part of the whole brook. It was a high-floored mountain valley with big yellow pine timber topping the hills on both sides. Down the slopes there were thickets of hazel and arrowwood and vine maple and mountain ash, separated by open stretches of grassland. On the flat bordering the brook there were fir and rock-maple, dogwood, alder, and wild raspberry bushes. The places where people lived were all half a mile or more up the hillside above it. The land along it had all been homesteaded for timber along in the eighteen-nineties, and had been abandoned after it was logged off. Most of the homestead buildings were still standing, with old half-wild overgrown orchards that still bore rusty pears and blue and yellow plums and little red-striped apples all through the late summer and fall. They were mostly merely deserted frame houses, a little spooky to stay in after dark, but there was a one-room log cabin a few miles farther up, so much older and simpler in design that there was something impersonal about it, where

I spread down for the night sometimes when it was cold or threatening rain. Its door wouldn't go all the way shut and its window was nothing but a square hole cut in the logs, but it had a stone fireplace at one end and a fir-tip bed in one corner, and keeping a fire going made it seem warmer than outdoors, even if the difference in actual temperature was too small to argue about. A fir-tip bed was made by filling a rectangle of logs with the small end-tips of fir-boughs, stood upright and packed tight so they couldn't lean over or flatten down under one's weight. It took a fair-sized fir tree and a day's hard work to make one, but they were luxurious to sleep on, and since the twigs got springier and more resilient in drying out, they would last for years.

It was a pleasant place to stay in, in spite of porcupines that sometimes came poking in through the half-open door at night after the fire had burned low, on a little grass-flat grown up in clumps of vine maple, facing a half-wrecked pole bridge that led across the brook to a thicket of chinquapins—the only trees of that species I ever saw in the Northwest—and on past them to a little draw where there were masses of huckleberries, and usually, in the season when they were ripe, one or two black bears. It was at its best in the fall, when the vine maples had changed color and the air was tinged bluish from the fallen leaves drying and fruit ripening in the old orchards. Sometimes, being usually off work in late September and October, I used to take books up to read during the slack afternoons, and there are poems of Rossetti and Browning that I couldn't look at now without remembering the vine maple clumps flaming deep red like geraniums, the bluish air tinged with the fragrance of huckleberries, and the sound of the brook washing among the old bridge-timbers and underneath a fallen tree a little distance downstream, much more clearly than I remember anything in the poems. It was tempting to speculate sometimes on what the man had been like who had put up the cabin to begin with: some early-day pelt-hunter, possibly, since its workmanship was more that of a camp than a permanent residence, and there were racks built for drying meat in the fir grove above it, and no sign around it of the flubbed-up pretense at agriculture required by the General Land Office for issuing a homestead patent. He hadn't bothered about ownership, seemingly. The country was too overgrown to amount to much for hunting, but there was hunting country within reach of it, and he may have picked it as a site for his cabin because it was a place to be, which it was.

The settlers who had taken homesteads up the hillside away from the brook were mostly small cattle raisers, with a few seasonal sidelines like cutting wild hay for a big cattle company on the far side of the valley and hauling cordwood down to sell in the town when it was going through one of its regular winter fuel shortages. The land they had taken up was not particularly good, but it adjoined open country where they could run their cattle without having to involve themselves in leases or grazing permits, and it had the additional advantage that they could occasionally knock over one or two cattle company steers and lay the blame for it, if it was noticed, on mountain lions or wolves or half-breed Indians. The company cowboy assigned to patrol that section of its range worked hard at it, but it was a big area to keep tab on single-handed, and he had never been able to work up sociable relations with the settlers because, though he knew his work and looked like something out of Frederic Remington's paintings, he couldn't speak any language except Welsh.

They were a shy, loud-voiced, old-fashioned set of people—their school was probably the last place in the country where the youngsters still played such obsolete games as hat-ball and black-man and bull-pen—expert at out-of-date skills like axemanship and ten-horse-team skinning and diamond-hitch packing, and given to old-time forms of social diversion that sometimes tended to upset all the standard notions of what old-time social diversions were like. I went one winter to a neighborhood candy-pull at one of their houses, sup-posing, from various patronizing allusions in old books and magazines, that it would amount merely to boiling molasses down to a caramel, setting it out in buttered plates till it cooled, handing it out for the guests to pull till it got pale-yellow and brittle, and then sitting around licking it and playing something like forfeits, or clap-in-and-clap-out. It turned out to be not in the least like that. The only form of group diversion it could have been compared to was a knock-down-and-drag-out riot. The point of the entertainment was that after the molasses had cooled and been handed around to start pulling, the men started trying to steal gobs of it from everybody and getting into fights with the other men over it. The spectacle of two sedate-featured men of middle age locked in a clinch and wrestling their way down the front steps into a snowdrift with one hand apiece while clutching a mass of coagulated molasses in the other would have been funny if they hadn't been in such dead earnest about it. None of the candy ever got pulled, and the casual-ties for the evening included two broken ribs, a dislocated shoulder, some smashed knuckles, a set of lacerated fingers that got into somebody's mouth by mistake, and everybody's clothes completely wrecked. None of the guests seemed to think the tally of injuries was anything unusual; it was about average for a candy-pull, they agreed, especially one where the people were all in high spirits and not holding back from enjoying themselves.

They showed the same strenuousness in their notions about hunting. Once I ran into a half-dozen of them taking a wagon up to the end of the road to start a three-weeks' hunt in the mountains, and their entire equipment for it, besides guns and ammunition, consisted of flour, salt, coffee, two belt-axes, a frying pan, and a tin bucket. There were no blankets, no tent, no bed-canvas; their system for keeping warm at night was to put up a fir-bough lean-to with a fire in front of it, which worked as well or better. As for food to supplement the flour and coffee, that was what they were headed into the woods for. A hunting party that couldn't bring in enough game to feed itself had no business going out on a hunt at all. Their faith in the country's game supply was stronger than mine would have been, but they came back at the end of the three weeks looking sleek and hearty, so it must have been well-founded. An outsider might have suspected them of filling in a few empty corners with huckle-berries and wild raspberries, which were ripe in the moun-tains at that season, but nobody who knew them would have given the idea house-room. They were not opposed to wild berries, but picking them was work for women and Indians, and a man who would do it to make up for his incapacity as a hunter was apt to find his standing in the community sunk too low to be recognizable for the next year or two.

Another of their prejudices had to do with fishing, which, without laying down any iron-clad doctrine on the subject, they were inclined to frown on as undignified for men and unladylike for women. The brook above the abandoned homesteads leveled off into a long reach of still water, so motionless and colorless that it looked shallow though in most places it was around four feet deep, full of big trout that refused to take the slightest interest in any fishing lure ever invented. I was at work trying everything on them one afternoon when a fifteen-year-old girl from one of the homesteads came past with an old .22 rifle, stalking a little native pheasant in the snow-brush up the hillside, and offered to show me how it was done. She rigged a horsehair noose on the end of a switch, and, by manipulating it carefully in the deep water close to the bank, yanked out six trout in less than twenty minutes. Then she got up, leaving them lying in the grass, and started on up the hill after her pheasant. A native pheasant, dressed, would weigh possibly a pound. The trout she had caught would have weighed easily five times that much. I tried to talk her into taking them, but she refused. Noosing trout was well enough for children to fool away their time at, but grown people didn't bother with such things. She was grown.

The place where the brook headed was only a few miles past the still place where the big trout were. It was on the slope of a high mountain, so near the top that it seemed almost like a break in the skyline, near the edge of a great lawnlike sweep of open grassland that people in the Northwest used to call a mountain meadow: a half-dozen clear springs, so cold it hurt to drink from them, that joined together and ran down past the white snags of dead trees and the dark fir-clumps swiftly, but without a ripple to break the silence. Standing beside the little forest-ranger shack where the highest spring came out was like standing with one's head and shoulders drawn into the sky, completely separated from the far-off sound of wind in the firs that went on constantly under it; but the silence reached all the way to the ground, too—down into the grass and the dead tree-snags and the water racing past them toward the quaking aspens and the gray alders of the canyon below. It was not so much looking at a landscape as living through something of which the landscape and the silence were both a part. All the brook's miles of clatter and usefulness could not touch the silence, but it touched and deepened them, all the way down to the town and through the big culvert under the railroad tracks where it spread out into the river and vanished.

The Camp

Back in California a few months ago, a young man was telling me about a motor trip he and his wife had taken over a new road through the Cascade Mountains of Washington, all the way up from the Columbia River to the main highway running west into Seattle, and about the public camp-grounds that had been installed all the way along it and how well-equipped and comfortable they all were. They were spaced out at exactly the right intervals, they were clean and pleasantly situated, and what with tables, benches, piped water, lavatories, fireplaces to cook on, garbage disposal and telephone service, and other vacationists dropping in of an evening for company, they left the road-weary wayfarer nothing to think out or bother about except enjoying the scenery. Everything was all worked out, everything provided for and labeled and regulated so that it would have been impossible for anybody to run himself into any acute problems or difficulties anywhere.

It sounded attractive. I had worked in that mountain country years before, putting in two summers at herding cattle on some grazing land in one of its national forests and another on a government survey, and if time had permitted I would have liked nothing better than to follow the new road back through it, using all the new and well-equipped

119

camp-grounds, obeying all the signs, and liking it all the more because everything had been so well provided for that no thinking was necessary anywhere. At my age, that would have been natural enough; every man reaches a point somewhere in his life when tranquillity and uneventfulness seem more appealing than all the wild and raucous emergencies in Nature, but it did strike me that the young man who was telling about the new road had missed a part of his birthright in having been left without any emergencies to face on it at all.

Of course, he must have had to face some in the everyday business of making a living, but the emergencies a wild country can come up with are different: they are sharper, livelier, and pleasanter to remember even when they turn out, in retrospect, not to have amounted to much, after all. There was one fall when I was camped on a little creek in the Mount Adams country, herding a few dozen cattle on some logged-off land bordering what must be the line of the new road now, and, according to the road-maps, not far from one of the well-equipped overnight camps the young man had told about, if not squarely on the site of one. In those days, of course, there were only horse-trails anywhere within miles of it, and supplies had to be brought up by an elderly camp-tender with a string of pack-horses from one of the towns down on the river.

He was supposed to show up regularly every two weeks, though he usually made a point of being a few days late to show his contempt for authority. A moderate amount of tardiness didn't matter much, but finally, when it was well into fall and the grazing season was almost over, he stayed gone for a full ten days beyond his schedule, and the food supply in camp got so low that I took to riding out on the trail toward town of an evening to watch for him and pick hazelnuts, which, though more trouble to husk and crack than they were worth, were at least something to fill in with. Then, late one evening when I was about to start back to camp, he did pull in, dusty and haggard and on foot, with a breathless and overelaborated story about having all his horses stampeded by a bear jumping out at them from the big huckleberry clearing at the edge of the timber while he was at the creek getting himself a drink of water. I didn't take much stock in it, never having heard of a bear showing itself when there was a man around, but there was no use arguing it with him. We walked back along the trail through dark second-growth fir and brown-yellow hazel thickets toward camp to rustle something for him to eat out of what little there was. The hazels ended at the top of a long slope that reached down to the creek, and, looking down through the scattering of arrowwood and snowberry and yellowing tamarack, we saw that the camp had a visitor. A large black bear was standing at the cook-table, trying to reach the sack of flour that was hung by a baling-wire from a tree-limb directly over his head. He was so deliberate and the light was so far gone that for a moment I thought it was a man. The camp-tender took hold quicker. He grabbed the rifle from the saddle, muttered, "By God, it's him!" and threw down and shot.

It was foolish to risk a shot in that light and at that distance with a food-shortage facing us, but it came out better than I had expected. He overshot the bear by several feet, and ripped the bottom completely out of the floursack and dumped our last half-gallon of flour squarely on the bear's head. It must have got clotted in his eyes, for he rubbed at them, dropped on all fours and rubbed again, and then lumbered blindly over among the tent-ropes, pulled the tent down on top of himself, and started wallowing and clawing it over toward the remains of the campfire. He was still hopelessly tangled in it and one corner of it was badly scorched and smoldering when we got down and finished him off.

It was not much to feel triumphant about, with the camp stood on end, our flour wasted, and the tent half-ruined, but we did feel triumphant, and lived uncomplainingly on bear-meat and boiled cottonwood bark for the week that it took us to track down the pack-horses and search out the places where they had rolled their packs off. The best part, thinking back, was that there was no really desperate bedrock necessity about any of it. We couldn't have starved, with sixty-odd head of company steers pasturing within walking-distance of camp, or, if that had seemed like overdoing it, one of us could have ridden the saddle-horses back to town and drawn new supplies and a new pack-string to bring them back on. Either way would have been allowable under the circumstances, but either would have been like running in some extra cards in the middle of a game to keep from losing. Getting the bear to fill in with was playing it through with the cards that were on the table. We felt pleased with ourselves for it, and we had every right to be.

The tent, though it was badly torn and chewed and scorched, turned out to be less of a loss than it had looked. Only half of it had taken any serious damage, and we split it down the middle and used the undamaged half as a lean-to. In some respects it was a more comfortable shelter on chilly nights than the whole tent had been. Keeping a closed tent warm in cold weather required a fire inside it, and the fire always set up a floor-draft that kept everybody in it suffering from chronically cold feet, as any old-timer who ever went through a spell of winter weather in an Indian tepee would be able to testify, with trimmings. A lean-to was warmed by a fire from outside, and the heat, instead of being carried up away from the ground, was reflected down against it. Even with the temperature around zero, it could absorb enough heat from an evening's campfire to make it uncomfortably warm to sleep in. For overhead warmth, a fire had to be kept going through the night, but a heavy backlog and a few knotty chunks took care of that easily enough. A big leaping blaze made more heat than was needed, and was hard to get to sleep by. A slow and steady smolder was always better.

The best season for camping in the woods was always fall, when the first rains had laid the dust and ended the danger of forest fires, and there was enough frost at night to do away with flies and mosquitoes and make a fire and shelter mean something. All the wild berries and nuts were ripe then, and the bear and deer and grouse out fattening on them were handsomer than at any time during the summer, and easier to catch sight of because of the thinning foliage and the leaves that shed down in clouds when an animal moved among them. It was apt to be damp in the creek bottoms, with frost in the shady places that sometimes stayed on all day, but the water between the stones was like dark glass, some trout would still rise if they were gone after with a small pearl spinner instead of a fly, and even in the deep evergreen forests of the Northwest the autumn colors in the undergrowth flamed out in the patches of sunlight like spreads of Indian beadwork—pink dogwood, scarlet vine maple, crimson wild blackberry, ghost-white stone-maple, pale-yellow elder with masses of blue berries, dark yellow mountain ash with masses of red ones. There were always things about it to remember: once, at Bennett's Meadows on the flank of Mount Hood in Northern Oregon, a black bear sneaking across a big timber-fall toward a flock of mountain quail feeding on some wild cherries that grew up from among the tangle of dead logs and, at the last minute, having a log tip under him and dump him ten feet down into the mass of thorn-bushes and dead tree-limbs underneath. Once, in the Sawtooth Mountain country of Northern Idaho, a couple of startled elk slamming full tilt into a quaking asp thicket bordering a little creek, and knocking down a great shower of restless pale-gold aspen leaves that settled into the water with a rustling sound like snow sliding off a roof; and, in the silence that followed, a little six-inch trout lifting itself clear out of the creek and standing for a couple of seconds with only its tail touching the surface, straining after a dead spider dangling from a twig an inch beyond its reach. And again, there was the winter on the upper White Salmon River in Central Washington when the snow that usually came toward the end of October held off all through November and most of December, and the snowshoe rabbits, going by the calendar instead of the weather, changed their coats from brown to white as usual, and went hopping around among dark firs and naked undergrowth looking as conspicuous as if they had worn headlights. They seemed completely unaware that the season's freakishness had made their protective coloration useless, and would squat down motionless against a bank of dark fir-needles at some suspicious noise as trustingly as if it had been the flank of a snowfield on Mount Adams, twenty-odd miles away. Sometimes, watching all the white splotches moving through the openings in the timber as far as the eye could reach, it was hard to believe that there could be that many snowshoe rabbits in the country, or in the world.

Of course, more emergencies can come up in late-season camping than during the summer; or at least, the ones that do come up are apt to be more serious. Having some irresponsible member of the family lost in the woods in July or August need not be any reason for immediate uneasiness: the trails are all open and marked, there are other campers scattered around the area, the forest service telephones reach everywhere, and even if the searching parties have trouble picking up the right set of tracks, a few nights in the open at that season shouldn't hurt anybody. That has all changed by mid-October: back-trails fallen into disuse and blotted out with dead leaves and drift, the constant possibility of all tracks being rained out or snowed under or blown over by a passing windstorm, nights too bitter and threatening for anybody to lie out in without food or shelter. If a man has to get himself lost in the woods, late fall is one of the poorest possible seasons to pick for doing it.

Getting lost can be avoided, of course, by a little more care and attentiveness than a lot of people are capable of, but there are some hazards of a mountain autumn that nothing will help with except luck. I once stood out a three-day hurricane in mid-October in a cattle-camp on the edge of a big pine forest north of Trout Lake in Central Washington, peeking most of the time through a half-inch crack in the tent-flap at the wind tearing forty-foot boughs from the pines and sending them screeching and flapping through the air in what looked like a deliberate and sustained attempt to wipe the camp and everything in it out of existence. The camp came through undamaged—tents stretched perfectly tight and pegged down solidly all around the bottom will stand a harder wind than most houses—but the feeling of complete helplessness while the pine branches were sailing at us was a strain, and when it was over we had to spend close to a week cutting our fourteen miles of horse-trail clear of trees that had blown down across it before we could even reach the wagon-road to town. There was an afternoon in another October, hurrying in from a surveying trip in the Blue Mountains of Eastern Oregon, when the pack-horse carrying our notes and records lost his footing on a slippery section of trail, slid eighty feet down into a creek canyon, and wound up underneath a log-jam at the bottom. We worked most of the night with a snowstorm whipping at us to saw an opening in the logs big enough for him to get out through. He didn't want to leave when it was done, preferring the shelter underneath to the weather outside, and we had to haul him out by main strength, a couple of inches at a time. Getting him back up to the trail through the snow in the dark was no picnic, either. The question whether to take pack-horses on a camping-trip is one that can never be completely settled, one way or the other. They can keep going in country where the best four-wheel-drive truck would be helpless, but they have to be grazed, watered, and watched against straying, fighting, stampeding, and running away, so that half the time it is open to debate whether they are not more trouble than they are worth. It depends on what one gets out of the trip, probably. If it turns out to have been worth taking, the horses are not enough to spoil it. Emergencies are bound to come up, and getting the best of all of them would be like watching a horse-race with the results posted at the start, or fighting a war with bean-bags tied to sticks. One has to risk losing for winning to mean anything.

I am inclined to think, looking back over a good many years spent at it, that though a large part of the good one derives from camping is in triumphing over its incidental emergencies, an even larger part is in the emergencies themselves, win or lose. No camping-trip lingers in my memory more pleasantly than one I went on with my parents and step-grandfather in Southern Oregon when I was ten, following the Little River Fork of the Willamette River along an old stage-road that reached far on up into the Cascade Mountains to a string of sheep-camps near the summit. We had borrowed a spring-wagon and horses from one of the neighbors, with the understanding that my step-grandfather was to help us unload and pitch camp and stay with us a day, and then take it back where it belonged, and that he was to bring it back for us at the end of three weeks. We planned on picking wild blackberries to fill in the time, and most of the space in the wagon was taken up by a big preserving kettle and boxes of fruit jars to put them up in. We had come out short of provisions, intending to stock up with essentials at a small crossroads store where the old stage-road struck up into the mountains, and to fill in with game from the country around camp. Other people had done it without any difficulties. The difficulties, it appeared, had all been left to accumulate for us.

The first one was the crossroads store. It was padlocked and empty, and a snappish old graybeard who ran the blacksmith shop next to it said it had closed down because the sheep-camp supply season was almost over and the proprietor didn't like to lower himself by selling things to ordinary people. Having got that left-handed dig on the record, he inquired where we were going and what for. My father told him, and mentioned deer-hunting. He said there was nothing up Little River worth going there for, deer-hunting or anything else. My father looked uneasy at that. He didn't hunt much because a childhood lameness made it hard for him to get through the woods, but he was one of the best rifle-shots in the country, barred from all the rural turkey-shoots because he used up turkeys faster than they could be brought in, and we had counted on him for a deer at least. We turned up Little River along the old road bulging with tree-roots and cushioned deep with fir-needles, watching the woods on both sides for some sign that might indicate the old blacksmith to have been mistaken, but there was nothing except chipmunks and a few little pine-squirrels. The river was good-sized for the mountains, ten or twelve yards across, full of black-and-silver rapids tumbling down a rock-littered gorge twenty feet below the road, and the forest on both sides could have stood for a model specimen of Northwestern deep woods at their best—big first-growth Douglas firs spaced out from twenty to thirty yards apart, with the ground between them filled in with elder, mountain ash, willow, sweet-balm, wild lilac, madroña, salal, and big-leaved thimbleberry. It was beautiful country, with little springs alongside the road and black haw and wild raspberry dangling ripe fruit out into it, but it wouldn't be easy to sight game in, if the blacksmith's rundown of the prospects turned out to be mistaken. If signs meant anything, he hadn't told us anything that wasn't the strict copper-riveted truth.

The camping-place was a small clearing cut out of the undergrowth and enclosed in a rectangle of big fir logs, with a spring coming out of the ground close to the road and a view of some white-water rapids in the river across it. There was a small pole-corral a couple of hundred yards farther on, and my step-grandfather took the horses up to it for the night and then came back to help with the unpacking before it got dark. An elderly homesteader with a G.A.R. button in his coat came down the road driving a cow on foot as they were finishing stretching the tent, and my father asked him about the old blacksmith's report on the hunting. The homesteader was milder about it, but no more encouraging. There might be some game, he thought, but a party of hunters three or four miles on up the road had been banging away at everything in sight all week, and they had probably scared most of it into cover or else out of the country. My step-grandfather asked about the fishing in the river, and he said there wasn't any. He had seen parties of anglers try it dozens of times, some with imported equipment worth thousands of dollars, and none of them had ever caught so much as a minnow. He thought it might be because of some sulphur springs that emptied into the river a few miles on upstream. Whatever it was, there weren't any fish.

He went on his way, and while my father and step-grandfather were discussing what to do our first break of luck happened. Somebody in town had lent my father a shotgun for the trip, and in unpacking he had laid it across one of the enclosure-logs with the muzzle pointed at a salal thicket a couple of hundred feet up the road. It was the first hammerless gun I had ever had a chance at, and while they talked I began furtively experimenting with the trigger-pull and let off both barrels. There was a nerve-rattling boom, a patter of shot on leaves, and a jingling and whir of wings as a covey of blue grouse flew up from the salal and lit in a big fur tree a dozen or so yards farther on. My step-grandfather moved away from the shotgun, which had kicked back almost against his feet, and laughed. He had been through the whole four years of the Civil War in the Army of Northern Virginia, had been wounded two or three times, and had come out of it with an aversion to firearms that lasted all the rest of his life. He wouldn't touch a gun, not even to pick it up when it had fallen down. His enthusiasm was fishing, which was quiet and stimulating to a man's inventiveness. My father gave me a long look, reached the rifle out of the tent, and hurried up the road to the big fir. It was getting near dark, and a blue grouse against a background of fir boughs is one of the hardest objects in Nature to see, even in broad daylight, but he had a system for it. He watched for a white spot at the base of the grouse's throat, which moved and showed up clearly against the tree-foliage. It was not much to shoot at, being about half the size of a pip on a playing-card, but there was grouse on all sides of it, so it didn't have to be hit dead center. He shot three times before the covey got alarmed and flew away, and we came back with three grouse, each the size of a full-grown hen. They were enough to keep us going for at least two days; more important, they were game, and two supposed authorities had assured us that there was no game in the country. My father said hopefully that it looked as if they hadn't known what they were talking about, and my step-grandfather said he had felt all the time that the river had fish in it, sulphur or no sulphur. The story about the angling parties failing to catch anything with their imported equipment didn't mean anything. They might not have used the right bait.

He went down to the river before sun-up the next morning, with a fresh-cut willow pole, a cotton line, a couple of rusty hooks, and the livers from our three grouse in case the trout were holding off for something new, and he stayed gone all day while my father and I beat salal thickets in search of the remaining grouse from the covey. We heard shooting from up the road several times during the afternoon, found no sign of any grouse at all, and got back to camp empty-handed and tired about sundown. My step-grandfather came in a half-hour later, lugging a string of trout so long it dragged the ground behind him. The grouse-liver had been the right checker, he said: the trout had come after it as fast as he could bait and throw in. He was mightily pleased with himself, mostly because he had shown the homesteader up for an ignoramus, and he talked about it all through supper and afterward while we cleaned the trout and sank a bucket in the spring to put them in so they would keep. It was something to be pleased over; there was not quite the feeling of seriousness and dignity and saving the old homestead about it that there had been to bringing in the grouse, but there were trout enough to tide us over the rest of the week, and it would give us leeway to work the country out a little. He got the team and wagon ready to leave the next morning, took a regretful look down at the river and the first spots of sun picking out patches of crimson Oregon grape and blue elderberries between the gray fir-trunks, and said he thought we would last.

"The wagon from the sheep-camps ought to be past here along next week, anyway," he said. "You can send word down by it if you decide to leave ahead of time, and I'll come up after you."

My father said we could get the sheep-camp wagon to move us out, if we needed to, and my mother put her foot down on even the possibility.

"We're not leaving ahead of time," she said. "We're here to stay three weeks, and we'll do it. You can come for us when it's up."

My step-grandfather bowed his head and said three weeks it was. "There might be some place around where you can buy truck," he said. "That homesteader must eat sometimes. Well, I don't blame you."

The trout were our second stroke of luck. The third came a week afterward, when they and the grouse were used up and we were watching for the sheep-camp wagon in the hope that it might bring a few things out from town for us. My father and I had climbed a bald knoll above a fir-balsam thicket to watch for quail that sometimes came to a roadside spring at sundown. They were late, and as it was beginning to get dark we heard a scattering of shots from the woods back of our camp, and, after several minutes, another shot and the sound of brush crashing and men's voices calling. My father told me to sit down in case there was more shooting, but he remained standing and the shooting had stopped, so I stood up again, watching a little half-acre patch of sun-bleached grass a couple of hundred yards back in the timber. It was the only part of the landscape where anything was visible so near nightfall, and, as I watched, a small buck deer came out of the trees on one side, trotted halfway around it, and then walked to the center and lay down. I pointed it out, whispering for fear of scaring it, and my father said in an ordinary tone that he saw it. It was wounded; badly, it looked like. A deer would sometimes head for a clearing when it was hard hit, thinking the cougars and coyotes wouldn't dare come out into the open after it. He took another look and a long breath. "It's dead, I believe."

I was mortally sorry. Still, there was nothing anybody could do, and there were practical things to think about.

"We could go down and get it," I said. "Those men won't find it now."

My father had been raised among hunters, and some of his deepest principles had been acquired from them. "A deer belongs to whoever shoots it," he said. "They shot it, and it's theirs. . . . No, now, wait a minute."

I waited while he wrestled it out with himself, hunting ethics against my mother's determination to keep the camp going, and against what she would say about leaving a whole deer lying out in the woods to spoil or be dragged away by wild animals or torn up by buzzards.

"Go on back to camp and bring the lantern," he said finally. "We'll take it. It'll spoil if we don't."

"We could say you shot it," I said.

"If anybody asks, we'll tell them the truth," he said. "Go on."

We worked over half the night getting the deer dressed and cut into sections and carried up the road to camp. After it was all in and hung up, we lay awake expecting somebody from the hunting party to come storming in and accuse us of stealing it and try to take it away. We could hear men talking and calling to each other from the woods, and see a lantern moving in the underbrush, and we knew that if they stumbled on the clearing where the deer had stopped they could follow our trail to camp merely by lighting a few matches. I had never much liked the idea of killing deer, but several times toward morning when the men seemed to be moving closer I felt that killing one might be the easiest way of doing it. They quieted down toward dawn, but daylight made the cut-up deer hanging from the tree-limbs back of our tent stand out like a Bull Durham sign, and it was not till mid-morning, when the sheep-camp wagon came past from up the river, that we were able to breathe easy again. It went past at a trot, with the men of the hunting party crouched in the back around a long bundle of blankets, looking worn and uneasy. About noon, the homesteader came past and told us that one of their men had shot himself in the leg trailing a crippled deer through the brush about dark. The others had a hard time finding him, and a worse one finding their way back to camp with him in the dark, and since he had to be got out to a doctor, they had decided to load up and leave with him. They were all badly shaken, and had left most of their supplies scattered around camp— flour, sugar, dried apples, one thing and another. My mother asked interestedly how far up the road their camp was, but taking their deer was as far as my father intended to go.

"Whatever's left in their camp can stay there," he said. "It's not ours, and we don't want it."

Coming back to a statement of his principles made him feel better. He even felt better about hijacking the deer, and when the homesteader asked about it he said I had jumped it out of a blackberry patch a few mornings back, which made us all feel better.

The rest of our stay was so quiet and even-toned that except for its contrast with the strain of the first week it might have seemed draggy. My mother canned wild blackberries and we helped pick them; my father tried the fishing two or three times without much luck, and puttered at splitting clapboards from a fir log for a cook-table; I manufactured a bow and arrows and sniped at the jaybirds and pine-squirrels around camp with it. The hunting had improved with the hunting party gone: we could hear buck-deer stamping back in the timber every morning, and several times the covey of quail we had hunted so patiently during our first week came to drink at the spring we dipped water from for the camp, but with our period of emergency ended there was no feeling of any real need or purpose in shooting them, and usually we merely looked and let them go. My step-grandfather was the only one of us who made his seriousness of purpose last. He came in a couple of days ahead of the three weeks we had agreed on, and called to my father to bring the rifle and come on, there was a big flock of blue grouse feeding in a mountain ash thicket down the road, and he needed a few of them for bait to catch trout with. My father said we didn't need blue grouse or trout either, and that they would merely spoil in the heat on the road home. My step-grandfather said he didn't intend to catch any big grist of them.

"A dozen or so, maybe, to wave in that old homesteader's face the next time he comes past," he said. "I want to show that bluebellied old coffee-cooler that he don't know anything."

The Forests

BECAUSE a forest is made up of living organisms competing incessantly with each other for soil and space and light, it is subject to the same process of growth, death, change and renewal that goes on in any of the other communities in nature: ants, bees, pigeons, wild geese, crows, or human beings. Sometimes the change carries on a natural order of rotation: a stand of fir trees flattened by a windstorm or wiped out by fire is replaced not by new firs, but by some small deciduous growth like hazel, dogwood, alder or mountain ash. It is only when these have lived out their time and died that the firs, having given the ground time for rest and refertilization, come back and start all over again. Sometimes the process is speeded up or turned in some special direction by such forms of human intervention as logging, road-building, backwoods farms and clearings, or reforestation. In the past and in some parts of the country, human intervention has operated to slow down the process of change, and even to hold it off for a time, as the Indians of the Pacific Northwest and the Southern mountains did in the years before white settlement by burning off the year's accumulation of dead leaves and small underbrush regularly every fall.

Any such practice nowadays would be reckless, destructive and dangerous, but with the Indians, it was entirely practical. Getting rid of leaves and undergrowth took much of the uncertainty out of hunting and tracking, made travel and running trap-lines through the woods easier, and helped to preserve the big timber by clearing out inflammable material while it was still too small for a fire in it to do any damage. The timber got off with only a light scorching on its outer bark, and the ground under it was kept clear and open so that a man could travel almost anywhere through the woods on horseback, or even with a team and wagon.

It would not be possible to go back to the Indian system now. The underbrush has grown so dense and heavy, and the accumulation of dead leaves and fallen branches so deep, that setting a fire to run loose in it could clean out a whole countryside: timber, livestock, roads, farms, wild life, everything. The disappearance of open woodland brought about by civilization is one of the changes that the old settlers, who were responsible for most of them, used to find inexhaustible food for conversation in complaining about. To people of a later generation, who never knew the woods in their pristine state, it didn't seem especially serious. Things had probably been better when there was no underbrush to fight through, but there were ways of getting around it, and, tangled or not, it was still forest, and it was better to take it as it came than to fret and bellyache about how much more agreeable it used to be.

The same principle holds, I think, for many of the changes in the Eastern forests. The extermination by some mysterious European blight of the great chestnut groves that once reached all the way from Western Pennsylvania through the Virginia mountains and far down into North Carolina and Tennessee must certainly rank as a national disaster, but to one who never had the opportunity of seeing them before the blight moved in, the stone-littered ridges where they once grew seem nothing more than pleasantly varicolored strips of young woodland growth spreading out over the stumps and root-sprouts of some worked-out logging operation. The chestnut trees were undoubtedly beautiful, especially in the fall when the leaves fell and wild animals flocked in by the thousand to grub for nuts in them, but the redbud and shadbush and mountain laurel and second-growth pine that have come in to replace them are so handsome and inviting that only the old residents who remember what the pre-blight era was like would even miss them.

There is the same feeling about traveling through some of the old white pine country in New England, or Michigan, or Minnesota, all long since logged off and grown up to small hardwood and bushes—birch, alder, maple, hazel, butternut, beech, willow, boxberry, with scatterings of young spruce and hemlock mixed in. The white pine must have been impressive. It is a pity that some of the big stands could not have been spared, merely as exhibits; but, to judge from the small clumps that somehow were spared, the original vast forests of it must have been monotonous, as well as discouraging to wild life. Even such small game as foxes and rabbits and squirrels need a certain amount of open country to range in, and it is not unlikely that there are more of them among the tangle of saplings and bush-thickets covering the old stumps than there was in the big timber before the logging-crews ever came near it. Of course, second-growth brushland can be overdone, too, but the cycles of Nature never stop working, and it might very well happen that in another hundred years or so the white pine will be on its way back again, as thrifty and as monotonous as ever, and that the old residents of that day will be putting in their time muttering nostalgically about the good old times when the country was all varicolored brushland, abounding in deer, bear, quail, cougars, wild berries, color and sunlight.

Much of the low ground fronting on the sea in the Southern states is grown up in pine, which, in large areas, always runs to a certain sameness; but the coastal forests of South Carolina break away from that pattern with a brightness of contrast and variety that puts them easily among the loveliest in the country. The lowland—one of the wildest and prettiest parts of it bears the odd name of Britain's Neck —is run through by little estuaries from the sea, separated by ridges covered with live-oak and hickory. Farther back, in what is called the barrens, are stands of small pine. Along the marshlands the variety of trees is uncountable—laurel, bay, palmetto, dogwood, black cherry, and nobody knows how many others, all bound together into a gigantic hedge by runners of smilax, supple-jack, and a species of wistaria called Carolina bean, the stems of which are so tough and pliable that they were used by Indians and early settlers as a substitute for rope. The live-oak and pine and laurel stay green all winter; in the spring, the wild cherry and jessamine blossoms load the air with a fragrance so heavy that an off-shore breeze will carry it miles inland; in the fall there is color everywhere.

The Southwestern Louisiana lowlands are much the same, with the palmettos left out and locust, gum, maple, cypress, elm, willow, pecan, persimmon, mulberry and magnolia added in, and so are sections of Southern Mississippi. An uncle of mine used to tell about taking a train-trip from Jackson to New Orleans in the early eighteen-eighties, and of feeling that every mile was a deeper plunge into a wilderness so gigantic and remote that the train itself had got lost and was wandering around frantically trying to find a place to butt its way out. Finally, when he had given up hope of ever seeing home again, he discovered that the forest had dropped away, and that the train was rolling into New Orleans as serenely as if nothing had happened at all, as, in fact, nothing had.

It would be interesting to lay out a whole series of studies on the forests of the Southern mountains—ten or a dozen, possibly, with room in each to spread out. There would be material enough for it; a whole book—*The Mountains*, by D. H. Strother—has been written about merely the small area of West Virginia lying between the South Branch of the Potomac on the East and the headwaters of the Monongahela on the West. Dozens of forests farther south could stand as much, and some deserve more. One that is fairly representative—out of forty others that would sound altogether different, and do as well—is the sweep of mountain country reaching up from Waynesville in North Carolina to the western flank of the great Balsam Peaks in the Pisgah National Forest, and then north following the beautiful Pigeon River through the Great Smokies into Southeast Tennessee. The woods along the river bottoms are at their best from late summer into mid-autumn, with a blue tinge in the shadows bringing out the yellow and brown and crimson of ash, sugar-maple, oak, hickory, alder, poplar, chinquapin and black walnut; walnuts and hickory-nuts beginning to drop, and half-leafless vine-runners dangling clusters of frost-grapes and 'possum-grapes from the tree branches overhead. Even the bottom-lands here have an altitude of over 2500 feet, and there are clumps of small pine and spruce around all the hilltops; but the dark balsam after which the mountain range is named seldom grows below 4000 feet, and farther up, extending all the way to where the timber ends in a fringe of stunted and half-dead pines, is one vast thicket of rhododendrons, blazing in the blossoming season with crimson flowers, picked out along the little watercourses with purple rosebay and azalea and pinkish-white mountain laurel.

An odd thing about the Southern high-mountain forests is that even in places where the timber is mixed, some one species will stand out so vivid and dominating as to leave the impression that there is nothing else anywhere around. There must be at least a few specimens of scrub-pine and spruce scattered among the balsams, at least at the edges, but it is impossible afterward to remember anything about them, as it is to remember anything about the rhododendrons except the great flower-masses crowding up the slope and littering the ground with crimson petals, though some of them, by actual count, range all the way from pale pink to bright purple.

The same thing is noticeable in the mountains of Southwestern Virginia, where the woods, which must have included trees of a dozen different species, appeared to me from a short half-mile away to be nothing but oak; and on the cliffs around the eye-staggering Tallulah Falls in Northern Georgia, where evergreens of probably half a dozen different species persisted unanimously in looking like hemlock; and around the less dizzying but lovelier Toccoa Falls some twenty miles away, where they all looked like black alder. It is a strange and beautiful region. The impressions of it that one carries away are unforgettable, and almost invariably inaccurate.

There are other forest areas that deserve at least the same skimpy measure as the Southern mountains, though they must be allowed even less: the great wooded regions of Arkansas and Southern Missouri, from the cottonwood, pecan, elm, holly, maple, buttonwood, honey-locust, and Kentucky coffee of the lowlands to the open woodlands of the Ozarks and the deep evergreen forests of the Boston Mountains; the wild places in the Trinity Bottoms in Texas, with gigantic cottonwood and water-oak overgrown with long streamers of pale Spanish moss and laced together with runners of mustang-grape and bull-briar and trumpet-flower; the old post-oak groves of the Mississippi Valley where the great wild-pigeon flocks once had their nesting-grounds—Indiana has several: one in Decatur County, 28 miles long by 14 miles wide in which the trees were not over ten steps apart, had at least fifteen nests to every tree; and, in the hill country of the same state, the beautiful oak woods between French Lick and Hardinsburg; the vast sweep of pine timber lifting from Western Montana across the Bitter Roots and down to Lake Pend d'Oreille in Idaho; in Eastern Utah, the high-altitude pines bordering an old side-road along the scarp of the Vintah Mountains between Fort Duchesne and Heber City, with bays and inlets of yellow and blue and pink and scarlet wildflowers between long stripings of unmelted snow; the great redwood groves in Northern California, which make a man feel uplifted and majestic when viewed from a distance or in passing and, seen at close range, fill him with a sense of puniness and humiliating insignificance on discovering that he is, after all, something less than twenty-five feet tall.

Of all these forests, the best, to my way of thinking, are the prairie groves along the part of the old Santa Fe Trail in Eastern Kansas known as The Narrows: places like Rock Creek and Pool Creek and the old wagon-camp at the Cottonwood Fork of the Arkansas River. They are not big, or scientifically interesting, or especially valuable, but the little streams wandering through the deep shade under the burr-oaks and cottonwoods and wild plum and cherry thickets, the bright sprinkling of arbutus and windflowers, bellwort and lobelia, yellow wood-sorrel and red cranebill and whitish-pink partridge-berry, the sounds of running water and of birds and squirrels moving in the branches overhead, make it a kind of refuge from the blaze and stillness of the open prairie around it, where a man sees too far to see really much of anything. In the groves, the trees shorten his field of vision. Seeing less, he notices more and remembers it longer.

A man always describes best what he knows best. Since I was born and brought up in the Cascade Mountain country of the Pacific Northwest, it seems worthwhile to go into some detail about its different types of forest and the changes they go through with the changes in altitude and exposure and climate, from the mild winters and moist summers and heavy rainfall of the western slope to the deep snows and violent extremes of climate on the slopes that face back toward the east. As good a beginning as any is to head east from Yoncalla in the Upper Umpqua Valley in Southwestern Oregon, and pick up an old abandoned emigrant-road, now mostly impassable except on foot, that strikes on east across the mountains beyond Elkhead by way of Black Butte and the old Bohemia gold diggings.

The foothill groves of scrub-oak come first, crowding the stony ridge-tops at any altitude up to 800 feet. Their sparse greenish-brown foliage and twisted grayish trunks are not much for color, but the spring wildflowers that come up among the old layers of dead leaves show all the brighter for being set against a drab background: long-stemmed yellow violets; a small white-and-blue species of sego lily called cat-ear, the bulbs of which are edible; stalks of fritillaria hung with delicate green-and-brown-spotted flowers like little bells, usually eaten by deer as fast as they open; black-and-crimson bird-bills; the graceful cream-white trout-lilies called lamb-tongues (on the Great Plains, where they are small and colored a liverish-purple, these are known as dog-tooth violets), and masses of wild strawberry blossoms under the bracken and old grass that in another month will be strawberries as big as a man's thumb. It may be that some chemical property in dead oak-leaves brings so many different flowers out of soil so stony and lifeless, or it may be that for some kinds of vegetation soil is less important than sunlight. In the low-lying swales farther up, where the deposit of black leaf-mold is almost bottomless, these upland flowers never grow at all.

In the swales, where the creeks spread out along the foot of the mountains, there are groves of smooth-barked rock-maple, their masses of gray-green foliage bouncing with bluejays and red-headed woodpeckers and big silver-gray squirrels. The low ground has clumps of huge-branched white ash, with taller clumps of black oak striking up past them, and in the damp places, big dark-green myrtles spreading out over a groundwork of green-and-black puddles circled with buttercups and wild yellow snapdragons and mottles of purple swamp-iris, so dark and elusive that one has to look several times to make sure they are not shadows.

Where the old emigrant-road begins, a few miles beyond Elkhead, in a you-be-damned alternation of chuckholes and fallen logs and intruding underbrush, is the beginning of the real mountains and the first stands of big timber, separated from the foothills by thickets of hazel, arrowwood, elder, dogwood, the wild azalea that used to be called calico-bush, sleek red-barked madroñas hung full of green-white flower-sprays, some small Oregon yew trees, and a long sweep of dark salal with white blossoms that look exactly like heather-bells, a great gathering-place for upland game-birds in the fall when the berries ripen, and finally through sword-fern and rank waist-high thimbleberry whose big soft-textured leaves were a standing substitute for toilet-tissue among the early pioneers, down to a shallow creek bordered with alder and flowering dogwood and big red cedars dangling loose strands of the long-grained fibrous bark that Indians used to beat together with rabbit-fur and wild-goose down into a kind of stiff felt for robes and mats and blankets.

For the Indians, the red cedar had a range of usefulness only surpassed in later years by rawhide, which could be fabricated into almost everything needful to housekeeping, from door-hinges and suspender-buttons and combs to stove-pipes and window-panes. Cedar bark was used not only for blanket-felt, but also for beds, thatching and weatherproof-ing, moccasin stuffing, and lining for saddles. The small roots were woven into baskets, and the soft straight-grained wood was the standard material for winter houses, arrow-shafts, canoes, water-buckets, hide-stretchers, pack-frames, and drums. The crushed foliage was also used as a flea-repellent: not always successfully, but it may have helped.

The Douglas firs grow taller than the cedars, and heavier at the base—a full-grown timber fir will average eight or ten feet through on the stump, as against not much over half that for a cedar. The firs show up at their best along the shaded canyons where they have to grow to reach the sun-light, far enough back from the creek to be safe from spring freshets, close enough to it not to be harmed by prolonged dry spells or excessive heat. There are many different kinds of ground and climate where Douglas fir can take hold and flourish so profusely as to be a nuisance, and sometimes even a downright menace to life. Not many experiences are more unpleasant than cruising a stand of half-grown fir, with trees from a foot to a foot and a half in diameter spaced barely far enough apart for a man to squirm between them through the ground-tangle of dead branches, with, every few hundred yards, a dead tree toppled sideways against some of the living ones and hanging on a precarious slant, all ready to fall at a touch and flatten a man underneath like a pile-driver flattening a bolt-head. Among lumbermen, such leaning trees are known as widow-makers. Wild animals never get caught under them, because wild animals never venture into the thickets where they are, knowing better than some human beings that there is nothing worth going there for. Birds light in the treetops sometimes, usually for not more than a few minutes, but the ground underneath is lifeless, sunless, colorless, and useless except as a proof that overspecialization can create dreariness in a wilderness as easily as outside it.

There is no lifelessness or overcrowding in the big fir timber. The trees grow from a hundred to a hundred and fifty feet apart—the distance is usually about equal to their height—with room between them for splashes of sunlight filled with runners of vine-maple, clumps of glossy Oregon grape hung with sprays of little round yellow flowers like acacia, red huckleberry bushes, beds of short-stemmed wild violets, neither yellow nor purple, but the most intense sky-blue, wild black raspberries along a rock-outcrop, and wild blackberries—not the tangled evergreen brambles of the Coast country, but native wild blackberries, ripening on tall canes to the size of a .45–90 rifle cartridge. Wild life is everywhere: blue grouse feeding on fir-buds in the treetops, mountain quail wallowing in the dust of a clearing, bears grubbing in the berry-patches for yellowjackets' nests, families of whitetail deer among the salal, rabbits, ruffed grouse, marten, weasels, bobcats and little blue foxes in the thickets along the creek; hawks, jays, doves, kingfishers, rain-owls, hummingbirds, woodpeckers, band-tailed pigeons, wood-ducks, porcupines, skunks.

It is never quiet among the big firs. Even on a still day,

the upper air currents keep up a continuous roaring in the treetops, like a distant waterfall or a train running wide open a half-mile beyond the next hill. One gets used to it in time, and can even come to miss it when taken away from it. Douglas fir bark is very thick: a section from a good-sized tree will measure a foot and a half through, and it burns with a smoldering heat like charcoal. The pitch, which is thin and colorless like that of the balsam fir, is preservative and antiseptic, and is used commercially in optics and in the manufacture of synthetic flavoring extract. A tree that has had its heart-wood injured will secrete pitch in vast quantities as a healing agent. My grandfather once, falling a good-sized fir for floor-planking, chopped into a hollow inside the trunk that ran more than twenty-five gallons of pitch, which filled every utensil the family owned and brought in enough to buy the floor-planking and leave the tree standing for use as a beehive.

The big fir timber reaches to an altitude of about 2500 feet. Beyond that level, which is a little under halfway to the summit of the mountains, the trees dwindle in size and grow closer together. The deep layer of fir needles on the ground takes up all sound except the roaring of the treetops, and the close-laced branches overhead shut out the sun so that even in the middle of the day it is scarcely more than a pale half-twilight. The mountain lakes lie close to the summit, which is usually level except for the peaks, and swampy because the cold of the heights condenses moisture from the rain-clouds blowing in from the Coast. Coming down to one of the lakes from the dusk and silence of the deep timber is like breaking through a time-barrier into a different geologic age. The cold glare of the open water reaches back among the trees like a searchlight; a half-dozen blue herons rouse up and splash frantically through the shallows and take wing, screeching and flapping; some wild ducks streak out of the tules and clatter past at almost eye-level; a beaver-colony lookout down by the lake outlet sounds an alarm by whacking his tail against the mud with a report that shakes all the tree-branches; a half-dozen buck-deer start up from cooling their budding antlers in the mud of a marsh and go banging off through a cottonwood thicket, falling over snags and shattering dead branches with a racket like a rock-crusher. The suddenness of the transition from stillness and half-light to so much glare and hellaballoo is enough to leave anybody a little shaken. Wild animals are silent enough in country frequented by human beings, but in their own territory they can be as noisy, and as blatant about it, as human beings habitually are in theirs.

The trees around the mountain lakes are usually small. Fir and cedar take hold sometimes, but they are usually broken down young by some big fall of snow or drowned out by a rise in the lake-level. Except for mountain laurel and the big sweep of huckleberry bushes up the hill at the far end of the lake, the trees are quick-growing soft-woods like alder, favored by wild bees for its honey, which is clear white, very heavy, and a little tasteless, and the dwarf cotton-woods which, besides supplying the beaver-colonies with food and building material, can be used as horse-feed in places where the grass is scant or washy.

The mountain huckleberry patches were regular assembling places for Indians from the entire surrounding country in pre-settlement times, much as the maple-sugar groves were for eighteenth-century settlers in Western Pennsylvania and the Southern mountains. The little mountain lakes were especially favored as camping places because, in addition to the huckleberries, the mud-flats and tule-marshes bore masses of yellow pond-lilies, the seeds of which were harvested and pounded into a cereal decoction called *wokas,* excellent in cases of prolonged starvation because, though nutritious, it was so flat and unpalatable that nobody could eat more of it than was good for him. The lakes swarmed with trout, but there was no sign around them that the Indians ever tried their hands at angling. They may not have understood about lures and tackle, or it may have been that handling two different jobs of food-gathering simultaneously was all they felt equal to.

Because the top of the mountains is usually a marshy table-land, one usually passes the summit without knowing it except by the change in the forest growth as the slope drops off east toward the inland plateau country and the sagebrush deserts. There are masses of pink rhododendron crowding among the alders; then, in the creek canyon leading down from the lake, there are red cedars growing out of a tangle of poison laurel, ground vine maple, wild columbine, black-stemmed maidenhair fern, and snowberry and huckleberry bushes. The dark bottom of the canyon is piled deep with the trunks of fallen cedars, cribbed and angled and crisscrossed over one another so that getting over them requires seesawing back and forth along the top logs twelve or fifteen feet above the ground, like a ship tacking into the wind. Some of the lower logs must have lain buried in mud and decaying vegetation for several centuries, but the wood in all of them is as sound and firm as if they had fallen no longer ago than last week.

The cedar swale tapers out in a thicket of tall steel-gray mountain ash, whose clusters of bitter scarlet berries are much favored by bears in the fall as an astringent and stomach tonic. Beyond it, the canyon opens out, the undergrowth thins to scattered clumps of laurel, and the trees take on range and variety: bushy incense cedar, lancelike red fir, silvery white fir, balsam fir, its pale-gray bark studded with pitch-blisters as big as a child's fist, deep-green spruce, bristling with close-set needles as stiff and as prickly as briers; dark hemlock; spindly tamarack, with thin black-green needles that look skimpy and anemic in the summer, but make up for it by lighting the woods with tall black-speckled pyramids of pale-yellow in the fall.

Changes come fast along these eastern slopes. It takes only a few minutes of clambering to reach the top of the canyon, and the level ground reaching back from it is columned with tall Western white pine, so clear and open underneath that a man can look out through the spaces between the trees and see tall stalks of pink foxglove at the edge of a sunlit meadow a mile away. There is no ground-clutter of dead branches or fallen snags. The trunk of a white pine, its hard dark-gray bark divided into regular diamond-shaped figures like the markings of a rattlesnake, goes up from the ground as straight and as clean as a gun-barrel, ending in a tuft of short dark-green needles that, though a good-sized house could easily be buried in it, looks, from a hundred and fifty feet down, to be scarcely bigger than a feather duster. The trees never crowd each other. There is always a long expanse of clear ground between them, and always a background of distant sunlight where they end and the smaller timber begins. Wild animals seldom frequent white pine country, because there is nothing in it that they can eat. People invariably take to it eagerly because there is so much about it that they can spoil.

The smaller timber opens out into scattered copses of spruce and small Douglas fir circling a mountain meadow where there are a few bleached snags and a litter of fallen logs half-buried in tall herdsgrass, pink-flowered wild pea-vine, gray-and-rose fireweed gone to seed at the top and still flowering lower down, and spotted tiger-lilies, a temptation to pick, but a useless one, since they wither in less than an hour when picked. The spruce and fir copses never face the open meadow full-length. They are always covered halfway up by an edging of wild blackberry, dogwood, blue elderberry, and white quaking aspen, which ranks with the white pine as one of the most beautiful trees in the world. Sometimes it grows in half-acre clumps, and the almost-round thumbnail-sized leaves, which turn buttercup-yellow at the first touch of fall, stand out in the heavy timber of a mountainside five or six miles away like massed flowers. More commonly they grow singly, planting themselves close around a stand of fir or spruce as if they knew the striking contrast their leaves made, twirling and shimmering against the dark evergreen background with merely the wind of a bird flying past. Looking at one from a distance on a still day, a man could almost swear that it was quivering from some deer rubbing against it, but it can go on quivering without any help from outside. It is merely the same sensitiveness to light air currents that keeps up the roaring in the fir-tops when there is not wind enough near the ground to stir a feather.

Crossing the Cascade Mountains by unused roads, and in places by no road at all, and allowing time enough to take in the country along the way, can easily use up an entire summer. A man is entitled to feel that he has made fairly good time from a start up the west slope in the late spring if, looking down across the eastern rimrock ridges to the lower pine timber, he can see no more signs of cold weather moving in than unmelted hoar-frost in the shadows of the scarlet vine-maples, and some yellow leaves falling from the wild pin-cherry thickets where the grouse and wild doves are rummaging through them for a last scattering of frost-shriveled red cherries.

The pine timber begins at somewhere near 3000 feet

altitude, and reaches almost down to where the mountains level off into open country, 1000 feet farther down. Pine timber is apt to be dusty and warmish in summer, but it is handsome and pleasant in the fall. The trees do not change coloring with the season, and the turpentine in the fallen needles keeps down the heavy underbrush that flourishes farther up the mountain, but there is enough autumn coloring scattered around to show what time of year it is: sweeps of whitish pine-grass, patches of brown bracken, crimson trailers of Oregon grape, yellow willow and deerbrush along the dry watercourses, clumps of lupine blackened by frost along the edges, black seed-heads of wild sunflowers, and their tumbled dry leaves that rustle in a nightwind like old brittle newspaper. The trees are of two species: lodgepole pine, a tall slender-trunked hardwood that reaches up the mountain clear into the lower limit of the firs, and red-barked Western yellow pine—one of the most widely distributed trees on the continent, since it grows as far east as Georgia and North Carolina and all the way through Texas and Arizona and into Northern Mexico—which spreads down to the foot of the mountains and the belt of warty black acorn-oaks with which the forest ends.

There is not much to see in a pine forest. The trees are all of an even size and shape and coloring, and the undergrowth tends to repeat itself after two or three days of plodding around in it. The oak woods are better, because of the wild animals that flock to them in the fall, some to feed on the acorns, and others, like the cougars and lynx-cats and coyotes, to feed on the feeders. It was along the margin of the oaks that we used to camp when we were bringing cattle down from the mountains for the winter, beside a little creek edged with red willow and wild plum and mountain mahogany, where we could watch for the deer and bear that came prowling among the dead leaves toward daylight, and look out over the bare treetops at the gray sagebrush and the lights of cars streaking along through it on the main highway, ten or a dozen miles away.

After a long summer in the mountains, wild game didn't mean much. It was the lights that held us. One of the men got up and stirred the fire, watching them, and then roused himself and said we were back in civilization. It struck me that we had accomplished something in being able to concoct civilization out of a distant strip of pavement and a dozen or so car-lights streaking along it. Without the forest back of us, we couldn't have done it.

Sheep Herding

AN ARTICLE in a magazine recently, discussing sheep-raising and various allied subjects, suggested that the reason the sheepherder had always lagged far behind the cowboy as a popular motion picture figure was his less picturesque rig-out and equipment. It went on to note that, unlike the cowboy, the sheepherder wore no gun, didn't ride a horse, didn't totter around bowlegged in high-heeled boots, and didn't do much of anything to set himself apart from ordinary humanity except tramp around vast expanses of disagreeable country with nothing between him and the hostilities of Nature except a few rocks, a bedroll, and a frying pan.

Nobody could quarrel with the basis of the argument. It is perfectly true that the sheepherder has never acquired anywhere near the standing in the nation's hero-mythology that the cowboy has grown into almost without an effort. But to me, looking back over some youthful years spent at protecting sheep from their own unflagging moronism, the explanation seems unrealistic. In my time, most sheepherders did carry some kind of pistol—the Luger 9 mm. automatic was especially favored, as being light and hard-shooting—and they were always outfitted with an old-model .30–30 carbine, to use against such forms of predatory life as bears, cougars, coyotes, and acquisitive backwoods settlers. They always had horses, because in places where the grass was scant the sheep would scatter out over so wide an area that it would have been impossible for a man on foot to keep track of them. The cowboy's clothes were, of course, more picturesque, though not as much so as the movies nowadays make them out, but it is open to argument whether they helped with his rise to popularity or whether he may not have helped with theirs.

There are two other explanations that might bear more closely on the question of prestige between the two professions. One is that sheepherders, having no distinguishing costume or conventionalized form of dialect, had to be shown attending to their job to be identifiable as sheepherders, and since work is always a repellent subject to a motion picture audience, they necessarily lose out to the cowpunchers, who are never shown punching any cows, or doing anything else that could be considered useful except to shoot each other occasionally. In addition, it should be remembered that the public likes its stock heroes to be not only economically useless, but also to show a noticeable density between the ears. For a genuinely popular folk-hero to exhibit signs of intelligence is a contradiction in terms: the rule for such things is that if he does he isn't, and if he is he doesn't. There are many cases in which a cowboy has risen to eminence in his profession without brains enough to blow his nose. A sheepherder who didn't have them or didn't use them wouldn't last three months.

The difference between the two callings was always especially noticeable in places where they were thrown into contact with each other. There used to be a small crossroads town in the section of Southeastern Arizona known as Sixshooter Flat which, being too straitened financially to afford a regular jail, had sunk a post in the middle of the main square with a log-chain bolted into it, to which disturbers of the public peace and dignity were handcuffed till they cooled off. The device was called a trot-line, and it was not unusual after a big Saturday night to see as many as half a dozen cowboys shackled to it, muttering and looking bitter and suffering from heat, hang-overs, and each other's company. Early one summer, a sheepherder from some camp back in the hills got sentenced to four days on it for fighting. Instead of following the cowboys' routine of serving his time out in rankling and vexation of spirit, he waited till dark and then dug the post up and walked thirty-five miles back to camp, carrying it on his shoulder. He could have lightened his load considerably by burning it, which would have left him only the chain and the handcuffs to carry, but he didn't like the idea of destroying public property, and besides, it would have held him up a long time and he didn't want to be late for work. Most of them used to be on that pattern: hasty and impulsive sometimes, but resourceful, not afraid of work, and law-abiding on principle, even at the expense of real personal inconvenience.

It is interesting, looking back into history, to note how many far-reaching changes in America were brought about not by any human need or public-spiritedness, but by human frivolity. The eighteenth-century fashion for fur *pelisses* broke the first pack-trails from the Atlantic seaboard into the trans-Allegheny wilderness. The vogue for buckskin breeches in Regency England carried white civilization on west into the Mississippi Valley, and the Western European demand for beaver hats pushed it all the way across the Rocky Mountains to the Pacific. The Western sheep business started its real flowering when some authoritative-sounding expert came up with the discovery, back in the early nineteen-twenties, that ladies with a tendency to heftiness could slim themselves down by going on a diet in which the main article of nutriment was lamb chops.

Whether there was anything to it or not I don't know, but its effect on the country's sheep production was not unlike that of the internal combustion motor on the petroleum industry. Wool became a by-product. Sheep changed from the fine-wool Merino and Rambouillet types, long-fleeced and light-built, to big-boned Hampshire and Lincoln crossbreeds, bearing shorter wool and less of it, but running so far ahead in meat production that their six-month lambs would outweigh the fine-wool sheep when they were full-grown. Sheep prices tripled and quadrupled. The demand for pasture-land grew until sheepmen were leasing waste stumpage that lumber companies had let go for taxes, and fighting over it. Sheep have a sharp-pointed hoof structure that can destroy the best pasture almost beyond redemption unless they are closely and expertly herded, and since sheep at over twenty dollars a head were more worth looking after than sheep at six, herders' wages increased in proportion and beyond it, along with their responsibilities.

For the older sheepherders, the change was not so much a moral vindication as an embarrassing nuisance. To be jumped from sixty-five dollars a month to five times that much without having done anything for it, gave them a feeling of uncomfortable self-consciousness and hypertension over their own importance. Most of them tried it two or three years, and then turned it over to younger men with more hustle and more interest in the money end of the business, and scattered out into lighter forms of employment—janitors, warehouse foremen, elevator operators, livestock buyers, mortgage appraisers, night-watchmen. None of them ever seemed especially regretful over their abandoned calling. They were mostly old, and it was not so much that they had left it as that it had left them. They couldn't have gone back to it: there was nothing to go back to.

A lot of them had been worth knowing, in one way or another. I remember an old Yaqui Indian herder in Southern Arizona who was clairvoyant and could tell three hours beforehand when anybody was coming out to his camp, who it was and what for, and exactly what point in the road he had reached and when and for how long he had been held up by having to change a tire or tinker a balky motor. Besides having second sight, he was an expert in native medicines, and I remember being especially struck once by his efficiency in doctoring a cowboy from a neighboring outfit who had dislocated a shoulder wrestling with an ill-tempered yearling bull. He stirred up an anesthetic of tequila and crushed jimsonweed, knocked the cowboy cold with a big snort of it, and yanked the shoulder back into place while he lay glassy-eyed and limp, babbling happily of green fields. He did his herding on foot and without a dog, using, as a long-range persuader, an old-fashioned leather sling like the one shown in Sunday school pictures of David and Goliath. His ammunition was a pebble about the size of a large walnut, and he could kill a jackrabbit with it at any range up to fifty yards, or jolt a sheep into a high gallop at a hundred and fifty. It was better than a dog would have been, considering the circumstances. A dog intelligent enough to be kept under control at that distance would have been too valuable to risk in a country abounding in poisonous reptiles, scorpions, eight-inch centipedes, javelinas, mountain lions, an occasional jaguar from south of the border, and seasonal visitations of trigger-happy sportsmen from the nearby towns.

I never found out exactly when the old fellow quit herding, but I did run into him once afterward, on a wild pack-road near the White Mountain Indian reservation. He was dressed in an informal but effective costume consisting of rawhide moccasins, a loin-flap, a dirty head-cloth, and an old-model .44 rifle, and he explained that he was helping some Apache trackers in a hunt for a couple of convicts who had escaped from the state penitentiary at Florence and had been spotted by an airplane in the scramble of ocotillo and cactus and dry gullies along the foot of the mountains. He doubted if they were really there: his spirit control, or whatever it was, had intimated clearly that they were headed south toward the Mexican line (where, as I recollect, they actually were picked up a few days afterward) but the trackers were getting paid by the day and he didn't like to spoil things for them. Besides, he was having a good time at it himself.

There was another old-time herder from the pine timber country farther north, where a herd-dog was almost indispensable, who used to maintain that the most useful kind of dog a man could have was one that was cowardly. He told of one time when, having got off his horse to examine some bear-tracks in the pine needles, the bear suddenly loomed up at him from behind a bush, scaring his horse into stampeding with his rifle still on the saddle, so that he had to take to a tree. Any dog with normal courage would have sailed into the bear and got knocked into gun-wadding at one slap. His dog, being yellow to the core, tucked its tail and lit out for home, taking twenty feet at a jump and yelping in terror whenever it got scraped by a passing twig, and brought a hunting-party back from the main ranch along in the mid-afternoon, which shot the bear and helped him down. Cowardice saved him. With a dog courageous enough to get itself killed, he would have remained up the tree for the rest of his life, which probably would not have been extensive.

Cowardly or not, a dog is handy to have around in wild country, where a man working alone can be put in peril by some ordinarily trivial accident—a sprained ankle, a mis-lick with an axe, even a bad stomach-ache—that in more settled areas would amount to no more than a temporary inconvenience. There was a fall, in a deer-hunting camp in the Blue Mountains in Eastern Oregon, when we were roused up about daylight by a lank and bedraggled black-and-white shepherd dog that appeared out of the rain-soaked underbrush and jumped around us barking, refusing to be caught or fed, until we gave in and let him pilot us out through the woods to an abandoned old trap-line cabin where we found, first a saddle-horse stretched out dead by the door with a bullet-hole between its eyes, and inside, a herder lying on an old straw-pallet with an injured ankle that was so badly inflamed and swollen that he couldn't bear his weight on it.

It had all been a combination of accident, bad luck, and overimpulsiveness. He had been out hunting stray sheep a few miles from his camp, and stepped into a rusty old wolf-trap under some dead bushes, which cut him badly and took him a long time to pry loose. Since it was late and raining, he took shelter for the night in the old cabin, which was sup-posed vaguely to be haunted. During the night, he turned loose with his gun at a blazing-eyed apparition that loomed up in the doorway and glared at him, only to discover, when the pain in his ankle waked him at daylight, that he had shot his own horse. He hadn't eaten for two days, his ankle had got so bad that he couldn't rustle fuel to keep up a fire, and he hadn't the slightest hope that anybody would think of looking for him for at least a week, when his camp-tender was due in. He couldn't understand how we had ever thought of it. We explained about the dog, and he lay back and shut his eyes thankfully.

"I'll buy that dog the biggest beefsteak that ever come off a steer," he said. "A whole pile of 'em, if he wants 'em. . . . Is he yours?"

We never found out whose he was, or whether he belonged anywhere. He stayed around till we finished dressing the herder's ankle and started back with him on the road to town, and then, in spite of every inducement we could think of, he loped off into the undergrowth and disappeared: apparently some excitement-hunting hobo type that could never stay put anywhere more than a few days. There were a good many hobo dogs around the open country. Most were highly intelligent, and it is likely that confidence in being able to take care of themselves had something to do with their taking up a roving life to begin with.

Not all of them were hoboes, of course. Some were skilled and self-respecting livestock specialists, cruising around in search of a place where their talents would be properly appreciated. I worked one summer with one of those, a big brown half-collie that came tagging in with an itinerant crew of sheep-shearers, went to work helping to herd our sheep while they were waiting their turn at shearing, and apparently found the place so stimulating that he decided to stay on. His sense of devotion to his work was downright exasperating sometimes. There was one late spring when he was helping me move a herd of six hundred ewes with lambs down a flat stretch of the Deschutes River canyon, with the river on one side and an eight-hundred-foot wall of basalt cliff on the other. I was riding among the lead sheep, to keep them from getting jammed together in the places where the flat narrowed. The dog was back with the tail-enders, to keep them from scattering out to graze where it widened. Everything was going well except for the dust and the infernal heat of the canyon, when I saw, glancing back, that a lamb had got crowded off into the river and was floating downstream toward me. It was moving moderately fast, but it was close to the bank, the water looked pleasantly ripply and cool and not deep, and I had on only a shirt and overalls and moccasins, which wetting couldn't hurt and might even improve. I hung my hat on the saddle-horn and emptied my pockets into it while the lamb floated even with me, and then dropped the reins on the ground and stepped off into the current to grab it.

Nothing worked out as it was supposed to. The water, which had looked shallow, was at least fifteen feet deep and so paralyzingly cold that it cramped me up like being kicked in the stomach by a mule, and the current, which had looked invitingly brisk and stimulating, snatched me off downstream so fast that it felt like falling out of a sixth-floor window. It was snaking me along, cramped and helpless, when the dog came racing down the bank past me and jumped in. It was a perfect opening for a story-book rescue, but he didn't pay the slightest attention to me. He was after the lamb. He swam right out into the current and shouldered it toward the bank, and then caught it by the scruff of the neck and lugged it into shallow water and stood over it, watching while I managed to flounder sideways onto a gravel-bar a couple of dozen yards below him. It really had been a close call, and he looked so serene and pleased with himself over the idiotic lamb that I was tempted to dig some rocks out of the gravel-bar and throw them at him, though it would have been completely pointless and useless. He had done nothing to be punished for. His business was to look after sheep, not men, and he had every right to feel pleased over having done it so capably. Not many sheepdogs would have noticed the lamb in time to reach it, and some of them wouldn't even have tried to.

A dog must learn some complicated reflexes before he can be considered expert at handling sheep. He must learn, against all the normal instincts of his species, that it is wicked to chase sheep for fun, and downright criminal to bite them. Having got that instilled into him, he must back up and learn that he is supposed to chase sheep under proper supervision, and that it is his duty to nip them sharply enough to make them move when he is sent out after them. He must have it drilled into him that an interest in wild life is all well enough in off moments, but that it must be shoved into the background when there is work to do, and that when some predatory animal is shadowing the sheep, his job is to get them either started out of danger or else bunched in a close circle with the bucks on the outside, ready to stand it off, even though he would much prefer to go high-tailing out after the enemy and try to whip it or drive it away. Coyotes always try to work on this instinct in a young or overimpulsive dog, by first sending one of their number to the flank of a herd as a decoy, waiting till the dog has gone pelting out after him, and then moving in on the opposite flank and grabbing whatever sheep they can work loose.

Coyotes are the most intelligent and resourceful of all the animals that prey on sheep, and the most destructive because, unlike the others, they understand the advantage of teamwork. Another of their tricks, when the sheep were bunched and the dog refused to be inveigled away, was to round up two or three antelope or jackrabbits or wild scrub ponies and bring them in at a run in the hope that the sheep would break formation to let them through, which, if not watched closely, they sometimes did. The coyotes' repertoire of shifts and trick-plays was almost endless, and they showed such a spirit of detached research about it that it sometimes seemed sordid and unsportsmanlike to break up one of their experimental combinations by turning loose on them with a gun, though there was little enough sportsmanship about them when they managed to corner a sheep out of rifle-range. Mountain lions were sometimes a nuisance, but they were too cowardly to do much damage when the sheep were well herded. I once saw one twelve feet long turn tail and run like a rabbit from two six-month-old puppies and a ten-year-old boy—me—armed with nothing but a stick. Bears were more nervy, but not any great problem, because they always worked alone and always steered shy of a camp where there was a dog. Even a dog that didn't have much sense was a convenience to have around in wild country, because of the things that might have happened if he hadn't been there.

Some of them were subject to streaks of temperament that wore on the nerves. I worked in the Deschutes National Forest in Oregon one summer with a white collie that some Indians had rescued from a wrecked stock-trailer on one of the old mountain freight-roads. With sheep, he couldn't have been more hard-working and conscientious, but he had evidently been brought up in some part of the country where red squirrels were considered game animals, and the worthless little fox-squirrels of the deep timber steamed his hunting instinct up so that he spent most of his spare time chasing them up the big fir trees and barking impatiently for somebody to come and shoot them. Finally, when nobody paid any attention to him, he gave us up and left, probably to hunt for some place with a higher level of taste and intelligence. It never seemed to enter his head that he might be mistaken in the kind of game he was treeing. No doubt he went to his grave believing that he had been right about it, and that we were either stupid or ignorant.

Another sheep-dog, a handsome brown-and-tan Australian shepherd, was uncanny at rough country herding. He could understand exactly what was wanted by merely being waved at from a half-mile away, and do it perfectly. His trouble was that when it was done, his enthusiasm wouldn't let him stop. He would charge off into the timber and, after an hour or so, come pelting back through camp driving whatever he had managed to scare up—two or three deer, some half-grown foxes, a snowshoe rabbit, anything to show that he felt like celebrating. Once he drove in some pack-mules from a government road-camp, and once he came larruping in with a dozen scrub ponies from an Indian huckleberrying camp up the mountain. It kept things lively, but finally, after he had tried to round up a family of big black mountain skunks, we sent him back to the headquarters ranch at the end of a long rope and got through the rest of the summer without him; less smoothly as far as work went, but more peacefully.

Sometimes, instead of eccentricity or wrong-headedness, a dog would come up with a streak of smartness that was beyond accounting for. I worked for a couple of summers in Oregon once with a big rough-coated old sheep-dog that had wandered into the ranch one night, sorefooted and smeared with crude oil, which we took to mean that he had fallen off some stock-train down on the railroad, and made himself so indispensable with the sheep that we took to keeping him out of sight when any strangers showed up, for fear some of them might lay claim to him.

He was as good at hunting as he was with sheep, and used to wander out and kill rattlesnakes for the fun of it when nobody was watching him, but the performance that knocked us endways happened early one summer in the national forest west of Ellensburgh in the state of Washington, when we were moving a herd of ewes across a cable suspension bridge over a deep canyon with rocks and a little thread of creek a couple of hundred feet down at the bottom. The sheepman was on the far side, to keep the sheep moving in the right direction as they came off. I was back behind, shooing them down the trail so the dog could keep crowding them on. Possibly a hundred and fifty had already crossed, somewhere near a hundred more were clattering along on the bridge-planking, and the rest, some six hundred, were jostling down through the red fir-needle dust toward it, when the dog stiffened, wheeled and drove them back, and then clawed and clambered his way to the middle of the bridge and began biting and shouldering the packed sheep on it as if he wanted to keep them from going anywhere. I would have thought the country had unsettled his mind except that he kept up the high-pitched barking he always took to when he needed help in a hurry. Finally he got the sheep all stalled, edged them off the bridge, half in one direction and half in the other, and stationed himself in the middle to keep any of them from getting back on.

That did seem like carrying things too far. I slid down into the trail and stopped to pick up a stick to use on him, and then, happening to glance at the cables under the bridge, decided to let it go. It had never struck me before —it evidently hadn't struck the forest service, either—what effect the vibration of sheep trotting could have on a structure resting on wire cables held under tension. The entire bridge-planking had been jiggled sideways so that only a bare half-inch at one edge held it from sliding off and plastering over two thousand dollars' worth of mutton on the rocks below. It was so precarious that I couldn't bear to watch when the dog shifted his weight to scratch himself. We never found out how he had learned about tensions and vibration-points, or whether he had acted on the kind of instinct that makes a horse balk at a tottering bridge when there is no visible sign that it is tottering. He seemed to consider it obvious, and treated us with dignified contempt for two or three weeks afterward because we hadn't seen it when he did.

There are long spells of isolation in sheep herding, but they are not nearly as hard to get through as most people imagine. The hardest part of the business is when the whole crew has to pitch in together on the heavy work in the spring. Lambing, which comes between late February and early April, depending on latitude, is one of the hardest. There is not much to say about it except that, like calving-time on a cattle-ranch, it is a large-scale form of midwifery, subject to all the usual accidents of the profession and a lot of unusual ones that only a sheep could think up. Marking lambs could be made to sound even more forbidding if it were described in detail, though it lacks the high-pressure rush and drive of lambing. Shearing, which supposedly comes at the beginning of warm weather (though it seldom works out exactly), requires keeping the sheep herded within range of the shearing sheds and bringing them in as they are called for, though the actual tonsorial operation is performed by highly skilled migratory shearing crews, who start from Western Texas in February, work their way through New Mexico and Arizona and then north through California into Oregon in late April, loop back across Idaho and Montana in May, and turn southeast through the Rocky Mountain states back to their starting place, which they usually reach early in July.

Sheep shearing is a hard round, mean, dull and dirty, but it pays well, and it touches so many different aspects of the country's life, character, tastes and temperament and levels of civilization that any bright young man setting out to write about such abstractions might profit by trying a couple of seasons at it. Whether the sheep would profit as much is another matter. A professional sheep-shearer has to know his business. With power clippers, which have been used in all big-scale shearing for over thirty years, an experienced man can shear a hundred sheep in an eight-hour day: a little under five minutes per sheep, including handling. The old-fashioned scissor-style hand-shears could do it even faster, but they required more skill than most shearers are capable of nowadays, and there was always the risk of a restive sheep being badly mangled by the sharp points.

Herding took in a much narrower range of country, in which there were fewer people; sometimes there were none at all. But it did range over a big spread of widely varied scenery and climate, and it touched each at its best. The sheep stayed in the open sagebrush as long as the grass stayed green and the water-holes full. After shearing, when everything was beginning to dry up, they were started for the summer pasture in the mountains where it was still spring, and they followed the spring grass and wild strawberries up through successive belts of oak, yellow pine, Douglas fir, spruce and rhododendron, to within sight of the final belt of jack-pine and pink salal bells where, in mid-August, a man could scrape off two or three inches of fallen needles almost anywhere and find snow still packed deep under them.

They moved back down to the sagebrush in early October, following the young grass that had been brought up by the first heavy fall rains, which in the high mountains sometimes took the form of snow. Striking camp to move out of the mountains in an early snowfall was always something to remember: the sheep crowding down the white road with gray vapor from their wet fleeces spreading among the dark snow-spotted firs, the dripping dogs working to keep the herd moving, stopping hurriedly sometimes to bite the hardened snow-clots from their feet, the horses shifting and steaming under their wet packs, the heavy snowflakes whitening the square of bare ground where the tent had been, and covering the pile of wood we had cut for fuel, and the trail we had worn in the dead grass down to the spring, and the trampled ground where we had corralled the pack-horses; places we had made and used until they seemed ours being covered over and taken away from us into a life and identity of their own for all of a long winter that, as it turned out, kept them hidden deeper and longer than we could ever have imagined.

The Kettle of Fire

THE kettle of fire story was told to me at different times during the summer when I was eleven years old and working at typesetting for a patent-inside weekly newspaper in Antelope, Oregon, though it didn't end with the telling and, I think, has not ended even now. The man who told it to me, a rundown old relic named Sorefoot Capron, held the post of city marshal except when there was somebody loose who needed to be arrested, and also managed the town water system, because he was the only resident who had been there long enough to know where the mains were laid. He used to drop in at the newspaper office sometimes when things were dull around town, which was often, to borrow a couple of dollars to get drunk on, and he would kill time by digging up experiences from his youth while he waited for the editor to show up and open the safe.

As he told it, he had run away from a respectable home in Ohio in the early eighteen-sixties, out of disgust with his parents because, after he had beaten his brains half out winning some prize in school, they had merely glanced coldly at it and reminded him that he was almost a half-hour late with his milking. The war was beginning then, but the enlistment boards turned him down because he was only fourteen and slight of build even for that age. He castigated his itinerary on west to St. Louis, where he supported him-self during the winter by gambling at marbles and spit-at-a-crack with the colored youngsters around the stockyards, and by running errands for a Nevada silver-mine operator named Cash Payton, a heavy-set man with a short red beard, a bald spot on top of his head like a tonsure, and a scar across the bridge of his nose from having mistimed a fuse, who was hanging around waiting for the Overland Mail route to reopen so he could freight some mining machinery west over it.

He had two partners who were waiting in St. Louis with him, one a blocky little Cornishman with bow legs who talked in a chewed-up kind of bray, the other a long-coupled German with a pale beard and gold earrings, which in those times were believed by some people to be a specific against weak eyesight. They were both pleasant-spoken men, though hard to understand most of the time, but Cash Pay-ton was not the kind of man to let his good nature stop with mere pleasant-spokenness. He took a special liking to young Capron, believed or let on to believe all the lies he told about being homeless and an orphan, and made plans to take him west with the mining machinery as soon as the road got opened up. When it turned out that the road was apt to stay closed for several months longer, he arranged to sign young Capron on as a herder and roustabout with a train of emigrants from Illinois and Missouri who were organizing to sneak past the frontier outposts and head west for a new start in unspoiled country, and also, though none of them brought the point up, to get themselves somewhere out of reach before they got picked up in the draft.

Travel across the plains to Oregon was forbidden at the time, because the military posts along the emigrant route had been abandoned and there was no protection against Indian raids, but the train managed to work its way out into open country while the border garrisons were busy with some rebel foray, and it rolled along on its westward course without any sign of trouble until it struck the Malheur Desert, not far from the line between Oregon and Nevada. It had moved slowly, and summer ends early in that part of the country, so it struck bad weather and had its horse-herd stampeded by Snake and Bannock Indians, who also killed a couple of night-herders by filling them full of arrows. The emigrants had hired some mountain man to steer them through the bad country, but the killings made them scared and suspicious, and they talked so loud and pointedly about hanging him for treachery that he picked up and pulled out in the night, leaving them stalled without any idea where they were or any draft-animals to haul them anywhere else.

It was a doleful place to be stuck in with bad weather coming on: merely a little muddy water-hole at the bottom of a rock-gully with nothing in sight anywhere around it but sagebrush and greasewood and rocks. They had vinegar to correct the alkali in the water, but several of the women got sick from drinking it, the dead sagebrush that they picked up for fuel was so soggy they couldn't get it to burn, and when they tried starting it by shooting a cotton wad into it they discovered that all their powder had drawn damp and got unusable except what was in the guns. They didn't dare squander that, and some of them opposed shooting of any kind for fear of drawing more Indians down on them, so they held a meeting and decided, since young Capron was not of much use to them and had nobody depending on him, to send him down toward the Nevada mining settlements for help, if he could find any. In any case, and whatever he found or did, he was to bring back an iron kettle full of live coals with which they could start a fire in damp wood.

It was a risky mission to put off onto a youngster, and several of the men, all elderly and in no danger of being let in for it themselves, dwelt with some sarcasm on the idea of selecting anybody so young and inexperienced for a job that they were all willing to offer advice about but not to undertake in his place, but nobody came up with anything better, and as far as young Capron was concerned he didn't in the least mind being picked for it. He was tired of the whole pack of them by then, and would have welcomed anything, dangerous or not, that could serve as an excuse to get away from them. He was not especially uneasy about the risks, or about the chance of finding any fire to bring back. His only difficulty, all through the time when they were arguing back and forth about sending him, was trying to decide whether to come back and expose himself to them again even if he did find it.

The strain and solemnity of starting settled that for him. He knew, even before he had finished saddling up and had climbed on the saddle-pony they had caught up for him, that he would have to come back. They had made him wait till after dark to start, and he couldn't see any of the men around him, though he knew that they were all there. From the ground, he had been able to make out their figures against the sky, but looking down at them from the saddle was like trying to keep track of a foam-streak after it had been swept under in a deep rapid. One of them reached out and clattered the kettle-bale over his saddle-horn, and he heard them all draw back to leave the way open for him. Except for that, they were all silent. There was no sound in the camp except for the herd-ponies shifting to keep warm, and a child blubbering listlessly in one of the wagons, and the choking sound of a sick woman trying to vomit. A curious apathy comes over people facing death when they know it and know what form it will take, even when they still go through the form of refusing to admit that they know anything about it. Afterward, when the reality begins to show itself, they are likely to fall into a panic and do things too disgusting to bear telling or thinking of. Young Capron knew that he had to get back with the fire, and that if he failed to get back with it before they reached that point it would be useless. Saving the lives of people who had made themselves unfit to live would be work wasted, and possibly worse than wasted. It would not help merely to keep on going, either: that would mean carrying the sounds of the camp along with him, the woman choking, the child blubbering, the silent men shuffling as they drew back in the dark, through all the years that he could reasonably expect to live, and maybe even beyond them. He had to find fire, and he had to get back with it while they were still able to hold themselves together. They might have been wrong and selfish in picking him, and they might be hard to like or live with, but there was nothing else for it. With that in his head, and with the kettle on his saddle-horn and a sack of food strapped on the cantle, he rode out between the wagons into the sagebrush.

Getting out of the gully into open country was slow and precarious work. The Indians turned out to have an outpost line drawn all the way around the camp a half-mile back from it, and he had to keep to the draws and move cautiously, leading the pony and inching along in places a step at a time, to dodge them. The pony saved him once, by balking and refusing to move even when spurred. He got off and crawled ahead to investigate, and discovered that he had been riding straight into a watch-post at the top of the ridge. The Indians had dug a hole and covered it with a blanket to keep the warmth in, with a head-slit cut in the middle to look out through. It took him over an hour to back-track, find the pony in the dark, and circle around it. Afterward he heard dogs yapping in the Indian camp, and he put in another two or three hours edging around that, dismounting and putting his ear to the ground every dozen yards or so to keep from running into squaws out rummaging firewood.

Toward daylight the desert around him looked clear, and he dropped down into a creek-wash and slept in a little thornberry thicket while the pony filled up on salt-grass around a mudhole, but when he got saddled up to start off again he saw mounted Indians casting around in the sage-brush for his trail a couple of miles away, so he kept to the draws, crawling and hauling the pony along by main strength where the thorn-bush grew heavy, until almost noon. Then he mounted and struck up a long lope and held it, stopping only to rest for an hour when he struck a water-hole, all day and most of the night and all through the next day, with no sleep except when he forgot and dozed in the saddle and no food except a sage-hen which he knocked over with a rock and ate raw. Toward nightfall he made out some scattering pine timber with shadows that looked palish blue as if smoke were coloring them. He headed for it, hoping to find some camp that was burning charcoal for the Nevada mines, or possibly a dead tree smoldering from being struck by lightning. Night came while he was still a couple of miles away, but he kept going because, in the darkness, he could see that it was a real fire, and that the reddish pine trunks lit up and darkened as it flickered back and forth across them.

He dismounted, playing it safe, tied the pony to a boulder and hung the kettle from his belt, and crept forward on his hands and knees, keeping the sagebrush clumps between him and the light and stopping behind every clump to sight out the ground before inching on ahead. It was a good thing he did, for he saw when he got close that the fire had men around it. The light was too fitful and uneven to show what they looked like, but he could make out a wickiup behind them, a round-topped basketwork structure covered half-way down with skins and tattered pieces of old canvas. It was enough to make him hug the ground and peer through the tangle of sagebrush instead of looking out around it. Only Snake Indians built basketwork wickiups, and the Snakes were the most warlike of all the tribes in that part of the country. He felt pleased at being able to remember about wickiups at such a time, and started looking for more signs that the men really were Indians, ignoring whatever evidence there was that might have hinted at anything else.

The fire itself was a clear sign that they were Indians. It was not the kind of towering holocaust that white travelers always set going when they were camped for the night in wild country, but a wan little flicker of only three or four small sticks, so puny and half-hearted that he wondered how its light could have been visible so far out in the open desert. It was not nearly big enough for the men to keep warm by, but it seemed what they wanted, for they kept piling ashes on it to hold it down, and once one of them picked up a stick that was beginning to blaze up and quenched it by sticking it into the dirt. Only Indians would have gone to so much trouble to keep a campfire low, and when the man who had quenched the stick stood up to rake the coals back to-gether young Capron saw that he was wrapped in a blanket and that there was a gleam of something whitish as he turned his head that looked like an Indian headband.

There might have been other signs if he had looked for them, but they were not needed, and he didn't dare wait any longer. The smallness of the fire had led him to miscalculate his distances, and his pony was tied close enough so that they might hear it if it started stamping or pawing. There was nothing to hold back for, anyway. Indians were Indians. They had not wasted their time arguing about killing the emigrant train's two night-herders and running off its live-stock, and the train needed fire worse than they had needed wagon-horses. He rummaged out his pistol, poked it carefully through the middle of the sagebrush clump, and waited till the man with the blanket stood away from the fire so he would have the light to sight against. He drew for the center of the blanket a handbreadth below the man's shoulders, leveled up till the foresight filled the back notch, and let go. The smoke of the black powder filled the tangle of sagebrush like gray cottonwood-down settling from a wind, but he lay and glared through it and through the smoke still dribbling from the pistol muzzle without even noticing it.

The man stood motionless for a long second while the blanket slid from his shoulders and piled up around his feet. Then he swayed, flapped his elbows and tipped his head back as if getting ready to crow, and fell face-down across the fire and plunged the whole camp into pitch darkness. He must have died falling, by the slack-jointed thump his body made when it hit in the ashes. If he had still been conscious he would have tried to avoid the fire, and he didn't; he merely let go all holds and whopped down and gathered it to his bosom like a hen covering her chickens from a hawk.

The other men jumped up and legged it for cover. Young Capron could hear brush cracking and dead branches ripping at their clothes as they galloped off into the timber. He waited till the light from the dead man's clothes taking fire showed him that he had the camp all to himself. There was something faintly worrisome about the smell of the clothes burning. It was like wool, and Indians never wore anything except cotton cloth and buckskin. Still, it might be from a corner of the blanket burning, and there was no time to speculate about it, whatever it was. He scrabbled in the

---

176

dead sagebrush needles for the kettle, had an awful moment of thinking he might have lost it, and then found it by the clatter it made against his pistol, which was still clutched in his hand. He grabbed it and scrambled up and ran in, flubbing the pistol into his holster between strides, and rolled the body clear of the ashes and stirred the blackened embers together and began scraping dead pine needles from the ground to pile on them. They were almost out. He had to pile on small twigs and fan up a glaring blaze to keep them from dying on him, knowing that every twig that caught would make him an easier target for the men who had taken to the timber, and not daring to stop feeding in more sticks to make it flame up stronger.

Ministering to the flame and strained between dread when it gained and panic when it sank, he did some wondering about what the dead man looked like, but when it finally took a solid hold and burned high enough to see by, he decided that he would rather not know, and moved back into the shadows and sat with his back to it, except for one moment when some sound, possibly of tree limbs rubbing together, made him glance around to see if it had moved. There was no sign that it had, but he didn't turn away quite fast enough to keep from noticing that what he had taken for an Indian headband was a bald spot and that a stiff beard down one side of the face had been burned to a pale gray ash that the draft from the fire kept crumbling into powder so that it looked, in the slanting light, as if it was twitching.

The sight was unnerving, though he had hard work to hold back from looking at it again, and its significance was not much help, either. Indians did not have beards or bald spots. The smell of wool had been the man's flannel shirt scorching. He had been white: possibly some Indian trader,

Shot a white man

177

or gun-peddler, or mining promoter; possibly somebody with political influence, and friends, and relatives; even possibly—

There was no use running possibilities all the way up the string. It was done, and there was no help for it and no use in thinking about it. It was not even certain that there was anything about it to regret. There were white men in the country who needed salting worse than most of the Indians, and a man shacked up in a Snake Indian lodge in that remote corner of the desert must have had some business in hand besides organizing classes in Bible study or quilt-piecing. Still, shooting him had been overhastiness, and young Capron was sorry about it, and scared. He scooped half the fire into the kettle, though the bigger pine sticks in it had not yet burned down to coals, and hung it on a dead tree-limb and ran for his pony. He was thankful that he had his errand to hurry for. Without it, his excuse for hurrying would have had to be something less dignified: fear that the two men might be creeping up through the trees to bushwhack him, fear that if he stayed any longer he would not be able to hold out against looking once more at the dead man's face.

The fire on the ground had burned low when he rode back, but the pitch-knots in the kettle were flaring up so the pony refused to edge within reach of it, even with spurring. Finally he got down and covered the kettle with a piece of bark, and then rode past at a trot and grabbed it from the limb before the bark had time to take fire. He moved up in the saddle, raked the pony down the ribs, and lit back into the desert with the kettle held out at one side and the flame from the bark caressing his hand and arm as vengefully as if the dead man had prayed it on him for a parting retribution.

When he got a couple of miles out, he reined up to let the flame burn down, but he heard hoofbeats from the trail behind, so he merely dumped a couple of the hottest knots out into the sagebrush and shoved on. Afterward, looking back at the glare they were making, he could have kicked himself for leaving so plain a marker for the men to steer by, though the truth was that it didn't matter much. Uncovering the coals he had kept made them flare high enough to be visible two miles away, and when he tried holding the kettle low they scared the pony into a paroxysm of rearing and pinwheeling that threatened to scatter all the fire out of it.

He had to go back to holding the kettle at arm's length before the pony would move ahead at all. It looked like trying to flag a steamboat, and the foolishness of it started him to reflecting bitterly on the things he should have done and had lacked the sense to think of till too late. He should have hunted out and stampeded the men's saddle-horses while he was waiting for the fire to get started. He should have picked greasewood for the fire instead of pitch-pine. He should have covered the kettle with dirt instead of bark. He should have used his brains instead of letting them run to imagining things that merely scared him. He should have kept his nerve, figured things out ahead, made himself into something steadier and more far-sighted than he ever had been. He should not have been in such a hurry to play the hand Providence had dealt him to establish his future on. It would have been better if he had held back and tried to change the spots on the cards by making faces at them, or possibly by crying over them. A man had to live up to what he was, weaknesses and all. Finding out what they were was probably not worth shooting a man for, but it was a gain. The kettle had returned him that much for his trouble, at least.

He held the pony to a high trot for a couple of miles, and then pulled up to let it catch its wind. He could no longer hear hoofbeats back of him, so he took time to pull off his coat and wrap it around his hand as a protection against the heat from the coals. Then a rock clattered back in the distance, and he knew the men were still coming, and closing the range. The pony heard it too, and he had to rein back hard to keep it from breaking into a run and getting wind-broken. It would have been easy to lose them if his hands had been free: he could merely have walked the pony down into some gully and laid low till they passed. The kettle killed that possibility; they could line him in by the light from it, no matter which way he turned or what track he took. He thought of covering it with gravel, or with a sod from some mudhole, but decided against that for fear of smothering the fire completely.

At the end of six or seven miles more, he realized that it was not far from going out all by itself. The coat wadded over his burned hand had kept him from noticing how much the kettle had cooled down. One welcome part of it was that the light had got too weak to be visible at a distance, but he was too much afraid of losing the fire to take comfort in its debility. He slowed to a walk for awhile, and then turned sharp away from his course down a long draw, dismounted and tied the pony in a thicket of giant sagebrush, and felt his way down the slope hunting for dead roots that could be used for kindling. There was nothing dry enough until, in the low ground where the draw widened out, he bumped into some stunted junipers. Juniper wood is too light and porous to be much use as fuel, but the trunks were run through with dead streaks from which, by gouging with his knife, he managed to pry loose a handful of splinters that would take fire easily, even if they didn't hold it long.

The kettle was cool enough to touch by the time he finished collecting them, but with careful blowing they condescended to flicker up so that he could lay on heavier fuel from the dead branches. When that caught, he rammed the kettle down into a badger hole, piled whole branches over it to make sure the fire would last, and went on down the dry watercourse to find hardwood that would burn down into coals. The light from the branches glared like a haystack burning, and he had no trouble finding greasewood roots and a dead chokecherry tree and loading himself up with chunks from them. The flame behind him filled half the sky by then, so he circled back cautiously and hid under a low-branched juniper fifty or sixty yards from it, in case it drew anybody to come investigating.

It happened quicker than he had counted on. He had got himself settled among the juniper boughs, which smelled bad, and was smearing his face with wet dirt to blend with the shadows when two men came down the slope from his trail, stopped where the sagebrush thinned out, and stood watching the fire and shading their eyes against it. They were a hundred yards away, and they looked unearthly tall in the sheeting glare of the fire, but he could see that they were white men. They had on ordinary work clothes, and they wore hats and had their hair cut short. That was nothing much; he had expected that they would turn out to be white, and he was not afraid of them except for a slight feeling of strain inside him. It gouged harder to see that one of them was blocky and reddish and bowlegged, and that the other was tall and thin and pale-bearded, with earrings on which the light sparkled when he moved his head. Young Capron would not have noticed the earrings at such a distance if he had not been expecting them. The men were the sawed-off Cornishman and the tall German who had been Cash Payton's partners. He had liked Cash Payton better than both of them—better than anybody else, as far as that went—but he had liked them. Because he had shot Cash Payton, he dared not move for fear they would pick out his hiding place and kill him. They stood peering across the fire-light into the junipers, the German wagging a long army cap-and-ball revolver and the Cornishman holding a rifle as if he were fixing to rake hay with it, all primed and set to open up on anything that moved.

They loomed up against the shadows like clay pipes in a shooting gallery. If they had been strangers, if the firelight had not outdone itself to show who they were beyond the possibility of a mistake, he could have cleared his way back to the emigrant train with two cartridges, besides acquiring possession of two unjaded saddle-horses which he could have used very handily. What they had been doing camped in the timber so far from anywhere he didn't try to guess. Nothing to their credit, likely, or they would not have gone to so much trouble to run him down. Catching Indian children to sell as slaves in San Francisco was a flourishing business then, and if it was that, they deserved shooting for it. So did Cash Payton, except that points of ethics no longer counted. All that did count was knowing that the man who had befriended him and kept him alive over a whole winter was lying dead back in the pine timber with half his face burned off, all be-cause of a scary young squirt's clubfooted foolishness. Bad or good, right or wrong, he had deserved better than to be shot down from cover when his back was turned. Young Capron shut his eyes and buried his face in the dirt, won-dering, to end a painful train of reflection, whether he could ever smell juniper boughs again without getting sick, as in fact he never could, in all the years afterward.

When he looked up, the men were leaving, probably hav-ing realized the sappiness of standing in the full glare of the fire when the man they were hunting might be lurking some-where close enough to take advantage of it. The tall German stopped at the edge of the sagebrush and examined the caps in his revolver to make sure they were all in place. That meant that they were not giving up, and that they would probably post themselves somewhere along his trail, figuring to knock him over when he came back to it. If it had not been for the shooting they would have been glad to see him and, if they could, to help him. If it had not been for the fire kettle there would not have been any shooting. Of course, he could leave it where it was and ride after them and let on not to know anything about it, so they would blame the shooting on somebody else. They would probably take his word for it: foreigners were trustful about things they didn't understand very well, in contrast to Americans, who were always the most suspicious in matters they knew the least about. He could go with the two men and be safe, and be rid of the emigrants and their sniveling and domineering for good.

The only trouble was that he couldn't bring himself to do it. It would mean that Cash Payton had died for nothing, for mere foolishness, because a streak of light hit him in the wrong place. The only way to make his death count for anything was to get the fire back to the train. He shook loose from his seesawing and went into the tall sagebrush for his pony.

The fire had burned down when he came back with the pony, and the juniper boughs were falling into coals that the stir of air fanned into flaky ashes. It was hard to lose time building them back, but he had to have some kind of fire that would last, and the pony would hold up better for being left to graze and rest a little longer. He piled on the greasewood and wild cherry, waited to make sure it caught, and then lay down upwind from the junipers and slept until the glare of the new fire woke him. He fished the kettle out with a forked tree-limb, left it to cool while he caught and bridled the pony, and scooped it full of new coals and tried to mount with it.

The pony had recuperated too well. It shied back and fought so that he had to put the kettle down to keep from being yanked off his feet. He tried covering the coals with ashes, but the glow still showed through, and the pony fought back from it till he set the kettle back on the ground and climbed aboard without it. He rode past it and tried to pick it up from the saddle, but the pony shied off so he couldn't reach it. Finally he found his forked tree-limb, circled back, and hooked the kettle at long range and hauled it in. Even then it took all his strength on the reins to keep the pony from pinwheeling and running away from the heat and light following along even with its off-shoulder.

He had held his feelings back too long, probably. He was crying by the time he got the kettle hoisted up and felt the heat on his burned flesh again. He got angry with himself for crying, and his anger made him forget about the two men waiting for him somewhere along the trail ahead. He remembered them after he had ridden a few hundred yards, and swung back along the draw on a wide circuit to keep clear of them. Half the coals in the kettle had got spilled out in his manipulations with the forked tree-limb, and he had no idea how he would manage about renewing them when they burned low again, but there was no use killing snakes till they stopped hibernating. He put it out of his mind, along with what seemed a lifetime of other useless reflections and apprehensions, and rode on.

The coals burned low about daylight, when he was crossing a long level plain on which even the sagebrush grew so thin that he was in plain sight of anybody two or three miles away in any direction. Sagebrush roots burned out almost like wadded newspaper, but there was nothing else, and he got down and gathered an armload of them and nursed the fire back to life. They were damp, and the smoke from them rose in a whitish column that could be seen for miles, but at least the open plain made it impossible for anybody to sneak up on him. It was about fifteen miles across, and he could see anything that moved on it. A man on horseback would have loomed up like a steeple, even at the edge of it.

Nothing came in sight. The plain was lifeless except for horned toads. With the daylight, the pony had got over its fright of the kettle, and it struck up a trot when he remounted, as if it were as anxious to see the last of the place as he was. The plain broke into a long ridge, speckled at its base with little rusty junipers and with a tangle of mountain mahogany marking the line of a dry gully. He halted and broke some of its dead boughs for fuel, since they were hot and slow-burning. They took away his anxiety about the fire for the moment, and it began to be brought home to him that he had circled into country where nobody had ever been before. A herd of antelope came out of the junipers as he passed, looked after him with their back-tufts twitching with inquisitiveness, and then followed along after him, edging downwind to catch his scent and then moving in to gawk at him from such close range that he could have hit them with a rock. The pony watched them uneasily and stumbled over so many rocks and roots trying to keep out of their way that he was halfway tempted to do it, except that it would have meant having to stop and dismount to find something to throw.

Beyond the ridge, he lost them. The ground leveled off into a long expanse of naked earth, pocked and honeycombed with sage-rat burrows. It must have been a mile across, and the country around it for a half-dozen miles was stripped as bare as if it had been plowed and harrowed. There were sage-rats all over it. Some sat up and stared at him as he passed, and then dropped almost under the pony's feet and went on about their business, whatever it was. Some scurried for their holes as if scared, but then they sat up and stared too, and finally sauntered back where they had come from, evidently feeling that whatever was happening at the pony's level was no concern of theirs, and that, when all was said and done, the proper study of ratkind was rats. There was nothing anywhere near their ground that could be used for fuel to keep the fire up, and the ground itself was treacherous because the pony kept breaking through it where they had tunneled it for their nests.

They were not much company. The worst of it was not their strangeness and preoccupation with themselves, it was the loneliness of the country that made young Capron adapt himself, without being aware of it, to their values and scale of living. A few more miles of them, he felt, and he would find himself growing feeler-whiskers, squeaking, and rearing up on his hind-legs to watch himself ride past and try for a second or two to figure out what he was. He turned down a dry gully to get clear of them and the waste they had created, and came to a long scarp of low gray cliffs, broken into rifts and ledges for its entire length. Every rift and every ledge was occupied by great pale-gray owls. None of them moved as he rode past. They sat straight and impassive, hooting to each other briefly sometimes with a hollow sound like blowing into an empty jug, their blank yellow eyes staring past him into the sun without seeing it or him and without knowing or caring what he was. They could see objects only in the half-dusk or in the dark. Nothing that passed in the sunlight made any impression on them.

The cliffs fell away, and the gully spread out into a wide flat covered with stubby clumps of old weatherstained rye-grass. The ground between the clumps was dark and water-soaked, but it was covered so densely with jackrabbits that it looked gray and moving like a spread of water. The jackrabbits moved sluggishly, some of them waiting till they were almost under the pony's feet and then dragging themselves barely out of the way and settling down again. Their trouble was one that usually hit jackrabbits in the years when they had run themselves down by overbreeding. They were swollen with wens from bot-flies, and so weakened by them that they couldn't have moved fast if they had wanted to.

A curious thing about it was that though disease had undermined their instinct for self-preservation, it had left their appetites unimpaired, or only a little slackened. They were still able to crop all the green sprouts out of the dead rye-grass clumps, and they had not lost their interest in copulation, whatever might have happened to their ability. They were not noticeably energetic about it, but they stayed with it faithfully, working as the pony picked its way among them at the absorbing task of perpetuating their kind, bot-flies and all, and regarding nothing else as deserving of notice.

The flat fell away into a long rise and fall of stony desert, and then to a broad grass-slope that reached down to a bright-green little alkali lake, with dark wire-grass in the shallows and patches of willow on the damp ground back of them. The slopes and the shallows were covered solid with wild geese, mottled like a patched quilt with their different colors—brown Canada geese, white snow-geese, dark little cacklers, blue honkers, ringnecked black brant—rocking placidly on the bitter water or crowded solid along the swell of short grass overlooking it. Young Capron would have liked to avoid them, but the fire was low in the kettle, and there was dead wood among the willows that would make good coals and no way of getting it except to ride straight through them.

Of all the forms of life the country had put him up against, they were the worst. They held their ground till he could have reached down and touched them, and then rose with a horrible blast of screeching and banging of wings, darkening the sky overhead and spattering him and the pony and the kettle and the fire in it with filth to show how much he had upset them by turning out to be something they had not been expecting. Then, as the next flock went squalling and clattering up with a new shower, the one behind him settled back onto the grass as unconcernedly as if nothing at all had happened, as, no doubt, in the tablets of their memory, nothing at all had.

They should have quieted down and gone back to resting when he dismounted and went to work preparing the dead willow limbs for his fire, but they seemed unable either to stand him or to let him alone. Every few minutes, though he moved as little as he could and the pony scarcely stirred out of its tracks, some of them would stalk close to him, rear up and look him over again, and then let out a horrified squawk and put the whole flock up to spatter him with filth all over again. It was not hostility so much as indignation. They were outraged with him for being there, without having the ghost of an idea what he was doing or the slightest interest in finding out.

Getting clear of the wild country took a long time. He had circled farther than he realized, and crossing the long swells of ground beyond the lake took up the whole afternoon, counting two or three times when he had to skirmish up dead limbs of cottonwood and service-berry to stoke the kettle. There was one more small flurry of wild life, a little creek bordered with short grass that was being stripped off by huge wingless Mormon crickets. They were slippery for the pony to step on, but there was nothing else to them except appetite. Some little darkish rattlesnakes picked languidly at them around the edges, without any great show of interest in doing it. Young Capron spurred away from the place, feeling with some self-pity that a man had to fall low to be siding with rattlesnakes, but wishing them well even in wanting to be rid of them for good.

He would have liked to keep going when it got dark, but the pony was sunken-flanked and laboring on the slopes, so he turned into a little stand of cottonwoods and unsaddled and turned it out to graze. He found some half-dead wild plum and dumped the coals from the kettle and built up a fire with fuel from it, first dead sticks and then bigger green ones, which burned slower but made long-lasting coals. When the fire took hold, he ate some salt pork that the emigrants had given him, downing it raw because cooking wasted it, and spread out on a patch of dampish ground and slept.

Something brought him awake along in the night. He didn't know what it had been, but he could tell by the waning fire that he had slept for several hours, and he noticed that the silence around him was deeper than it had been when he was going to sleep. Building the fire back, he realized that what he missed was the sound of the pony grazing. He piled kindling into the kettle for a light and went out to see what had become of it. The grass showed where it had been grazing, but it was gone. He tried farther out, remembering gloomily that Indians always ran the horses off from a camp that they were getting ready to jump, and found a shallow mudhole that had been trampled all around by horses. The tracks were fresh, which disturbed him for a minute, but a smoothed-down place in the mud where they had been rolling showed that they were running loose. Not all of them were Indian horses either; some of them were shod, and the calk-marks were big enough to have been made by wagon-teams, possibly from the emigrant train, not that it mattered. The pony might have been scared off by some cougar stalking the herd, and it might still be hanging around. That didn't matter either. All that mattered was that the pony had gone with a loose horse-herd, and that there was no use trying to get it back on foot and burdened with a kettle of fire that it had been scared of from the beginning. One from one left nothing, no matter what had been responsible for it.

He ate salt pork again, hung his saddle and bridle from a tree limb, filled the kettle with new coals and cut a stick to carry it by, and started on afoot without waiting for daylight. In some ways, traveling was easier with the pony gone. There was no worry over having it snort or stamp or whinny at the wrong time, or over having to find grass or water at the stopping places, or having it shy and fight back when he tried to mount, and being able to carry the kettle close to the ground made it less easily seen at a distance. More than that, he was freed from the temptation to throw it away and head out for himself. Without a horse and without food enough for another day, the emigrant camp was the only place he could go. Having to concentrate on one thing instead of seesawing between lurking alternatives made everything simpler: not easier, but easier to summon strength for.

In the afternoon, plodding down a wide valley that opened into draws where there was small wood and water, he found the first sign that he was nearing human beings. It was not a brightening one, merely a dead horse spread out on a patch of bare ground with some buzzards lined up waiting for the sun to burst it open, but it did show that he was headed right and that he was making distance. It turned his thoughts to the emigrant camp, and he began to notice, thinking of the emigrants waiting for him, that the dead sagebrush tops were drying out and that the ground underfoot was strewn with little chips of black flint. He refired the kettle and hurried on, driven by fear that the emigrants might have run into the same thing near their camp, that they might have found dry kindling and lighted a flint-and-steel fire for themselves.

Thinking of that possibility and discovering what his own feelings about it were opened a new area of self-knowledge to him, and not an especially comforting one. He tried to think how much suffering and fear and despair they would be spared if they had thought of trying it, and could get no farther than the reflection that it would make his own suffering and fear and despair useless: a man dead, and his pain, terror, weariness, humiliation and hunger all gone for nothing. He took more consolation from thinking that, if his knowledge of the emigrants was a sign of anything, they wouldn't have sense enough to think of hunting for flints to start with, even if they had the courage to venture far enough out to find them.

It was humiliating to realize that his values had all been turned upside down, when he could welcome seeing a dead horse with buzzards around it and be downcast to think that people he knew might be keeping warm and cooking food and drying out their gunpowder, but the fear held on in spite of him. When he looked down from the last rise of ground on the Indian camp he had skirted around in starting out, he saw a smoke rising from beyond it that appeared to come from the emigrant train, and it set him shaking at the knees so that he had to sit down to keep from collapsing. It was near sundown by then, and when it got dusk he crept on through the sagebrush and discovered that it was not from the wagons at all, but from the hole where the Indian watch post had been on the night he left camp. The hole had been abandoned, it appeared, and the Indians had made a smudge of damp sagebrush roots in it to scare the emigrants into staying where they were. He took time to pile wet earth on the smudge, to keep the emigrants from finding out how easy it would have been for them to get fire if any of them had thought of it, and he felt relieved and uplifted in spirit to think that none of them had.

The camp seemed dead when he came stumbling down into it, but after a few minutes he began to hear sounds from the wagons: children whimpering with the cold, a man praying in a loud monotone under a wagon, the sick woman still trying to vomit. He remembered that the sounds were the sweetest music he had ever listened to. No ninety-eight-piece orchestra in the land could have come within flagging-distance of them. Even after so many years and so many changes, remembering it still stirred him inside, something like jumping off a barn-roof after swallowing a half-dozen humming jew's-harps.

That was all of the story. He used to build up different parts of it at different times while he sat waiting in the printing office for the editor to arrive, but at the first telling he told it all straight through, and he ended it, as he was right to do, with the concluding emotion instead of stringing it out into the subsequent events that dulled it all down. I asked what had happened afterward, and he said nothing worth telling about. The emigrants had scraped up nerve enough to go out and run in their teams, or most of them, and they were so pleased with themselves for doing it that they forgot all about his fire that had given them the necessary courage. Then they had moved on, and finally they had come out at a river-crossing that took them into the old Barlow Road. They were not worth much, on the average, any of them.

"They made me pay for the pony I lost," he said. "And the saddle and bridle, too. Took it out of my wages, what little there was of 'em."

"It don't sound like you'd got much out of it," I said. At

the time, it didn't seem to me that any story with such a frazzled-out ending was worth spending all that time on. "It sounds like everybody had come out ahead except you."

"That was what they all thought, I guess," he said. "They're welcome to their notions. None of 'em come out as far ahead as they thought they had, and it's the only thing I've ever done that I got anything out of that was worth hellroom. It's the only thing I'd do over again, I believe, if I had to. Not that I'll ever get the chance. Things like that don't happen nowadays."

He was wrong about that, of course. Such things change in substance and setting, but they go on working in the spirit, through different and less explicit symbols, as they did through the centuries before emigrations West were ever heard of, and as they will for men too young to know about them now and for others not yet born. There will always be the fire to bring home, through the same hardships and doubts and adversities of one's life that make up the triumph of having lived it.

Note

ALL of these stories were originally published in various magazines. They were all written a long time ago and over a long period, as the dates of magazine publication printed after each will indicate. The most recent is from 1940, the earliest from away back in 1928. This spreads the entire collection over some thirteen years, and puts all of it within the period poetically referred to as *l'entre deux guerres*. It is a period that seems very remote now: in some ways more remote from the present than many eras that lie much farther back in actual time. I had expected, in looking over the stories after many years away from them, to find marks of the illusions and stresses and preoccupations of the time in which they originated, but they don't seem to show many. Their emotions stand up as solidly as ever; the well-written passages still read well; the weak spots seem, if anything, considerably less embarrassing than they used to, which may mean merely that I have grown less touchy about such things. And the stories don't seem noticeably dated. They don't give the impression of having gone out of fashion, but then they never were altogether in fashion to begin with.

It was back in 1928 that I started writing them, under the patient guidance and encouragement of H. L. Mencken, then, of course, editor of the *American Mercury*. I had only written poetry then, and had sent him a poem — or maybe several — as a possible contribution. He took it — or took one, at least — and remarked in his letter about it that I ought to try something in prose for him, and had I anything in mind that seemed interesting? As it happened, I had nothing whatever. I was working for a Seattle radio network at the time, and the combined afflictions of the Puget Sound climate and radio exigencies left no room for any bright ideas within miles of me. However, I put up a bold front, grabbed the first thing that came into my head and wheedled it into an outline under the title *A Town in Eastern Oregon,* and sent it in to him. Then, having gained time to reflect a little, I labored out three stories and sent them, figuring that, as in a sweepstakes, the more entries the better the percentage.

None of the stories bore the slightest resemblance to the one I had outlined (as I learned later, it is always disagreeable to work on a story after it has been outlined; doing the outline knocks all the suspense out of it) but he took all three of them. He didn't mention the one I had outlined except to express the hope that it was coming along; it had stuck in his mind, he said, and he was anxious to see how it worked out. I assured him that it was coming along catawamptiously, which was false, and wrote two more stories to keep from thinking about it. He suggested some changes in them and inquired again about the one I had outlined, but he took them both, and they are among those reprinted here. Rereading them now, I can feel a vague restlessness and strain underlying them that must have been that outline hanging over me while I wrote them. It is true that I had plenty of other anxieties to bother about, then and thereafter, but they did sometimes change. It didn't; it merely hung on and on.

There were a few further inquires about it from Mencken during the ensuing months, and I finally got desperate and finished it, though it was over a year before I got it worked into shape to send in. It is curious, with those preliminary incidents still so vivid in my mind, that I haven't the faintest recollection what he said about it when it reached him. He took it, so he must have said something, but not a trace of what it was remains in my memory. I do remember that my relief at getting the thing done and off my hands was tempered by disappointment that it fell short of what I had wanted it to be, though by magazine standards it was probably successful enough. It came out in the *Mercury* in the Fall of 1929 under the title I had given it in the original outline, *A Town in Eastern Oregon*, and since the Pacific Northwest had already entered on a period of troublous and irritable times by then, it stirred up something of a hellaballoo among the newspapers of the region. Most of their indignation, I suppose, was probably shock at encountering something they were not accustomed to. Irreverent and astringent commentaries on their culture were a new thing to them in those days, and the process of readjustment was necessarily a little unsettling. Most of them have since taken to irreverence and astringency themselves, when occasion calls for it, and they are probably the better for the change.

The piece, at any rate, is as vaguely disappointing to me now as it was when I first finished it, though it has lasted better than I ever dreamed it would. People still write me about it, usually mentioning (probably without intending to be irritating) that it is better than anything I have written since, and suggesting a sort of sequel to bring its historical background up to date. It would be easy enough to do one, I suppose. The country in these past years has piled up any amount of material for it, and it might be highly diverting if it were handled right. Still, I can't feel that it is worth doing. Nothing new would be proved by it; it would be merely piling up more evidence to make the same point that the magazine piece made to begin with. What is needed is not more material, but a more deeply-studied thesis. It makes its case well enough as it stands, but there is something more to it than that, some flicker of deeper truth that it does not quite reach down to.

Maybe it can't be reached; learning to write is largely a process of finding out how many things there are that writing is incapable of handling. Still, it is something to keep in mind. The truth is always worth trying for, and it is still there.

Having *A Town in Eastern Oregon* drag on so long and turn out so disappointingly upset my confidence in all writing for a long time. It was a couple of years before I really got it back again, with the little sketch entitled *Team Bells Woke Me* which is the title story in this book. Even that went through vicissitudes. I was living on a ranch in Southern Arizona when I wrote it, and had started it with the determination to make it a strictly commercial magazine story and let art go chase its tail for a while. It turned balky almost from the start, and after tussling with it for several months without getting anywhere, I gave up and let it ramble along to suit itself: anything to get the thing finished and be done with it. I finished the rough draft of it at four o'clock one morning, after a stretch of grinding on it that had lasted for eighteen hours, and bunched the pages into a used manuscript envelope addressed to the *American Mercury,* intending to copy it out after I had got some sleep. When I came to late the next afternoon, the envelope was gone. One of the ranch-hands had seen it on the table, and, thinking to be helpful, had taken it down to the postoffice and mailed it. There was no return address on the envelope and no name on the manuscript, and I had no copy of it. I was not sure whether it amounted to anything or not, but I had spent a lot of work on it, and it was gone.

It was too late to get a letter off about it that day. I sent one the next afternoon, explaining how it had all happened and what the manuscript looked like, but it turned out that it was not really necessary. A letter about it came from Mencken before mine had time to reach New York. The story had got there all safe, he said; there was no signature on it, but he had recognized the writing without the least difficulty, and it was being put to print under my name and a check for it would follow in a few days. It was a relief to know that it hadn't got lost, and to discover afterward that it really was well-written. I still like it, but I still like the story it made in its wanderings better. It encouraged me to begin taking writing seriously, as I have done unremittingly ever since.

The other stories in the collection need little comment. Some are better than others, but they all have enough to be worth keeping, and they all mean something. Years ago, when I was a youngster in Southwest Oregon, I lived for a couple of Summers on an old pioneer homestead that dated back to the times when people in the back-country had to manufacture most of the things they needed or else go without them. There were relics of that vanished era all over the place—soap-kettles, scalding-troughs, an ash-hopper, a smoke-house, brine-vats, an old forge and charcoal-pit, and in one corner of the old barn there was an assortment of abandoned homemade haying-implements: rakes, cradles, pitchforks, all handturned out of straight-grained white ash and worn shiny with use. They were beautifully made, but they were no longer of any use to anybody, and we decided to plane one of the pitchfork-handles into a bow to shoot wild ducks with. We got it out and were starting to take it apart when the old man who owned the place came wandering around and caught us. He ordered us to put it back where we had got it, and leave it there.

"Never mind how old it is or whether it's any use now or not," he said. "I made them old wooden hay-tools myself, and it was hard work and I learned a lot from it. I learned more from 'em than you'll ever learn in all your lives, and if I don't have 'em around where I can look at 'em sometimes I might not remember it. Go put it back."

We put it back. It was better to keep it. It would have been a pity to lose it, with all the associations it had back of it; and it would still pitch hay.

H. L. D.
Chapala, Jalisco.

Open Winter

THE drying East wind, which always brought hard luck to Eastern Oregon at whatever season it blew, had combed down the plateau grasslands through so much of the winter that it was hard to see any sign of grass ever having grown on them. Even though March had come, it still blew, drying the ground deep, shrinking the watercourses, beating back the clouds that might have delivered rain, and grinding coarse dust against the fifty-odd head of work horses that Pop Apling, with young Beech Cartwright helping, had brought down from his homestead to turn back into their home pasture while there was still something left of them.

The two men, one past sixty and the other around sixteen, shouldered the horses through the gate of the home pasture about dark, with lights beginning to shine out from the little freighting town across Three Notch Valley, and then they rode for the ranch house, knowing even before they drew up outside the yard that they had picked the wrong time to come. The house was too dark, and the corrals and outbuildings too still, for a place that anybody lived in.

There were sounds, but they were of shingles flapping in the wind, a windmill running loose and sucking noisily at a well that it had already pumped empty, a door that kept banging shut and dragging open again. The haystacks were gone, the stackyard fence had dwindled to a few naked posts, and the entire pasture was as bare and as hard as a floor all the way down into the valley.

The prospect looked so hopeless that the herd horses refused even to explore it, and merely stood with their tails turned to the wind, waiting to see what was to happen to them next.

Old Apling went poking inside the house, thinking somebody might have left a note or that the men might have run down to the saloon in town for an hour or two. He came back, having used up all his matches and stopped the door from banging, and said the place appeared to have been handed back to the Government, or maybe the mortgage company.

"You can trust old Ream Gervais not to be any place where anybody wants him," Beech said. He had hired out to herd for Ream Gervais over the winter. That entitled him to be more critical than old Apling, who had merely contracted to supply the horse herd with feed and pasture for the season at so much per head. "Well, my job was to help herd these steeds while you had 'em, and to help deliver 'em back when you got through with 'em, and here they are. I've put in a week on 'em that I won't ever git paid for, and it won't help anything to set around and watch 'em try to live on fence pickets. Let's git out."

Old Apling looked at the huddle of horses, at the naked slope with a glimmer of light still on it, and at the lights of the town twinkling in the wind. He said it wasn't his place to tell any man what to do, but that he wouldn't feel quite right to dump the horses and leave.

"I agreed to see that they got delivered back here, and I'd feel better about it if I could ride across to town yonder, and see if there ain't somebody that knows something about 'em. You could hold 'em together till I git back. We ought to look the fences over before we pull out, and you can wait here as well as anywhere else."

"I can't, but go ahead," Beech said. "I don't like to have 'em stand around and look at me when I can't do anything to help 'em out. They'd have been better off if we'd turned 'em out of your homestead and let 'em run loose on the country. There was more grass up there than there is here."

"There wasn't enough to feed 'em, and I'd have had all my neighbors down on me for it," old Apling said. "You'll find out one of these days that if a man aims to live in this world he's got to git along with the people in it. I'd start a fire and thaw out a little and git that pack horse unloaded, if I was you."

He rode down the slope, leaning low and forward to ease the drag of the wind on his tired horse. Beech heard the sound of the road gate being let down and put up again, the beat of hoofs in the hard road, and then nothing but the noises around him as the wind went through its usual process of easing down for the night to make room for the frost. Loose boards settled into place, the windmill clacked to a stop and began to drip water into a puddle, and the herd horses shifted around facing Beech, as if anxious not to miss anything he did.

He pulled off some fence pickets and built a fire, unsaddled his pony and unloaded the pack horse, and got out what was left of a sack of grain and fed them both, standing the herd horses off with a fence picket until they had finished eating.

That was strictly fair, for the pack horse and the saddle pony had worked harder and carried more weight than any of the herd animals, and the grain was little enough to even them up for it. Nevertheless, he felt mean at having to club animals away from food when they were hungry, and they crowded back and eyed the grain sack so wistfully that he carried it inside the yard and stored it down in the root cellar behind the house, so it wouldn't prey on their minds. Then he dumped another armload of fence pickets onto the fire and sat down to wait for old Apling.

The original mistake, he reflected, had been when old Apling took the Gervais horses to feed at the beginning of winter. Contracting to feed them had been well enough, for he had nursed up a stand of bunch grass on his homestead that would have carried an ordinary pack of horses with only a little extra feeding to help out in the roughest weather. But the Gervais horses were all big harness stock, they had pulled in half starved, and they had taken not much over three weeks to clean off the pasture that old Apling had expected would last them at least two months. Nobody would have blamed him for backing out on his agreement then, since he had only undertaken to feed the horses, not to treat them for malnutrition.

Beech wanted him to back out of it, but he refused to, said the stockmen had enough troubles without having that added to them, and started feeding out his hay and insisting that the dry wind couldn't possibly keep up much longer, because it wasn't in Nature.

By the time it became clear that Nature had decided to take in a little extra territory, the hay was all fed out, and, since there couldn't be any accommodation about letting the horses starve to death, he consented to throw the contract over and bring them back where they belonged.

The trouble with most of old Apling's efforts to be accommodating was that they did nobody any good. His neighbors would have been spared all their uneasiness if he had never brought in the horses to begin with. Gervais wouldn't have been any worse off, since he stood to lose them anyway; the horses could have starved to death as gracefully in November as in March, and old Apling would have been ahead a great deal of carefully accumulated bunch grass and two big stacks of extortionately valuable hay. Nobody had gained by his chivalrousness; he had lost by it, and yet he liked it so well that he couldn't stand to leave the horses until he had raked the country for somebody to hand the worthless brutes over to.

Beech fed sticks into the fire and felt out of patience with a man who could stick to his mistakes even after he had been cleaned out by them. He heard the road gate open and shut, and he knew by the draggy-sounding plod of old Apling's horse that the news from town was going to be bad.

Old Apling rode past the fire and over to the picket fence, got off as if he was trying to make it last, tied his horse carefully as if he expected the knot to last a month, and unsaddled and did up his latigo and folded his saddle blanket as if he was fixing them to put in a show window. He remarked that his horse had been given a bait of grain in town and wouldn't need feeding again, and then he began to work down to what he had found out.

"If you think things look bad along this road, you ought to see that town," he said. "All the sheep gone and all the ranches deserted and no trade to run on and their water threatenin' to give out. They've got a little herd of milk cows that they keep up for their children, and to hear 'em talk you'd think it was an ammunition supply that they expected to stand off hostile Indians with. They said Gervais pulled out of here around a month ago. All his men quit him, so he bunched his sheep and took 'em down to the railroad, where he could ship in hay for 'em. Sheep will be a price this year, and you won't be able to buy a lamb for under twelve dollars except at a fire sale. Horses ain't in much demand. There's been a lot of 'em turned out wild, and everybody wants to git rid of 'em."

"I didn't drive this bunch of pelters any eighty miles against the wind to git a market report," Beech said. "You didn't find anybody to turn 'em over to, and Gervais didn't leave any word about what he wanted done with 'em. You've probably got it figured out that you ought to trail 'em a hundred and eighty miles to the railroad, so his feelings won't be hurt, and you're probably tryin' to study how you can work me in on it, and you might as well save your time. I've helped you with your accommodation jobs long enough. I've quit, and it would have been a whole lot better for you if I'd quit sooner."

Old Apling said he could understand that state of feeling, which didn't mean that he shared it.

"It wouldn't be as much of a trick to trail down to the railroad as a man might think," he said, merely to settle a question of fact.

"We couldn't make it by the road in a starve-out year like this, but there's old Indian trails back on the ridge where any man has got a right to take livestock whenever he feels like it. Still, as long as you're set against it, I'll meet you halfway. We'll trail these horses down the ridge to a grass patch where I used to corral cattle when I was in the business, and we'll leave 'em down there. It'll be enough so they won't starve, and I'll ride on down and notify Gervais where they are, and you can go where you please. It wouldn't be fair to do less than that, to my notion."

"Ream Gervais triggered me out of a week's pay," Beech said. "It ain't much, but he swindled you on that pasture contract too. If you expect me to trail his broken-down horses ninety miles down this ridge when they ain't worth anything, you've turned in a poor guess. You'll have to think of a better argument than that if you aim to gain any ground with me."

"Ream Gervais don't count in this," old Apling said. "What does he care about these horses, when he ain't even left word what he wants done with 'em? What counts is you, and I don't have to think up any better argument, because I've already got one. You may not realize it, but you and me are responsible for these horses till they're delivered to their owner, and if we turn 'em loose here to bust fences and overrun that town and starve to death in the middle of it, we'll land in the pen. It's against the law to let horses starve to death, did you know that? If you pull out of here I'll pull out right along with you, and I'll have every man in that town after you before the week's out. You'll have a chance to git some action on that pistol of yours, if you're careful."

Beech said he wasn't intimidated by that kind of talk, and threw a couple of handfuls of dirt on the fire, so it wouldn't look so conspicuous. His pistol was an old single-action relic with its grips tied on with fish line and no trigger, so that it had to be operated by flipping the hammer. The spring was weak, so that sometimes it took several flips to get off one shot. Suggesting that he might use such a thing to stand off any pack of grim-faced pursuers was about the same as saying that he was simple-minded. As far as he could see, his stand was entirely sensible, and even humane.

"It ain't that I don't feel sorry for these horses, but they ain't fit to travel," he said. "They wouldn't last twenty miles, I don't see how it's any worse to let 'em stay here than to walk 'em to death down that ridge."

"They make less trouble for people if you keep 'em on the move," old Apling said. "It's something you can't be cinched for in court, and it makes you feel better afterwards to know that you tried everything you could. Suit yourself about it, though. I ain't beggin' you to do it. If you'd sooner pull out and stand the conse-quences, it's you for it. Before you go, what did you do with that sack of grain?"

Beech had half a notion to leave, just to see how much of that dark threatening would come to pass. He decided that it wouldn't be worth it. "I'll help you trail the blamed skates as far as they'll last, if you've got to be childish about it," he said. "I put the grain in a root cellar behind the house, so the rats wouldn't get into it. It looked like the only safe place around here. There was about a half a ton of old sprouted potatoes ricked up in it that didn't look like they'd been bothered for twenty years. They had sprouts on 'em—" He stopped, noticing that old Apling kept staring at him as if something was wrong. "Good Lord, potatoes ain't good for horse feed, are they? They had sprouts on 'em a foot long!"

Old Apling shook his head resignedly and got up. "We wouldn't ever find anything if it wasn't for you," he said. "We wouldn't ever git any good out of it if it wasn't for me, so maybe we make a team. Show me where that root cellar is, and we'll pack them spuds out and spread 'em around so the horses can git started on 'em. We'll git this herd through to grassland yet, and it'll be something you'll never be ashamed of. It ain't everybody your age gits a chance to do a thing like this, and you'll thank me for holdin' you to it before you're through."

II

They climbed up by an Indian trail onto a high stretch of tableland, so stony and scored with rock breaks that nobody had ever tried to cultivate it, but so high that it sometimes caught moisture from the atmosphere that the lower elevations missed. Part of it had been doled out among the Indians as allotment lands, which none of them ever bothered to lay claim to, but the main spread of it belonged to the nation, which was too busy to notice it.

The pasture was thin, though reliable, and it was so scantily watered and so rough and broken that in ordinary years nobody bothered to bring stock onto it. The open winter had spoiled most of that seclusion. There was no part of the trail that didn't have at least a dozen new bed grounds for lambed ewes in plain view, easily picked out of the landscape because of the little white flags stuck up around them to keep sheep from straying out and coyotes from straying in during the night. The sheep were pasturing down the draws out of the wind, where they couldn't be seen. There were no herders visible, not any startling amount of grass, and no water except a mud tank thrown up to catch a little spring for one of the camps.

They tried to water the horses in it, but it had taken up the flavor of sheep, so that not a horse in the herd would touch it. It was too near dark to waste time reasoning with them about it, so old Apling headed them down into a long rock break and across it to a tangle of wild cherry and mountain mahogany that lasted for several miles and ended in a grass clearing among some dwarf cottonwoods with a mud puddle in the center of it.

The grass had been grazed over, though not closely, and there were sheep tracks around the puddle that seemed to be fresh, for the horses, after sniffing the water, decided that they could wait a while longer. They spread out to graze, and Beech remarked that he couldn't see where it was any improvement over the tickle-grass homesteads.

"The grass may be better, but there ain't as much of it, and the water ain't any good if they won't drink it," he said. "Well, do you intend to leave 'em here, or have you got some wrinkle figured out to make me help trail 'em on down to the railroad?"

Old Apling stood the sarcasm unresistingly. "It would be better to trail 'em to the railroad, now that we've got this far," he said. "I won't ask you to do that much, because it's outside of what you agreed to. This place has changed since I was here last, but we'll make it do, and that water ought to clear up fit to drink before long. You can settle down here for a few days while I ride around and fix it up with the sheep camps to let the horses stay here. We've got to do that, or they're liable to think it's some wild bunch and start shootin' 'em. Somebody's got to stay with 'em, and I can git along with these herders better than you can."

"If you've got any sense, you'll let them sheep outfits alone," Beech said. "They don't like tame horses on this grass any better than they do wild ones, and they won't make any more bones about shootin' 'em if they find out they're in here. It's a hard place to find, and they'll stay close on account of the water, and you'd better pull out and let 'em have it to themselves. That's what I aim to do."

"You've done what you agreed to, and I ain't got any right to hold you any longer," old Apling said. "I wish I could. You're wrong about them sheep outfits. I've got as much right to pasture this ridge as they have, and they know it, and nobody ever lost anything by actin' sociable with people."

"Somebody will before very long," Beech said. "I've got relatives in the sheep business, and I know what they're like. You'll land yourself in trouble, and I don't want to be around when you do it. I'm pullin' out of here in the morning, and if you had any sense you'd pull out along with me."

There were several things that kept Beech from getting much sleep during the night. One was the attachment that the horses showed for his sleeping place; they stuck so close that he could almost feel their breath on him, could hear the soft breaking sound that the grass made as they pulled it, the sound of their swallowing, the jar of the ground water under him when one of the horses changed ground, the peaceful regularity of their eating, as if they didn't have to bother about anything so long as they kept old Apling in sight.

Another irritating thing was old Apling's complete freedom from uneasiness. He ought by rights to have felt more worried about the future than Beech did, but he slept, with the hard ground for a bed and his hard saddle for a pillow and the horses almost stepping on him every minute or two, as soundly as if the entire trip had come out exactly to suit him and there was nothing ahead but plain sailing.

His restfulness was so hearty and so unjustifiable that Beech couldn't sleep for feeling indignant about it, and got up and left about daylight to keep from being exposed to any more of it. He left without waking old Apling, because he saw no sense in a leave-taking that would consist merely in repeating his common-sense warnings and having them ignored, and he was so anxious to get clear of the whole layout that he didn't even take along anything to eat. The only thing he took from the pack was his ramshackle old pistol; there was no holster for it, and, in the hope that he might get a chance to use it on a loose quail or prairie chicken, he stowed it in an empty flour sack and hung it on his saddle horn, a good deal like an old squaw heading for the far blue distances with a bundle of diapers.

III

There was never anything recreational about traveling a rock desert at any season of the year, and the combination of spring gales, winter chilliness and summer drought all striking at once brought it fairly close to hard punishment. Beech's saddle pony, being jaded at the start with overwork and underfeeding and no water, broke down in the first couple of miles, and got so feeble and tottery that Beech had to climb off and lead him, searching likely-looking thickets all the way down the gully in the hope of finding some little trickle that he wouldn't be too finicky to drink.

The nearest he came to it was a fair-sized rock sink under some big half-budded cottonwoods that looked, by its dampness and the abundance of fresh animal tracks around it, as if it might have held water recently, but of water there was none, and even digging a hole in the center of the basin failed to fetch a drop.

The work of digging, hill climbing and scrambling through brush piles raised Beech's appetite so powerfully that he could scarcely hold up, and, a little above where the gully opened into the flat sagebrush plateau, he threw away his pride, pistoled himself a jack rabbit, and took it down into the sagebrush to cook, where his fire wouldn't give away which gully old Apling was camped in.

Jack rabbit didn't stand high as a food. It was considered an excellent thing to give men in the last stages of famine, because they weren't likely to injure themselves by eating too much of it, but for ordinary occasions it was looked down on, and Beech covered his trail out of the gully and built his cooking fire in the middle of a high stand of sagebrush, so as not to be embarrassed by inquisitive visitors.

The meat cooked up strong, as it always did, but he ate what he needed of it, and he was wrapping the remainder in his flour sack to take along with him when a couple of men rode past, saw his pony, and turned in to look him over.

They looked him over so closely and with so little concern for his privacy that he felt insulted before they even spoke.

He studied them less openly, judging by their big gallon canteens that they were out on some long scout.

One of them was some sort of hired hand, by his looks; he was broad-faced and gloomy-looking, with a fine white horse, a flower-stamped saddle, an expensive rifle scabbarded under his knee, and a fifteen-dollar saddle blanket, while his own manly form was set off by a yellow hotel blanket and a ninety-cent pair of overalls.

The other man had on a store suit, a plain black hat, fancy stitched boots, and a white shirt and necktie, and rode a burr-tailed Indian pony and an old wrangling saddle with a loose horn. He carried no weapons in sight, but there was a narrow strap across the lower spread of his necktie which indicated the presence of a shoulder holster somewhere within reach.

He opened the conversation by inquiring where Beech had come from, what his business was, where he was going and why he hadn't taken the county road to go there, and why he had to eat jack rabbit when the country was littered with sheep camps where he could get a decent meal by asking for it?

"I come from the upper country," Beech said, being purposely vague about it. "I'm travelin', and I stopped here because my horse give out. He won't drink out of any place that's had sheep in it, and he's gone short of water till he breaks down easy."

"There's a place corralled in for horses to drink at down at my lower camp," the man said, and studied Beech's pony. "There's no reason for you to bum through the country on jack rabbit in a time like this. My herder can take you down to our water hole and see that you get fed and put to work till you can make a stake for yourself. I'll give you a note. That pony looks like he had Ream Gervais' brand on him. Do you know anything about that herd of old work horses he's been pasturing around?"

"I don't know anything about him," Beech said, sidestepping the actual question while he thought over the offer of employment. He could have used a stake, but the location didn't strike him favorably. It was too close to old Apling's camp, he could see trouble ahead over the horse herd, and he didn't want to be around when it started. "If you'll direct me how to find your water, I'll ride on down there, but I don't need anybody to go with me, and I don't need any stake. I'm travelin'."

The man said there wasn't anybody so well off that he couldn't use a stake, and that it would be hardly any trouble at all for Beech to get one. "I want you to understand how we're situated around here, so you won't think we're any bunch of stranglers," he said. "You can see what kind of a year this has been, when we have to run lambed ewes in a rock patch like this. We've got five thousand lambs in here that we're trying to bring through, and we've had to fight the blamed wild horses for this pasture since the day we moved in. A horse that ain't worth hell room will eat as much as two dozen sheep worth twenty dollars, with the lambs, so you can see how it figures out. We've got 'em pretty well thinned out, but one of my packers found a trail of a new bunch that came up from around Three Notch within the last day or two, and we don't want them to feel as if we'd neglected them. We'd like to find out where they lit. You wouldn't have any information about 'em?"

"None that would do you any good to know," Beech said. "I know the man with that horse herd, and it ain't any use to let on that I don't, but it wouldn't be any use to try to deal with him. He don't sell out on a man he works for."

"He might be induced to," the man said. "We'll find him anyhow, but I don't like to take too much time to it. Just for instance, now, suppose you knew that pony of yours would have to go thirsty till you gave us a few directions about that horse herd? You'd be stuck here for quite a spell, wouldn't you?"

He was so pleasant about it that it took Beech a full minute to realize that he was being threatened. The heavy-set herder brought that home to him by edging out into a flank position and hoisting his rifle scabbard so it could be reached in a hurry. Beech removed the cooked jack rabbit from his flour sack carefully, a piece at a time, and, with the same mechanical thoughtfulness, brought out his triggerless old pistol, cut down on the pleasant-spoken man, and hauled back on the hammer and held it poised.

"That herder of yours had better go easy on his rifle," he said, trying to keep his voice from trembling. "This pistol shoots if I don't hold back the hammer, and if he knocks me out I'll have to let go of it. You'd better watch him, if you don't want your tack drove. I won't give you no directions about that horse herd, and this pony of mine won't go thirsty for it, either. Loosen them canteens of yours and let 'em drop on the ground. Drop that rifle scabbard back where it belongs, and unbuckle the straps and let go of it. If either of you tries any funny business, there'll be one of you to pack home, heels first."

The quaver in his voice sounded childish and undignified to him, but it had a more businesslike ring to them than any amount of manly gruffness. The herder unbuckled his rifle scabbard, and they both cast loose their canteen straps, making it last as long as they could while they argued with him, not angrily, but as if he was a dull stripling whom they wanted to save from some foolishness that he was sure to regret. They argued ethics, justice, common sense, his future prospects, and the fact that what he was doing amounted to robbery by force and arms and that it was his first fatal step into a probably unsuccessful career of crime. They worried over him, they explained themselves to him, and they ridiculed him.

They managed to make him feel like several kinds of a fool, and they were so pleasant and concerned about it that they came close to breaking him down. What held him steady was the thought of old Apling waiting up the gully.

"That herder with the horses never sold out on any man, and I won't sell out on him," he said. "You've said your say and I'm tired of holdin' this pistol on cock for you, so move along out of here. Keep to open ground, so I can be sure you're gone, and don't be in too much of a hurry to come back. I've got a lot of things I want to think over, and I want to be let alone while I do it."

IV

He did have some thinking that needed tending to, but he didn't take time for it. When the men were well out of range, he emptied their canteens into his hat and let his pony drink. Then he hung the canteens and the scabbarded rifle on a bush and rode back up the gully where the horse camp was, keeping to shaly ground so as not to leave any tracks. It was harder going up than it had been coming down.

He had turned back from the scene of his run-in with the two sheepmen about noon, and he was still a good two miles from the camp when the sun went down, the wind lulled and the night frost began to bite at him so hard that he dismounted and walked to get warm. That raised his appetite again, and, as if by some special considerateness of Nature, the cottonwoods around him seemed to be alive with jack rabbits heading down into the pitch-dark gully where he had fooled away valuable time trying to find water that morning.

They didn't stimulate his hunger much; for a time they even made him feel less like eating anything. Then his pony gave out and had to rest, and, noticing that the cottonwoods around him were beginning to bud out, he remembered that peeling the bark off in the budding season would fetch out a foamy, sweet-tasting sap which, among children of the plateau country, was considered something of a delicacy.

He cut a blaze on a fair-sized sapling, waited ten minutes or so, and touched his finger to it to see how much sap had accumulated. None had; the blaze was moist to his touch, but scarcely more so than when he had whittled it.

It wasn't important enough to do any bothering about, and yet a whole set of observed things began to draw together in his mind and form themselves into an explanation of something he had puzzled over: the fresh animal tracks he had seen around the rock sink when there wasn't any water; the rabbits going down into the gully; the cottonwoods in which the sap rose enough during the day to produce buds and got driven back at night when the frost set in. During the day, the cottonwoods had drawn the water out of the ground for themselves; at night they stopped drawing it, and it drained out into the rock sink for the rabbits.

It all worked out so simply that he led his pony down into the gully to see how much there was in it, and, losing his footing on the steep slope, coasted down into the rock sink in the dark and landed in water and thin mud up to his knees. He led his pony down into it to drink, which seemed little enough to get back for the time he had fooled away on it, and then he headed for the horse camp, which was all too easily discernible by the plume of smoke rising, white and ostentatious, against the dark sky from old Apling's campfire.

He made the same kind of entrance that old Apling usually affected when bringing some important item of news. He rode past the campfire and pulled up at a tree, got off deliberately, knocked an accumulation of dead twigs from his hat, took off his saddle and bridle and balanced them painstakingly in the tree fork, and said it was affecting to see how widespread the shortage of pasture was.

"It generally is," old Apling said. "I had a kind of a notion you'd be back after you'd had time to study things over. I suppose you got into some kind of a rumpus with some of them sheep outfits. What was it? Couldn't you git along with them, or couldn't they hit it off with you?"

"There wasn't any trouble between them and me," Beech said. "The only point we had words over was you. They wanted to know where you was camped, so they could shoot you up, and I

215

didn't think it was right to tell 'em. I had to put a gun on a couple of 'em before they'd believe I meant business, and that was all there was to it. They're out after you now, and they can see the smoke of this fire of yours for twenty miles, so they ought to be along almost any time now. I thought I'd come back and see you work your sociability on 'em."

"You probably kicked up a squabble with 'em yourself," old Apling said. He looked a little uneasy. "You talked right up to 'em, I'll bet, and slapped their noses with your hat to show 'em that they couldn't run over you. Well, what's done is done. You did come back, and maybe they'd have jumped us anyway. There ain't much that we can do. The horses have got to have water before they can travel, and they won't touch that seep. It ain't cleared up a particle."

"You can put that fire out, not but what the whole country has probably seen the smoke from it already," Beech said. "If you've got to tag after these horses, you can run 'em off down the draw and keep 'em to the brush where they won't leave a trail. There's some young cottonwood bark that they can eat if they have to, and there's water in a rock sink under some big cottonwood trees. I'll stay here and hold off anybody that shows up, so you'll have time to git your tracks covered."

Old Apling went over and untied the flour-sacked pistol from Beech's saddle, rolled it into his blankets, and sat down on it. "If there's any holdin' off to be done, I'll do it," he said. "You're a little too high-spirited to suit me, and a little too hasty about your conclusions. I looked over that rock sink down the draw today, and there wasn't anything in it but mud, and blamed little of that. Somebody had dug for water, and there wasn't none."

"There is now," Beech said. He tugged off one of his wet boots and poured about a pint of the disputed fluid on the ground. "There wasn't any in the daytime because the cottonwoods took it all. They let up when it turns cold, and it runs back in. I waded in it."

He started to put his boot back on. Old Apling reached out and took it, felt of it inside and out, and handed it over as if performing some ceremonial presentation.

"I'd never have figured out a thing like that in this world," he said. "If we git them horses out of here, it'll be you that done it. We'll bunch 'em and work 'em down there. It won't be no picnic, but we'll make out to handle it somehow. We've got to, after a thing like this."

Beech remembered what had occasioned the discovery, and said he would have to have something to eat first. "I want you to keep in mind that it's you I'm doin' this for," he said. "I don't owe that old groundhog of a Ream Gervais anything. The only thing I hate about this is that it'll look like I'd done him a favor."

"He won't take it for one, I guess," old Apling said. "We've got to git these horses out because it'll be a favor to you. You wouldn't want to have it told around that you'd done a thing like findin' that water, and then have to admit that we'd lost all the horses anyhow. We can't lose 'em. You've acted like a man tonight, and I'll be blamed if I'll let you spoil it for any childish spite."

They got the horses out none too soon. Watering them took a long time, and when they finally did consent to call it enough and climb back up the side hill, Beech and old Apling heard a couple of signal shots from the direction of their old camping place, and saw a big glare mount up into the sky from it as the visitors built up their campfire to look the locality over. The sight was almost comforting; if they had to keep away from a pursuit, it was at least something to know where it was.

V

From then on they followed a grab-and-run policy, scouting ahead before they moved, holding to the draws by day and crossing open ground only after dark, never pasturing over a couple of hours in any one place, and discovering food value in outlandish substances — rock lichens, the sprouts of wild plum and serv-

iceberry, the moss of old trees and the bark of some young ones —
that neither they nor the horses had ever considered fit to eat
before. When they struck Boulder River Canyon they dropped
down and toenailed their way along one side of it where they
could find grass and water with less likelihood of having trouble
about it.

The breaks of the canyon were too rough to run new-lambed
sheep in, and they met with so few signs of occupancy that old
Apling got overconfident, neglected his scouting to tie back a
break they had obliged to make in a line fence, and ran the horse
herd right over the top of a camp where some men were branding
calves, tearing down a cook tent and part of a corral and scattering cattle and bedding from the river all the way to the top of the
canyon.

By rights, they should have sustained some damage for the
piece of carelessness, but they drove through fast, and they were
out of sight around a shoulder of rimrock before any of the men
could get themselves picked up. Somebody did throw a couple of
shots after them as they were pulling into a thicket of mock
orange and chokecherry, but it was only with a pistol, and he
probably did it more to relieve his feelings than with any hope of
hitting anything.

They were so far out of range that they couldn't even hear
where the bullets landed.

Neither of them mentioned that unlucky run-in all the rest of
that day. They drove hard, punished the horses savagely when
they lagged, and kept them at it until, a long time after dark,
they struck an old rope ferry that crossed Boulder River at a place
called, in memory of its original founders, Robbers' Roost.

The ferry wasn't a public carrier, and there was not even any
main road down to it. It was used by the ranches in the neighborhood as the only means of crossing the river for fifty miles in
either direction, and it was tied in to a log with a good solid chain

and padlock. It was a way to cross, and neither of them could see anything else but to take it.

Beech favored waiting for daylight for it, pointing out that there was a ranch light half a mile up the slope, and that if anybody caught them hustling a private ferry in the dead of night they would probably be taken for criminals on the dodge. Old Apling said it was altogether likely, and drew Beech's pistol and shot the padlock apart with it.

"They could hear that up at that ranch house," Beech said. "What if they come pokin' down here to see what we're up to?"

Old Apling tossed the fragments of padlock into the river and hung the pistol in the waistband of his trousers. "Let 'em come," he said. "They'll go back again with their fingers in their mouths. This is your trip, and you put in good work on it, and I like to ruined the whole thing stoppin' to patch an eighty-cent fence so some scissorbill wouldn't have his feelings hurt, and that's the last accommodation anybody gits out of me till this is over with. I can take about six horses at a trip, it looks like. Help me to bunch 'em."

Six horses at a trip proved to be an overestimate. The best they could do was five, and the boat rode so deep with them that Beech refused to risk handling it. He stayed with the herd, and old Apling cut it loose, let the current sweep it across into slack water, and hauled it in to the far bank by winding in its cable on an old homemade capstan. Then he turned the horses into a counting pen and came back for another load.

He worked at it fiercely, as if he had a bet up that he could wear the whole ferry rig out, but it went with infernal slowness, and when the wind began to move for daylight there were a dozen horses still to cross and no place to hide them in case the ferry had other customers.

Beech waited and fidgeted over small noises until, hearing voices and the clatter of hoofs on shale far up the canyon behind him, he gave way, drove the remaining horses into the river, and swam them across, letting himself be towed along by his saddle horn and floating his clothes ahead of him on a board.

He paid for that flurry of nervousness before he got out. The water was so cold it paralyzed him, and so swift it whisked him a mile downstream before he could get his pony turned to breast it. He grounded on a gravel bar in a thicket of dwarf willows, with numbness striking clear to the center of his diaphragm and deadening his arms so he couldn't pick his clothes loose from the bundle to put on. He managed it, by using his teeth and elbows, and warmed himself a little by driving the horses afoot through the brush till he struck the ferry landing.

It had got light enough to see things in outline, and old Apling was getting ready to shove off for another crossing when the procession came lumbering at him out of the shadows. He came ashore, counted the horses into the corral to make sure none had drowned, and laid Beech under all the blankets and built up a fire to limber him out by. He got breakfast and got packed to leave, and he did some rapid expounding about the iniquity of risking the whole trip on such a wild piece of foolhardiness.

"That was the reason I wanted you to work this boat," he said. "I could have stood up to anybody that come projectin' around, and if they wanted trouble I could have filled their order for 'em. They won't bother us now, anyhow; it don't matter how bad they want to."

"I could have stood up to 'em if I'd had anything to do it with," Beech said. "You've got that pistol of mine, and I couldn't see to throw rocks. What makes you think they won't bother us? You know it was that brandin' crew comin' after us, don't you?"

"I expect that's who it was," old Apling agreed. "They ought to be out after the cattle we scattered, but you can trust a bunch of cowboys to pick out the most useless things to tend to first. I've got that pistol of yours because I don't aim for you to git in trouble with it while this trip is on. There won't anybody bother us because I've cut all the cables on the ferry, and it's lodged down-stream on a gravel spit. If anybody crosses after us within fifty miles of here, he'll swim, and the people around here ain't as reckless around cold water as you are."

Beech sat up. "We got to git out of here," he said. "There's people on this side of the river that use that ferry, you old fool, and they'll have us up before every grand jury in the country from now on. The horses ain't worth it."

"What the horses is worth ain't everything," old Apling said. "There's a part of this trip ahead that you'll be glad you went through. You're entitled to that much out of it, after the work you've put in, and I aim to see that you git it. It ain't any use tryin' to explain to you what it is. You'll notice it when the time comes."

VI

They worked north, following the breaks of the river canyon, finding the rock breaks hard to travel, but easy to avoid observation in, and the grass fair in stand, but so poor and washy in body that the horses had to spend most of their time eating enough to keep up their strength so they could move.

They struck a series of gorges, too deep and precipitous to be crossed at all, and had to edge back into milder country where there were patches of plowed ground, some being harrowed over for summer fallow and others venturing out with a bright new stand of dark-green wheat.

The pasture was patchy and scoured by the wind, and all the best parts of it were under fence, which they didn't dare cut for fear of getting in trouble with the natives. Visibility was high in that section; the ground lay open to the north as far as they could see, the wind kept the air so clear that it hurt to look at the sky, and they were never out of sight of wheat ranchers harrowing down summer fallow.

A good many of the ranchers pulled up and stared after the

horse herd as it went past, and two or three times they waved and rode down toward the road, as if they wanted to make it an excuse for stopping work. Old Apling surmised that they had some warning they wanted to deliver against trespassing, and he drove on without waiting to hear it.

They were unable to find a camping place anywhere among those wheat fields, so they drove clear through to open country and spread down for the night alongside a shallow pond in the middle of some new grass not far enough along to be pastured, though the horses made what they could out of it. There were no trees or shrubs anywhere around, not even sagebrush. Lacking fuel for a fire, they camped without one, and since there was no grass anywhere except around the pond, they left the horses unguarded, rolled in to catch up sleep, and were awakened about daylight by the whole herd stampeding past them at a gallop.

They both got up and moved fast. Beech ran for his pony, which was trying to pull loose from its picket rope to go with the bunch. Old Apling ran out into the dust afoot, waggling the trig-gerless old pistol and trying to make out objects in the half-light by hard squinting. The herd horses fetched a long circle and came back past him, with a couple of riders clouting along behind trying to turn them back into open country. One of the riders opened up a rope and swung it, the other turned in and slapped the inside flankers with his hat, and old Apling hauled up the old pistol, flipped the hammer a couple of rounds to get it warmed up, and let go at them twice.

The half darkness held noise as if it had been a cellar. The two shots banged monstrously, Beech yelled to old Apling to be care-ful who he shot at, and the two men shied off sideways and rode away into the open country. One of them yelled something that sounded threatening in tone as they went out of sight, but neither of them seemed in the least inclined to bring on any general engagement. The dust blew clear, the herd horses came back to grass, old Apling looked at the pistol and punched the two exploded shells out of it, and Beech ordered him to hand it over before he got in trouble with it.

"How do you know but what them men had a right here?" he demanded sternly. "We'd be in a fine jack pot if you'd shot one of 'em and it turned out he owned this land we're on, wouldn't we?"

Old Apling looked at him, holding the old pistol poised as if he was getting ready to lead a band with it. The light strengthened and shed a rose-colored radiance over him, so he looked flushed and joyous and lifted up. With some of the dust knocked off him, he could have filled in easily as a day star and son of the morning, whiskers and all.

"I wouldn't have shot them men for anything you could buy me!" he said, and faced north to a blue line of bluffs that came up out of the shadows, a blue gleam of water that moved under them, a white steamboat that moved upstream, glittering as the first light struck it. "Them men wasn't here because we was trespassers. Them was horse thieves, boy! We've brought these horses to a place where they're worth stealin', and we've brought 'em through! The railroad is under them bluffs, and that water down there is the old Columbia River!"

They might have made it down to the river that day, but having it in sight and knowing that nothing could stop them from reaching it, there no longer seemed any object in driving so unsparingly. They ate breakfast and talked about starting, and they even got partly packed up for it. Then they got occupied with talking to a couple of wheat ranchers who pulled in to inquire about buying some of the horse herd; the drought had run up wheat prices at a time when the country's livestock had been allowed to run down, and so many horses had been shot and starved out that they were having to take pretty much anything they could get.

Old Apling swapped them a couple of the most jaded herd horses for part of a haystack, referred other applicants to Gervais down at the railroad, and spent the remainder of the day washing, patching clothes and saddlery, and watching the horses get acquainted once more with a conventional diet.

The next morning a rancher dropped off a note from Gervais urging them to come right on down, and adding a kind but firm admonition against running up any feed bills without his express permission. He made it sound as if there might be some hurry about catching the horse market on the rise, so they got ready to leave, and Beech looked back over the road they had come, thinking of all that had happened on it.

"I'd like it better if old Gervais didn't have to work himself in on the end of it," he said. "I'd like to step out on the whole business right now."

"You'd be a fool to do that," old Apling said. "This is outside your work contract, so we can make the old gopher pay you what it's worth. I'll want to go in ahead and see about that and about the money that he owes me and about corral space and feed and one thing and another, so I'll want you to bring 'em in alone. You ain't seen everything there is to a trip like this, and you won't unless you stay with it."

VII

There would be no ending to this story without an understanding of what that little river town looked like at the hour, a little before sundown of a windy spring day, when Beech brought the desert horse herd down into it. On the wharf below town, some men were unloading baled hay from a steamboat, with some passengers watching from the saloon deck, and the river beyond them hoisting into white-capped peaks that shone and shed dazzling spray over the darkening water.

A switch engine was handling stock cars on a spur track, and the brakeman flagged it to a stop and stood watching the horses, leaning into the wind to keep his balance while the engineer climbed out on the tender to see what was going on.

The street of the town was lined with big leafless poplars that looked as if they hadn't gone short of moisture a day of their lives; the grass under them was bright green, and there were women working around flower beds and pulling up weeds, enough of them so that a horse could have lived on them for two days.

There was a Chinaman clipping grass with a pair of sheep shears to keep it from growing too tall, and there were lawn sprinklers running clean water on the ground in streams. There were stores with windows full of new clothes, and stores with bright hardware, and stores with strings of bananas and piles of oranges, bread and crackers and candy and rows of hams, and there were groups of anxious-faced men sitting around stoves inside who came out to watch Beech pass and told one another hopefully that the back country might make a good year out of it yet, if a youngster could bring that herd of horses through it.

There were women who hauled back their children and cautioned them not to get in the man's way, and there were boys and girls, some near Beech's own age, who watched him and stood looking after him, knowing that he had been through more than they had ever seen and not suspecting that it had taught him something that they didn't know about the things they saw every day. None of them knew what it meant to be in a place where there were delicacies to eat and new clothes to wear and look at, what it meant to be warm and out of the wind for a change, what it could mean merely to have water enough to pour on the ground and grass enough to cut down and throw away.

For the first time, seeing how the youngsters looked at him, he understood what that amounted to. There wasn't a one of them who wouldn't have traded places with him. There wasn't one that he would have traded places with, for all the haberdashery and fancy groceries in town. He turned down to the corrals, and old Apling held the gate open for him and remarked that he hadn't taken much time to it.

"You're sure you had enough of that ridin' through town?" he said. "It ain't the same when you do it a second time, remember."

"It'll last me," Beech said. "I wouldn't have missed it, and I wouldn't want it to be the same again. I'd sooner have things the way they run with us out in the high country. I'd sooner not have anything be the same a second time."

May 6, 1939

Feeling of respect, accomplishment
when riding through town w/ herd.

The Homestead Orchard

THE patch of sagebrush which young Linus Ollivant's charge of six hundred lambed ewes had selected as a bed ground for themselves and their progeny was an old starved-out homestead halfway down the slope of Boulder River Canyon, with a few broken-down sheds, a naked slope of red conglomerate that had once been plowed, and a slow trickle of water, small, but holding its flow steady in spite of the drying wind that had driven most of the country's water supply off into the unknown, and a considerable proportion of the country along with it.

It lacked a good deal of being an ideal location for a range camp, being altogether too far from pasture. The sheep, in the three days they had been there, had put in most of their waking hours plodding out to feed and trudging back to water, but they refused to omit either end of the circuit; and Linus, trying to handle them alone until an extra herder could be raked loose from a box car and sent out from town, shoved his old herding horse along behind them in the hard glare of a windy twilight and pulled up on the slope above the bed ground to count them into camp before going down into the shadows after them.

The intense blackness of the shadows in that clear air made the camp so dark that even the white tent looked ghostly against the gloom. There was one clear patch of light where the sky reflected in the pond of water, and the mass of dark-wooled old ewes and white-fleeced and inquisitive lambs trailed down into it and stood patterned against it clear and distinct as they drank and crossed to their bed ground for the night.

When they had all crossed, Linus strained his eyes back over the naked rock ridges of the canyon, hoping, because he was too inexperienced at sheepherding to know that it contained no pleasant surprises, that some tail-end bunch of late feeders might still come moseying along in time to bring his count up somewhere near where it belonged.

As might have been expected, he saw nothing except the ridges, ranked one behind another, as frail-looking as if they had been shadows in the pale red sky, darkening to gray at the edges where they touched it. The country's lifelessness was a new thing to Linus. His family had homesteaded on the divide back of that river canyon in his childhood, and one of his few pleasant recollections from that time was of standing on high ground at dark and counting the lights of other homesteads where families had settled to grow up with the country. Now there were no signs of life visible anywhere except in the range camp, where the sheep fidgeted themselves into position for the night and where Linus' father, suffering from a case of dust blindness from the alkali flats back in the desert, fumbled matches into a pile of greasewood in an effort to get a fire started for supper.

His fire building didn't make much headway. His eyes were so inflamed that they were not only useless but so agonizingly sensitive that they had to be kept heavily bandaged against the least light or wind or irritation. Most of his matches blew out while he fumbled around for fuel to touch them to, and Linus, seeing that he was about to run a fit of temper over his own helplessness, gave up hopes of the stray sheep and hurried down to help him out. The fire started easily enough, with a little coddling, and old Ollivant settled gloomily back against the tent pole, hauled his bandage down into place as if he were conferring a favor on society by tolerating the thing, and supplied what entertainment he could by offering conversational leads as Linus got their cooking under way.

"It ain't right for you to have all this work put on you," he said. "It looks like them people in town could have raked up some hobo herder to ship out here, if they had any consideration for a man. How did the sheep handle today? It didn't sound to me like there was as many come in as usual. Did you get a count on 'em?"

Linus raked the fire, clattered buckets and said he had counted them in carefully. He didn't mention what his count had come to. He thought of owning up to it, and then reflected that it would be better to hold back until daylight, when he could make sure that the strays were actually lost and not merely yarded up in the brush, waiting to be sent for.

"They pulled in too tired to make much noise, I expect," he said. "They had a long lug in from pasture tonight. Three or four miles, anyhow."

Side-stepping one disturbing circumstance, he ran squarely into another. His father picked on his estimate of the distance to pasture as if it were a dynamiting he had confessed to.

"We can't carry these old pelters where they've got to trail four miles to pasture," he said. "They'll wear themselves to death on it. If I could trust you to stay out of trouble with people, I'd be about in the notion to hold the whole bunch here in camp for a day or two, till you could scout up some better place to bed 'em. You'd probably land up in some fight, though. Blame it, what does a man have to depend on sheep for, anyhow?"

That was something of a dig; it was Linus' fault that he had been reduced to depending on sheep. Ordinarily, he wouldn't have made a point of that, but enforced inaction made him short of patience. Linus knew enough to humor him.

"It wouldn't do any good to scout around here," he said. "There ain't any other place around here where we could camp sheep at all. You'd see that if you could see what this country looked like."

"If I ever get these old buzzard baits sheared and turned off to ship, I'll kill the next man that says 'sheep' to me," old Ollivant said. "There ain't a jury in the land that would cinch me for it, the provocation I've had." He stopped and lifted one hand for silence for a minute. "I heard horses," he said. "If them people in town have sent out a herder, I'll never complain about my luck again."

It was a handsome offer, and Linus hated to sound as discouraging about it as he felt obliged to.

"It can't be anybody to see us," he said. "We've moved camp five times since you sent for a herder, and the people in town wouldn't know where to send one. You heard some bunch of wild cayuses. Maybe it's Indians out to dig camass."

"It was a shod horse I heard," old Ollivant said.

They both listened, saying nothing and even taking care not to rattle the dishes as they ate supper. Neither of them heard a sound, and Linus fell to thinking over their homesteading days up on the ridge, and of the long string of accidents that had led him back to it against his will. His father had come to that country to homestead a likely quarter-section of sagebrush and find out whether high-altitude soil and climate couldn't be adapted to raising domestic fruits, and he had been obliged to give that up, the orcharding and the homesteading together, through a run of misfortune for which Linus was a good deal to blame.

Afterward he worked around a feed yard in one of the river towns long enough to figure that it led nowhere, and finally he allowed himself to be tempted into taking a half interest in a flock of rickety old ewes, on a chance that, given a decent year and careful handling, they might bring in a crop of lambs worth three times his original investment in them, with the wool figuring at enough extra to cover incidental expenses, taxes, and possibly even day wages for his work.

It had been a tempting project, with little risk showing on its exterior, to begin with. But there had been enough risk about it to make it a gamble, and, like most gambles undertaken by people who couldn't afford to lose, things had gone wrong with it almost from the outset.

The roster of bad luck began with a feed shortage and a rise in hay prices, proceeded onward into an outlandishly protracted dry spell and a shortening of the country's water supply, and held on into a failure of all the spring pastures at the exact time when the entire country had counted on them as a last hope to keep going on. A vast invasion of cast-off scrub horses used up what little coarse grass the land had managed to hold on to, and old Ollivant's dust blindness had topped off the whole structure of calamities and left, as far as Linus could see, scarcely any possibility of their pulling through to shearing time with any sheep at all.

He had done his best to keep going singlehanded, and though he had been forced to several emergency measures that his father would not have approved of, he had kept the herd up better than most professional herders would have bothered to do.

He hadn't wanted to pasture back so near the scene of his father's abandoned experiments with dry-country orcharding. That was one of the emergency measures he had not been able to avoid. The sheep had wandered down from the alkali desert with no notion in their heads except to move where they could find something to eat, and the line of grass had led them, almost as if it had been set out for the purpose, straight down into Boulder River Canyon and through it to the water hole where they were bedded. It wasn't a good place for them, but it was the only water in the neighborhood where sheep could be held without running into opposition from the resident landowners.

One of the few useful things Linus had got out of his homesteading years on the ridge over Boulder River was a knowledge of the country and its limitations and prejudices. He knew the region well, and he knew there were no open camping places in it that had even as many advantages as the one where they were.

One of the points about it was that there were thirty head of his father's sheep running loose somewhere around it, and he couldn't leave until he had taken some kind of a stab at finding them. He roused out of his train of reflections and remarked that it was a cold wind to be sitting out in with a case of inflammation of the eyes. Old Ollivant said morosely that he wasn't responsible for the temperature of the wind.

"It's a blamed funny thing we don't hear any coyotes," he remarked. "This is the first night since we've been out here that there ain't been a dozen of 'em on the yip all around us. They couldn't all have left the country in a day."

"You can't tell about coyotes around these blamed rock piles," Linus said vaguely. The coyotes had not left the country, and he knew the reason they weren't making themselves heard from as they usually did. With thirty head of sheep wandering at large, they had something better to while away their time on than hunkering on a cold rock to howl.

He tried to decide whether to own up about the strays, and heard metal grate on rock somewhere up on the ridge. He held up his hand for silence, heard it again, and let the strays slip out of his thoughts with a feeling of relief at not having to make up his mind about them.

"Somebody with horses," he said. "You'd better fetch out the gun. It might be some of these neighborhood busybodies come to drag us out of here in a sack."

"Guns can make more trouble for some people than draggin' in a sack," old Ollivant said, without moving. "I told you I heard shod horses fifteen minutes ago. It's somebody from town come out to see what's happened to us, I expect."

The wind shifted, and for a long time they heard nothing more at all. Then the hoofs clattered on the ridge above them, and they could tell that it was several horses in charge of one man who was humming a loud mixture of three or four different tunes as an indication that he was not trying to sneak up on anybody. Linus stirred the fire into a blaze, and he stopped his humming, shaded his eyes against the glare, and rode down into the full light, so they could look him over before he offered to dismount.

"They told me in town that some people named Ollivant wanted a herder," he said. He was a large-built man with a saddle a couple of sizes too snug for him, and he had three pack ponies strung, head and tail, behind him. He kept yanking their lead rope to keep them from trying to lie down.

"My name is Dee Radford. I'm a herder, and I ain't ever worked this country before, so I come out to see what your layout looked like. They had this order of groceries made up for you, so I brung it along. This place ain't fit to camp sheep on. I'll bet you've lost a couple of dozen head in the last two days, if you'll count."

Linus didn't consider it necessary to mention what the correct statistics on his shortage were. "How did the people in town know where to send you?" he asked.

"They didn't. I had to work out your trail from the scenery," Dee Radford said.

He dismounted so heavily that he almost pulled the weary animal over on top of himself, and proceeded to unsaddle and unpack in the dark, working as confidently as if nobody had ever told him what a lantern was for.

"When you've been in this business as long as I have, you don't need to know where people are to find 'em," he explained, unraveling a complicated four-way hitch from a pack. "A man that can't find what he wants without help ain't entitled to call himself a herder. This ain't any place to camp a band of sheep like these of yours. They walk off their feed gittin' to water, and they dry out thirsty trailin' back to feed, and they're too old to stand it. I picked out a place up on the ridge where they'll handle better. There's an old homestead with a patch of run-down orchard around it, and there's water enough to make out on if we're careful. You can git your camp struck and packed, and we'll move up there the first thing in the morning."

To Linus, it seemed a little high-handed for even a skilled herder to drop into the middle of a strange camp and start issuing orders as if it belonged to him.

Old Ollivant was less touchy and more interested. At mention of a ridge homestead surrounded by an old orchard, he sat up and said he had been agitating to have their camp moved, and that Linus had assured him the thing was impossible.

"It is," Linus said. "That ridge country ain't open land. It belongs to people that use it to feed cattle on. If we move in with sheep, they'll throw us out, and maybe run the sheep to death for good measure. I know the people around here. I know how they act with pasture thieves, and I don't blame 'em for it."

"We won't be pasture thieves, because there ain't any pasture on that ridge to thieve," Dee Radford said. "There's been cattle over every foot of it, and they've cleaned the grass right down to the roots. The only thing about it is that there's a big scatter of grass seed blowed around into horse tracks and under rocks where the cattle couldn't reach it. Sheep can, and there ought to be enough of it to run us for three weeks or more anyhow. We won't be trespassers, because the place don't belong to anybody. I asked some men in the road about that. I told 'em I was a mind to buy it, and they said it hadn't ever been proved up on. We'll move up there in the morning, if it's all right with both of you."

It was not all right with Linus and he said nothing, but his father said there was no use palavering around about a move so plainly commendable and necessary.

"We'll move any time you say, and don't pay any attention to anything this boy says," he said. "He's always balky at the wrong times, and there ain't much you can do with him. He's done well to handle the sheep by himself without any losses, but he's got to learn to listen to other people sometimes, and he can't start any younger."

Linus still remained silent, so he fumbled his way inside the camp tent and began rattling small articles into his war bag to save having to pack them in the morning. They heard his boots thump and the blankets rustle as he spread down in them, and then the noises subsided as he went to sleep.

Dee Radford remarked that they had better be thinking about rest themselves, if they were to make it up to the ridge homestead in a day's trailing. Linus replied that he didn't plan to make it to any ridge homestead, and that he would rest when he felt like it. He tried to sound chilling, but Dee Radford merely sat back and studied him thoughtfully.

"I've seen young squirts act like this when I've pulled into some camp to help through a bad season," he said. "You're a different cut from that, if looks is anything. You don't look like a squirt, and you ought to know that you'll lose all your sheep if you try to handle 'em down here. You don't think I'd be in this business if I didn't know something about it, do you?"

"You know your business, I guess," Linus conceded, a trifle sullenly. "What you don't know about is this country. You've got it fixed to land us all in trouble with the people in it. That old ridge orchard you've picked for us to move to ain't open land. If any men told you it was, they lied. It used to be our homestead. My old man planted that orchard, and I took care of it, and I could draw you a picture right now of every tree in it. We'd be there yet, but I got into a rumpus, so the old man had to sell out his homestead rights and leave to get away from lawsuits. I shot a man, if you want to know what it was. Maybe that homestead ain't been proved up on, but it ain't ours, because we sold the rights to it. If we take sheep onto it we'll have trouble, and people around here will swear I started it to show off. The old man don't know about that, because he don't know what part of the country we've drifted back to. He'll probably claim I sneaked back here to hunt up some more cussedness, if he ever finds it out."

Dee Radford stirred the fire and said that cleared up two or three points that he hadn't understood at first. He added that old

Ollivant's dust blindness had looked serious, and that they might manage to get the sheep sheared and off their hands and get clear away from the Boulder River country before he cured up enough to realize that they had been there.

"It would be playin' underhanded with him, but that ain't any business of mine," he said. "Sheep is all I claim to know anything about, and there ain't but one thing to do with this bunch of yours. We can keep 'em alive on that ridge homestead, and we'll try to handle 'em so people won't find out we're there. If they have to stay here they'll die, and if you'd sooner they done that, say so and I'll leave you to handle 'em. You'll go broke, but that ain't any of my put-in. How many head have you lost since you've been here that you ain't told your old man about?"

That was a sharp surmise, and Linus took no risks in replying to it. He nodded toward the tent, and stated in clear tones that he had lost no sheep at all. Then he opened and closed the fingers of his hands three times, traced the course of one setting sun down the sky, and waited to see if Dee Radford had ever stopped long enough in one place to know what Indian sign talk was.

Dee indicated his comprehension with a nod, and remarked cautiously that he would have expected the shrinkage to have run higher and started sooner. If they had dropped out only that afternoon, they might still be alive. Having turned in that reflection, he got up, got his horse out of the corral, and reached down his saddle.

"I'm goin' to show you that a man don't need to know a country to handle sheep in it," he said. "You show me which direction you pastured today, and I'll find them strays for you. You git packed and line the sheep for the ridge the first thing in the morning, and quit this shiverin' around for fear of trouble. People ain't fools enough to fight us over a place as worthless as that homestead. If they do, I'll tend to 'em, and if we damage the premises, I'll stand good for it. We won't hurt your old man's orchard, if that's what you're uneasy about."

"I don't care what you do to the orchard," Linus said. "I put in four years' hard work on it, and all I ever got for it was a pile of trouble, and all I want is to make sure we won't get into any more. Trouble ain't easy to dodge out on in this country."

"Trouble ain't easy to dodge out on in any country that you spend too much of your time in. You ought to learn your trade and travel around with it, like I do, and then you wouldn't have to bother about what people thought of you."

Linus and his father packed camp an hour or so before sunup. Linus getting everybody's personal belongings together into one of the packs, and reflecting that it did look as if Dee Radford's system of short-staking around had paid better than any protracted residence in one place.

Dee's outfit included such show pieces as a leather-faced bed roll, double-lined goatskin chaps, and a hand-carved rifle scabbard, all of which were expensive and none of which either Linus or his father possessed at all. His rifle was a new flat-shooting rig with box magazine, oiled stock, peep sight with micrometer scale, buckhorn tips, and all the trimmings. Linus' father had a common little saddle carbine with iron sights and a squared-off butt, and Linus not only had no gun at all but wasn't even supposed to handle one except under his father's personal supervision.

Except that it showed what he had missed by staying too long in the shadow of his youthful reputation, the contrast in the rifles didn't bother Linus much. The old piece of momentary recklessness that had ended his residence on the ridge homestead had also destroyed most of his interest in guns, and the sight of one was generally enough to bring the whole unlucky episode back to him clearly and painfully.

Its beginning cause had been the old homestead orchard. He had put in an entire spring on it, pruning, cultivating, whitewashing and spraying for insects, and, as he was applying a few final touches against twig borers, a contingent of old Lucas

Waymark's cowboys pulled in and camped a herd of starved-out old cows right against a weak place in the fence where they were certain to break through the minute they were left to themselves.

Linus was alone on the place at the time and, not feeling disposed to let a pack of scrub cows grab what he had barely finished rescuing from all the other pests in the country, he forted up behind some baled hay with the family musket and ordered the Waymark minions to be gone.

The minions hadn't kept up with their reading sufficiently to realize that they were supposed to slink away in baffled rage, so they offered to spank him if he didn't take the gun straight indoors and put it back where it belonged. One of them straddled the orchard fence to illustrate how they would go at it, and Linus tightened down and cut loose, intending to hit the post under his hand as a final warning. The fore sight of the old gun had got knocked out of line and, instead of jarring the post, he spread the Waymark man across the top wire of the fence with a smashed collarbone.

There was never any general agreement in the country over which of the parties to the incident had been most to blame for it. The homesteaders blamed old Waymark for running his cattle around the neighborhood as if he owned it. The Waymark men blamed their stricken co-worker for trying to walk down a gun in the hands of a frightened youngster. Linus blamed the gun for not shooting straight, Linus' father blamed Linus for pointing it at a man he didn't intend to shoot, and several people blamed Linus' father for keeping a firearm on the premises without making sure the sights were lined up properly.

All the bestowals of blame were probably partly justified, but none of them could clear Linus of the responsibility for injuring a fellow man with a deadly weapon, and old Waymark played that fact for all there was in it. He worked up claims for doctors' bills, wages for the wounded man's lost time, physical suffering and mental anguish, and complaints against Linus for everything from juvenile delinquency to attempted manslaughter. In the end, Linus' father gave up, sold him the homestead relinquishment, and moved away.

The change was no particular misfortune, but Linus' mismanagement in bringing it on was something he never liked to be reminded of. The old gun that had done the shooting was so painful a memento that he stuck it back of a rafter in the homestead cabin, out of sight, and neither he nor Linus thought enough of it to get it down when they moved. They never mentioned the shooting afterward, and there was always a little strained note in their conversation with each other, because they so painstakingly avoided any subject that seemed likely to lead into it.

They both steered around handling the two herding rifles while they were packing up. After Linus had got them wrapped in some bedding and stowed quietly on one of the packs, his father went out and felt carefully over the horses to make sure where they were. It wasn't that he suspected Linus of having stolen them; he merely wanted to see that they hadn't been overlooked, and he preferred to hunt them out rather than open a subject which neither of them took anything but distrust and uneasiness in thinking back over.

Trailing the sheep was slow, but not troublesome. The cold kept them well bunched, and since there was not enough grass to tempt them to loiter, they moved along without needing any encouragement beyond a little rock throwing to keep them pointed right.

Old Ollivant dragged along behind with the pack horses, holding his eye bandage down against the wind with one hand and his reins, trail rope and saddle horn with the other.

Linus pulled into the homestead about an hour past sundown, and found Dee Radford waiting. Dee sat beside a fresh-banked pond, watching it fill up from the spring. He had turned the little quarter-inch trickle of water away from the sink back of the orchard where it disappeared into the ground, and he was storing it for the sheep to drink.

"We may have to ration it out, the way it's runnin'," he said. "We'll know about that after they've watered a couple of times. You notice I collected your strays."

There was probably not another man in the country who could have found those strays in that river canyon in the dark. Linus paid his respectful acknowledgements to the feat, and looked doubtful about the arrangements for conserving the water. The thing that came into his mind, in spite of him, was that the trees must have come to depend on the flow of the water into the ground. They looked so wild and worthless, all broken and tangled and killed down by cattle and heavy snows and freezing, that he kept his thoughts to himself, for fear of sounding sentimental. He did remark that the trees belonged to somebody, and Dee took him up hard on that.

"You've got a patch of fruit trees that ain't worth anything, and a band of sheep that'll bring your old man ten thousand dollars if they stay alive," he said. "You've got an old orchard that nobody thinks enough of to prove up on, and you've got sheep that your old man has run himself alkali-blind over, besides the work you've put in on 'em yourself. I don't see how you can even argue about turnin' this water. I'd be ashamed to be that big a fool about any place I'd ever lived."

"I ain't any fool about this place," Linus said. "You may have to answer a claim for damages to these trees before you're through here, that's all. Don't think you'll be able to argue yourself out of it, either. There's harder outfits around here than you might think."

Old Ollivant drew up with the pack horses, and Dee searched his box-magazine rifle out from under the bedding and hung it ceremoniously on a fence post.

"If anybody shows up to be fought, he's mine," he said. "I don't

240

notice any signs of heavy travel around here, so it ain't likely that anybody will. You don't need to look that far ahead for anything to worry about, anyhow. When you've stood a week or two of feedin' sheep on grass seed in these rocks, you'll wish you had a good quiet fight to rest up on. We'll make a herd camp here where we can take turns standin' guard over the bed ground, and we'll put the tent off yonder in the orchard where your father can be out of the wind."

Old Ollivant didn't think much of that arrangement, insisting, with a stubbornness of conviction that turned out to be almost clairvoyant, that Linus would land in some trouble if he stood guard over the bed ground without somebody to stand guard over him. He gave in only when Dee, having pitched the tent in the cove, helped him down from his horse and led him into it, with instructions to stay there until his eyes felt better.

The ridge was not so abundantly supplied with either grass seed or water as it had looked to begin with. It had barely enough of both to keep the old ewes from bawling loud enough to be heard clear down to the road, and even that frugal measure of sustenance didn't last well.

Trouble started one evening when Linus brought the herd in by himself; Dee having gone down to the road to put up a flag for the shearing crew. Instead of bedding down quietly, the sheep milled, changed ground and collected in little bunches, blatting tunelessly and persistently. Linus was too tired to hear them, and Dee, getting back late, didn't discover till daylight that they had run short of water. Some animal—a skunk or a sage rat, by the signs—had burrowed into the ditch between the spring and the catch pond, and the entire night's supply had seeped out into the ground behind the orchard.

He patched up the break, but that was no immediate help. The ditch and pond basin had dried out so deep that getting them primed and getting the pond filled afterward took the entire day. The sheep waited and continued their blatting, and, to get out of listening to them, Linus went out and cut bundles of willow and wild-cherry sprouts as something for them to practice eating on, even though it couldn't be considered food.

Coming back through the high sagebrush behind the camp with his harvest of shrubbery, he heard men talking and Dee's voice rising in an argument which, to judge by the sound of horses moving restlessly, didn't seem to be commanding much attention. He dropped his brush and crept up behind the old homestead cabin for a look, knowing beforehand who the visitors were and what they had come for.

Old Waymark's bad-news committee hadn't changed its membership in the years that Linus had been away. There was old Waymark himself, undersized and savage-looking. Behind him was his foreman, a sandy-haired man with red eyes who kept fiddling with his rope; back of him were a couple of ordinary herders, and off to one side was old Slickear Cowan, who would have classed as an ordinary herder, except that he was the man whom Linus had rimmed with the shot heard round as much of the world as old Waymark could command a hearing from.

The injury hadn't damaged Slickear Cowan's vitality much. He carried a long jute woolsack on his saddle fork, and he kept working his horse sideways, getting, as if accidentally, between Dee and the post where he had hung his rifle. Linus' father was asleep in the tent, out of range of the conference, and Dee was so absorbed in handling the case for the defense that he didn't notice the maneuver being organized against his peace and dignity.

He proved that he was not stealing pasture, pointed out that, instead of damaging the homestead, he had kept it from falling apart, and touched on various phases of the land-title question with so much authority that old Waymark acted apologetic about being there at all. His sandy-haired foreman shook out a turn of his rope and looked thoughtful, Slickear Cowan gathered his reins and sat forward in his saddle, and old Waymark studied the tent in the orchard as if half wondering whether there was anybody in it who ought to be invited to see the fun.

It was clear enough what they were up to. Dee Radford was about to be taken through the rural ceremony known as a sheepherder's sleigh ride. Slickear Cowan would make a run and snatch his rifle; when he turned to see what was up, the foreman would hang a rope on him and dump him. The woolsack would be yanked over him and tied shut, and he would be dragged behind a horse over the rugged countryside, with special attention to those portions of it that would bounce him highest.

That was the standard treatment for men who ran sheep on somebody else's land, and there was only one way to head it off. Linus tiptoed inside the old homestead cabin, noticing, with a little half-homesick feeling, that a worn-out pair of his own shoes were still on the kitchen floor where he had dropped them on leaving, and how woebegone they looked with the strings trailing loose and the dust heavy on them.

He had not been tall enough to reach the rafters the day his father hid the old rifle back of them. Now he put his hand up to it without even having to stretch. The rifle was dusty and the action was rusted shut, so it wouldn't work, but that didn't disturb him. He didn't intend to shoot, and it added something to his confidence to know that he couldn't, even if he felt tempted to. He tiptoed to the back door, kicked it open and stood in it with the rifle trained, in involuntary deference to the past, on the fork of Slickear Cowan's collarbone.

"Pull up that horse and drop them reins," he ordered. "Put your hands under your belt and take your feet out of the stirrups. Now move out of here, the whole bunch of you."

If he had appeared draped in a sheet and clanking a chain, he couldn't have quenched the delegation's high spirits more completely. Everybody stared, and nobody moved. Linus motioned Dee Radford toward the rifle on the post, and Dee roused himself, got it and backed off, still staring.

"Where in creation did you find that gun?" he asked. "You ain't robbed any Indian graves, have you?"

"It didn't come out of any Indian grave," Linus said. His voice, with the empty house backing it up, sounded so spooky that he hardly recognized it himself. "We left this gun here when we moved away, and I remembered where it was." He turned apologetically to old Waymark. "I don't want to shoot any of your men. All I want is for you to let us alone. We'll pay for any damage we've done here."

Old Waymark edged his horse sideways, picking up his spirits a little.

"You're that young Ollivant hoodlum that like to killed one of my men once before," he said, as if he expected Linus to deny it. "You ought to have gone to jail then, and I'll see that you do go now. I bought this place from your father, and I want these men to witness that you've ordered me off of it at the point of a gun. You'll hear from it, you and your father both."

He picked up his reins, and Dee asked him to hold on a minute.

"There's a point or two about this trespass business," he said. "This boy has told me that his father moved out of here before he got this homestead proved up on. What you bought was his relinquishment, wasn't it?"

Old Waymark conceded that it was, and said that had nothing to do with the main issue. "One of my men went down and filed on it. You'll find that out plenty soon, if you've got any doubts about it."

"I've got a few," Dee said. "There's a residence requirement about homesteads, and your man ain't ever lived here. This boy's father left that gun in the house when he moved out, and it ain't been touched till now."

Old Waymark's whiskers pointed slightly astern again. It was not unusual for people in remote districts to be a little neglectful about residence on their homesteads. The fact that his man had followed the general custom was the main reason he had come there. There was nothing on the homestead worth squabbling over, and he wouldn't have cared how many sheep camped on it if his title had held a little closer to legal standards, but a counterentry on the place was worth going to some trouble to head off. He said an old gun being overlooked in some hiding place meant nothing, and picked up his reins again.

His men were all staring down into the orchard. The tent had come open, and Linus' father came slowly up from it, holding his bandage clear of one tortured eye, so he could see his way between the tangle of neglected old trees that he had set out to be a light and a beacon to horticultural expansion in the sagebrush. He drew up and fixed Linus with a glare that was all the more impressive because it was so obviously agonizing to him.

"This is the kind of high-handed thuggery you've sneaked in on me, is it?" he demanded. "You tore loose with a gun once, and got yourself in trouble till I had to sell out and leave here to get you clear of it. A man would think that would have been enough to last you, but here you're back for more. You wait till I get my eyesight crippled, so I can't see what you're up to, and then you gallop straight back to the same place to do the same trick all over again. You promised me never to touch a gun unless I was around to watch you, and you know it. You know we ain't got any right to be here too. You know this old skunk bought this place off of me, and you've got no right to order him to leave it. Put that gun down."

Linus leaned the gun against the wall outside the door. The Waymark men watched thoughtfully as he stood back from it, and Slickear Cowan lifted his hands clear of his belt. Dee Radford advised him to avoid rashness, jiggled the safety catch on his rifle to indicate that he was serious and told Linus' father to cover his eyes from the light and show a little sense.

"You didn't sell anything to this outfit but your homestead rights," he said. "Nobody has ever used 'em, and we can prove it.

This homestead is open to anybody that wants to live on it the legal time. This boy of yours has got a right to occupy it and he's got a right to use a gun on anybody that tries to run him off of it. He may intend to file a contest on it himself, how do you know?"

"It was on his account that I sold it to start with," old Ollivant said. He did cover his eyes from the light. "How would it look if he come back and took it away from the man I sold it to? It wouldn't be honest."

"You didn't sell his rights to it, because he was too young to have any," Dee said. "He's old enough now to file on any open land he wants to, and it ain't anybody else's business. It ain't even yours."

Old Waymark started to say something about principles, and Linus put in ahead of him, seeing that the argument was reaching a little too far into metaphysics to be practical.

"I don't want to file on any homestead and I wouldn't file on this one if I did," he said. "I've put too much time in one neighborhood already, and I don't aim to do any more of it."

That was a sentiment that Dee Radford had done a good deal of arguing in favor of, and yet he seemed disappointed.

"I'll be blamed if I'll see this place go back to this outfit, after the way they've acted," he said. "I'll file on it myself, if I have to. I want you men to take notice that there's a contest to be entered on this claim and you can keep off of it till the law settles it. Now move, before I shoot up a few of your horses for you." He watched them until they were a little distance away, and then turned to Linus. "Pick up that old pacifier of yours and touch it off somewhere over their heads. I'd like to hear what it sounds like, and I'd like to see how they take it."

"It won't touch off," Linus said, feeling a little foolish over having to admit it. "The breech is rusted shut. I didn't bring it out to shoot with. Them men was about to drag you in a sack, and all I wanted was to head 'em off till you could get clear of 'em. It come out all right."

Linus' father pulled his bandage clear of one eye, looked the old gun over and tried unsuccessfully to budge the hammer. He put it down again and looked at Linus. The light and wind must have been agony to him, and yet he didn't appear conscious of any particular pain.

"It did come out all right," he said. "Not but what it took a blamed long time to it. I've distrusted you all these years, and the Lord knows how much longer I'd have kept on at it if you'd got hold of a gun that would shoot. You've turned out dependable in spite of me, it looks like. If you've got a mind to take this homestead for yourself, I've got no right to forbid you. It used to be a sightly place, when it was kept in shape."

"I don't want it," Linus said. "There never was anything to it except that patch of orchard, and the trees is all killed out. I whittled into some of 'em, and they're as dry as a wagon spoke."

"Not any more," his father said. "That was what I started up here to tell you, and then I hear them men. There's been a funny kind of a noise outside that tent ever since the sheep blat let up. It got so loud I couldn't rest, so I went out to see what it was. It was bees. Them old fruit trees has all come into bloom. You didn't waste all the work you put into 'em, after all."

"I wouldn't call it wasted, even if them trees all dried up and fell down," Dee Radford said. "If you hadn't recognized them men and remembered about that old rifle, we'd have lost them sheep sure. It would have been the first herd of sheep I ever lost in my life, and I wouldn't want that on my record."

The breaking up of that drought was not especially beautiful in itself, but it ended the long monotony of dust and dry wind and cold sun, and its contrasting mildness and silence made it seem one of the most beautiful things imaginable. A night rain laid the dust, the sky clouded over, the air was so still that the sheep shearers didn't even bother to anchor their burlap corral panels down, and the sheep, having come through their pasturing season, turned from a care and a burden into a salable asset that strange workmen labored over and strange buyers bid for and strange feed yards were almost embarrassingly gratified to advance wagonloads of hay on.

Dee Radford knelt outside the old herding tent, packing up to leave the sheep he had half killed himself to save from the buzzards. That was an old ceremony for him, and he took it tranquilly. Linus couldn't feel quite so lighthearted about it. He detested sheep, but there seemed something unnatural about working so hard over something that had to be given up afterward, with nothing left to show where his work had gone. There were wages, but they were the same for bad work as for good.

He walked down into the orchard, thinking about that, and saw, in the scrubby tangle of old trees in bloom, something he had worked hard on that had not disappeared afterward, but had lived and developed courage to bring forth its clumps of perfect flowers, pink apricot and apple, green-white plum and white pear and cherry, through all the tangle of dead and broken and mutilated limbs that showed how hard it had been to live at all. That much of his work had not been wasted, since it had helped to bring into life a courage and patience and doggedness in putting forth such delicate beauty against all the hostility of nature and against even the imminence of death.

Linus' father was sitting under one of the trees with his bandage lifted from one eye, and Linus sat down beside him. "I've decided to try this old homestead for a while," he said. "It's—"

He didn't bother to finish.

His father nodded. "I know how you feel," he said. "I know how it feels to have something you've raised turn out better than you expected."

July 29, 1939

Team Bells Woke Me

THE wagon-freighters into Eastern Oregon in 1906 had a night-camp on the Upper John Day River, in a country which, having since turned its population over to the payroll towns on the Coast and all its land to the Federal Farm Loan banks, now has neither freight-camps, freight-haulers, nor freight-users. Economic progress has made it merely another hole in Nature's pants; but it was a paying section in the teaming days. Prosperous and dissatisfied farmers worked every creek-bottom, putting up hay for the freight-teams at $50 a ton, and the freight-camp at dusk in the Spring wool-hauling season, with all the cooking-fires shining through the wagon-spokes like a Chicago jail burning down, made me uneasy the first time I saw it. I was eleven years old, playing hookey from the bucksaw detail at home to help Tamarack Jack Pooler haul wool, and the animation and racket in the freight-camp made me feel that humanity had already jammed the country till it popped at the seams. If they kept on coming at this rate, I thought, they would crowd the open country out of existence, and I didn't want them to.

Unharnessing, Tamarack Jack told me that I needn't worry. The willow flat did sound like payday at a cavalry post, with fires, arguments, whiskers, bedclothes, tinware, stray dogs, sucking colts trying to locate their mothers, and chorded copper team-bells plunking as a late string wheeled in to feed up and spread down; but there were only about thirty outfits in the camp. They covered considerable ground, on account of the sixty wagons and three hundred horses; but they were nothing to compare with the crowds that he had seen there. In the '90s, the place had camped sixty outfits a night regularly. In the Indian outbreaks of the '70s there had been more life on this one road than there was now in the country. Counting Indians, of course. An old Piute buck who hung around the freight-camp to panhandle the left-over scraps had once headed a village of twenty wickiyups. Now he claimed title to four, inhabited by a bunch of cavernous-gutted grown sons who stayed with him because he rustled their victuals for them. They weren't worth killing, and the old buck, who would undoubtedly call on us before the evening was out, knew it, and boarded them anyway.

"Because it makes him feel like he's still a chief," explained Tamarack Jack, spreading out harness, "even if it's only over a set of bums . . I'll tie them horses. Some of 'em fight, and you don't know which ones to keep separated. Tag around and learn things, that's what a boy your age ort to do. You study about Indian fightin' in school, don't you?"

Tamarack Jack was one of the best freighters on the line. He caught his teams straight out of the wild bunch on the range, and broke them to work by dragging them into harness and working them. The blacksnake whip around his neck was merely a badge of office: he never whipped his horses. If their gait needed correcting, he threw rocks at them. Heaving from the saddled near-wheeler, on the go, he could hit as many as three with one rock. He never apologized for taking a drink of whiskey in the presence of a youngster, or volunteered long explanations about how it was only good for elderly men broken by exposure and sorrows. Instead, he always reached his flask back as if offering a swig, and then corked it and put it away, pretending solemnly that it had been refused. All the kids liked him in spite of the interest he affected in their schooling, which came either from politeness or because he had never had any schooling himself.

"This old Siwash can learn you things about Indian fightin' that I'll bet that school-teacher of yourn never heard of," he said. "I'll poke a couple of drinks down him, and you prop your ears and pay attention. You'll learn some history to take home with you. *Klahowyam*, Spencer!"

The old Piute was wrinkled and skinny, with two braids of gray hair end-bound with drugstore twine. He was all faded except at the eyes, which were black as obsidian. The Mother Goose conceit about beggars on horseback couldn't have been among his memory gems; but he was a beggar, and he not only rode a horse, but led two pack-ponies to take his plunder home on. His saddle had been inherited from the United States Army, and he ate a two-handed piece of apple pie with enjoyment until Tamarack Jack winked and stuck up one thumb. Then he dismounted, stowed the pie on a pack, and started the two pack-ponies home with a cut of his quirt. His people, it seemed, were fussy about getting their meals on time. Was there any brandy? For four drinks he was willing to do a scalp-dance with genuine scalps. For a bottle, he would —

"To hell with your scalp-dance," Tamarack Jack told him. "I'll give you two drinks, and then I want you to tell this kid about Indian fightin'. He's studyin' it in school, and it'll help out with his education. There ain't anything historical about watchin' you get drunk and jump around with your clothes off. Come around back of the wagon where everybody can't see us."

Whiskeying an Indian had to be done on the sly, because of the law which, in those days, was respected even when it wasn't obeyed. The old Piute came back, wiping his chin and breathing deep, and sat down. "White man *kultus*," he announced, after a little thought. "Bad! Me kill 'em — shoot 'em, cut 'em, stick 'em —" He ran through a list of other things he had done to them in the days when he had his strength. It was pretty stout stuff. I hadn't imagined that Indian hostilities ever took quite such a personal form. The only Indian stories I had heard were from people the hostiles had failed to catch. Of the Indians, I had seen only a hard-riding, goodnatured set of berry-peddlers who embarrassed townspeople by nursing papooses and settling family rows in the middle of the business district. Here was a new side to the subject. I stopped feeling uneasy about the country's waning wildness. There was such a thing as having a country too damned wild.

I must have looked shaky, for the old buck went back again to his table of premises, which he had laid down as a kind of ethical foundation to excuse his enormities. All white men, he reminded me, were bad. Columbus had been bad, for not staying at home and minding his own business. The freighters were bad. He waved his hand to take in all the men whose large-handedness with cooking measures kept him and his whole gang from starvation, or, worse, from having to go to work. They were all *kultus*, all lowdown sons of leglifters. Murders, mutilations, rapes, tortures and unnatural abuses were too good for them. Shoot 'em. Cut 'em.

And so on. The two drinks were beginning to take hold and talk up. The freighting trade was pretty well mangled by the time Tamarack Jack appeared from behind the wagon, about two-thirds drunk, and explained that he was going to leave us two to entertain each other. "I'll go over and borrow a piece of fresh beef for supper," he said, standing over us with one foot in the fire. Among the wagons, somebody sang "The Dying Ranger" to a fiddle, while a couple of his audience threw rocks at the dogs so they wouldn't howl and spoil it. Tamarack Jack took his foot out of the fire and put one hand on my head benignly. "Spencer'll tell you about this history business," he assured me. "Once he gets started, all hell can't stop him till he's finished. All he tells you is gospel truth. All them freighters got exterminated, just like he's told you."

He had, of course, mistaken Spencer's ill-natured spouting for historical reminiscence. Still, he was merely a few years ahead of time, for, though it wasn't history then, it is now. All the freighting traders did get exterminated, just as the old Piute who lived on their extravagance hoped they would.

II

Tamarack Jack claimed freighting as his profession, but he made most of his money out of his genius for horse-breaking. Of his string of ten horses at the start of a trip, six would be wild, new-shod cayuses that had never before felt iron or leather. At the end of three hundred miles of road, they would be honest, well-broken work-horses, worth from $50 to $80 apiece; and he would sell them and run in another bunch of fence-breakers from the bunch-grass. Three days in a dark barn, and they would step into the collar for him as if they had been doing it for twenty years, without a spark of meanness except to strangers and to one another.

He named them after public characters, probably because it gave a flavor to their habit of fighting on the picket-line. On the trip I went with, Frances E. Willard couldn't be staked with the rest of the *caballada* because she insisted on biting big hunks out of William Jennings Bryan; Laura Jean Libby and Susan B. Anthony got along excellently with the Great Commoner, but they bit each other, and would also slip their halters to chase off after any barefooted stallion that came within wind of them; and Alice Roosevelt and Emilio Aguinaldo had a mortal feud on, which ended with Emilio caving in three of Alice's ribs so that she had to be shot.

The name, it is gratifying to add, didn't perish with her. Tamarack Jack changed his horses a dozen times a year, but he never changed the names at all. His off-pointer, regardless of sex, color or disposition, was always Alice Roosevelt, and all the other monickers stuck as inflexibly. The horses didn't mind, and it saved Tamarack Jack the trouble of inventing and learning a whole set of new names every time he sold his string down.

Freighting and horse-breaking wasn't a usual combination on the road, but there were personal marks by which each freighter could be remembered. Big Simon and Little Simon Madance were father and son who looked alike, ran opposition lines to a little watertrough town in the Lava Beds country, and hated each other with a fury all the deadlier because neither was able to give any reason for it. They could neither stand each other nor let each other alone, and they ended along in 1909 with a challenge race down the old Sherar toll-grade, which Big Simon won by hubbing his firstborn, outfit and all, over a three-hundred-foot pitch to die under his pile of tangled horses. The only thing about it that the other freighters appeared to mind was that it hadn't happened sooner, and that it hadn't killed both of them. Sociability died wherever they were, as it did around Big Foot Larsen, who, loyal to his racial tradition of Scandinavian gloom, had married a squaw and then eaten her during a hard and lonely Winter.

According, that is, to the story they told on him behind his back. It may have been merely their way of accounting for his expression, which was so Strindbergian that even squaw-eating seemed scarcely an excuse. I didn't believe he had eaten her, because he didn't look bright enough to have thought of it; but I was afraid of him anyway. I wasn't afraid of Greene Tucker, though he was even meaner on account of having been an Indian war hero. He had held a stone milk-house full of women and girls against a Shoshone warparty in 1877, and whipped the whole band with a neckyoke and two kettles of boiling water, fighting most of the set-to with a knife-rip across his abdomen.

It crippled him for life, for the rescued women all got sick when he called on them to sew it up, and he had to do it himself. Unused to needlework, he sewed too deep. The muscles drew up, and the only reward his heroism got him was a lifelong stoop, like a man looking for a four-leaf clover, and a lifelong grudge against creation for not doing something about it.

His sour temper would have made him a continental pest, if it hadn't been for the rip-staving set of tunes he could whack out of a fiddle. Nothing could have been a more compact study in over-lapping humors than old Greene Tucker bowing it up on a wagon-tongue, his eyes set in a gall-shot glare as if he hoped his thrums and double-stops would poison everything they struck, while the tune itself — usually a slippery old hoe-down like "Leather Breeches" or "Hell Among the Yearlings" — cackled to his face that he was a liar, and that he didn't hope anything of the kind.

It would have been easy to have played badly if he had sincerely wanted people to feel badly; and it would have been impossible to heave himself into a mere piece of dance-music if his arteries had really contained as much bile as he pretended. I never heard him play any tune coldly or indifferently. Probably he never realized that his perkiness leaked out on him through his fiddling; probably he didn't even know that there was any perkiness in him at all. Good humor, it seemed, didn't always lie at the surface of the mind, nor bitterness always among the profundities; and either, if it set deep enough, could be involuntary and incurable.

Frank Chambeau was the only example, in the entire Eastern Oregon freighting country, of a man who babied his horses. Not merely to work them humanely and see that they got enough to eat. Everybody did that, for the same reason that a carpenter takes care of his tools. Chambeau hugged and kissed his horses, carried pones of bread to deal out to them every two miles, rubbed them down with expensive hair-tonic, and bought silver harness-studs, conchas, spreaderrings, hame-knobs, and even a full set of silver-alloy team bells with housings of bright orange goatskin.

An ordinary team, strung with such a Siwash get-up would have run away, out of self-consciousness. Chambeau's horses had no run in them. They were overfed, grizzle-headed old straw-bellies that couldn't be left standing unwatched for ten minutes for fear they would all go to sleep and fall down. Resting them at the foot of a grade, he would distribute bread and endearments all round, and then address the string of dozing, limp-lipped old plugs with a personal appeal.

"Now, babies," he would explain, "here's this hill, and here's papa dependin' on you to pull it for him. You're goin' to do that for papa, ain't you?"

They did it for him, even over humps that other outfits were double-teaming to get over. He claimed it was because they appreciated sentiment and hand-holding, which I didn't believe then or thereafter. Yet he must have had some tap on them, or why should they have held his wagons dead still on the steep Shaniko grade for eleven hours while he lay drunk in the road with his head a foot from the wheel? No other horses would have done that, petting or not.

Windy Missou was the biggest-built man on the line — six feet seven, three hundred pounds with his shoes off and his pockets empty, and strong enough to dehorn a bull barehanded. He was also the biggest coward. He slept in his wagon because he was afraid of snakes on the ground, and he kept a lantern burning all night because he was afraid of the dark. He ended by killing a young feed-yard hay-peddler who had tried to shut him into an unlighted granary for a joke, and never came back from the penitentiary. Big John Payne had served in the Philippines, and carried a collection of dark, gristly objects which he claimed were dried ears of the gu-gus whom he had personally dispatched for Civilization and Liberty.

Uncle Ike Bewley had been a lieutenant in the Civil War, had buried seven wives — nearly all of them white — and he chafed with uneasiness for fear his manly fire might cool before he could land an eighth. There was some excuse for feeling nervous, for he was seventy-four years old, and he had proposed to every girl in the country so often that they had all stopped being polite to him. His persistence was a regional joke; and yet there was a lot more to him than mere senile obsession. Uncle Ike had seen enough of death, between his wives and the Civil War, to know it well. Knowing it would land on him, he wasn't in the least afraid of it; only of life, for fear he wouldn't manage to spend the little he had left of it as he wanted to.

Those were freight-camp men. Not all of them, nor a just impression of any as I saw them in the clearing around Greene Tucker's fiddling-stand. They had unloaded a keg of whiskey from a saloon shipment, and, with a gimlet to tap it and a straw to imbibe it through, had given the place a tone of shading from camp-meeting exuberance to camp-meeting prayerfulness. The keg helped the effect. It had become, because of the kneeling position in which they had to tackle it, a kind of sacramental altar, theological, compelling, and awful. The liquor was low. To reach it, each man in turn knelt, pressed his forehead against the keg-staves in a long, breathless fervor, and pulled loose with a soul-riven gulp that would not have disgraced any experience-meeting in the land.

Minors, however, were not welcome. Tamarack Jack wove over and ordered me back to our wagon. I embarrassed the men, he explained. They couldn't cut loose with me around, for fear it would be a bad influence. I had better go back to the old Indian, who, besides being educational, needed to be watched so he wouldn't prowl around and steal loose property.

"Go on back, now" said Tamarack Jack firmly. "Cook yourself a feed, and put enough in the pot so the old Siwash'll have something to take home with him, and give him what's left of the small bottle. It's in Alice Roosevelt's nosebag on the trail wagon. Give him that, and he'll tell you some things that'll help with your schoolin'. You learn about Indian fightin' in school, don't you?"

I went back, feeling misused. Nowadays, I would treat a ten-year-old kid about the same way he treated me; but I would still deny that there was much sense in doing it. The freighters were, it was true, a little off-color in their merriment, and they played one game with a row of ten-cent pieces laid out on a wagon-tongue that was certainly no treasure to describe to the home-folks.

But the Indian wars had run through stuff that made even the freighters' little sub-surcingle competitions seem as harmless as antey-over. Why bar me from one and ram my nose in the other? I hoped the old Indian would have stolen himself a load and left with it.

He hadn't. He had found the small bottle, and had been bitten through the hand fooling around the horse-line in the dark. But he had no notion of quitting me with his homicide record half-told. With the tooth-marks red on his skin and whiskey dripping from his breath, he told me about Indian wars, past and to come, in a long, blurred monotony of murders and manglings that ended when the first team bells jingled for the road at daylight.

III

The one season of the year when freighting was pleasant, with the happy, busy importance of peace-time maneuvers at an Army headquarters or protracted meeting in a cracker settlement, was the Spring rush of wool-hauling. Then, with the roads springy and dustless, new grass and water, and a sure cargo both ways for every rig that could carry one, the wagons packed the road with a close, double-columned line, flowing between horizons like a river. The team bells shook out their first clatter at daylight, tolling dry goods, groceries, fence-posts, spring millinery, and Cyrus Noble's Favorite Prescription from railhead to the

Shoshone deserts, with cow-town kids from the home bucksaw to tag along and see where they landed. The freighters welcomed company, or pretended to; and the bells, ringing so far out on the road that one could only locate mid-column by the far drift of vapor the teams shed into the sky, were too much to hold out against.

They were not the common bellyband castanets that one sees in pictures of sleighing scenes. Freight teams were too tony for such fifteen-cent-store tinware. They carried real music-making bells, with the same accuracy of tuning and much the same range as the chimes of a modern orchestra. Mostly, they were cast in thin bronze, and set five bells in a strap which fitted over the hames to ring in time with the horse's shoulders. Each set of five struck one major chord, as C, E, G, C, E. To protect them from the weather, and to prevent them from sounding harsh or tinny, they were muffled in a housing of goat's wool. It made them ring sweet and delicate and woody, like water dripping in a barrel spring.

All the freighters belled their teams, but no two of them ever gave the same reason for doing it. Tamarack Jack explained that the tone and rhythm enabled him to keep track of the team's action with his eyes shut. No horse, he pointed out, could drag back or fall out of step without registering the irregularity on the bells, and also identifying himself, so that Tamarack Jack, by noticing which chord was acting queer, could tell where to administer correction with his rock. Frank Chambeau, who never threw rocks at his horses, claimed the bells helped the teams gait themselves together; somebody else thought they were there to keep the driver from going to sleep, and somebody else that they were a kind of warning signal to notify stations ahead that a freight outfit was coming, so the girls would have time to find their hairpins and get downstairs before it pulled in.

That jibed with an old cow-town story about a freight-horse stampede in the night, which, old-timers related, had been headed by a quick-thinking citizen who wrapped a red bandanna around a lantern and tittered girlishly until the horses, thinking they were up against a red-light house, stopped meekly to wait for the boss to come out and pass around the nose-bags. But both story and explanation seemed a little too pointed to be true. The team bells were part of freighting because they sounded pretty and gave style and ceremony to the business.

To the whole country, for that matter. There was never a wool-hauling column that all the towns didn't turn out for, yelling at the lead-wagons to ask where their freighter was, and mobbing his wagon when it wheeled out of line to weigh in and unload. Between towns, lying on the trailwagon out of range of Tamarack Jack's conversation, watching the sky turn round the earth like a flywheel around a slipping driveshaft, I would hear the smooth, even-toned beat of the team bells break, cast off, and swing into a sharp-stepped drumtime, which meant that the horses had sighted country people and were putting on dog to give them an eye-full.

If it was a ranch, Tamarack Jack would put on dog too, stiffening to set straight and light in the saddle, left hand to hat, right hand on the brake-rope as if he expected his whole outfit to light off at a run any minute. The small kids would be lined along the fence by the watering-trough, the big girls by the front-gate, the women bareheaded by the house, shading their eyes and flapping their aprons in welcome, not merely to new dress-patterns and canned goods and phonograph records, but to the whole United States after a Winter of homesick separation. It was a dry line into that Duck Valley section, and there were times when the homestead watering-troughs looked mighty tempting; but not one of the horses ever spoiled the dignity of the occasion by trying to snatch a drink. They arched their necks and hoofed high and went thirsty to give those people the ceremonious parade their enthusiasm deserved.

They showed off the same way in front of the Indian camps,

which Tamarack Jack never straightened up for except when some elderly buck made the recognition-sign of slapping himself open-handed across the mouth. Even then his response was only formally polite. The Indians came out to look at us, exactly as the farm women did; but the farm women came because seeing us meant something. To the Indians, we meant merely another object to gawk at, or, if it was a big day, to cheat in a horse-trade.

We meant that much to the other wild life of the country. Little herds of antelope skirmished along the skyline to look us over, pitching back their heads to get our wind, and snapping their tails nervously, all cocked to run if we acted too interested. Coyotes hung out of range, sociable, but cautious, hoping we would lose something they could eat; and bald eagles dawdled along overhead watching for the jackrabbits that our team bells scared up out of the brush. Wild horseherds drifted along the line sometimes, closing in after dark when the stallion could try his sales-talk on the picketed mares without getting himself shot. If the camp was small, the ground clear, and the mares respon-sive, he was likely to push his courtship along by stampeding his herd across the picket-line to destroy the peg-ropes. The weight of such a charge would destroy them, all right, and usually it destroyed the mares along with them.

The freighters didn't bother much about wild-horse scares. In open country they always corralled wagons; but none of them ever lost anywhere near as many horses to the wild herd as they got back from it. The wild horses, indeed, were one of the biggest assets the country had. Without them, the Indians, tied to their camps, would have become objects of charity fifty years earlier than they did; a cowboy could no more have afforded to own a saddle-horse than an airplane; horse-breakers like Tamarack Jack — and there were plenty of them — would have been stuck with a talent as unprofitable as writing poetry. Homesteaders would have been hurt even worse. In their lives, the wild herd was as essential as the sago palm to the South Sea Islanders. Broomtail horses were their hog-feed, chicken-feed, dog-rations, garden-compost; the hair made riatas, hackamores and mattress-stuffing; the hides were chair-bottoms, floor-coverings, water-buckets, belt-lacing, and cold-weather vests. Babies in the High Desert were born on horsehair, raised on horse-milk, blooded on horseback, and pretty regularly, hanged from the neck of one horse in a noose braided from the hide of another.

There were beautiful nags in the wild bunch. The good ones, of course, were the hardest to run down, which accounts for the general notion that all wild horses were hammerheaded scrubs. Only the riffraff got caught. Runts and runners, they are all gone now, fenced out by the wheat-farmers and either starved or else sold in bunches to fertilizer-factories at $3 a head. The country can't be the same without them, and it doesn't deserve to be.

It can't be the same without the old side-hill Indian burying-grounds, either. Even in the freighting days, they were going to pieces fast; but the spots where the dirt shoveled easiest all had them. They were dug shallow and skimpy, probably because the Indians enjoyed manufacturing corpses better than getting rid of them; and the old skeletons, washed out of the earth and wind-polished among the old burial trinkets — grinding-stones and fleshing-knives for the women, bowstaves and horse-furniture for the men, and little toy saddles, papoose-carriers and grass-stuffed buckskin dolls for the children, with big cylindrical stone beads for everybody — had so little of the ordinary graveyard unearthliness that we youngsters would have looted and wrecked them ourselves, merely for curiosity, if the freighters hadn't prevented.

Robbing graves, they explained, was bad luck, and we could either let them alone or else get off and walk. If it had been a fenced-in plot with white posts and epitaphs, money couldn't have tempted us to disturb even the rusty wire of an old wreath. We weren't callous about dead people. Only, they had to keep their skeletons out of sight and show certain conventional trimmings, or we simply couldn't tie them up with the fearful and spooky objects which, instinctively, we believed that death turned people into.

IV

The years 1905-1907 brought the West its heaviest spell of rainfall in recorded history. Draws and gullies flooded, cattle mired on the range, clothes mildewed, and crops, planted mostly by newcomers in ignorance and with a prayer for the deserving, boomed and bore enormously. Momentarily, the anomaly was a nice little stroke of luck. Its eventual effect took longer to work out, and played hell; for the crop-raisers, exultant over their big harvests, refused to listen to old settlers' forecasts for future precipitation, and sat right down to write back East to folks about the bonanza in sagebrush farming.

The folks, also disregarding warnings, rolled in. Mostly, they didn't stay very long; but there were enough of them to mill heavy while they lasted; and they killed the freighting business colder than a wedge before they left. Crops were poor from the start; but they overlooked that, and concentrated their uproar on the right of a settled farming section to decent communications; and their combined thunderings brought in the branch railroads.

They brought plenty of them. The Shaniko branch, the Condon branch, the Heppner branch, two Deschutes branches, a stub-line East to Prineville, and a narrow-gauge north from the Humboldt River Basin, all piled in as if answering a riot-call; and the freighters jacked up their wagons, rolled the big wheels down to soak in the creek, turned their teams out to the wild bunch, and went out dismally to hunt for jobs.

Curiously, the improved communications didn't help the rainfall of the country at all. The weather turned dry, and, as had been its off-and-on habit for several thousand years, it stayed dry with the completest indifference to all the preparations that had been made to have it wet. The High Desert turned into a nest of hide-outs and cattle-thieves, the Wagontire and Owyhee sections into a God-forsaken, do-as-you-please waste. Neither faith, complaints, petitions, nor farmers' protest-meetings helped a particle. The railroads were there, and there was nothing to use them for. A late-started line, rushing steel east across the Cascades from the Rogue River Valley, got scared to a standstill after it had built about twenty miles. Ten years after the rush an auditor for one of the Deschutes lines told me that his company was going behind $15,000 a mile annually, and wishing that it had never been born.

The clamorers had all gone by that time. Their miracle hadn't happened; and their scheme of making it rain on their fields by the Indian system of informing God that it ought to, had worked as badly for them as their doctrine had for the Shoshones, the Bannocks, and the Northern Piutes of 1877, in the outbreak about which old Piute Spencer told me his stomach-turning stories in the freight-camp on the John Day River.

It had been a medicine-war, he told me. A lot of tribes went into it that year — the Sioux, the Utes, the Comanches — everybody. On account of an idea which their theologians had swiped from the white man's ghost book that a man holds up in front of you when they intend to put you in jail. The idea — he had fallen for it along with the rest of them — was that a man could get killed and then come back to life again.

None of the medicine-men claimed credit for inventing such a notion. They admitted that a white man appeared to have done it first, but they argued that, if a white man could do that much, an Indian could do more and better. All that was needed, they promised, was faith. With that, they could lick the whites, restore to life all the warriors who got killed doing it, and bring back all the buffalo herds that had been slaughtered and crowded out by the cattle. Transubstantiation figured in the campaign, for they were ordered to slaughter all the cattle they could, so that the buffalo would have some kind of integument to come back to.

For six months, old Spencer bragged, he had lived on nothing but the tongues of slaughtered cows, leaving the rest for the buffalo to inhabit. It was plenty of fun, but it hadn't worked out. The buffalo hadn't showed up. None of the casualties had been restored to health. A lot of them, trying to swim the Columbia ahead of an infantry column, had run into a gatling-gun detail on a steamboat and got cut all to flinders. When the enthusiasm started, he was chief of a big village. Now it kept him humping to stay chief of anything.

He went over a list for me of the men of his village who had got killed and crippled on false expectations, but he didn't mention, except to brag drunkenly, how many white people his witch-doctor plagiarism had got tortured and outraged and murdered.

It was the same with the freighters, driven out of their livelihood by the settlement-rush and railroad-splurge that ended in 1910. The financiers and farmers felt sorry for themselves, but none of them ever mentioned the freighters except to brag about having got the country rid of them. Things hadn't panned out, it was true; but, if they had done nothing else, they had brought modern communications to the sagebrush, and that was something.

It was a whole lot. Merely to have taken away the team bells at morning ought to be enough to get them all immortality. I hope it will.

April, 1931

Old Man Isbell's Wife

THE cow-town started as an overnight station on the old Military Road through Eastern Oregon into Idaho. The freighters wanted a place to unhitch and get the taste of sagebrush out of their mouths. They were willing to pay for it, and one was built for them by the people who like, better than anything else, money that has been worked hard for—not to work hard for it themselves, but to take it from men who do.

The cow-town itself was a kind of accident. When they built it, they had no idea beyond fixing up a place where the freighters could buy what they wanted. They fixed it up with houses—houses to eat in, houses to get drunk in, houses to sleep in, or stay awake in, houses to stable horses in; and, as an afterthought, houses for themselves to live in while they took the freighters' and cattlemen's money. And money came—not fast, but so steadily that it got monotonous. There were no surprises, no starvation years, no fabulous winnings or profits; simply, one year with another, enough to live on and something over. They got out of the habit of thinking the place was an overnight station to make money in. They began, instead, to look at it as a place to live in. That, in Eastern Oregon, meant a change of status, a step up. The risk of the place being abandoned was over; there, straddling the long road between Fort Dalles on the Columbia and Fort Boise on the Snake River, was a town.

The new status had no effect upon its appearance. Ugly and little it had begun, and ugly and little it stayed. The buildings were ramshackle and old, and with the paint peeled off; and, including the stack of junk behind the blacksmith shop, the whole thing covered an area of ten blocks. Two acres of town, in the middle of a cattle range of ten thousand square miles. Yet in those ten blocks a man could live his entire lifetime, lacking nothing, and perhaps not even missing anything. Food, warmth, liquor, work, and women; love, avarice, fear, envy, anger, and of a special kind, belonging to no other kind of life, joy.

Over the ten thousand miles of range, whole cycles of humanity—flint Indians, horse Indians, California Spaniards, emigrants, cattlemen—had passed, and each had marked it without altering its shape or color. The cow-town itself was one mark, and not the biggest, either; but that was a comparison which none of the townspeople ever made. They were too much used to it, and they had other things to think about. What interested them was their ten blocks of town, and the people who lived in it.

All country people keep track of each other's business—as a usual thing, because they haven't anything else to think about. But the cow-town people did it, not in idleness, but from actual and fundamental passion. They preferred it to anything else in the world. It was not in the least that they were fond of one another—though, of course, some of them were. That had nothing to do with their preference. It was merely that what their town did was life—clear, interesting, recognizable; and nothing else was. They stuck to what was familiar. It must be remembered that these people were not chance-takers. They were more like the peddlers who follow an army, not fighting themselves, but living on the men who do. The freighters and cattlemen, and the men from the range, were a different race; the range itself was a strange element; and they were too small to have much curiosity about either. The women were the smallest. It was they who backed the movement to ship Old Man Isbell out of town.

II

Old Man Isbell lived in the cow-town because there was no other place he could live. He had ridden the range, at one job or another, for more than fifty years, and the town would have been strange and foreign to him, even if it had made him welcome. It did not. For one thing, he was not a townsman, but a member of the race which they preyed on. For another, he was eighty-five years old, slack-witted, vacant-minded, doddering, dirty, and a bore. It took an hour to get the commonest question through his head, and another hour for him to think up an answer to it. He never tied his shoes, and he had to shuffle his feet as he walked, to keep them from falling off. Nor did he ever button his trousers, which fact was cited by the women as indicating complete moral decay. He ought to be sent away, they said, to some institution where such cases were decently taken care of.

The clerk in the general store agreed with them, and perhaps he, at least, had a right to. It was his job, every day, to sell Old Man Isbell a bill of groceries, and the old man could never remember what it was he wanted. Sometimes it took hours, and while he was there ladies couldn't come in the store, on account of his unbuttoned trousers and his pipe.

His pipe was another just ground for complaint. It was as black as tar and as soggy as a toadstool, with a smell like carrion and a rattle like a horse being choked to death. To get it lit took him hours, because his hand shook so he couldn't hold a match against the bowl. It was his palsy, no doubt, that was to blame for his unbuttoned trousers, his dangling shoestrings, and the gobs of food smeared on his clothes and through his whiskers. But that was not conclusive evidence that he was feeble-minded. Even a sane man would have trouble tying a bow-knot or hitting a buttonhole if his hands insisted on jumping two inches off the target at every heart-beat. The ladies added it to their evidence, but it should not have been allowed to count. Old Man Isbell's chief abnormality was of longer standing. He was simply, and before anything else, a natural-born bore.

The dullness of his speech was a gift of God. He had lived his eighty-five years through the most splendidly colored history that one man could ever have lived through in the world — the Civil War, the Indian campaigns in the West, the mining days, the cattle-kings, the long-line freighters, the road-agents, the stockmen's wars — the changing, with a swiftness and decision unknown to history before, of a country and its people; yes, and of a nation. Not as a spectator, either. He lived in the middle of every bit of it, and had a hand in every phase. But, for all the interest it gave to his conversation, he could just as well have spent his life at home working buttonholes.

"I remember Lincoln," he would say. "I drove him on an electioneerin' trip, back in Illinoy. Him and Stephen A. Douglas. I drove their carriage."

One would sit up and think, "Well! The old gabe does know something good, after all!" Expecting, of course, that he was about to tell some incident of the Lincoln-Douglas debates — something, maybe, that everybody else had missed. But that was all. So far as he knew, there hadn't been any incidents. They electioneered. He drove their carriage. They rode in it. That was all that had impressed him.

Or he would remember when there had been no Military Road, and no cow-town, nor even any cattle; only, instead, great herds of deer pasturing in grass belly-deep to a horse. A herd of over a hundred big mule-deer trotting close enough for a man to hang a rope on, right where the town was. But when you tried to work him for something beside the bare fact that they had been there you struck bottom. They had been there. Hundreds of them. He had seen them, that close. That ended the story. I asked him, once, if he remembered anything about Boone Helm, an early-day outlaw and allround mean egg. He considered, sucked his pipe through a critical spell of croup, and finally said, "They used to be a road-agent by that name. He cut a feller's ears off."

It was not a prelude, but a statement of what he remembered. Some old men remember more than what actually happened; some remember things that never happened at all. Old Man Isbell remembered the exact thing, and, that being done, he stopped. He ought to have been writing military dispatches. Or had he? It never came into his head to tone up or temper down the exact and religious truth, and amplifying what he had seen simply wasn't in him.

To events that went on in town he never appeared to pay the smallest attention. Indeed, he paid none to the people there, either, and, though they laid that to the condition of his wits, it irritated them. Yet it was no more than an old range-man's indifference to things which he considers immaterial. He was sharp enough when anything was going on that interested him — cattle-branding in the corrals below town, or the state of the water on the range. South of town was a long slope, with a big spring almost at the top, ringed with green grass except when the spring went dry. Then the grass turned brown. The old man never failed to notice that. He would stop people in the street and point it out.

They laughed at him for it, behind his back. What did it matter to him whether the cattle had a dry year or not? He had an Indian War pension to live on, and he would get it whether the cattle throve or died to the last hoof. But, of course, he remembered what cattle looked like when they died of thirst, and swelled and popped open in the unmerciful heat, their burnt tongues lolling in the dust. It excited him to think of it, and he made a nuisance of himself about it. Sometimes he would stop strangers to tell it to them, which gave the town a bad name. Beside, his critics added he smelled bad. The place for him, they agreed, was in some nice home where he could be waited on decently. He needed looking after.

In that they were right. He did need looking after. The trouble was that their plan involved sending him away from the sagebrush country, and that would have been the same thing as knocking him in the head with an ax. He was an old sagebrusher. To take him out of sight of his country — the yellow-flowered, silver-green sage, the black-foliaged greasewood, blossoming full of strong honey; the strong-scented, purple-berried junipers, and the wild cherry shrub, with its sticky, bitterish-honeyed flowers and dark sour fruit; the pale red-edged ridges, and the rock-breaks, blazing scarlet and orange and dead-black — to lose them would have killed him. By these things, an old sagebrusher lives. Out of reach of them, silly as it sounds to say so, he will die. I've seen them do it.

Old Man Isbell, incapable and slack-witted, helpless with age, and, so far as anybody could tell, without any suspicion of what the townspeople were thinking about him or that they were making designs against his life, did the one thing that could save him. He had nobody to take care of him. It was to see him taken care of that they wanted to send him away; and, surely without knowing it, he stumbled on the way to head them off. He got married.

The wedding threw the town into a perfect panic of delighted horror. This was one of the things that made life a fine thing to live. Other people, other communities, had diversions which the cow-town did without; this made up for them. The justice of the peace, having performed the ceremony, put out for home on a gallop to tell his wife the news. Hearing it, she came out with her hair down, and canvassed the houses on both sides of the street, knocking at every door, and yelling, without waiting for anybody to open — "Old Man Isbell's got married! You'll never guess who to!"

271

III

The bride alone would have made a rich story. She was about twenty-eight years old — Old Man Isbell being, as I've mentioned, eighty-five — and the rest of her was even more incongruous than her youth. She weighed close to three hundred pounds, being almost as broad as she was tall, and she had to shave her face regularly to keep down a coarse black beard, which showed in the wrinkles of fat where a razor could not reach.

As Old Man Isbell was the town nuisance, she was the town joke. Even in that scantily-womaned place, where only the dullest girls lived after they were big enough to look out for themselves, she had never had a suitor. The men were not too particular, but nobody dared pay court to her, for fear of getting laughed at. She was so fat that to walk downtown for Old Man Isbell's order of groceries took her almost an hour. It made one tired to watch her. Even the Indian squaws, riding through town, their matronly bellies overhanging the horns of their saddles, drew rein to admire Old Man Isbell's bride for an adiposity which laid theirs completely in the shade. They were fat, all right, but good heavens! They cackled and clucked to each other, pointing.

Housewives ran to peep through the curtains at the twenty-eight-year-old girl who had been hard up enough to marry an old, dirty, feeble-minded man of eighty-five. Store loafers perked up and passed remarks on her and on the match. But in spite of them all, in spite of the tittering, and the cruelty and the embarrassment, and her own exertion, she carried home the groceries every day. She cooked and cleaned house, too; and kept it clean; and one of the first things she bought after her marriage was a clothesline. It was full every day, and the clothes on it were clean. So were Old Man Isbell's. He sat on his front porch, wobbling matches over his black gaggling pipe, without a thing in the world to bother his mind except his pipe and the spring on the slope south of town. His trousers were fully buttoned, his shoes tied, and his beard and clothing washed, brushed and straightened, without a speck upon them to show what he had eaten last, or when.

Town joke or not, the fat woman was taking care of him. She was being a housewife, attending to the duties of her station exactly as the other married women in town attended to theirs, and that was something they had not expected. There wasn't any fun for them in that. They wanted her to remain a joke; and they couldn't joke about her housework without belittling their own. They took it out on her by letting her alone. There was no woman in town for Old Man Isbell's wife to talk to, except my mother, who, being the school-teacher's wife, didn't quite belong to the townspeople, and would probably have repudiated their conventions if she had. Across the back-fence she got all of the fat woman's story — not all of it, either, but all its heroine was willing to volunteer.

The fat woman had come to the country with her father, who took up a homestead on Tub Springs Ridge. But he got himself in jail for vealing somebody else's calf, and she moved into town to live till he served out his time. For a while she lived by selling off the farm machinery he had left. But it didn't take very long to live that up — "not that I eat so much," she hastened to add, "I really don't eat as much as . . . as ordinary folks do . . ."— and when that was gone she was broke. That was what induced her to listen, she said, to Old Man Isbell, when he first began to talk about getting married. She was desperate. It seemed the only resort, and yet it was so unheard of that she hesitated.

Finally, she borrowed a lift from a stage-driver, and went to the county jail to ask advice from her father. He knew the old man. It would be all right, he said, for her to marry him. But not unless she realized what kind of job she was taking on, and was game to live up to it. She mustn't bull into it and then try to back out. The old man would have to be tended exactly like a small infant — the work would be just as hard, and just as necessary —

and, in addition, he was uglier, meaner and dirtier. If she wanted to undertake the contract, all right; but she must either stick to it or let it entirely alone. When Old Man Isbell died, she would get what money he had saved up, and his Indian War pension. Enough to keep her, probably, for life. But it was up to her to see that she earned it.

"He made me promise I would," she told my mother, "and the Lord knows I have. It's just exactly like pa said, too. He's just like a little baby. To see him set and stare at that spring for hours on end, you wouldn't believe how contrary and mean he can be around the house. All the time. He'll take a notion he wants something, and then forget the name of it and get mad because I don't guess it right. I have to pick up things and offer 'em to him, one at a time, till I manage to hit the one he's set his mind on. And him gettin' madder every time I pick up the wrong thing. Just like a baby. And his clothes—they're the same, too." She sighed into her series of stubby chins. "It keeps me goin' every minute," she said. "It's mighty hard work."

"You do keep him clean, though," my mother said. "He was so dirty and forlorn. Everybody's talking about how clean you keep him now."

"They talk about how I married him to get his pension," the fat woman said. "How I'm just hangin' around waitin' for him to die. I know!"

"That's only some of them," my mother said. "They don't know anything about it. You work right along, and don't pay any attention to them."

"None of the ladies ever come to call on me," said the fat woman.

"I shouldn't think you'd want them to," my mother suggested. "You must be so busy, you wouldn't have time to bother with visitors. They probably think you'd sooner not be disturbed at your work."

"I do want 'em to, anyway," said the fat woman. "And they call on all the other married ladies, whether they're overworked or not. They call on Mis' Melendy, across the way, and she's got teethin' twins."

"Well, I wouldn't care whether they came to see me or not," said my mother.

"I do, though," the fat woman insisted. "I've got a house, and a husband, just the same as they have. I do my housework just the same, too. I'd like to show 'em all the work I do, and what a care it is to keep things clean, and how clean I keep 'em. If they'd come, they'd see."

My mother assented. There was no earthly chance that any of them would come, and she knew it. But the fat woman didn't know it, and it was the one thing in the world that she had her head set on. Everything else that women take pride in and nourish conceit upon she had given up; and for that very renouncement she stuck all the more fiercely to the idea of being visited by the neighbor ladies — of being received as an established housewife, like the rest of them. There might not be any sense in the notion, but she wanted it. No matter how they came, or why, she wanted them. Even if they came prying for things to discredit her with, to trot around and gabble about, she wanted them anyway. When other women got married the neighbor ladies came to call. Now she was married, and they didn't.

The worst of it was, there was no way of breaking it to her that they weren't going to. My mother made several tries at letting her down easy, but got nowhere. She wanted it too much to give it up. Some days she would come to the fence elated and hopeful, because one of the ladies had nodded to her; sometimes she would be depressed and glum.

"I know what's keeping 'em away," she told my mother. "It's him!"

She yanked a fat arm in the direction of her husband, sitting in the sun with his mouth hanging open.

"Oh, no!" my mother protested. "Why—"

"Yes, it is!" the fat woman insisted. "And I don't blame 'em, either! Who wants to come visitin', when you've got to climb around an object like that to get into the parlor? I don't blame 'em for stayin' away. I would, my own self."

"But you've got to take care of him," my mother reminded her.

"Yes. I've got to. I promised pa I wouldn't back out on that, and I won't. But, as long as I've got him around, I won't have any visitors to entertain. I might as well quit expectin' any."

She sighed, and my mother tried to console her, knowing how deep her idiotic yearning was, and how impossible it was to gratify it. She had tried to persuade the neighbor ladies to call. There was no use wasting any more time on them. Yet, to come out bluntly with the fact that they had all refused would be silly and cruel. My mother was incapable of that. Concealing it, she did her best with promises and predictions, taking care to be vague, while Old Man Isbell dozed, or poked matches at his choking black pipe without any thought of human vanity or hope or disappointment, or anything but the Winter stand of grass on the range. Nobody could believe, from his looks, that he could have asked the fat woman to marry him. It was much more likely that she had hazed the notion into him. Some day, I thought, we might find out, when he could forget the range long enough.

But we never did. He died before the Winter grass got ripe enough for the cattle to sample.

IV

It was on a morning in October that my mother was awakened, about daylight, by yelling and crying from the Isbell's house. She got up and looked across, and saw, through their window, a lamp still burning, though it was already light enough to see. As she looked, the lamp went out — not from a draft, but because it had run dry. That meant that something was up which was keeping them too busy to tend to it. My mother dressed, and hurried over.

Old Man Isbell was dying. The fat woman had been up watching him all night. She sat beside the bed, while he plunged and pitched his thin hairy arms and yelled. Across her knees lay an old, heavy Sharp's plainsman's rifle.

"Watch 'em, watch 'em!" yelled Old Man Isbell. "They cut sagebrush, and push it along in front of 'em to fool you while they sneak up! If you see a bush move, shoot hell out of it! Shoot, damn it!"

The fat woman lugged the immense rifle to her shoulder and snapped the hammer. "Bang!" she yelled.

"That's you!" approved the old man, lying down again. "That's the checker! You nailed him that time, the houndish dastard! You got to watch 'em, I tell ye."

"He thinks he's standin' off Indians," the fat woman explained. "He's young again, and he thinks he's layin' out on the range with the hostiles sneakin' in on him. I've had to — All right, I'm watchin' close," she told him. "Bang!"

My mother got her something to eat, and built a fire, so that when the neighbor ladies came to help they could have a warm room to sit in. Their resolution to stay away held good only in life. When anybody was dying, social embargoes collapsed. Beside, a death was something they couldn't afford to miss. They came; all the women whom the fat woman had set her heart on being friends with; and nobody thought to remark that, instead of being responsible for their staying away, it was Old Man Isbell who had the credit of bringing them there, after all.

But the fat woman was past bothering about whether they came or stayed away. Even their remarks about the cleanness of her house went over her unnoticed. She had livelier concerns to think about. The old man was driving stage. He was going down the Clarno Grade, and a brake-rod had broken. The stage was running wild, down a twenty percent grade full of hairpin switchbacks. He was flogging his horses to keep them out from under the wheels. He yelled and swore and pitched and floundered in the bedclothes, screaming to his wife that she must climb back and try to drag the hind wheels by poking a bar between the spokes.

"And hurry, damn it!" he yelled. "Drag 'er, before that off pointer goes down!"

The neighbor women gaped and stared. This was something they had never heard of. They didn't even understand what kind of emergency the old man was yelling about. But the fat woman paid no attention to them, and did not hesitate. She climbed along the edge of the bed, reached a broom from the corner, and, poking the handle down as if into a wheel, she set back hard. Her mouth was compressed and firm, and she breathed hard with excitement. She appeared to be taking the game almost as seriously as the old man did, crying back to him that she was holding the wheel, as if it meant the saving of both their lives, though hers was in no danger, and his was burning out like a haystack flaming in a gale.

The women brought food and put it into her mouth as if she was something dangerous. They weren't used to games like this, except in children and dying men. Being neither, the fat woman had no business playing it; and they poked buttered bread into her mouth sharply, frowning as if to show her that they saw through her nonsense, and considered it uncalled for. Neither their buttered bread nor their disapproval made any impression on her. The old man was yelling that she must hold the wheel, and she, with her chins trembling with fatigue and sleeplessness, cried back that she had it where it couldn't get away.

In the afternoon he had another one going. He was in a range-camp at night, and there was a herd of wild mustangs all around his fire, trying to stampede his pack-horses. The fat woman pretended to throw rocks to scare them off.

"There's the stud!" he mumbled. "Where in hell is that gun of mine? Oh, God, if it wasn't for bringin' down them damned Siwashes, wouldn't I salivate that stud? Don't shoot! Don't you know them Injuns'll be all over us if they hear a shot? Hit him with a rock! Watch that bunch over yon! Look how their eyes shine, damn their souls! Throw! Do you want to lose all our horses, and be left out in Injun country afoot?"

All day, and till after dark, the neighbor women watching her, she threw when he ordered; and when, at dark, he switched to heading a stampede of cattle, she charged with him to turn them, swinging an imaginary rope with her fat arm, yelling and ki-yi-ing as he directed, and jouncing the bed till the whole house rocked.

About midnight he had burned his brain down to the last nub, and there the fat woman was no longer needed. He lifted himself clear of the bed, and said, "Well, hello, you damned old worthless tick-bit razor-back, you! How the hell did you get out to this country?" He sounded pleased and friendly. It had never occurred to the townspeople that he had ever had any friends. Even as it was, the fact was lost on some of them, for while he spoke he looked straight at one of the visiting women, as if he were addressing her. Somebody tittered, and she left indignantly, banging the door. Everybody jumped, and looked after her. When they looked back, Old Man Isbell was lying on his pillow, dead.

The fat woman did not want to leave him. She was dull and almost out of her head with weariness, but, when they took hold of her, gently, to put her to bed where she could rest, she fought them off.

"He might come to again," she insisted. "You can't tell, he might flash up again. And he might think of something he'd need me for. You leave me be!"

They explained to her that it wasn't possible, and that, even if it was, she must have some sleep. She mustn't kill herself to humor a man out of his mind.

"I want to!" she said. "I want to do that! All them things he's done, and been in, and seen — he never let on a word to me about 'em, and I want to hear 'em! I never knew what an adventured and high-spirited man he was. I like to do what I've been doin'!"

She fought them until they quit trying, and left her. When they came back, she had gone to sleep by herself, beside her dead husband; a fat woman, twenty-eight years old, beside the corpse of a man eighty-five.

V

She came to call on my mother after the funeral. Her mourning habit had come from a mail-order house, and, though there were yards of it, enough, I judged, to make three full-size wagon-sheets, it needed to be let out in one or two places, and she wanted advice.

"How to fix it so I can wear it, right away," she explained. "I could send it back, but I don't want to wait that long. I want to show 'em that my husband was as much loss to me as theirs would be to them. He was, too. He was a sight better man than any of theirs."

She rubbed the tears out of her eyes with the back of her wrist. My mother consoled her, and mentioned that now, at least, everybody knew what care she had taken of him.

"I don't care whether they know it or not," said the fat woman. "None of 'em come to see me, and they can all stay away for good, as far as I'm concerned. The way they acted the one time they did come settled 'em with me."

"But they helped out during your bad time," my mother said. "They meant kindly."

"Yes. Helped out. And then they come smirkin' and whisperin' around how I ought to be glad my husband was out of the way. How I must have hated takin' care of him, and what a mercy it was to be rid of him. I told 'em a few things. They'll stay away from me a spell, I can promise you that!"

She sat straight in her chair, and dropped the mourning dress on the floor.

"I was glad to take care of him," she said. "Yes, sir! I was proud of my husband. The things he'd done, and the risks he'd been through, when the men in this town was rollin' drunks and wrappin' up condensed milk . . ."

She drew a breath, and, forgetting that my mother had been there, began to tell about the time when he had been surrounded by the Indians, creeping in on him with sagebrush tied to their heads. He fought them back and outgamed the whole caboodle of them; and her voice rose and trembled, shrilling the scenes she had enacted with Old Man Isbell when his numb old brain was burning down through the pile of his memories, spurting a flame out of each one before they all blackened and went to nothing.

She shrilled the great scenes out defiantly, as if it were her place to defend them, as if they belonged to her, and were better, even at second hand, than anything that any of the townspeople had ever experienced. None of their common realities had ever touched her. Beauty had not; love had not; nor even friends. In place of them, she had got an eighty-five-year-old dotard and the ridicule of the townspeople. Watching over the old man when he died was the one time when she had come anywhere within reach of heroism and peril and splendor; and that one time, being worthy of it, she passed them all. And that one time was enough, because she knew it.

"The hostiles a-prowlin' around," she cried, her voice blazing. "The houndish dastards! . . ."

February, 1929

Back to the Land—
Oregon, 1907

THE opening of Spring, which, in most parts of the North Temperate Zone, comes in for an eager welcome and lots of minor poetry with heigh-ho in it, was the season which everybody in the sagebrush dreaded and hated. Winters were long, cold and mean, but then, at least the roads were good—hard and solid and smooth with packed snow, and better than at any other time of year. When the snow thawed, they went into bottomless, rubbery mud, and human activity stopped as if the country had been hit by a pestilence. There was not a road anywhere on which a horse could set foot without sinking to his belly. Travel was impossible. Nobody but fools ever attempted it.

The Spring the homesteaders attempted it was the longest and dullest and most hopeless of all. Perhaps it seemed worse because of the job I had. I was typesetter on the cow-town weekly, and there was nothing to set except patent-medicine locals and a few miners' location-notices. News there was not a trace of. Nobody in the country was doing anything. The printing-office was like a cave which even the bats have deserted. The editor went out into the gumbo, to try to collect enough subscriptions to get drunk on. There were three degrees in his collecting. If business was slow, he hoped for enough to get drunk on; if it was fair, he tried for enough to stay drunk on; and, if things were rushing, he kept on until he had rustled enough to pay me my wages. There was no chance of that happening, I knew. Nothing else had any interest. I set type drowsily, and wished, not knowing about the homesteaders, that the Indians would come.

The coming of the Indians meant that travel would start again. Indians were supposed to have some instinctive way of knowing the exact moment when the roads had dried shallow enough for a horse to pull his feet through. They probably guessed at it, the same as anybody else; but they did manage to hit close enough for people to depend on, so it had got to be a habit to wait for them. When the first band of squaws, bucks, papooses, pack-horses and dogs jogged through the street, the cow-town people woke up and unlocked and put on clean shirts and got ready for business. The ranchhands, they knew, would have seen the Indians, and might be expected before night. There would be news, traffic, reunions, fights, hubbub and gaiety and celebration. People would call at the printing-office and pay up their subscriptions and get their names in the column of items of local interest, and the editor would pay me my wages.

It was the best possible kind of festival, because it depended upon natural causes. The enthusiasm was spontaneous, not pumped-up for some artificial occasion. I wouldn't have traded it for ten Independence Days, which always came when the weather was so scalding hot that even hell-raising seemed forced. The coming of the Indians was an occasion when people blew off steam, not from patriotic duty, but because they had accumulated more than they could hold. I loved it. I can be charitable with the homesteaders for spoiling my career as a journalist, but their destroying that Spring festival is something that history will hold against their memory forever.

The whole country was a mass of quivering blue mud. Melted snow undermined it, and rain pounded the surface to froth. It was the lonesomest, dirtiest season in the whole year; and, right in the height of it, when not even the most morbidly silly Indian would have stirred out of his wickiyup on a bet, the homestead rush started.

I had heard of homestead rushes before, but had never seen one. I had imagined they meant noise, excitement, competition, a thousand wagons racing each other through the sagebrush at a dead gallop. The reality knocked all that in the head. There were not a thousand wagons, but only three, so rickety that a moccasined Siwash could have kicked them to pieces. The horses wallowed through the mud an inch at a time, whimpering with weariness. Every whip-cut almost knocked them down. The people were dirty, sallow and starved. They drubbed the horses savagely, like a man chopping a knotty stick of wood. Sheets of rain slammed in their faces, and they looked glary and scared. In all three wagons were cold, half-naked children who sat and bawled monotonously, without opening their mouths.

They stopped in town only long enough for one of the men to trade a silver watch for some plug tobacco at the store. Then they plunged forward into the mud, leaving the town bewildered. Should the people take the homesteaders as a sign that the roads were open, and get ready for business? Would the ranchers go by this signal, as they had by the Indians? Suppose the town got ready and the ranches didn't? Suppose the ranches got ready and the town didn't? Argument and debate, founded on guesswork, filled every man's mouth, and the end was confusion and disunity, with everybody playing a separate hunch. Some got ready; some got half-ready; and about half of them refused to make a move until they had something better to go on than surmises. That the homesteaders had got through the roads proved nothing except that the homesteaders themselves were fools. The ranchers who saw them, it was argued, would so conclude, and would wait for the Indians, just as they always had done. As for the other homesteaders who, it appeared, were coming along behind, they weren't worth fixing up for. None of them ever had any money, and, besides, all homesteaders were teetotalers.

The same disunity, it appeared, existed among the ranchers. Some of them insisted upon striking out for town immediately, some were for waiting, and some sent in a couple of riders to see how things stood, and report. Being valved off in this aimless way, the old enthusiasm and trustfulness vanished. There was no big day to look forward to. The ranchers, by ones and twos, straggled in, bought what they wanted, gazed around wistfully, and went home. There was nothing to see except the homestead rush — a rickety wagon, or two, or a half-dozen, wallowing through the street; women and bawling children and sallow, middle-aged men beating the tired horses forward with the brutality of a desperate hope.

And they were not much to look at. They were coming to take up farms, which the government was willing to give away; and everybody in the country knew that there were no farms worth having as a gift. There was no hundred and sixty acres of land that a man could farm a living out of. Not knowing that, or that their two hundred miles of mud-wallowing were useless, the homesteaders were pitiable; and the sight of a pitiable man is embarrassing.

II

On me they bore the hardest of all, because of my job. I had to set in type the stories about them which the editor, hoping for new subscriptions, banged off whenever a new wagon struggled into town, and it griped my sense of honesty even to read such a set of lies, false surmises and impossible predictions as he let loose about them: This influx of sturdy latter-day pioneers and substantial home-builders. The country faced an agricultural future second to that of no section in the world. It would become the granary of America, and all Hell couldn't stop it. I don't know whether he believed it or not. There were times when I suspected he did. For instance, when he explained to me that we must do everything we could to make the new settlers feel welcome, because it wouldn't be long before they would be running the country.

It was that policy that forced me out of a typesetting career. The rush had lasted about a week, the mud and the weather were about the same as ever, and I had helped print one lying issue of the newspaper, feeling like an accomplice to a fraud, when a new and very diffident latter-day pioneer entered, tracking mud all over the floor (I had to sweep the place) and trying to work up nerve enough to ask a favor. The editor greeted him effusively, and interviewed him forthwith.

He was tall and thin, with a little head on a long neck, big feet, and a rascally-looking black mustache. The right things about him might have made pretty good reading. The coat he was wearing, for example. It was a long-tailed cutaway, with silk facings and cloth-covered buttons. They were black. The coat was yellowish-green. Where had it come from? Did he buy it new, and why? Was it a hand-me-down, and from whom?

But the editor had a mind above such things. He yanked his interview out of the man like a district attorney buttering a State's witness. The homesteader blushed at his own prominence. He had come to take up a claim from the government. It was a hard, horse-killing trip, but he was in a hurry to get in before all the good land was taken. It was the advertisements that had decided him to come. The railroad was advertising for homeseekers to join the movement back to the land. And he had fetched his wife and six children. Which reminded him, he said, that the editor could help him out some, if he was a mind to. The idea was that it seemed like his wife was going to have another, and it looked like she might need a doctor, or something. Well, a doctor would charge—

"We haven't any doctor," said the editor. I thought he acted relieved, in spite of his continuing, "It's a disgrace to the country to be without one, too. A confounded disgrace. But, well, now, for matters of this nature the people usually call in some of the housewives around town. For matters of this nature they seem to serve pretty well. And, besides, they don't charge anything."

The homesteader remarked that that was a mighty handy thing to know. But he looked worried, as if he still wanted something.

"Well, now, it's a mighty fine thing to know you're welcome in the country, like you said," he began. "Bein' a stranger here and so on . . . not acquainted around, nor nothin' . . . uh . . . whut'ud be the matter ef you was to ask some of them housewives to help a stranger out, kind of?"

For a moment, the editor looked panicky. He was a middle-aged bachelor, and women scared him to death. Then he looked at me, peacefully distributing type, and the glassy look left his eyes. He became cordial again. "Certainly," he said. "Assuredly. Most decidedly. My compositor, here, needs a little fresh air, anyhow. We'll get him to tend to it."

They both looked at me, and I climbed down from my stool and got my hat. "Get family ladies, remember," cautioned the editor. The town had a small collection of ladies of another kind.

"And it wouldn't hurt ef he was to kind of hurry up with 'em, neither," added the homesteader.

I slammed the door, and stood in the rain feeling abused and outraged. What business did he have ordering me to hurry? Why did I have to rustle his midwives? How should I go about rustling them? That was the worst. All the housewives I knew were grim, cranky, and suspicious of practical jokes. How could I word my errand so they would believe it? I thought up speeches to open on them with. Everything sounded either licentious or flip.

The homesteader's wagon stood in the street, the back full of bawling children, and a woman holding the reins in the front seat. I couldn't see anything wrong with her, except that she looked notably shrewish and ignorant. She turned and rebuked the sniveling children with threats and cusswords that would have sent a ten-up team of mules into a stampede. If she was in need of help, I'd certainly have hated to be her little boy when she felt healthy. What would the housewives think of me for fetching them down to wait on a woman who swore like that?

I never found out, for suddenly my mind cleared, and I saw the best way was simply to walk out on the job, and not fetch them at all. I wasn't married to typesetting and I didn't have to go back unless I felt like it.

I closed my newspaper career there on the sidewalk in the rain, with the homestead woman glaring at me like a pet hawk; and it was so great a relief to have it over with that I felt grateful to her for having brought me to a decision. How she came out with her prospective maternity I never learned, for I rode out through the mud to a cattle-ranch and got a job that afternoon. They lit in some part of the country, probably.

III

If the homestead rush was to blame for my losing one job, it was equally responsible for my getting a new one. The cattle-ranch had been torn by disputes, stirred up by the settlers' wagons passing. Were the roads open, or not? The foreman claimed they weren't, and forbade anybody to take a horse out until he gave the word. About a third of his force rebelled, quit, and waded into town afoot, where they remained, squandering their wages on dullness, leaving the ranch short-handed, and wishing, no doubt, that they could kick themselves till their noses bled. The foreman was pleased about that. About the homesteaders, he merely remarked that they had been overdue for a long spell.

"It's one of the things we figger on about every ten years," he explained. "It ain't anything a man can help. One thing, though; you'll have to be careful how you leave things layin' around."

I could see the sense in that, all right, but something more seemed to be called for. "Won't they fence off all the range?"

"Some of it, I reckon. Not enough to hamper us much. And they'll mostly all be starved out inside of a year after the roads they had to buck to git here. You don't know about homestead rushes, I reckon."

I told him that I knew as much as I wanted to, and hoped I never saw a homeseeker again.

"They don't run on sense, like ordinary homesteadin'. They can't, because there ain't any sense to 'em. A homestead rush runs on what the old-timers used to call afflatus. It's a kind of an edge, you might say, and they have to keep goin' till they git it worked off. If the roads was good now, like they was when the rushes come in '84, and '92, we'd have some land-buyin' to do to git rid of 'em. They'd tough it out the full five years till they proved up. But the way it is, it'll use up all the afflatus they've got to pull through that mud. They won't have none left for anything else. I know 'em."

I remarked that these might be a kind he wasn't used to.

"A little more up-to-date, maybe, but no better," he said. "Any of 'em tell you how the rush started? They seen an advertisement! You know what kind of people answer advertisements, don't you? They're the kind of humans that start in to raise hell and put a block under it, as long as their afflatus holds."

He went on talking, but I stopped listening. There was a sound of wheels ricketing, horses wheezing and children blubbering. It was a homesteader; maybe the prospective father in the cutaway coat coming after me. I stood ready to duck out of sight in case it was. But it was a different outfit—a young couple, with a long-chinned, black-eyed old virago of a grandma coiled up in the seat between them. The young woman couldn't have been over eighteen, and nursed a gaunt, braying baby, beside fussing with two other children at her feet. The young man was pink-faced, filthy and talkative, and had a crippled foot bundled around with strips of gray blanket. He opened the conversation. One of their wagon-wheels was coming to pieces, and they wanted to swap it for a sound one. When the foreman declined to deal, the long-chinned old grandma leaned out and shrieked abuse — she would have called it giving him a piece of her mind — until he retired into the bunkhouse.

"Let her run," he advised me, though I had no intention of trying to stop her. "I'm used to it these days. Besides, it uses up some of her afflatus. The more she gits rid of, the less she'll have left to bother us with . . . . Are they leavin'? Stick your head around the corner and notice whether they try to pack anything away with 'em."

I reported that, by the looks of it, we were getting rid of them without loss.

"That's where you're wrong," said the foreman, emerging. "That's one kind of people there ain't such thing as gittin' rid of. Some of 'em, maybe, but there's always plenty where they come from."

I had quit a job that owed me wages for no other purpose than to keep from having to deal with them.

"I used to feel that way, too," he said. "I give up the notion. You can't git rid of 'em. The best you can hope for is to git used to 'em. It ain't their fault. It's afflatus."

IV

It was easy enough to talk about getting used to them, but trying to do it was different. As individuals they were simple enough to understand. A set of misfits, who had come homesteading because they could not be any worse off, and would try anything once. But, collectively, they had the weight and dignity of some great force of nature. The way the country filled up with them was frightening. They traveled so slowly, and at such intervals. Yet, before the roads got fit to travel, they had overrun the sagebrush from one horizon to the other. I don't understand yet how they could have seemed so few and been so many. A schoolhouse on Cherry Creek opened the year with five pupils. It closed in the

Spring with an enrollment of eighty and an epidemic of head-lice. There were families everywhere.

There was another anomaly. They had gone to so much work and misery to get in before the good claims were taken, and when they got there they took anything that happened to be close. Whether it was good or bad didn't appear to make any difference. They would work their wagons through a ten-mile creek-bottom, almost killing their teams doing it, and take their claim on a rock sidehill where there wasn't enough earth to hold up a fence-post. An uncle of mine who crossed the plains to Oregon in 1852 has told me that the early pioneers did the same thing. So perhaps the editor, in calling them latter-day pioneers, wasn't so far out, after all.

They took after the pioneers, too, in their tendency to help themselves to whatever they happened to need, without inquiring whether it belonged to anybody else or not. With the pioneers, that worked very well, because there was nobody to object, except Indians, and nobody to pay any attention to them if they did. But the wild game which the pioneers had appropriated was all gone. There was nothing left to eat but cattle, and they belonged, not to the Indians, but to white people who had votes and a pull with the sheriff. Still, it was either steal cattle or starve; and, though some of the homesteaders were extremely strong churchmen—one, I recall, held family prayer every evening—I don't remember a single case of death from famine. They did get pretty hungry sometimes; but the great thing is to keep alive, and that even the family-prayer man managed to do.

He was one of the toughest stock-stealers that we had; not that he was hard to catch, but that, when we did catch him, he always had some kind of yarn fixed up to slide the blame somewhere else. He never attempted to deny that a steer wasn't his, or that he had killed it. But there were always extenuating circumstances— the brute had attacked one of his children, or he had found it tangled in barbed-wire, and so badly cut that he shot it as an act of humanity. He was a tall, slab-sided man with gray side-whiskers and a hard blue eye, dull and shallow like a marble. He had started out as a preacher—Nazarene, as I recall—and he felt that he oughtn't to be expected to work at anything else.

That accounted for him, all right; but what about the rest of them? They weren't preachers, and they didn't work, either. Not that they could have made a living, if they had plowed and seeded the whole country; but, after the prodigious labor of bringing themselves there they might have given it a try.

But they tried nothing of the kind, and by the beginning of Summer we began to hear their wagons ricketing past the cattle-ranch in the night, leaving the country, as the foreman had predicted. Sometimes we would hear a woman crying in a wagon. All the suffering and hardship they had gone through to get to a place where, it turned out, they hadn't wanted to live—one couldn't blame them for crying, though a little more of that at the start would have saved a lot of it in the end. While they were wasting their effort was the time to have shed tears; not after it was wasted.

Some of them were left, like puddles after an overwhelming sea. There was an old bearded man who lived by cobbling boots, though he himself went barefooted. And a shriveled-up little wart who charmed rattlesnakes, and was believed to eat them; and a man with long black hair and two thumbs on each hand— the extra ones growing, very small but perfectly formed, in the heel of his palm—who made brooms which he couldn't sell, because women were afraid of him.

There were only those three, and why even they stayed nobody could tell, least of all themselves. They could have done better at their respective trades almost anywhere else in the world. They admitted as much themselves; but they stayed on. Except for them, the country was exactly as it had been to start with; and nobody minded them much. They never washed; but they were harmless, and even, as oddities, interesting. And they were

totally without vices of any kind; but, indeed, all the homesteaders were. Drunkenness, any of the anti-social excesses, were
unknown among them. To a man, they were kind husbands and
indulgent fathers, for which circumstance, I have more than once
thanked God. If they hadn't been, I might have been running a
country newspaper and getting backache once a week from pulling a Washington hand-press until death. And died knowing this
people only as nomadic nuisances. I've been lucky.

V

The range left by the 1907 homestead rush looked much as it
had before they came. They had exhausted their energy on the
roads, and had none left to spend on altering the country. When,
being rested, it returned, they used it to pick up and leave. If the
roads had been good, what would they have done with it? But the
homestead rushes of 1884 and 1892 had better roads to travel
over. They brought their afflatus to the country unimpaired and
yet they, too, had picked up and left. Why hadn't it done them
any good? The time came to graze cattle on the home range,
among the claims of '84, and the first one I visited showed all I
needed to know.

It lay at the bottom of a deep river canyon — a fenced field with
a house in the middle. Only the bare legal requirements. All the
extra touches had been spent upon the road that led down to it.
The road was fifteen miles long, graded out of crumbling basalt,
with all cuts and fills complete! Every inch of it had been done by
hand! I refused to believe that it was the work of less than ten
men. The foreman swore that it had been built by one, and a very
average-looking one, at that. Fifteen miles! To replace it would
cost, today, ten thousand dollars. One could buy all the land in
sight of it for less. What did he build it for? To get to his claim, in
the canyon. And it wasn't worth getting to. It wasn't worth
anything.

Riding down into the blue shadow between the broken cliffs of the river canyon, I used to try to imagine what he must have looked like, gouging at that naked-flanked red sidehill with one small shovel. The foreman hadn't remembered, and I could never manage to form a picture that satisfied me. All I could be sure of was that he had been middle-aged, for a young man would never have undertaken a job so monumentally dull and endless, and no old man would have lasted till it was finished. And also, he was a bachelor. No woman would ever have stood for his wasting that much of his time. The homestead women may have been ignorant of reality, but they were never indifferent to it, as this road-builder was.

I have given up hopes of ever figuring that man out. Didn't he know anything at all? He must have, or he could not have built his road. It took more than high spirits to go through with a job like that. Yet, if he did know that much, how did he contrive to avoid knowing anything else? How did he preserve himself from the evidence, spread around him for thirty miles in every direction, that the earth he was shoveling a road to wouldn't raise a crop? In that red, gravelly soil even the sagebrush dies yearly. Did he convince himself that wheat was hardier than sagebrush?

The best I can do with these questions is to surmise that he never even thought of them until his road was completed. And then he didn't have to bother making tests and drawing inferences. All he had to do was to seed his field and see. At the end of the road was the place where he had done it. There was a field of old stubble, a pile of old threshed-out straw, and, a little to one side, a mound of caked, queer-smelling earth, covered with sickly sprouts of wheat. That had been his crop.

It was not enough to be worth hauling to market, and he had poured it out on the ground and pulled up and left. The smallness of the strawstack showed that he had considered one fizzle enough, and had not tried a second. His cabin, too, was too clean to have been lived in long. Its rafters were not smoked, and the assortment of wreckage which accumulates wherever a homesteader has lived any length of time — old clothes, newspapers, patent-medicine bottles, scraps of machinery — was missing.

Maybe he realized that he had been a fool, and hated to go on living where he would be reminded of it. Maybe — I am still trying to figure him out — maybe the hopefulness and ardor of making his road had been so pleasant that he couldn't bring himself down to cheapen his work by making it the line of communication for a mere ordinary starve-out wheat-crop. Maybe he moved off on to another range, and used his last energy on building another road.

VI

These vacant homestead houses were used by the cattle-ranch as range-camps. All the hands were required to know where each place was, what its name was, and how to find it. Getting them all straight in my head was one of the first jobs of my apprenticeship. Eventually, I got so that I could have ridden to any one of them in the darkest night; but while I was learning, I had to depend more on luck and signs. One of the most reliable guides was a windmill. It was easy to see, hard to lose site of, and a sure indication of a homestead.

Only the homesteads had them. For this, there were two reasons. They were a great deal of trouble to install, and, during the season when water was scarce, they were perfectly useless, because there was not enough wind to make the paddles go round. Why didn't they find out about that before they put them up? Why did they do any of the things they wasted their labor on? Building corncribs on land that wouldn't raise a tassel; ash-hoppers and smoke-houses in a country where the only fuel is juniper, which makes neither ash nor smoke; cordelling farm-machinery up to the top of a mountain, where there wasn't enough earth to bury a dog; planting orchards at an altitude where the fruit froze, every year, before it was even thoroughly green.

The orchards were one thing that I wholeheartedly liked. They never matured any fruit, but I liked to go and look at them when they were in bloom. There was one apple tree that over-hung a spring, so deep and still that the water was black. The sight of the white petals floating down into it was too beautiful to miss. I used to spend whole days there, on the sly. One needs smallness in beauty for a change, sometimes, from the majesty of a big country.

Another thing I liked was the material the homesteaders papered their walls with — namely, newspapers. I like it still. Nothing gives a house so definite a character. It is not only less monotonous than wallpaper, but infinitely more interesting. What conventionalized foliage, or English hunting-scene, could have duplicated the delight of finding a cabin in the brush on Cherry Creek, papered with issues of a newspaper for which I had set the type? Could any number of family portraits give a man more background than a few carefully-selected copies of his home-town weekly? Beside, it encourages literacy. I learned to read at the age of four, through being stood in a corner, for punishment, squarely against an illustrated advertisement for a one-man stump-puller. Most farm-children of my time acquired their letters in much the same way, to the subsequent joy of small politicians, and similar pamphlet peddlers, the country over. That is, of course, regrettable, but I would be willing to put up with even that, rather than lose the custom.

And even the thinnest reading-matter gains from being papered on a wall. A house southeast of the Three Sisters, where I wintered once, was lined with pages from the Saturday Evening Post, and they gained a real ascendancy over me. Not by the print, which I can't even recall, though I read it all through; but by the illustrations. They were by A.B. Wenzell, and depicted a complete assortment of tall, hatchet-faced men, exquisitely attired in long-tailed coats, choke-bore trousers, and white vests. I can remember how their scornful regard made me flinch when, during a spell of zero weather, I was weak enough to go to bed without taking off my pants.

There was a house west of Ridgeway that was papered with an account of the battle of Shiloh. It came from Memphis, Tenn., and its politics were vehemently pro-Southern. So were — and are — mine; but I did think this editor carried his a little bit farther than the facts warranted. His headlines were at least eight inches high — "VICTORY! VICTORY!! VICTORY!!! The Yankees Defeated And Routed!!!!"

Which, as I knew from Barnes' School History, they weren't. Not that it would have made things any better if they had been. A victory in a lost war is the saddest of all. It merely protracts the agony, slaughters men uselessly, and causes editors to make fools of themselves. It was unpleasant to think of my people being whipped at Shiloh, but at any rate the whipping had got them somewhere, which was more than a victory would have done. The prematurely triumphant hurrah of those headlines used to get on my nerves. It was like a child laughing in a house where somebody has died. Yet I never went near the place without stopping in to read the thing again.

It was on the homestead adjoining that one that I encountered a wonder of an altogether different kind — not sad, like so many of the other signs were, but grimly capable. It was an enormous old gray gander. His owners had gone away and left him, and he had held the place, single-handed, against all comers, for at least fifteen years. He held it against me, too. I had knelt to drink out of the spring, and, without the slightest preliminary, he charged me and tried to stab his big yellow beak into my eyes. When I mounted, to get rid of him, he sailed into my horse, almost scaring the poor animal to death.

I had to either leave, or kill him; so I left. He was too good to kill. His keeping alive for so long in that lonely place, among so many wild animals that might have preyed on him, was real heroism. He was neither swift nor cunning, and there were hawks,

eagles, coyotes, wildcats, lynx-cats, snakes, skunks and owls, by
day and by night, that were both, and stronger than he to boot.
Yet he had managed to evade, or to whip, all of them. As far as
courage went, he could have whipped a whole pack of coyotes.
But how had he managed against their brains?

Apparently, though, he was used to getting the best of fights.
He plainly didn't consider that he had performed anything
unusual in licking me. When I retreated, he stretched his neck,
gobbled a few spears of watercress from the spring, and retired
into a sagebrush thicket to digest them. Fifteen years. If the
homesteaders had possessed half his determination—

VII

Or the adaptability of their cats. Cats, it appeared, were the
one thing they always brought and never took away. They throve
and multiplied until there was one behind every sagebrush in the
country. Food there was no lack of—chipmunks, sage-rats, birds,
jackrabbits and snakes were even more plentiful than the cats.
The amount of hell that one family of adventurous kitties could
raise around a range-camp after dark appeared limitless. They
prowled boldly over our beds, knocked things over, yowled mur-
derously and fought and squabbled among themselves, and when
we scatted them they ran under the horses, getting us up in our
shirt-tails to quell a stampede, while they strolled back to camp
and fought in our blankets. We hated them, and should have
killed them. Why didn't we? Everybody threatened to, but
nobody ever did. It appears to be a human failing everywhere to
hate to kill a cat.

Another pest around homestead houses was the pack-rat. One
imagines, commonly, that animals are gifted with instincts to
help them get food, or escape their enemies, or continue their
species. But what advantage can a pack-rat derive from the
instinct that causes him to carry away and hide all the old junk he
can get his claws on—spoons, keys, broken crockery, old harness-

buckles, bottle-necks, bent nails — anything, so long as it is portable and perfectly useless? I slept once in a cabin where the pack-rats worked all night carrying rifle-cartridges from a wooden packing-case, and hiding them under a saddle at the opposite end of the room. Out of curiosity, I left the cache undisturbed; but I learned nothing, for they left it undisturbed, too, and never came near it again.

Since then, I have seen the same thing happen many times. If there is any reason for it in nature, I don't know what it is. Race-aberration, maybe; or a holdover from an instinct that did once have some sense in it. One guess is as good as another. The foreman probably hit as close as any when he called it afflatus. Maybe the pack-rats had hatched up some magnificent scheme in which the rifle-cartridges were designed, vaguely, to figure; and when they got the cartridges moved all their zest was gone and they decided to play something else. If moving the cartridges had done them any good I shouldn't have minded putting them back. As it was, I cursed them for a set of addle-headed little pests, and talked about putting out poison for them.

I never got round to doing it, though, and I suppose they did get some good out of moving the cartridges, after all. They had the fun of planning big; maybe that was all they wanted or expected. If that is so, their living in the homestead houses was the most appropriate of all earthly coincidences, for they, more perfectly than any other created thing, exemplified the people whom they supplanted. If there is ever a monument to busted homesteaders, the pack-rat deserves to be on it. He is nature's one victim of the homesteaders' never-failing curse — a fury for beginning things and leaving them one-fourth done. It may have been from them that he learned his habits. I used to think so.

But the feeling that I had the oftenest, and the most clearly, when we rode in to make a night-camp in one of the old houses, among the ruins of work wasted, was one of abashment and shame. It was as if we were prying upon somebody's hurried, childish extravagances which were none of our business, and ought, out of decency, to be left secret. The people who built them had no need to be reminded of their mistakes, being either dead or too old to profit by them. And the newcomers had mistakes enough of their own, including the one they had made in coming there at all.

We used to hear them when they moved out, passing the cattle-ranch in the night, arguing to make their wives stop crying, and explaining that there was still a new section of country a couple of hundred miles further on, where a man stood a chance.

March, 1929

A Town in Eastern Oregon

THE early settlements in Oregon have had enough books written about them to patch the Oregon Trail its full length. Some of them are first-class reading; many are feeble-minded puling; but nearly all of them make, either explicitly or by implication, the mistake of crediting the whole keelwork of Pacific Coast civilization—such as it is—to the pioneers who crossed the plains to farm.

Such an injustice needs to be corrected. For one thing, farming lacked a great deal of being the pioneers' fundamental lust. It was, in general, their trade, but only in the most hopeless simpletons did it amount to an ambition. The true explanation would do the early settlers more credit, and would reveal, no doubt, a connection with the propaganda of Senator Thomas H. Benton, who was far-sighted enough to see the West as the gateway to the Orient, and to arrange that, if it came to a plebiscite on sovereignty, the United States should count enough heads to win it. There were, of course, other and deeper motives. The pioneers were not fools. Indeed, they averaged higher than any men the West is ever likely to see again, and to circulate the impression that they were a set of simple-minded, big-hearted goofs is to plaster them with an insult which they do not deserve. It is wrong, also, to give them credit for a structure on which other men did part of the work. In Western Oregon, the French-

Canadians of the Hudson's Bay Company had laid down settlements before any of the emigrations started. The pioneers, when they did come, merely took up the job where the *voyageurs* had called it a day.

In Eastern Oregon, they did even less. The country was wild, arid, lonesome as death, and swarming with strong, hostile tribes of Indians. More, it was 200 miles inland, and what the emigrants wanted was the gateway to the Orient, which lay along the coast. They went through the sagebrush without stopping. Civilization came to Eastern Oregon, not by farms, but by the institution of the town.

Towns jibed with the country. Even the Indians preferred to gang together in villages, and one of their *wickiyup* communities, in the gorge of the middle Columbia, has existed longer than any white man's town in America. Not even Saint Augustine or Santa Fe is older. The inhabitants look it. There are old Indians in it who appear to be not a day less than a hundred and twenty years old; and there are smells that can't possibly have started later than five centuries ago. Both smells and centenarians could, no doubt, be done away with by the use of chloride of lime, carbolic soap, and kicks in the trousers. But the Indians haven't the ideal of betterment. To them, both stinks and dotards mean something more valuable than a shiny outside: to wit, permanence and stability. They prefer to let things alone. That is why they have become a subject race. Ideals would probably have saved them, as they have so often saved the town of Gros Ventre.

Gros Ventre is a town on the south bank of the Columbia River, at the foot of the middle rapids, where the deep cliffs of the river-gorge break southward into low, pleasant hills. The amount of devilment and cussedness that its citizens have succeeded in whipping out of its corporate limits since it was founded would line Hell a hundred miles. From 1835 down to the present, it has been one long war for righteousness, and in that war the winning of a victory has meant only the opening of an offensive against something else. Just now, the fight is against allowing youths under twenty-one to play pool.

They will win that, as, of course, they ought to. Not that they have always won. The betterment campaign of 1835, which they undertook before they had learned to measure their meat, ended in defeat, because the job was too much for them. It would have been too much for anybody, for it was no less than the conversion of the Indians to Methodism.

The missionaries themselves were not to blame. It is true that they banked a good deal on journalistic veracity, but worldlier men than Methodist missionaries have fallen for sob-stuff about the Land of Opportunity, even in our own time, and in less reliable journals than the *Christian Advocate and Journal* and *Zion's Herald,* where, in the issue of March 1, 1833, an artist signing himself G. P. D. honed his quill and let himself go upon the subject of the Flathead Indians, who, he alleged, yearned for religious instruction.

They were so desperate for a dose of the true doctrine, he proceeded, that it was pitiful, and almost an impediment to travel. A delegation of them had even hiked all the way from Oregon to St. Louis to try to find a preacher who would expound the divine mysteries unto them. The worst of it was, they failed to locate one. To anybody who has ever trusted an Indian with an errand in town, that part of the yarn is entirely convincing. But the readers of *Zion's Herald* did not stop there: they swallowed the whole thing, and, in three weeks after the story came out, the Methodist Mission Board had begun to investigate where the Flathead Indians lived, and to receive applications from clergymen anxious to go there. In 1835, the Gros Ventre Mission opened for business, and found that there wasn't any. Indians there were in plenty, but their thirst after the Gospel had been all in the eloquent G. P. D.'s head. They did not hanker to be freed from "the chains of error and superstition." They did not want a preacher, or any number of preachers, and the assurance that they would go to Hell when they died made them laugh.

The Gros Ventre missionary was a good sport. He looked over the flock which he had been appointed to lure into the fold, and decided that, after all, if they didn't want salvation, they probably weren't worth it. He was ahead of his time, and he was also out of step with the tradition of improvement which Gros Ventre later took up and stuck to. The other missions which went into Eastern Oregon at the same time took their disappointment harder. At Lewiston and at Waiilatpu, where the savages showed equal obstinacy in running behind the dope-sheet, the two emissaries of Christianity went so far as to beat the Everlasting Mercy into their unwilling disciples with a cowhide. The disciples stood it as long as they could, and then hit back. They killed all the white men — there were fourteen of them — at Waiilatpu, and carried off fifty-three women and children as prisoners.

The avaricious and unchristian Hudson's Bay Company ransomed them, rescued the whites at other threatened missions, and managed to cool the Siwashes down; it is not unlikely that a fresh missionary would have been able to take up the work in perfect safety. But the divines of the Mission Board had been scared, an it was they who were putting up the money. They now called in all their men from all the missions, Gros Ventre included, and put Eastern Oregon on the blacklist as an apostolic field. When they next appeared in Gros Ventre, it was not to call souls to repentance, but to bring suit for damages against the United States War Department for putting a fort on part of their abandoned mission.

They got judgment for $24,000, for, even without them, the town had got over its setback, and was headed once more down the pathway to perfection. The pioneers were coming through, the government had garrisoned Gros Ventre to guard them out of Eastern Oregon, and with the soldiers came a class of men who were to bring to success the job at which the missionaries had failed; merchants, traffickers and money-changers, peddling at the heels of the army, were started at their task of boosting Gros Ventre to its final eminence in civilization.

II

The War Department, in garrisoning Gros Ventre, did only what diplomacy and strategy made compulsory. The Indians, who had taken nearly ten years to work themselves up to killing the strong-armed missionaries at Waiilatpu, had passed from the control of the Hudson's Bay Company to that of the Indian Bureau, and the change made them nasty. The district Indian agent was an ex-clergyman who, it appeared, still believed the unlucky piece in *Zion's Herald,* and so set out to provide the simple savages with a decalogue, a set of ethics, and the proper machinery of enforcement. The Hudson's Bay Company men had controlled the tribes by playing sub-chiefs one against the other. The new Indian agent got rid of all the sub-chiefs, who now spent all their time talking instead of making their tribes live up to his new code of laws, and, in their place, furnished each tribe with a despot, who, he figured, would get action.

Action was what he almost immediately got. A chief strong enough to keep his subjects out of mischief was also strong enough to force them into it, and all the new appointees took their men out to hunt for trouble. They shot up and butchered small emigrant trains, raided prospectors' camps, and even talked of crossing the Cascades to loot the Western settlements and run all the whites into the ocean. They needed, perhaps, to be well thrashed; but, for that, there were not men enough. The best the War Department could do was to garrison a point which commanded the Cascade passes and the emigrant trail to the East, and the deserted mission at Gros Ventre filled the bill. With a fort and two companies of infantry, the town once more loped forth upon its career of lofty destiny.

The soldiers, however, turned out to be the least important ingredient of the place. They were, of course, a kind of assurance

---

that the Waiilatpu episode would not be repeated; but, merely sitting around and looking ugly, they contributed nothing to the life of the municipality. The real civic bonanza lay in the camp-followers who had tagged into Gros Ventre with them—sutlers, peddlers, card-slickers and horse-holders, who, setting up their counters and chuck-a-luck tables as usual, found themselves distinguished and looked up to as propertied men. Not by the military, of course, but by the emigrants, to whom the sight of established business was like a piece of home in a country where everything else was against them. Gros Ventre became an emigrant rest-station, where they fattened their teams, patched their harness, boiled their bedding, and nerved themselves for the last lap of their trip across the Cascade mountains. It was a tough and dangerous road, and they regarded the Gros Ventre men, who didn't have to travel it, much as a hobo regards the proprietor of an eating-house.

It is not of record how much time it took for the ex-sutlers to get over their modesty and decide that the emigrants were right. It can't have taken long, however, for they next appear in history as signers of a petition to the War Department, asking that the soldiers be sent out to whip the Indians. As customers, the boys in blue had lost their standing. What was wanted now was not their trade, but their services. Why didn't they get out and do something? Why, instead of lying around a comfortable fort, stuffing themselves with government grub, didn't they go out and prune a horn or two on the Siwashes? How could a town ever hope to amount to anything with hostiles yanking off scalps practically at the city limits?

It was the spirit of Community Betterment speaking, for the first time in its own voice. Perhaps they were not yet conscious of an ideal. It was enough for them that there were other towns where a man could run a business and bring up a wife and children without the risk of having them tomahawked, and they wanted their town to be the same. The Army officers, however, lacked sympathy. They alleged that the Indians would mind their own business if the whites let them alone, and that, if they wanted to have wives and children, they had better go somewhere besides a frontier post to do it. The merchants' legitimate business dealings with the Siwashes were rudely termed swindling; they were always getting themselves into a private war, and then expecting the Army to finish it for them. This time they would get fooled.

The merchants took no notice of these ignoble charges. Instead, they went back upon Washington again, to get the department commander thrown out of his job. The whole campaign, up to the time hostilities actually began, lasted almost fifteen years, and even then the new commander, though he fought the Indians willingly enough, didn't tie into them to suit the citizens' notions. He wanted merely to thrash them into good behavior. The business men cared nothing about their behavior, good or bad, but wanted them exterminated. There were controversies about that, and a particularly vicious one about the regulars' objection to killing Indian women; but, in the end, idealism prevailed over squeamishness, the single standard of redskin-slaughter was enforced, and the hostile tribes were thrashed into helpless, starving mobs, and shipped off to distant reservations to die of homesickness. Except strays, and a few inoffensive fish-eating colonies along the Columbia, no Indians remained. Gros Ventre had made its first Civic Improvement.

The one flaw in the triumph was that the pacification had gone farther than it needed to. The Army had whipped the Indians from Gros Ventre, which was all right; but it had whipped them out of all the rest of Eastern Oregon, too, and that was not so good. The town's chief value had been as a refuge, and now there was nothing to take refuge from. Travel fell off. Since one road was as safe as another, the settlers took the Southern line, which was the least rutted. Gros Ventre lost out. Bad luck bred its like, for, on top of this, the soldiers packed up and left for good, under orders for a less peaceful section of country. It was a tough

Winter in Gros Ventre without them; but the tide was on the turn, and those who stuck and starved it through came in for their reward. For the settlers took the Eastern Oregon country almost at a grab; and the sternwheel steamboats of the Columbia began to unload for the freight-roads at Gros Ventre.

III

Neither the steamboat men nor the long-line freighters picked Gros Ventre for an unloading-point out of benevolence. The steamboats could get no farther up the Columbia, on account of the unnavigable rapids; and the low-sloping hills behind the town were the only ground for miles where one could take a freight-wagon from the high country to the beach, except by lowering it over a cliff. At the head of navigation, commanding all the roads south and east, Gros Ventre was the commissariat for a country as big as the German Empire, and a whole lot livelier. Its population had been under 500; the steamboat hands alone numbered 2,000, and the freighters, horse-handlers and roustabouts came to half as many again.

The town had not been organized to handle such a mob. Not, perhaps, that its citizens wouldn't have been glad enough to try, but they didn't get a chance to. A report that a town has turned good is like news of a gold-strike. Men came crowding into Gros Ventre to cash in, and the town built back over the hills so rapidly that a string of freighters, returning from the southeastern sheep country, wandered for two days among the new houses trying to find the way downtown.

It would seem natural if the old established citizens of the town had hated the new arrivals who came to claim a share in prey that was none of their killing. But not at all. Instead of opposing each other, they settled down as friendly as buzzards on a strychnined cow, to work on the freighters and rivermen. From that common bond they worked down to one more fundamental, namely, improving the social tone of Gros Ventre.

The freighters were the biggest drawback. For one thing, they charged high for their freight, and hauled slow, which hindered business with outside communities. What was more serious, they were a mob of rough, ill-mannered savages, almost as injurious to a City of Homes as the Indians had been, and far harder to deal with. The most respectable citizens were not safe from insult around them. They got drunk, picked fights, staged runaways down the main business street, shot off guns, broke windows, and, on one occasion, threw lighted kerosene lamps at each other and burned down half the town. One skinner had paralyzed church-goers by parading the street on the Sabbath morning with nothing on but a red flannel undershirt. No city could hold up its head while such persons infested it, and Gros Ventre was determined that, whatever else happened, its head should be full high advanced. The citizens chipped in, helped by the interior country, on subsidies to lure railroads to their city, and got two main lines and eight branches.

The main lines were, in all likelihood, inevitable, though two of them were more than they had any use for. Gros Ventre was so located that no east and west railroad line could miss it without wasting a fortune on grading and bridging. But the branches were something extra, which the citizens had angled for with all their art. It didn't seem possible that they could pick any other terminus than Gros Ventre. The freight roads hadn't, and a team could pull a harder grade than a train. Yet, when the steel went down, Gros Ventre was not the terminus of a single one of the entire eight. The people had trusted too much to their natural advantages, and they had been let down.

In one thing, at least, they had succeeded. They were rid of the freighters, for good and all. Yet, without them, business appeared to have fallen into slack times. The money wasn't coming in the way it used to. The trouble, they decided, was in their not having improved things enough. There were natural resources which needed to be worked over, and the citizens entertained suggestions about them which ranged all the way from a theological seminary to a set of factories to manufacture something. It didn't particularly matter what. For raw material, the country was a very skinny prospect; but the factory idea sounded so good that they built one, anyhow, announcing that they would make glass in it. There was plenty of sand, but something, it turned out, was wrong with it, and the factory became a place where, before the motoring age, Gros Ventre youths took their girls to neck. Their elders decided to put their improvements somewhere else, where they would show. It seemed a pretty good idea to go to work and fix over the Columbia River.

This was carrying Betterment into an entirely new field; for, up to now, the stern-wheelers had gone about their business without much caring where Gros Ventre bloomed or blighted. The railroads had touched them very little, for they were able to underbid almost two-thirds on way freight, and the Big Bend and Palouse wheat countries made up for the cargoes which they lost to the new branches. Gros Ventre was no longer a distributing point, but a portage, where the lower river steamers transferred their freight to another line of vessels above the rapids.

It was against this portage that the town began to plot, wire-pulling for a congressional appropriation to build a canal around the rapids. They got it. It cost the government $8,000,000, and killed Gros Ventre, as a steamboat terminal, as dead as a hammer. Why they should have wanted it is beyond the power of man to figure. They can scarcely have been infatuated enough to think it would help their commerce to send freight somewhere else, instead of handling it themselves. Nor could it have been a Spirit of Helpfulness, for Gros Ventre didn't think very much of the steamboats, nor of the men who worked on and with them.

Indeed, it may have been mere hatred of the steamboat men, who, like the freighters before them, did not belong in a quiet, respectable City of Homes. They were tough, loud, roughnecked and quarrelsome. They fought each other in the streets, and regarded murder as merely one of the unlucky episodes of a high old social evening. They were too wild to control, too numerous to whip, and, by a very slim margin, too human to shoot. A war like the one that knocked out the Indians would have been the very remedy for them.

Whether intentionally or not, the canal got the same results, for it took away their jobs, and they had to move. Relieved of their hell-raising ruffianism, the town gained in respectability almost as much as it lost in population — about one-fourth. Yet, the canal-builders seem to have been moved by a deeper cause than mere exasperation with a set of loud-mouthed roisterers. Perhaps that started it, but the direct motive was surely something more mystical. Neither profit nor propriety, I should guess, knowing them, but an instinct for fixing things over; for making their town, not what humanity at that stage of the West needed, but what they themselves could live in most comfortably — something safe, mild and predictable.

They wanted a city for home-lovers, in the midst of a country of high-rollers and wild-horse-peelers; and they could only make their town feel as if it belonged to them by making it over. The things they altered might not be any better, but at least they wouldn't feel that they owed them to the wild country in which, after a half-century, they were still actually strangers. I remember a magistrate of the place, to whose court I was hauled as a witness in a case of mayhem. A roistering cow-puncher had chewed a comrade's ear off, and the magistrate, before imposing sentence, explained sternly that what passed for high spirits in Three Notches might be a penitentiary offense in Gros Ventre.

"It's time you out-of-town men found out who this town belongs to," he informed us, as if he suspected us of having divided the ear among us. He was very stern, and the town reporter took notes. "This town belongs to us law-abiding citizens. It ain't yours at all . . . . Huh?"

He glared at the ear-chewing defendant, who had muttered

that he didn't want the damned place for a gift, and who now protested that he hadn't said a word, and that it was probably his stomach rumbling.

"It'll have something to rumble about before I'm through with you," replied the magistrate. "This ain't your town. It's ours. We let you use it, and you raise hob around and think you're smart! You!" He glared at all of us, and breathed hard with indignation. "You whip the police, hey? You carry concealed weapons, hey? You buck a cayuse through the main business part of town, hey? You —"

The prisoner had done none of those things. He had merely yielded to momentary impulse, before he noticed what his teeth were clamped on, and he said so. Besides, he ventured, the ear wasn't city property. The crack raised a giggle, and drew him a sentence of six months in the brig. Even that didn't satisfy the Gros Ventre sense of justice. Although we had done nothing except testify, he gave us one hour to leave town. One of the punchers brought our obvious innocence to his notice. But he was set as granite.

"Maybe you ain't done anything," he admitted. "That ain't sayin' you won't! No, sir! You go somewhere else for your hob-raising! The people of Gros Ventre don't intend to put up with it any more!"

The reporter had taken it down, but, at the time, we presumed that the magistrate had delivered it merely to hear his head roar. But, as the papers informed us within a fortnight, we had done him an injustice. He had been reading us an official bull. The people of Gros Ventre were cleaning house, and hob-raising, of even the most furtive kind, had gone on the death-list. Two companies of militia had appeared, surrounded all the brothels in town, and arrested everybody in them.

IV

The news of the raid filled all the newspapers in the State, but only in Gros Ventre itself was it received in anything but a spirit of levity, which was not unmixed, in the stock country where I worked, with thankfulness that the raid had caught somebody else. Not even the fact that the arrests turned out to have been illegal made any difference in the general self-congratulations. To be arrested was tough luck; but to be pinched in a wenching-house was horrible, because it was funny.

Gros Ventre, everybody agreed, was a good place to stay away from. If they had raided the red-light section once, they would very likely do it again, and it was too much of a chance to take. There were too many other places where people were not so per-nickety. The ladies, it turned out, felt the same way, for they all pulled up and left Gros Ventre as pure as the lily in the dell. It could not be learned that any of them even objected to leaving, for their business had not been paying interest on their preferred stock since the steamboat men left. As far as they were con-cerned, being run out of Gros Ventre was a favor, and not a defeat at all.

Indeed, it seemed that nobody had lost on the affair, except a few scattering individuals. The mayor of Gros Ventre got his name in all of the papers; the militia got credit, which they deserved, for having done what they were told; the men in the stock country were pleased that it had happened before they took their vacations in town; and nobody appeared to feel badly about it except the Gros Ventre bankers, who noticed a falling off in deposits and clearings, and three members of the Anti-Vice League, who had been snared by the militia while gathering evi-dence, and herded forth to public ridicule until churchmen could rush down and order them turned loose. True, the town had lost population, but the improved tone of cleanness and refinement more than made up for it, and, so far from repining, the citizens made ready to bounce out a few more, on the issue, naturally, of Prohibiton.

Up to now, the rum-handlers of the town had managed to hold themselves in place by voting all the cow-punchers who hit town just before election, and by running in hoboes, section-gangs, and all members of the dry party who liked beer, but didn't like to pay for it. All told, these reinforcements gave them just enough of a lead to win with. The dry party used to try to keep even by hauling in the inmates of the poor-farm, but there weren't enough of them. Now, with the cow-punchers gone, and the beer-lovers chastened, the odds were lost. I had been accustomed to make a little side-money from the wet election committee by hauling in stray buckaroos and swearing them in to vote; but now they were so confident of defeat that they wouldn't even authorize me to try. The whole thing was shot, they said, and putting up a fight would only make their licking look worse.

Since they were licked already, I didn't try to argue with them. But I thought then, and still believe, that they could have run Social Betterment a closer heat than any of them imagined. They had lost votes, it is true, but so had the drys, for, odd as it may sound, the bawdy-house inmates invariably favored the side of temperance, and voted it with strength and persistence. Their idea, of course, was not reform, but to remove competition. They sold whiskey, whether a town was dry or not, and the removal of the grogshops, which were more law-abiding, never failed to build up their trade with a boom.

Whether they had counted their votes correctly or not, there was one omen which they had figured right. That was the sudden acceleration of improvement and reform. Hitherto, changes had come only after years of fighting. Now there was almost one new one a day. Prohibition went over with a rush, most of the liquor interest disdaining even to vote; and a system of paved highways carried before the bootleggers had time to agree upon rates and prices.

The highways were Gros Ventre's first purely commercial improvement. They were intended to bring travel into the town, and give the merchants something more to live on than the distinctly waning population. The results from them were a little bit disheartening, for nobody had considered that the same road which brought trade into town would also carry it out. Even the farming population motored to the big city, instead of stopping, as of old, to make the Gros Ventre cash-registers jingle.

From this improvement, they proceeded to the soil itself, and undertook the job of turning their wheat lands into orchard. The bank which financed the project went broke; the land, which was worth $75 an acre for wheat, was worthless as orchard, and couldn't be put back in wheat without pulling out the trees, which could not be done except at a cost an acre of $90.

They tried stratagems to lure back their lost population. A Chamber of Commerce expert sat in, installed a full stock of wheat-samples, pamphlets and form-letters, and succeeded, before they fired him, in fetching upon the town some hundreds of indigents who straightway applied to the county for support, got it, and wrote to all their friends. Then they tried industries again, and subsidized a fruit cannery which had to shut down for lack of any fruit to can; and a sawmill which never ran because there was nothing to saw. Do these stunts sound like stupidity? They were something far more dignified and pathetic — the desperation of a people who, having whipped a wild corner of the earth into a gentility pleasing to their hearts, find that the process has stripped it of anything to live on.

No city in the West could count so many advantages to start with, and they cleaned off every last one of them. How could they have kept them? Indians, freighters, steamboat men, saloons, bawdy-houses — they had to destroy them, for with them life in their town would be too loud and uncomfortable to be worth living. They didn't, it is true, foresee that the consequence would be death, but it is altogether likely that they would have gone ahead with it, even if they had. It was the same instinct that operates in a soldier on the firing-line who, having turned down a hundred chances to rush a machine-gun and be a hero, will straighten up squarely in the line of fire to scratch a place on his leg.

Yet, admitting that their ninety years' campaign for home, fireside and family tranquility accomplished enough bad to balance every good, it cannot be denied that, without it, they would lack strength for the work before them still. It is not Betterment, in these days; they are even past trying to get back what they have lost. It is hard enough to hang on to what they have left. The population is down to 3,000, and nothing but the fiercest kind of work has held it there. A golf links has kept a lot of them satisfied to put up with the town until times get better; there is an athletic stadium to keep the young blood steady against the same eventuality; an up-to-date water system so the place won't burn down at the threshold of its reward, as it has several times threatened to do. These things came hard, because they cost money, and money is scarce.

The trouble is in the improvements voted when the town had a population of 10,000, and paid for, unluckily, with bonds. Up-to-date schools, $500,000; public auditorium (for receptions and speeches), $150,000; police force and commodious jail, so much; paved streets and highway system, so much. Ten thousand people could afford them; but, now that the bonds are beginning to come due, there are only 3,000 left to pay them. In 1910, the city's tax rate was 1½ cents on the dollar; in 1929 it was four times as much, and the actual increase was twice that, on account of book values having been boosted to make further bond issues look safe. I estimate that the privilege of remaining faithful to Gros Ventre this year will cost every man, woman and child inside its corporate limits about $1.50 a day in taxes. It wouldn't be so bad if they were making anything to pay them with; but nothing comes in. Their trade is almost entirely with each other. If past experience had not strengthened them to hope and endure, they wouldn't be able to stand it.

That, however, is their platform — to hope and endure, to tough the thing through, to hang on and wait for the boom which, after every improvement heretofore, has always turned up to save them. Somebody may strike petroleum in the hills; maybe a syndicate will come along and build a ten-million-dollar power plant on the rapids; the climate, experts say, is as nearly ideal for moving-pictures as that of Hollywood. Things will get better. Times have been hard before, and they always picked up and took a surge. Why leave, when every day, even at $1.50 a head in taxes, is certainly bringing the good streak that much closer? Why go to some other town, where the job of Betterment might have to be done all over again?

January, 1930

Appendices

Stemming the Avalanche of Tripe

Glen A. Love

*"It was not in the least of American barbarism
she was afraid; her dread had been all of American civilization."*
Henry James, *"Lady Barbarina"*

THE Pacific Northwest, while not the most recent section of the
continental United States to receive what Mark Twain sar-
donically called the Blessings of Civilization, has probably been
the last to develop a written literature worthy of the name. With a
few exceptions, such as the autobiographical works of Theodore
Winthrop and Joaquin Miller, Frances Fuller Victor's biography
of mountain man Joe Meek, some of Idaho-exiled Mary Hallock
Foote's fiction, and a scattering of poems from various hands,
practically no pre-1920 literature from the Northwest remains
readable today.

True, the region faced all of the physical and social checks to
culture of any frontier. Yet other parts of the nation sharing these
difficulties had at comparably earlier stages in their development
created a body of literary work far superior to that in the Northwest. The Northeast, the Old Southwest, the Middle West, the
California and Nevada of Mark Twain and Bret Harte—all had
given rise to literature of lasting interest and importance while

the Northwest remained largely silent and unstoried, or worse yet, given to vapid and pathetic twitterings.

One crucial difference may be that, to a greater degree than artists in these other regions, early Northwest writers seem to have attempted to hold themselves aloof from the actual primal conditions of regional life which surrounded them. In particular, they failied to incorporate into their work those elements of folk life and art, especially humor and bawdry, which formed an indispensable part of pioneering and homesteading life in the region, and which might have breathed life into their work. As Constance Rourke points out in her now-classic work, *American Humor,*

> *Great writers have often drawn directly from these [primal] sources; inevitably genius embraces popular moods and formulations even when it seems to range furthest afield. From them literature gains immensely; without them it can hardly be said to exist at all. The primitive base may be full of coarse and fragmentary elements, full of grotesqueries or brutality; it may seem remote from the wide and tranquil concepts of great art; but it provides materials and even the impulse for fresh life and continuance.[1]*

It is just this primitive base that is missing in Northwest literature through most of the region's history. Whether from the evangelical influence of the early missionary-led settlements, or from the regions's first sense of itself as having been so blessed by God and nature as to be destined for a higher civilization, or from the determination of early notables to make the wilderness safe for homes and commerce — whether from these or other causes, the literature of the shaping region suffers from a smothering moral earnestness, a yearning after refinement which effectively cut it off from contact with the revivifying primitive and folk traditions, and left it pallid and devoid of interest. "They wanted a city for home-lovers, in the midst of a country of high-rollers and wild-horse peelers," wrote H. L. Davis, who was to help lead the assault upon this barren respectability in the 1920s, about his home town of The Dalles. "They could only make their town feel as if it belonged to them by making it over. The things they altered might not be any better, but at least they wouldn't feel that they owed them to the wild country in which, after half a century, they were still practically strangers." Although Davis's target here is, as his essay's title indicates, "A Town in Eastern Oregon," his judgment might be expanded to encompass the entire region.

> *No city in the West could count so many advantages to start with, and they cleaned them off every last one of them. How could they have kept them? Indians, freighters, steamboat men, saloons, badwy-houses—they had to destroy them, for with them life in their town would be too loud and uncomfortable to be worth living. They didn't, it is true, foresee that the consequence would be death, but it is altogether likely that they would have gone ahead with it, even if they had.*[2]

The "death" here is the economic death of the town, but again Davis's words have a double edge to them, for they apply as well to the artistic extinction with which we are concerned here.

Perhaps no event in Northwest history so clearly portends the moral direction of the region's future culture as the reaction to the arrival of four Northwest Indians in St. Louis in 1831, interested in learning more about the white man's power, which to them was signified by his superior weapons and trading goods.[3]

But an account of this visit in the Methodist *Christian Advocate and Journal* interpreted their actions as evidence of spiritual hunger. What they wanted, what they needed, were missionaries to instruct them and their fellows in the ways of Christ. The story caused a great stir among the faithful and resulted in a number of applications from clergymen anxious to attend to the Indians' spiritual needs. This was soon followed by the establishment of missions in the Northwest. The missionaries, most of them, quickly discovered that the Persons Sitting in Darkness had no interest in freeing themselves from the bonds of ignorance and superstition. The sensible servants of God pulled out and went elsewhere. Where they persisted in their labors, the obstinacy of their charges was sometimes put beyond question, as the bloody massacre at the Whitman mission in 1847 was to demonstrate.

But it was the dream of conversion rather than the reality of tragic defeat which survived to shape and direct Northwest literature along its lines of spiritual improvement. Frederick Homer Balch, a young man from the Columbia River country not far from Davis's The Dalles, published in 1890 a book entitled *The Bridge of the Gods: A Romance of Indian Oregon*. It became the best-known and most widely-read novel of the Northwest country during the first century or so of white settlement. By 1935 it had gone through 29 editions and it is still in print today. To examine the book and its author more closely is to understand something of the high moral seriousness of the culture which honored them.

Appropriately enough, Balch came to the writing of *The Bridge of the Gods* after an agonizing spiritual conversion which included burning the manuscript of his agnostic novel *Wallulah,* and becoming a home missionary of the Congregational church in the settlements along the Columbia Gorge. In his conception of *The Bridge of the Gods* Balch is firmly in thrall to the old story of the Northwest Indians pining for conversion. His hero, a New England pastor at the end of the 17th century, is possessed by a powerful calling to carry the gospel to the Indians of the West.

The book's opening paragraph immediately establishes it as another of those impossible historical romances which led the sales charts at the end of the last century, and against which Howells and the realists doggedly inveighed:

> *One Sabbath morning more than two hundred years ago, the dawn broke clear and beautiful over New England. It was one of those lovely mornings that seem like a benediction, a smile of God upon the earth, so calm are they, so full of unutterable rest and quiet. Over the sea... came a flood of lights as the sun rose above the blue line of eastern sea. And still beyond, across the Alleghenies, into the depth of wilderness, passed the sweet, calm radiance, as if bearing a gleam of gospel sunshine to the Indians of the forest.* [4]

The genteel diction and the sentimentality are universal to inferior romance, but the note of piety is peculiarly Northwestern.

The Reverend Cecil Grey ("—for such was our young minister's name—") dreams portentously of a great arch of stone between mighty mountains, under which sweeps a wide western river, and upon which wild Indian horsemen race, shaking their plumes and lances. Grey resigns his New England pastorate and, with official ordination from his church, heads into the western wilderness, accompanied, curiously enough, by his old nurse, an Indian woman servant of his family who will not be shaken in her fealty. "One long last look, and he disappeared in the shadows of the wood, passing forever from the ken of the white man" (51). Having thus allowed his hero to carry out Hester Prynne's suggested escape to Dimmesdale into the obliterating wilderness, Balch is now free, as Hawthorne was not, to indulge in the maximum of romantic distortion. Grey and his old nurse eventually reach the Northwest, where he becomes a kind of white shaman among the Indians, despite his difficulties in making solid Christians of them. He finds the stone bridge of his vision, a bridge which Balch assures his reader in a learned preface actually existed over the Columbia in the Cascade Gorge. He attends a great meeting of the confederated tribes of the Columbia under Multnomah, chief of the lordly Willamettes. There he falls in love with Wallulah, the daughter of Multnomah and his wife, a shipwrecked Asian princess whose antecedents are not so wholly shrouded in mystery as to prevent classification of Wallulah as a "white woman," thus cushioning the shock for Balch and his audience of his hero's romantic attachment. Balch, himself the victim of an unhappy love affair in which his sweetheart had died after his renunciation of their love in favor of his evangelical duties, projects his own misfortunes upon the novel. Grey, alternating between his passion for Wallulah and his heavenly mission, at last gives her up to continue his preaching, while Wallulah is forced to wed a cruel Indian chief. She drowns in the Columbia following the collapse of the Bridge of the Gods, a sign of the breakdown of the confederation and of the passing from power of the Willamettes. The accompanying eruption of nearby Mt. Hood adds to the plethora of signs of heavenly disapproval and the advent of moral judgment upon the pagan culture.

Grey is seized by the Indians to be executed in retaliation for the killing of several Indians by a white trading ship near the coast, but he dies of heart failure after a final appeal to the Indians to renounce their barbarism for Christ's love. Amidst the smoke and ruin the tribes are broken and scattered. Plague and sickness and death descend upon them. "Mongrel bands from the interior and the coast," Balch summarizes, "settled in the valley after the lapse of years; and, mixing with the surviving Willamettes, produced the degenerate race our own pioneers found at their coming" (277). But Balch sends one golden shaft of sunlight to pierce the final gloom. One of the Indians has embraced Grey's faith at last. He goes off to live among the Flatheads, accompanied by Grey's aged nurse, trudging silently after yet another zealot. There, he and his followers made such a stir over the next one hundred and thirty years or so that, we are told, in 1832 (Balch's Indians are a year late, actually) four of the tribe are sent to Saint Louis to ask for teachers to come and instruct them in the ways of God. "Thus," Balch continues, "he who gave his life for the Indians, and died seemingly in vain, sowed seed that sprung up and bore a harvest long after his death," and "thousands of Indians are the better for his having lived" (279).

In fairness to Balch it should be added to the above summary of plot that his scenes of everyday Indian life and activity are sometimes realistic and convincing, based upon his own observations and his considerable research among pioneer diarists, anthropologists, and historians. But the realistic touches do not aid the novel in reaching the mythic status toward which it strains. We are able to disregard much of Mark Twain's attack upon Fenimore Cooper's wilderness romances because their mythic power transcends the list of bloopers that Twain cites. Balch's mythopoeic leap, however, never gets off the ground. His savages are ignoble by virtue of their casual cruelty and their infidel status, which are constantly thrown before us. His hero is physically a pansy and a man of no craft. His faithful Indian companion is not a stately Mohican warrior like Cooper's Chingachgook but a shuffling old crone, his *nurse*, indeed! He rejects the woman he loves, and who loves him, and watches her married off to a cruel and sadistic husband while he stands by, keeping his spiritual skirts clean, a poltroon and a cad. Above all, of course, the novel is overlaid with an evangelical religiosity of so earnest a character as to render the book unreadable today except to a Christian Endeavor literary discussion group of unusual dedication. And this is the masterwork of what Alfred

Powers — something of the Balch of Northwest criticism, to be sure — called in his 1935 *History of Oregon Literature* "the most gifted novelist . . . in a century of settlement."[5]

By the mid-1920s the Pacific Northwest literature seemed hopelessly refined and uplifted. Still lacking any firm regional identity or a major writer to help shape its direction, the region's official culture battened upon Writers' Clubs and Poetry Societies and even a Parliament of Letters in Seattle. The chief impresario of the latter gathering and the most vigorous force for moral poetry in this period was Colonel E. Hofer of Salem. Under the banners of his journal, *The Lariat,* Colonel Hofer saw himself leading the fight for "clean literature" in the Northwest, "sweet, readable songs that leave a good taste in the mouth and sweet jingling in the hearts of readers."[6] Of an issue of a rival journal, Hofer complained that "the whole number contained little of real beauty and hardly a half-dozen poems that did not have in them somewhere a risque suggestion."[7] Shades of Dreiser!" cried Irma Grace Blackburn in another review, citing a particularly scandalous passage from *Poetry* magazine.[8]

The Colonel was proud of the western virility of his journal's verse, claiming heartily — three years after Sinclair Lewis's *Babbitt* had taken literate America by storm — that "there is no good reason why a Western poetry magazine should not have some verses with some kick and pep, zip and zep."[9] Besides leading attacks upon the effete and sex-besotted East, and the teaching of literary modernism in colleges, the Colonel offered sound advice on how to sell verse, including market analysis, classification of prospective customers, and tips on producing snappy, readable copy.

One appreciative contributor, Delia Delight Pinney, opined that "*The Lariat* is . . . a beacon of light to the people of the eastern part of the United States, teaching them that we of the wild and woolly northwest have God given ideas, and are able to express them in an attractive way."[10] Such sentiments were supported by poems with titles like "My Chum God," "To a Bird," "Little Spider," and "When Muriel Smiles."

All of this was too much for James Stevens and H. L. Davis, two serious young Northwest writers whose work had already received some national attention, but who were ignored by the literati of their home region, tripping off after the likes of the charismatic Colonel Hofer. Acutely embarrassed to be geographically linked with such folk, Stevens and Davis, under the inspiration and example of H. L. Mencken, issued in 1927 an outrageous little pamphlet entitled *Status Rerum: A Manifesto, upon the Present Condition of Northwest Literature Containing Several Near-Libelous Utterances, upon Persons In the Public Eye.*

> *Other sections of the United States can mention their literature, as a body, with respect. New England, the Middle West, New Mexico and the Southwest, California—each of these has produced a body of writing of which it can be proud. The Northwest—Oregon, Washington, Idaho, Montana—has produced a vast quantity of bilge, so vast, indeed, that the few books which are entitled to respect are totally lost in the general and seemingly interminable avalanche of tripe.*[11]

Colonel Hofer's *Lariat* was quickly singled out by Stevens and Davis as the region's principal literary eyesore, "an agglomeration of doggerel which comprises the most colossal imbecility, the most preposterous bathos, the most superb sublimity of metrical ineptitude, which the patience and perverted taste of man has ever availed to bring between covers." Along with Colonel Hofer, *Status Rerum* indicted by name various teachers and administrators at the Universities of Washington and Oregon whose literary values, the pamphlet claimed, were commercial rather than artistic and whose own talents were limited to their successes on slogan contests and Chambers of Commerce jingles. They and their followers, " 'naturals,' mental weaklings, numskulls, homosexuals, and other victims of mental and moral affliction" formed a vast army of "posers, parasites, and pismires" from which Stevens and Davis boisterously declared their independence.

Status Rerum's importance is easy to underestimate if it is seen as only an attack upon a few literary nonentities of the region. Robinson Jeffers, to whom Davis sent a copy, regarded it thus, remarking that it was a "rather grimly powerful wheel to break butterflies on."[12] But the pamphlet takes on a broader importance as a kind of watershed moment in the Northwest's literary development.

As an artistic manifesto, *Status Rerum* declared the contempt of serious writers for the trivial gamesmanship and mutual back-scratching of the Northwest literary colony. Stevens and Davis were prepared to accept the regional banishment which would necessarily result from their outburst. They properly judged that their talents and opportunities were more than local. H. L. Davis had already won the prestigious Levinson Prize for his poems in Harriet Monroe's *Poetry* magazine in 1919. He had since continued to publish poetry in that journal and in *The American Mercury,* whose editor, H. L. Mencken, had also urged him to try fiction. James Stevens had published six sketches and stories in the first six issues of that same magazine, beginning in 1924, and Mencken continued to publish Stevens's work through the decade. By the time *Status Rerum* appeared in 1927, Stevens had also published with Alfred A. Knopf a well-received book on Paul Bunyan and a novel, *Brawnyman.* Thus, Davis and Stevens, as the region's foremost young writers, declared their own independence from it and asserted the weightier standards of "the East," that final arbiter of judgment for all Westerners, by which, they had good reason to believe, their own work and that of other serious Northwest artists might be more fairly valued.

As a cultural event, *Status Rerum* announced the death of the genteel tradition in Northwest literature. Stevens and Davis were both from rural and working-class backgrounds. Stevens, born in 1892, had been self-supporting since his boyhood in the Idaho sagebrush country, and had worked on farms, in the woods and mills, and as a mule skinner on construction projects across the Northwest. Davis, born in 1894, followed his country school-teacher father from town to town in rural Oregon, settling eventually in The Dalles. Davis's parents were educated but poor, so that the boy grew up well-acquainted with farm and ranch work; he claimed cow-boy, sheepherder, packer, typesetter, surveyor, and deputy sheriff as some of the occupations of his early years. In addition, he assimilated a prodigious knowledge of the region's folklore and history. Both were well-qualified to assert the primitive base of the Northwest's cultural life. *Status Rerum* reveals a kind of bawdy delight in their attack upon shrinking violets of the region's literary circles, who, lacking the compe-tence "to pile lumber, operate donkey-engines, or combined har-vesters; to shear sheep, or castrate calves," must be employed where they can do no harm, namely in the writing of stories and poems. Shocking, obscene, outrageous, unfair — *Status Rerum* was all of these, but at the same time, it loosened the dead hand of respectability which held the region.

The influence of H. L. Mencken on *Status Rerum* and the minor revolution which it signified takes several forms. First, on the broad national level, Mencken had prepared the stage for such free-swinging assaults on establishment values and institu-tions. He had in the 1920s an enormous influence upon young artists and intellectuals across the country. His well-known attacks upon the "booboisie," the Bible Belt, the college pro-fessors, and assorted American illusions found ready-made tar-gets in the Northwest as well. His sallies against Puritanism and the New Englander in art applied almost without alteration to the characteristic Northwesterner's devotion to moral uplift. For Mencken art was

> "a temptation, a seduction, a Lorelei, and the Good Man may safely have traffic with it only when it is broken to moral uses—in other words, when its innocence is pumped out of it, and it is purged of gusto. It is precisely this gusto that one misses in all of the work of the New England school, and in all of the work of the formal schools that derive from it."[13]

Mencken rewrote the American literary canon during the 'teens and twenties, devaluing the New England school and elevating the realists working in the colloquial tradition of Mark Twain, a tradition in which both Stevens and Davis could be placed.

Mencken's second point of influence upon Stevens and Davis was in his direct encouragement of their work as editor of *The American Mercury,* probably the most influential magazine for thinking Americans in the mid-1920s. Mencken had, as stated above, encouraged both young men to write fiction, and his magazine was receptive to their work all through the decade. Both Stevens and Davis acknowledged their debt to Mencken, Stevens in the introduction to his first book, *Paul Bunyan* (1925), and Davis in a preface to his collection of stories, *Team Bells Woke Me* (1935). Moreover, Mencken seems to have given Stevens, in a 1924 letter to the young writer, what might have been the germinal idea for *Status Rerum:*

> My advice is that you forsake Tacoma forthwith or retire to the woods. Unless you shake off the literary ladies constantly, they will presently have you in a velvet coat and some of the more

> *enterprising of them may actually attempt your*
> *person. The more literary contacts you make,*
> *the more you will write like a* Saturday Evening
> Post *editorial writer. Flee them as you would the*
> *devil.[14]*

Status Rerum shook off the literary ladies with a vengeance and served to further establish the early literary personae of Stevens and Davis as it appears in their essays and fiction for Mencken's *Mercury* in the 1920s. There, they are both tough but ironic and voluble types with a broad streak of humor and plenty of experience in the real world, a stance which must have pleased Mencken immensely, since it was so like his own.

The famous Mencken prose style offers a third area of influence upon *Status Rerum*. Stevens especially seems to have imitated Mencken's cocksure audacity, his sesquipedalian bumptiousness combined with his relish for plain, blunt words, his tongue-in-cheek archaisms and moralisms, his habit of scandalous overstatement. Much of Stevens's prose style in his early *Mercury* pieces is pure Mencken, such as these, which close "The Uplift on the Frontier," in which Stevens describes the sad decline of the new, tamed laborer:

> *Consider the spectacle of a paw-handed, anvil-*
> *shouldered toiler .... Hearken to his basso gig-*
> *gles as he rides down the highway with a gang of*
> *spooners! The suppression of his old spirit has*
> *brought him into a sugar age. The bulge in his*
> *pocket is a box of candy instead of a bottle. And*
> *the pamphlet he is reading is not the* Police
> Gazette, *but a work on etiquette!*[15]

Status Rerum is rich in Menckenian diction and rhythm. The use of a Latin title is a familiar Mencken device, as is the alteration of polysyllabic verbosity with Anglo-Saxon brevity. Piling up evidence until the reader howls for relief is another Menckenian strategy adopted in *Status Rerum*. So is the "goosed" language: nouns and verbs crackling with specificity, gaudy adjectives and adverbs to push them into greater prominence. ("Regard the versicles emanating from the poetry classes of Prof. Glenn Hughes, of the University of Washington — a banquet of breath-tablets, persistently and impotently violet!")

Finally, Mencken's influence may be seen in *Status Rerum's* close resemblance to one of his most famous essays, "The Sahara of Bozart," an attack upon the artistic and cultural vacuity of the South, first published in 1917 and expanded for *Prejudices: Second Series*. It quickly became something of a Mencken classic, and can hardly have escaped the notice of Stevens, whose letters reveal his close acquaintance with Mencken's work. Mencken's essay, with its brash assertion of the South's "unanimous torpor and doltishness, this curious and almost pathological estrangement from everything that makes for a civilized culture," and its search for the causes of this stupendous cultural sterility, seems a ready-made model for the sort of regional attack which Stevens and Davis undertook. Indeed, Bernard DeVoto had done just such a hatchet-job on his own homeland, entitled "Utah," which Mencken published in the *Mercury* just a year before *Status Rerum* appeared. ("How am I to suggest the utter mediocrity of life in the new Utah? How can I suggest its poverty in everything that makes for a civilization? ... Who, indeed, ever heard of a Utah painter, a Utah sculptor, a Utah novelist, or poet or critic, or educator, or publicist — who ever heard of a Utahn?")[16] Stevens wrote to Mencken praising DeVoto's article early in 1927.[17]

Status Rerum, then, follows Mencken's "Sahara of the Bozart" as an excoriation of regional cultural insipidity drawn in broad and outrageous terms. Like "Sahara," *Status Rerum* begins with an overview of the region's present benighted condition. Like "Sahara" it asks the reader to consider the panoramic cultural blight, a process which, in both works, breaks down in mid-paragraph with a too-hopeless-to-go-on wave of dismissal. Like "Sahara" it seeks and finds causes for this intellectual sterility, and like the earlier Mencken essay it offers something of a historical overview. Both pieces draw frequently on the imagery of natural disasters to heighten the sense of cultural catastrophe; drought, flood, avalanche, etc., serve to emphasize artistic failings by linking them to these cataclysmic natural events.

With all of these similarities it is still evident that *Status Rerum* is a cut below vintage Menckenese. Mencken's delight in the attack, his cheerful exuberance at being outrageous is missing in *Status Rerum*. The authors' stance in the pamphlet is unclear. Occasionally they slip out of the appropriate tone of ironic attack and begin to sound aggrieved or hortatory. There is an underlying exasperation in the work which blunts its satire. Moreover, their targets *are,* with the possible exception of the indefatigable Col. Hofer, "butterflies." Attacking by name a string of virtually unknown creative-writing professors hardly qualifies for great satire's function of laying low the proud, smug, mighty of the earth. Stevens, who was the closer of the two to Mencken, may have sensed these shortcomings, and for that reason perhaps seems not to have sent him a copy. But he did submit to Mencken and the *Mercury* a much-improved attack upon Northwest letters, this time limited to the Colonel and the maunderings of his *Lariat,* which Mencken enthusiastically accepted and printed in the January, 1929 issue.[18]

But if *Status Rerum* was not as brilliant as it could have been, it was sufficient. Its publication in 1927 marked the virtual demise of the Emmeline Grangerford school of Northwest writing. With or without the pamphlet's help, *The Lariat* passed from Col. Hofer's hands to those of a less able successor. A year later it ceased publication, the twitterings of its three-named warblers stilled forever. *The Bridge of the Gods* was still the Northwest's steadiest seller, but new stirrings in the region indicated that the old hold of genteel romance, moral uplift, and imitative fiction and poetry was weakening in favor of a strongly realistic literature which dealt honestly with the Northwest upon its own terms and through the lives and language of its own people. One of the most important of these stirrings, also in 1927, was the launching of *The Frontier* as a serious regional publication by Harold G. Merriam of the University of Montana. H. L. Davis greeted the new *Frontier* with a preface to its March, 1928 issue which marked out the old errors and the new territory ahead, concluding, "We began here with a new way of life, new rhythms, new occupations. We have failed to make that freshness part of ourselves," and calling for new writers to come forth.

Davis and Stevens themselves tapped this regional freshness in their finest work in the decades to come. Stevens's best novel was to be *Big Jim Turner,* a celebration of his own hard-knocks life in the woods and mills and big construction jobs, half poet and half alligator and Halleluiah, I'm a bum, holing up winters in the Portland Public Library and working at physical labor the rest of the year. Breaking out of his imitations of Mencken, he fashioned his own narrative voice, but in the familiar and appealing American fictional pose of the intellectual tough guy. One of the roughs, a Kosmos.

H. L. Davis was wary of being typed as "merely" regional ("Of all the traps for ruining Pacific Coast writers the deadliest is costume and dialect — briefly, local color"),[19] and his finest books and stories — *Honey in the Horn, The Winds of Morning, Team Bells Woke Me, "Kettle of Fire"* — assert the universality of human experience. But at the root of his best work is the folk voice and the anecdotal storytelling humor of the old Southwest. *Honey in the Horn* combined these qualities successfully enough to win the 1935 Pulitzer Prize and to be called by Mencken the best first novel ever printed in America.[20] Davis and Stevens alike were instrumental in weeding out the bookish talk of their Northwest predecessors and asserting the colloquial style as the dominant medium of literary expression. Their use of the metaphors and rhythms of folk speech unsettled the old verities and invited new values.

Davis kept an eye out for the old literary embarrassments of the region as well, and skewered them when he had the chance. A minor figure in *Honey in the Horn,* Uncle Preston Shiveley, a closet author, is the vehicle for Davis's jibes against *Bridge-of-the-Gods* Indian claptrap and the doggerel rhymers of the defunct *Lariat:*

> *He had written a novel-length romance about that very neighborhood in which an Indian chief's daughter ran off with a high-strung young warrior from a hostile tribe, and how, when the vengeful pursuers were closing in, she hove herself over a bluff to keep from being parted from the man of her choice. It was founded on solid statistics, too. An Indian woman in the early days had gone over a promontory on Little River, though some of the older Indians claimed she got drunk and fell over, and a few mountain men told it that her parents backed her over, not to prevent her marriage, but in an effort to hold her down while they washed her feet.*
>
> *Besides the romance, which was called* Wi-nem-ah: A Tale of Eagle Valley, *he had turned off a considerable raft of poetry. Most of it was for use in autograph albums, and was on the order of "May your jobs be as deep as the ocean, your sorrows as light as its foam"; but there were also pieces in which he had got mad and cut loose against retail merchants in town when, to his notion, they had dealt a little closer with him than they should have:*

Oakridge is a pretty little thing;
I say damn the whole damn thing.
John S. Chance and R. C. Young
And the whole damn bunch ought to be hung.[21]

Davis commands his backwoods-shrewd narrative voice in the classic style of western oral humor, combining an obvious delight in the folk idiom with an understated manner.

Curiously enough, just as Mencken's assault against the South was a major cause of that region's literary flowering in the years to follow, so *Status Rerum* helped to shake Northwest writing out of its arrested development into self-awareness and the beginnings of a firm cultural identity. Davis and Stevens, with Mencken not far offstage, provided the primal overture which genteel respectability had so long muffled. And the literature which has since come to define Northwest writing has continued to owe much to the primitive base, to the coarse or comic or physical elements of the region's land and life which Davis and Stevens first brought to light. The Northwest fiction of writers like Vardis Fisher, Anne Shannon Monroe, Betty MacDonald, Ernest Haycox, Dorothy Johnson, Archie Binns, Nard Jones, A. B. Guthrie, Don Berry, Ken Kesey, Norman Maclean, James Welch, Jack Hodgins, and William Kittredge springs from this primitive base. So, too, does the history and autobiography of Steward Holbrook, William O. Douglas, E. R. Jackman, and Ivan Doig, and the poetry of Theodore Roethke, William Stafford, Richard Hugo, Madeline De Frees, Carolyn Kizer, David Wagoner, and Gary Snyder, to name a few.

Kesey's novels, especially, recall the native comic traditions of Mike Fink and Davy Crockett. The irrepressible Randle Patrick McMurphy and Hank Stamper can jump higher, squat lower, dive deeper, and stay under longer and come up drier than any of their fictional contemporaries. And Joe Ben, the ebullient woodsman of *Sometimes a Great Notion,* pinned to the bottom

---

of a river by a runaway log, with the water rising, dies laughing, outfacing the relentless force of nature in the best tradition of western tall talk. Although Kesey may be more inclined than his fellow Northwesterners to grin the raccoons out of the trees, it is clear that the pagan virtues championed by Mencken and Davis and Stevens continue to flourish in God's country.

University of Oregon
Eugene

Notes

[1](1931:rpt. Garden City, New York: Doubleday Anchor Books, 1953), p. 130. Besides my general debt in this paper to scholars of American humor like Rourke, Walter Blair, and Kenneth Lynn, I have profited by the stimulating suggestions of Professor Richard W. Etulain. For a folklorist's view of the genteel Northwest, see Barre Toelken's "Northwest Regional Folklore," in *Northwest Perspectives,* ed. Edwin R. Bingham and Glen A. Love (Seattle and London: University of Washington Press, 1979), pp. 20-42.

[2]In *Team Bells Woke Me, and Other Stories* (New York: William Morrow, 1953), pp. 185, 190.

[3]Earl Pomeroy, *The Pacific Slope* (Seattle and London: University of Washington Press, 1965), p. 25.

[4]*The Bridge of the Gods: A Romance of Indian Oregon* (Chicago: A. C. McClurg, 1890, 1911), p. 13. Further page references will be included in the text.

[5](Portland: Metropolitan Press, 1935), p. 319.

[6] "How to Get Into The Lariat," *The Lariat,* 6 (1925), 304.

[7] "The West is Not the Real 'West'," *The Lariat,* 6 (1925), 243.

[8] "Sour Grapes," *The Lariat,* 6 (1925), 318.

[9] "Lariats," *The Lariat,* 6 (1925), 507.

[10] "Appreciations," *The Lariat,* 5 (1925), 89.

[11]Original copies of *Status Rerum* are somthing of a rarity. Fortunately, the text has been reprinted in Warren L. Clare's " 'Posers, Parasites, and Pismires': *Status Rerum,* by James Stevens and H. L. Davis," *Pacific Northwest Quarterly,* 61 (January, 1970), 27-30. Because of the brevity of *Status Rerum,* page references will be dispensed with.

[12]Quoted in Paul T. Bryant, *H. L. Davis* (Boston: Twayne, 1978), p. 20.

[13]Quoted in William H. Nolte, *H. L. Mencken: Literary Critic* (Middletown, Conn.: Wesleyan University Press, 1966), p. 112. Davis, with his Southern ancestry, shared Mencken's distaste for the New England personality. See Davis's *Kettle of Fire* (New York: William Morrow, 1959), p. 36, and his treatment of New England-type townspeople in *"A Town in Eastern Oregon,"* (n. 2) and *Honey in the Horn.*

[14]H. L. Mencken to James Stevens, July 11, 1924. James Stevens Papers, University of Washington Library.

[15]*The American Mercury,* 1 (1924), 418.

[16]*The American Mercury,* 7 (1926), 321.

[17]See H. L. Mencken to James Stevens, May 4, 1927. James Stevens Papers, University of Washington Library.

[18]Mencken's eagerness to receive this article is indicated by two letters of Mencken to Stevens while the essay was being written, August 24 and September 7, 1928, in the James Stevens Papers.

[19]Bryant, *H. L. Davis,* pp. 70-71.

[20]*Letters of H. L. Mencken,* sel. and ann. by Guy J. Forgue (New York: Knopf, 1961), p. 394.

[21](1935: rpt. New York: Avon, 1962), pp. 17-18. Winemah, incidentally, is a character in another Balch novel, *Genevieve.*

"Posers, Parasites, and Pismires"

Warren L. Clare

SOON after the American Expeditionary Force had diffused democracy in its wake across the continent of Europe and the embattled, battered engineers who last saw action in a questionable cafe in Saint-Nazaire were all but forgotten, James Stevens returned to the United States with a new scar on his scalp and discharge papers in his hand. The government had given him a free ride halfway around the world and back, sergeant's stripes, and eighteen months of excitement, as well as protection against smallpox and a guarantee of proper peristalsis. With a clean bill of health, he made his way back to Oregon and heavy construction work. But the drive to write that had received tantalizing support from the poetry which he had written in San Francisco in 1916 and from his contributions to the *Stars and Stripes* was with him more than ever.[1]

While Stevens worked, he not only read but wrote. He studied seriously the position of the laboring man and attempted to set down his observations. The first article he submitted to the *Saturday Evening Post* was "The Tormented Men," a provocative study which George Horace Lorimer, the editor, published almost immediately. A second article, "The Laborer's Lunch," appeared in the *Post* soon thereafter. Perhaps best of all, Stevens was now making friends with professional writers, men who would help him to form his own literary ideas.[2]

Soon after Stevens' articles began to appear in the national magazines, he met Richard Wetjen, another Pacific Northwest writer. Wetjen had been in the maritime service during his early years, and his fiction — primarily short stories — dealt with life in the merchant marine on the Pacific Coast of the United States. Wetjen was well known in the region as a writer, and he moved freely within the literary circles of the Pacific Northwest.

In the fall of 1927, Carl Sandburg was on a lecture tour through the southern part of the Pacific Northwest. He was also gathering material for a new book, which he would entitle *The American Songbag.*[3] When Sandburg came to Willamette University in Salem, he spent the night at Dick Wetjen's home. After the lecture there was an open house at which students and faculty met and visited with Sandburg. As Stevens recalled later:

> *There wasn't any drinking or anything. Sandburg ... would do his stuff, get his lecture fee, meet the people, be nice to them ... and early the next morning get the hell out of there. So we had this nice evening at Wetjen's house. A very sober one, much to Wetjen's disgust.*[4]

During the evening, Sandburg ("who could get awful loud") asked, "Where the hell is H. L. Davis? He's the only poet the Pacific Northwest has got. Where is he? Why isn't he here?" Davis and Sandburg had met previously when the Northwest poet had gone to Chicago to see Harriet Monroe and other members of the "New Poetry" group which was developing in the Midwest.[5]

Davis had drawn the attention of H. L. Mencken, then editor of the *American Mercury,* when he submitted an October poem. The poem was rejected, but it exhibited such precision and control that Mencken had encouraged the cowboy from Bend,

Oregon, to continue writing. Davis was fond of the rejected poem, even though it was not quite socially acceptable. And when he occasionally found himself in a group of friends and writers, he would read the work for pure entertainment.

The old ranch grandma climbed out of bed,
And tottered to the chuck room, and she said:

"You young harvest hands, you're might fiery-
gaited;
You're as high-lived a bunch as ever
congregated.
You get drunk, and you yell around after dark,
You pester all the kitchen girls a tryin' to spark.
I want to warn you now, before you mouth
another bite—
There's witches a bewitchin' us every blamed
night!
They bewitched my son, and they rode him with
a quirt
From here to Camas Valley in his undershirt!
They rode him all a lather, and they spattered
him with mud,
And they dug him with their toenails till his ribs
run blood;
When they wanted him to gallop, they twisted on
his private!
He says he never knew how he managed to sur-
vive it!

Well, as long as she believes him, that's all right.
Anybody's liable to get a little tight.
Any drunk'll get his shirt muddied and tore,
And be a little vague how his reuben got sore. [6]

This delightful but ribald poem had been enthusiastically accepted by the Chicago group and endeared the poet to Carl Sandburg. It is obvious, however, why the work has never appeared in print. The night following his lecture in Salem, Sandburg was scheduled to speak at the Oregon Agricultural College, as it was then known, in Corvallis. Willard Wattles, a young assistant professor of English at the college, was Sandburg's host. Knowing that the poet had asked about Davis, Wattles had taken the pains to see that an invitation to a reception for Sandburg had been extended to the not quite acceptable H. L. Davis.

As Stevens remembers the event, Wattles' guests were preparing to leave for the lecture when there was a knock at the door.

> *Professor Wattles went to the door and there stood a long, lank guy, hair dangling down in his face, and his cap pushed back on his head, and in a scrawny right hand he held a pint of what was obviously whiskey. Moonshine! Everybody looked at this apparition, you know, and Wattles was advancing to greet him, and holding out his hand when up went the whiskey bottle, and there came out this hoarse voice with a distinctly Eastern Oregon cowboy accent that Davis had. "Hi Carl! How the hell are you?" Then [the apparition continued], "Here's a drink for you." Of course Carl had a little drink, and Carl called me and Wetjen, and we all four had a little drink. And that was it. That was all the drinking that was done. Four drinks.* [7]

The party then moved to the women's gymnasium, where the lecture was to be given. The gymnasium was completely full.

Some sixteen hundred tickets had been sold in advance, although the capacity of the gym was only a thousand. At Sandburg's insistence, people sat on the stage and in the aisles. The poet captivated the audience as he read selections from *The Prairie Years.* He called Abraham Lincoln "The Strange Friend and the Friendly Stranger." He read selections from "Cornhuskers," "Smoke and Steel," "Wilderness," "Night Stuff," and he told one of his Rootabaga stories, "Gimme the Ax," about the country vegetable that moved to the city of liver and onions. Occasionally he would strum the guitar in a rendition of a folk ballad. The audience was enthralled, and for several days afterward, the student newspaper carried stories of Sandburg's visit.[8]

Sandburg, Wattles, and Stevens (who had given a lecture earlier in the day) returned to Wattles' home with Davis, the dirty cowboy, and Wetjen, who had driven down from Salem. Wetjen knew many sailor songs from his years in the West Coast maritime service. Davis could sing and play the guitar, and he remembered a great many ballads that he had learned when he last sang with Sandburg. Stevens, of course, also knew many songs, not the lusty sea chanteys of Wetjen, but the robust, occasionally off-color ballads of the laboring man and the condemning protest songs of the Wobblies. Neither Stevens nor Wetjen, however, could sing; but they tried anyway, rasping and roaring with the others until dawn, when Sandburg realized that he had missed his train and had only a few minutes in which to catch another.

The affair was not without embarrassment. Among the college students and faculty members who had not been in attendance and also among the more puritanical elements in the town itself, the story had started that there had been an old-fashioned, hell-roaring, hard-drinking, abandoned orgy at the home of the sedate professor. The unmistakable sound of raucous singing, people howling, and the clink of glasses had been heard. Long-haired tramps with guitars and bottles and a brawny hobo with a voice like a mule had been seen — and heard — leaving the home at a most inappropriate hour. "It was really rustic simplicity when you think of the songs. They couldn't have been less sophisticated."9

Stevens recalls that Professor Wattles lost his post at Oregon Agricultural College. But the important aspect of the evening was that James Stevens and H. L. Davis had met. And however raucous, the harmony of their voices raised in song was destined to continue as they raised their literary voices in open protest against the nature of things literary in the Pacific Northwest.10

H. L. Davis proved to be a vigorous literary companion for James Stevens, and soon the two men became close friends. Davis' carefree brand of recklessness appealed to Stevens. Stevens' views of regional literature appealed to Davis. One night in Davis' hotel room in Eugene, they began to talk of Pacific Northwest literature. With a typewriter between them, they revived an age-old genre of protest.

One can imagine Davis and Stevens — rebellious, strong-willed young authors, not accustomed to mincing words, and disliking the literary conventions of the time — as they sat in the small hotel room and entertained each other with derogatory observations regarding Northwest regional literature. Their remarks were probably general at first and then became more specific, until they were naming writers, editors, and publications and obviously enjoying themselves immensely. As authors who were well aware of the problems of regional literature, they appraised the Northwest's literary output as it was in 1926. The result was a spontaneous manifesto.

"Our first impulse," they agreed, "was to vow abstention from a pursuit which linked us with such posers, parasites, and pismires." As the evening wore on, their comments became more and more vitriolic. Since they had already established themselves as critics of an entire region, they felt that they should also point out what should be done to improve the literary output. What are the influences, they asked themselves, that have served to mold Northwest literature? Why were young writers producing pulp?

The first malignancy to be called to the attention of the public was the creative writing courses taught in the universities of the Northwest. More specifically, however, the professors themselves came under the fusillade of charges; it was they who propagated and metastasized the literary cancer; it was they who trained young writers to produce pulp material that was designed only to sell.

As the outburst of youthful enthusiasm continued, Stevens and Davis categorically criticized the enfeebled efforts of Pacific Northwest literati. They named names, attacked colleges and universities, examined the mire of specific classes, waded through the muck of literary groups, and examined, as an entomologist would examine a peculiar insect, the presidents (or purveyors) of the literary circles. They denounced the magazines, slammed the journals, and pounced upon the editors of these organs of tripe. They were instruments of literary outrage, preying upon the posers and parasites that inhabited a regional sway of mucky belles-lettres.

HERE, then, was the indictment that the two young men filed against the body of Pacific Northwest regional literature. They called their work *Status Rerum,* and when it occurred to one of them that it should have a subtitle, they added *A Manifesto, upon the Present Condition of Northwestern Literature: Containing Several Near-Libelous Utterances, upon Persons in the Public Eye.* With wit, a sesquipedalian verbosity, and caustic sarcasm, they completed the manifesto.[11]

Stevens and Davis were both pleased and excited over the manuscript. When it was finished, they presented it with pride to a publisher in Portland. He would not touch it. The text was too hot. It condemned too many of the Northwest's leading citizens of the day. And far too many of the objects of the Stevens-Davis ridicule were among the most powerful men in the West. Consequently, the two writers published approximately two hundred copies of the manifesto at their own expense and mailed copies to all the newspapers and literary men they could think of throughout the entire region.[12]

The text of *Status Rerum* makes it very plain that the two young men considered most of the creative efforts from the Pacific Northwest sub-literary. Nearly all Northwest writers, unlike those of other regions, failed in one way or another to express the spirit of the region. Regional literature suffered because it did not catch the historical or social milieu of the Northwest. Those who believed that the true milieu of the Northwest had little to offer in the first place, but still produced ostentatious tripe, were about to descend upon the two young raptorial birds who presumed to criticize the works of the mighty. The response from writers, editors, newspapermen, and professors of creative writing was electrifying. Much of the protest in *Status Rerum* was directed against the universities in Oregon and Washington. During an interview in 1963, Stevens said:

> *In every damn school at that time there were classes in short story writing. And in all that we'd ever encountered, it was not the study of the short story as an art form; it was a study of how to write the thing so as to get it published in a pulp magazine. So they would teach the pulp form. Then they made a great show of culture out of it.[13]*

Other targets of *Status Rerum* were the literary circles which flourished in the metropolitan areas and perpetuated the "great show of culture." Also subject to their scorn were the regional attempts to produce literary magazines, usually edited, Davis was certain, by some "ridiculous old bird" who did not have the qualifications to "castrate calves," let alone dictate literary taste to the region.[14]

All of these institutions, the manifesto implied, served only to encourage either highly emotional or purely mechanical belles-lettres. Either of these literary indiscretions was fully as bad as the other: "All these short story writers that we could think of, in terms of the welfare of regional literature, well, they just stank, that was all."[15]

Status Rerum is extremely important in the development of James Stevens as a writer. It is a definite indication of his maturity as a regionalist. The manifesto tacitly advances a theory of literature, an idea regarding creative expression to which Stevens still subscribes. "I think he [the writer] should write what he knows."[16] If the writer restricts himself to his knowledge and does not attempt to impose an artificial system or form upon his work, Stevens believes that the result will be far more significant. *Status Rerum*, then, advanced both the problem existing in Northwest literature and an approach to literature which would eliminate the problem.

The condemnation of Northwest literature itself received angry condemnation. In addition, the manifesto was embarrassing to some of the writers' friends. Stevens and Davis knew that it would be. For instance, one copy of *Status Rerum* (No. 201) is inscribed:

> *Stern Daughter of the Voice of God!*
> *O Duty! If that name thou love,*
> *Who art a light to guide a rod*
> *To check the erring, and reprove!*
>
> *... Better read the rest of it. W[ordsworth] can't*
> *hurt you. You are unworthy to gaze upon our*
> *sonnet, but we will drink with you.*

Furthermore, Dick Wetjen, who had introduced Jim Stevens to Carl Sandburg, was a close friend of Colonel E. Hofer, publisher of the *Lariat* and one of the men unfit to "castrate calves." But by far the most outspoken critic of the manifesto turned out to be Lancaster Pollard, a close friend of Stevens. Pollard wrote a daily "culture-corner" column for the Seattle *Post-Intelligencer.* The column, appropriately called "Potpourri," fed upon a salmagundi diet of things artistic and literary throughout the region. Pollard approached *Status Rerum* with more peevishness than thought. Spurred by the reaction, Stevens wrote to Pollard:

> *Why all the pother over* Status Rerum? *It appears to me that its reception is confirming its charges, even if conditions that existed before its composition did not confirm them. My three books have won me no recognition or position in the Northwest, aside from praises in your erudite columns . . . . I owe nothing to Seattle or Portland or any of its babbling birds or braying asses. I have never complained about the reception accorded the books I wrote my heart and guts out to create. I didn't particularly give a damn what anyone thought of them, and I don't now. But it certainly affords me a sardonic grin to behold you . . . retching and convulsing yourselves over a piece that required about as much thought and effort as taking a crap. News value, I suppose. Ah, well. Jesus wept over the inanities of mankind, its perfidy and et cetera. I haven't the soul of Jesus, so I can only be faintly amused.*[17]

Pollard's impressionistic response to the manifesto (a response which is still supported by some Northwest literary reviewers) unfortunately roused the mule skinner in Stevens. "I am entirely done... with being made publicly ridiculous and with being publicly abused by my friends," he wrote to Pollard. "I am not sore, but I am firm."[18]

As the debate with Pollard continued, Stevens expostulated:

> *Davis and I circulate a hundred copies of our attack, and you at once circulate a hundred thousand copies of a piece that is in no sense a reply to the manifesto, but a deliberate distortion of all its contents, and a personal attack upon Davis and myself.*[19]

Stevens wanted the debate to ascend to an examination of Northwest literature. Instead, he found himself the center of a personal attack, condemned as an irresponsible bum, and ostracized as a man who was not really an author. He warned Pollard that, if the trend of criticism continued, he was likely to get very angry. He reminded Pollard that he too could engage in "pithy personalities via newsprint."

> *I shall do a screaming article entitled THE WAR ON THE P-I BOOK PAGE. It will make rich reading. The former cyclops of the Seattle Klan, author of That Something, originator of the Purple Bubble Ball, defending the poetry societies, under the supervision of the editor of the Woman's Magazine.*[20]

Lancaster Pollard had spent nearly a year building up the quality of his book page in the Seattle *Post-Intelligencer.* Stevens and others had once held hopes that, when the page was well established, it would serve to bring together everyone in the region who was honestly interested in literature, everyone who hoped for a genuine Northwest fiction. "And this group is solidly behind you," Stevens had told Pollard in 1926.[21] A year later, when Pollard took the popular stand and defended subliterary treatments of unreal conflicts in a mythical history, painted with a romantic glow of nostalgia for something that had never been, he lost the support of the man he most needed.

Even though Stevens was disappointed in Pollard's position, he thought he could make the best of a poor situation by writing an article for the *American Mercury* about the literary foolishness of the Pacific Northwest. He sent an outline of the proposed article along with a copy of *Status Rerum* to H. L. Mencken. Mencken answered immediately: "It is capital news that you are at work on the article. Let me have it at your convenience. Certainly Colonel Hofer ought to be introduced to the Eastern literati."[22]

Two weeks later Mencken wrote again: "I surely hope that you have not forgotten the article on the literati of the Northwest. They deserve loving embalming."[23] The Mencken metaphor led Stevens to bleed the corpse of Northwest letters one final time. As an indictment, Stevens simply used material that had appeared in Colonel Hofer's *Lariat*. He pointed out, for instance, that the Colonel was rather modestly given to the publication of tributes to his own magazine.

TOAST TO THE LARIAT

Hail! Hail! oh Lariat!
Your length unfurl
With dashing twirl,
With snappy curl,
And lo! Off comes our hat!

Sing! Sing! oh Lariat!
Now here, now there,
Humming in air

A song so fair,
A song so rare
That lo! Heart follows hat![24]

Colonel Hofer was, conveniently, a millionaire. He could afford to ship bales of his own magazine to all parts of the United States. Stevens commented:

Editors of Eastern magazines devoted to the new poetry sniffed solemnly and at length in paragraphs designed to set the upstart in its place. True Westerners never turn the other cheek. Soon such counter blasts as these began to boom and smoke from the pages of the Lariat:

BLURBS

Anybody can make rhymes; but if they're easily understood
And have a meaning, why, they're no good.

To be a poet, you must write sonnets to ashcans and to bricks
Like Sandburg and Lindsay; those are their tricks...

Critics will hail you as a genius and marvel at your imagery.
But somehow, I don't know why, it's all bunk to me.[25]

With his article about the Colonel's contributions to Northwest poetry, Stevens buried his protest forever. Disappointment in the region's literature had brought Stevens to the point of violent protest, just as a common love for an uncommon poet had brought

H. L. Davis and James Stevens together in the first place. Thereafter the tacit protest manifest in Stevens' own fiction was disagreement enough. For he believed that he was learning to write the way men should write — about present conflicts and about current people, and couched in common language.

Notes

[1]Otheman Stevens, "Mule Driver Writes Dazzling Poetry: *Examiner* Finds Grading Camp Genius," San Francisco *Examiner*, Nov. 1, 1916. In November, 1916, James Stevens was driving a scraper blade as a teamster on major road construction in the Bay Area of California. He began to send occasional bits of verse to Otheman Stevens, the editor of the San Francisco *Examiner*. Like most newspapermen, Otheman Stevens tended to shy violently at the sight of poetry, and he decided not to print the material. Yet he felt that some of the poems were particularly good and sent them to George Horace Lorimer, editor of the *Saturday Evening Post*. Lorimer thought he saw a spark in the laborer's poetry and purchased four of them, one of which was featured in his magazine. See "An Old-Fashioned Ode," *Saturday Evening Post*, Vol. 189 (Nov. 11, 1916), 14.

[2] "Tormented Men," *Saturday Evening Post*, Vol. 197 (Nov. 1, 1924), 22, 54-56; "The Laborer's Lunch," *ibid.*, Vol. 197 (Dec. 6. 1924), 18-19.

[3]*Oregon Agricultural College Daily Barometer*, Jan. 19, 1927. Willard Wattles of the English department at the college was quoted as saying, "Mr. Sandburg is completing his collection of American folk songs while here. This collection will be published this year under the title, *The American Songbag*. Men from whom he obtained folk songs are Richard Wetjen of Salem, H. L. Davis of The Dalles, and James Stevens of Tacoma."

[4]Interview with Mr. and Mrs. James Stevens, Jan. 4, 1966.

[5]*Ibid.*

[6]H. L. Davis, "Witches," private papers of James Stevens (hereinafter cited Stevens Collection). The above is simply a fragment of the work. This is the first time any portion of the poem has appeared in print.

[7]Interview with Stevens, Jan. 4, 1966.

[8] "Famous Author Appears Tonight: Dean Grants Women Permission to Attend," *Oregon Agricultural College Daily Barometer,* Jan. 18, 1927; "Author of *Brawnyman* to Visit Campus Tonight," *ibid.;* "Large Audience Hears Sandburg," *ibid.,* Jan. 19, 1927; "Hobo Poet Leaves Lasting Impression," *ibid.,* Jan. 21, 1927.

[9]Interview with Stevens, Jan. 4, 1966.

[10]*Ibid.* Although Stevens believes that Wattles lost his post following the night-long party at his home, the *Oregon Agricultural College Bulletin* for 1927-28 carries Wattles' name as a member of the faculty.

[11]James Stevens and H. L. Davis, *Status Rerum: A Manifesto, upon the Present Condition of Northwestern Literature: Containing Several Near-Libelous Utterances, upon Persons in the Public Eye* (privately printed at The Dalles, 1927). Copies of *Status Rerum* are very difficult to find today. In the course of my Stevens research, I discovered one copy in the Tacoma Public Library and one copy in Stevens' possession. Stevens' copy is number 201, out of limited printing of only 200. I attribute this incongruity simply to Stevens' sense of humor. He sent No. 201 of *Status Rerum* to Richard Wetjen, his close literary friend in Salem. It was apparently returned to Stevens at a later date, possibly at Wetjen's death. Copies of the pamphlet are collectors' items today and should demand a premium price among bibliophiles. Yet, because the pamphlet remains virtually unknown, there is apparently little demand for it. Very likely, most of the copies were thrown into wastebaskets during the first few days after the pamphlets were received.

[12]Interview with Stevens, Jan. 4, 1966.

[13]Interview with Stevens, Nov. 23, 1963.

[14]Interview with Stevens, Nov. 23, 1963.

[15]*Ibid.*

[16]*Ibid.*

[17]Stevens to Lancaster Pollard, Nov. 12, 1927, Stevens Papers, University of Washington Archives (hereafter cited Stevens Papers).

[18]Stevens to Pollard, Nov. 13, 1927, Stevens Papers.

[19]Stevens to Pollard, Nov. 15, 1927, Stevens Papers.

[20]*Ibid.*

[21]Stevens to Pollard, June 21, 1926, Stevens Papers.

[22] H. L. Mencken to Stevens, Aug. 24, 1928, Stevens Collection.

[23]Mencken to Stevens, Sept. 7, 1928, Stevens Collection.

[24]James Stevens, "The Northwest Takes to Poesy," *American Mercury,* Vol. 16 (January, 1929), 65.

[25]*Ibid.*

STATUS RERUM

A Manifesto, Upon The Present
Condition of
Northwestern Literature

Containing Several Near-Libelous
Utterances, Upon
Persons In The Public Eye

by
JAMES STEVENS
of Washington

and

H. L. DAVIS
of Oregon

∴

Privately Printed For The Craft

1927

PRICE TWENTY-FIVE CENTS
Box 512 — The Dalles, Ore.

Status Rerum

I

THE present condition of literature in the Northwest has been mentioned apologetically too long. Something is wrong with Northwestern literature. It is time people were bestirring themselves to find out what it is.

Other sections of the United States can mention their literature, as a body, with respect. New England, the Middle West, New Mexico and the Southwest, California — each of these has produced a body of writing of which it can be proud. The Northwest — Oregon, Washington, Idaho, Montana — has produced a vast quantity of bilge, so vast, indeed, that the few books which are entitled to respect are totally lost in the general and seemingly interminable avalanche of tripe.

It is time people were seeking the cause of this. Is there something about the climate, or the soil, which inspires people to write tripe? Is there some occult influence, which catches them young, and shapes them to be instruments out of which tripe, and nothing but tripe, may issue?

Influence there certainly is, and shape them it certainly does. Every written work, however contemptible and however trivial it may be, is conceived and wrought to court the approbation of some tribunal. If the tribunal be contemptible, then equally contemptible will be the work which courts it.

And the tribunals are contemptible.

From Salem, Oregon, from the editorial offices of one Col. Hofer, issues, in a monthly periodical somewhat inexplicably called "The Lariat", an agglomeration of doggerel which comprises the most colossal imbecility, the most preposterous bathos, the most superb sublimity of metrical ineptitude, which the patience and perverted taste of man has ever availed to bring between covers. And Col. Hofer encourages it. He battens upon it. Somewhere within the dark recesses of this creature's — we will not say soul, but nebulous sentience — is some monstrous chord which vibrates to these invertebrate twitterings.

In a healthy condition of society, this state of things would be merely funny. As things are, it is not funny. It is deeply tragic. Northwestern poetry, seeking, in the ingenuousness of its youth, some center about which to weave its fabric, has done no less than bind itself in thraldom to Col. Hofer and his astounding magazine, and the results are all too pathetically apparent. Read some of it!

Or contemplate the panorama of emotional indigestion, the incredible conglomeration of unleavened insipidity, spread before your eyes in the works of the Northwest Poetry Society, the begauded pastries of the Seattle "Muse and Mirror", which surfeit without satisfying. Regard the versicles emanating from the poetry classes of Prof. Glenn Hughes, of the University of Washington — a banquet of breath-tablets, persistently and impotently violet! Regard — but enough! "Palms," exotic *frijole* congealing among the firs of Aberdeen, you need not trouble to savor.

II

If this were all, it would be too much. Regrettably, we have still to contemplate a literary influence which has been, if possible, even more degrading. The Northwest has not escaped, any more than other sections of the United States, its share of "naturals," mental weaklings, numskulls, and other victims of mental and moral affliction. Unfortunately, our advanced civilization has neglected to provide an outlet for their feeble and bizarre energies. Yet, many of these unfortunate creatures are unfit even to teach school. What are they to do? In Chicago, the problem would be simple. There, such unfortunates can devote themselves to the service of some gang-leader, and gain a livelihood in the professions of bootlegging, blackmail and murder. In the South, they are privileged to lead active lives as members of the Ku Klux Klan, and appear prominently at nocturnal whipping-parties and Fundamentalist crusades. Such inoffensive and normal employments have, unfortunately, no place in our Northwestern civilization. What, then, are these unfortunates to do? Such puerile faculties as they may chance to possess demand some exercise. To deny it them would be inhumane.

The earliest white colonies of the Northwest, more merciful than we, found them normal employment. The lumber companies of that age availed themselves of the unfortunates of their time, for the purpose of filing upon timber-lands, then in the possession of a too suspicious Government. They were found useful instruments for murdering Chinese laundrymen and tracklaborers, thus establishing the supremacy of the Caucasian race. For hanging Basque and Mexican sheep-herders, and destroying sheep, by theft, poison, firearms, or dynamite, civilization has gained much from their exertions. We do not grudge them their meed of veneration.

But civilization, with impersonal cruelty, has used them and passed on. The agricultural commonwealth has given place to the industrial empire. What can we give our own numskulls, "naturals", and mentally afflicted, to do? How can we even rid ourselves of the annoyance of their society? To our industrial leaders, the answer is simple. Put them where they will do no harm. Put them where their imbecility will be congenially occupied. Obviously, they could not be trusted to manufacture rocking-chairs, to pile lumber, to operate donkey-engines, or combined harvesters; to shear sheep, or castrate calves; in the operation of woolen, paper and flour mills, their employment would be a continual jeopardy, not only to themselves, but to the lives of men valuable in the industries which they serve. Fortunately, no doubt, for Northwestern industry, but calamitously for the welfare of Northwestern literature, an employment has been developed which offers the advantages of congeniality and inoffensiveness, without entailing the least risk to the continued prosperity of our factories, so much desired by all. That employment is, briefly, short-story writing.

III

From this cause, from the humane sentiments which desire to find harmless employment for these poor creatures, has come that pullulating institution, the short-story writing class. Teachers were, of course, easily recruited. As chiropractors, prohibition agents, saxophone players, radio announcers, and movie organists, have been seduced from more strenuous walks of life, such as pants-pressing, curve-greasing, track-walking, lumber-piling, tin-roofing, and cascara-bark-stripping, by the superior usufructs of a life of authority without backache, so, and from these or similar walks, have been recruited our teachers of short-story writing.

Nor have they succumbed to this seduction without honor. On the head and shoulders of the most eminent apostle of short-story writing, Dean M. Lyle Spencer, have descended, suffocatingly, the cap and gown of the Presidency of the University of Washington. Candor compels us to add, that President Spencer's rise to eminence was due no less to this leadership of youthful unfortunates of the State of Washington through the occult mysteries of short-story writing, than to his faithfully sustained administration of the office of Vice-President of the Seattle Chamber of Commerce. President Spencer's career has been aptly expressed in the slogans of the institutions with which he is allied, as follows:

"Get the Seattle Spirit;" "Advertise Education;" "Produce Pecu-
niary Prose."

The University of Oregon can boast of no short-story instruc-
tor of the eminent attainments of President M. Lyle Spencer. If
Professor W. F. G. Thacher's record includes a term of service as
Vice-President of any Chamber of Commerce, we possess no
knowledge of the fact. Professor Thacher has, nevertheless, certain individual claims to fame. He has been awarded honorable
mention in the list of winners in a Chicago tire-naming contest,
in which more than two and one-half million names were submitted. Professor Thacher has offered the fruits of his intellect in
other national name and slogan contests, and has won distinction
in practically all of them, for the winsomeness and *chic* of his
titles. A movement is reported to be on foot among Professor
Thacher's more devout disciples, to present him with a gift of 250
engraved calling-cards, bearing his name with the legend, neatly
engraved in elegant script, "You Can't Go Wrong with a Thacher
Title."

But these are the admirals, so to speak, of the service. To continue the figure, the lower decks offer a spectacle which, in charity, we do not encourage the reader to contemplate. What shall
be said of Mme. Mable Holmes Parsons, the illuminatrix of the
short-story writing department of the University of Oregon
Extension Division? Not for her the Vice-Presidency of the Seattle
Chamber of Commerce; not for her parched lips the fragrant
moisture of Honorable Mention in a Chicago tire-naming contest. For her, only the enfeebled sighs, the emasculate twitterings,
of the vapid ladies, trousered and untrousered, the mental unfortunates who inhabit the unstoried corridors in which her dictum
runs as law. Hers only to feed her soul, between intervals
pathetically wide, upon the empty honor of kiddie poem in the
Sunday Supplement of the Portland Journal. Let us not touch her
further. There is enough, ay, more than enough, to engage us
elsewhere. Scientists inform us, Nature is an excess. In the field of

the short-story classes in the Northwest, surely she has outdone herself.

Shall we descend still further into the recesses? We shall encounter the vertiginous galley in which Prof. Borah, of the University of Washington, concocts his flashy and injurious messes, to dazzle the eyes and ossify the intestines of the hapless intellectual paralytics of his short-story classes. What lies further? The stokehold! Formless shapes there labor and conspire, yearning for greater power to lead victims into the path of error. There bend the leaders of the Y. M. C. A. short-story classes. There toil, in groaning discontent, the teachers of short-story writing in the high schools. What lies further? Shall we look further? Dare we look further? In common pity, no! There is a point at which curiosity ends, and perversion begins. We had almost crossed it. Let us turn our faces away.

IV

Until lately, it was difficult — it was impossible — to have formed the faintest conception of the abysmal degradation into which Northwestern letters had fallen. We had noticed that, when we announced ourselves as practitioners of literature, people regarded us suspiciously, and treated us with a wariness which impressed us as unnecessary. We could not imagine why. We had not seen the Parliament of Letters in Seattle. It included all the Writers' Clubs, all the Poetry Societies. Now, we have seen it. We have seen it all.

We have sat in the gallery of the Parliament of Letters in Seattle, and gazed with dreadful awe upon the tossing sea of puerile and monotonous imbecility raging beneath us. Sterile and barren wave after wave of frustrate insipidity swayed beneath the apostolic trident of their pitiable Neptune, the above-mentioned Col. E. Hofer. As the presiding deity, so were the votaries. What hope that a bright-hued phrase might leap glittering from that desert sea? What hope of any act of reverence for life, for character? What hope of any fruition, except that of selling a plot, conceived in avarice, written in slavish and feeble-witted devotion to the dictates of a porcine mind, squalidly inhabiting the skull of a professor of a short-story writing class? We faced the appalling truth. This, then, was the image upon which the public had formed its impression of Northwestern writers!

But worse than this had to be faced. How many times had some tired Eastern editor, chained to his desk by the necessity of earning his daily bread, cringed from the gruesome monument of driveling manuscript, overshadowing, like some monstrous fungus, the desk which, perhaps, has felt the glory of the writings of such men as Theodore Dreiser, Sinclair Lewis, James Branch Cabell, Robert Frost, Carl Sandburg — men of whom American literature may be proud? How could we, as Northwestern writers, ever again demand courtesy of these editors? How could we ever again dare to commit our manuscripts to this devastating flood of imbecility? In our innocence, we had done that which the imagination rebelled to contemplate.

V

Our first impulse was to vow abstention from a pursuit which linked us with such posers, parasites, and pismires. Horror at contemplating a spectacle so blasphemous, so mortifying, so licentious, so extravagantly obscene, drove all sense of loyalty, duty and self-sacrifice from our minds. Our own thoughts were washed away in the black flood, and we could only repeat, with the Elizabethan, Webster:

> *"Thou hast led me, like a heathen sacrifice,*
> *With music and with fatal yokes of flowers,*
> *To my eternal ruin."*

But it need not be eternal. It lies with us, and with the young and yet unformed spirits, to cleanse the Augean stables which are poisoning the stream of Northwestern literature at the source. Our Hercules has not yet appeared, but hope is surely not lacking. We have had a vision, and we have gained faith boldly to prophesy his coming. We can yet cry, even in this darkest and most hopeless hour, from the mountain tops of vision—

> *"Yet, Freedom, yet thy banner, torn, but flying,*
> *Streams like a thundercloud against the wind!"*